TEESSIDE DREAMS

TEESSIDE
DREAMS

JOHN NICHOLSON
Nick Guymer Series
No.11

Published by Head Publishing
Copyright © John Nicholson 2016

Edition edit by Robert Marcum

Printed by CMP UK Ltd

ISBN 978-0-9933817-3-7

http://www.johnnicholsonwriter.co.uk

*As ever, I am supported in my writing by one excellent
hairy man and a team of wonderful women,
all of whom make me look better than I am.
So, thank you one and all:
Robert, my editor, backstop and general rock 'n' roll
groovemeister (Peanut Butter Conspiracy dept.)
Janet, my proof-reading Wonder Woman,
margin scribbler and pointer-out of wrong stuff.
Julie at Women's Aid East and Midlothian,
whose spirit, knowledge and encouragement was so
important in guiding how I wrote some important
parts of this book.
Winty, my Yorkshire siren,
whose wise words never leave me.
And, of course, more than anything,
Dawn for encouraging me just to sit around the flat
making stuff up, all day and night.*

**Content warning: This novel contains details of,
and references to, rape and stalking, which some
survivors might find upsetting.**

*"...and in the end
on dreams
we will
depend"*

CHAPTER 1

Nick sat bolt upright in bed, his heart pounding.

'It's alright, it's only me,' said a familiar voice.

He stared in disbelief at the figure sitting on the end of the bed.

'Mam...good god...what on earth are you doing here?'

She was sitting, her hands on her lap, wearing a tweed wool skirt and a pale blue roll-neck sweater. She looked like she used to look in the early 70s, before her descent into paranoid schizophrenia. Her hair still had colour to it and there was a healthy look to her skin that he hadn't seen since.

He looked to his left. Julie was asleep on her side, turned away from him.

'Settle down, our Nick. There's no need to worry, I just thought I'd look in on you.' She said it in a soothing and reassuring way.

He licked his dry lips. It was totally dark in the room but somehow he could still see her, as though she gave off just enough light to make her visible.

'But mam, you're dead. How are you here?' He spoke in a hoarse whisper, as though not to wake Julie, his heart still racing. She replied in her normal speaking voice. Julie didn't stir. Could she hear her?

'We're allowed to come back occasionally.'

'Allowed? Who allows you, mam?'

'We allow ourselves, Nick. Or rather, you allow it. But then, you always were a sensitive lad.'

She said it so matter of factly, then smiled at him with watery blue eyes that were devoid of even a hint of the madness that had engulfed her from the late 70s onward.

'So won't Julie see or hear you?'

'Not yet. How are you keeping then, luv?'

'Oh, well, fine.'

This was too weird. Was he asleep? He looked around the room. Looked at the glass on his bedside table. Looked at the clock. It read 4.27am. Then put his hand to his own face and felt the beard growth on his chin. No, he was definitely awake.

She looked around the room. 'It's nice in this house. Much nicer to be living on Norton High Street than in that place in Green Dragon Yard. I always liked Norton.'

1

'Oh, you saw us in the old flat?'

'Sort of. It's not seeing, really. More like knowing. It's a bit different. You don't have it when you're...you know...alive. It's right hard to use words for it. A bit like trying to describe what a strawberry tastes like. It's just strawberryish, isn't it? But I know what you've been up to. I'm sorry about what happened with Joni. That was sad for you both. You'd have made a lovely mam and dad.'

'Yeah, I'm used to it now. Still makes us both a bit sad. But we've got each other.'

She nodded and smiled. 'Aye. You're very lucky to have Julie. She's good for you. Such a passionate, loving girl. That was always your thing as a boy. You always did like passionate girls, didn't you? Used to get up to all sorts in that bedroom of yours.' She wagged an admonishing finger at him, but in a good way. 'You never brought a girl back that I didn't like. I remember thinking you always had lovely girlfriends.'

'Yeah, I was lucky. I used to like the fact you liked them. Do you really remember them, mam? It's a long time ago.'

'I don't *remember* anything, luv. It's not memory now, it's something else. I can't explain it. But I can see them all, as clear as day, though I don't recall their names. The short lass with blonde hair, she had lovely manners. The big busty one, she was funny. And there was that lovely, smiley, clever girl you were sweet on, who was both of those things; well-mannered and funny. Eee, you were daft about her. You used to come in from seeing her with bright, excited eyes, and stand in our bedroom telling me all about her and what she'd said and done. I think it annoyed your dad, but I liked seeing you so happy.'

'Yeah, she was great. You were still quite healthy then. Do you remember what you said about her? I wrote it in my diary at the time.'

'What did I say?'

'It was on my 18th birthday. You said you could tell that she had a really good soul. I didn't really understand what you meant at the time, but you were right. You knew far more than I understood, back then. I should have listened to you more. I got away from all your good advice for far too long. For decades, in fact.'

'Don't be so harsh on yourself. You were just a teenager growing into yourself, our Nick.'

'What about when I left home and all the years since then? Do you know about those years?'

2

'No luv. I was lost. My head was in the wrong place. I'm so sorry. I went...I don't know...I went away. I still don't know why or how.'

This all felt so real. So like talking to his mother when she was well. He didn't want it to end. It was the relationship he'd missed for all of his adult life; a relationship her illness had robbed them both of.

'I feel so sorry for you, mam. And I'm sorry I didn't come and look after you more. I was scared of your madness. I went my own way to hide from it, or to protect myself from it. I couldn't engage with you or it'd have upset me a lot and I was scared of being upset. So I closed myself down. I bottled up all the hurt and upset. It was cowardly, though. I should have been more brave. I'm really sorry, mam and I hope you can forgive me. You brought me up to be a nice lad, nicer than I actually turned out to be.'

Tears glazed over his eyes at the memory of it all.

She looked at him with distant but kindly eyes. 'There's nothing to forgive. I don't blame you at all. You were a sensitive boy, it was difficult for you. You had to get through it all somehow and to be honest, a lot of those years I hadn't a clue what was going on, even if you had been there. I was so drugged and then they gave me ECT and that just wiped my mind clean for years.'

'That was so awful. It was like you became a pale imitation of who you had been. Oh, mam...I wish it hadn't happened. It seems so unfair on all of us. I know I would have had a happier life if you'd been in it and been healthy. It makes me feel sad and angry all at the same time.'

He let out a sob and pushed tears from his eyes. Who cries in a dream? This wasn't a dream at all, this was something else.

'Sssh, there, there. Don't cry. It's alright. Remember, life is only a fleeting moment. It soon passes.'

She paused, then said, 'So you're going to London to see your publisher tomorrow. How wonderful. Writing your first novel must be exciting. You always had a vivid imagination. I remember when you told me and your dad that you were playing for the school football team and was the top scorer and even had a special pair of white boots bought by the school just for you to play in. You kept that story up for months. We even believed it for a while.'

It was Nick's turn to laugh a little.

'Yeah, well, reality has never seemed as much fun as the world I could make up in my own head. It's nice to be able to control the world in a book. I wish real life was like that.'

3

He looked at Julie again. She was still fast asleep and breathing deeply.

'Mam? Do you ever see dad? Or connect with him, or whatever it is you do?'

'Your dad? No. I don't know why. I'm not right sure how it works, our Nick. You just go into this different space and that's that. Maybe he's somewhere else. All the problems of life seem very brief and silly now.'

'And are you happy?'

'Well, I know it'll sound daft, but I can't tell. All of those sorts of things are just for when you've got a body. It's nowt to be scared of, though. It's just different, the way green is different from red. They're still both colours, just different. It's like that. You understand what I mean, don't you?'

He nodded.

'Of course you do. You always were a special lad. That's why I can talk to you now.'

'I've never felt special. At least not in a good way.'

'Oh, you are, our Nick. Very special. You just need to trust your instincts. I mean, take this publisher business in London. What do you think is going to happen tomorrow?'

He thought for a few seconds. 'Well, the bloke I'm meeting will be a middle class cardigan-wearer. I think they'll offer to publish the novel and give me a small advance but I'll feel alienated from them because I always feel alienated from London types, especially when they're middle class. I'll feel like a big vulgar Northern oik and that'll make me defensive and resentful.'

She nodded. 'How much will you get offered?'

'Two grand, I think and seven and half per cent royalty.'

She patted the quilt, tapping on his foot as she did so. If she was a ghost, she had a hand that he could definitely feel.

'That's right. Now that you know what's going to happen, think on and make the best of it. Make sure you make the right decision.'

'I don't understand, mam.'

'You will. You're special. If you think about it, you've always had it. Even when you were little, you had it.'

'Had what, mam?'

She stood up and brushed out the creases in her skirt.

'You know what's going to happen when you trust your instincts. You always did. You've just forgotten how to do it because the world puts so

4

many doubts in your mind that you don't have when you're little. Now, I'll try and look in on you now and again. Just be a nice lad and mind your manners, alright? Give my love to Julie.'

And with a little wave, she opened the closed bedroom door and walked out, shutting it behind her, or did she just fade away? It was hard to tell.

Nick leaned back on his hands, feeling hot, his heart racing. Scared. Or sort of. And yet so happy at seeing his mother again and seeing her as she once was: healthy, sane and kind.

He laid down, took a couple of deep breaths and closed his eyes. What did it all mean? Was this all some weird hallucination? Maybe it was a combination of whisky and his anti-depression drug? No, it couldn't be. It felt so real.

Glancing at the clock on the bedside radio, it still said 4.27am and had done so for the whole time he'd talked her, as if time was suspended. He was due on the 9am train from Darlington. His heart began to calm its pounding. He put his hands together on his chest, fingertip to fingertip and sucked in a deep breath of air.

'Have your tea. Then I'll run you to Darlo, before I go to work.'

Nick opened his eyes and groggily sat up. It was bright and sunny, the sun streaming into their east-facing bedroom. 'It's a gorgeous morning,' Julie said, standing naked at the window and putting on a white bra, then pulling on plain white underwear. She put her hands on her hips. 'Eee, it's cloudless out there,' she said, passing a big comb through her loosely curled shoulder-length, centre-parted blonde hair. 'Sleep well, luv?'

He took the paisley patterned mug of green tea and sipped from it. 'I'm not sure.'

She took a white shirt out of the wardrobe, put it on and buttoned it up as she looked out of the window again across an expanse of open, wild, scrubby grass covered in a scattering of trees and bushes, a little way beyond which were allotments. It was a nice bit of green space to be able to walk across from their own small back garden.

'It's a proper summer's day. I think it's going to get hot. Or hot by Teesside standards anyway, which means it'll be roasting down in London. You should wear those ecru linen jeans I got you for your birthday and your black stretchy t-shirt, so it won't show your wet armpits. You're such a sweaty boy. Eee, you and your copious bodily fluids, what are you like, eh?' She laughed to herself as she pulled his clothes out of the wardrobe and put them on the bed. 'It'll be stuffy in my office today. I'll be ready for a few ice-cold gins by the end of the day. Wouldn't mind one now, actually. Come on you, hands off cocks, hands on socks.'

He swung his legs out of bed and stood up. She slapped him on his bare backside and kissed him on the neck, running the palms of her hand over his chest and giving his balls a light squeeze, pulling a silly lustful face at him, as she often did, just to make him feel a bit special.

'That was a bloody good session last night,' she said. 'It's funny isn't it, when we were kids, I never imagined 50-year-olds would have shagging sessions like that. I think I thought you just lost interest in sex.'

'Maybe most people do. I'm sure my parents did. Maybe it's only me and you who haven't. And anyway, you're only 47. Still a mere lusty girl.'

'Nah, I reckon our generation is always at it. Sex is much better at our age. It is for me, anyway.'

'Aye, it's different to young lust, that's for sure. Lasts much longer, for a start.' He went to the bathroom to use the toilet and have a wash, returning rubbing his face with a red towel. Julie was sat in front of the dressing table mirror, rubbing moisturiser into her forehead and the crow's feet around her eyes, then rolling her hair up and clipping it on the back of her head, pulling a couple of long strands forward at the front.

He began to get dressed, pulling on the close-fitting black t-shirt and the lightweight jeans.

'Did you know they reckon men reach their sexual peak at 17 and women in their late 30s? Though quite what "peak" means, I don't know,' he said, finding some socks.

'That can't be true. 17-year-old lads are rubbish at it. It's like being assaulted by a dribbling, panting, overexcited puppy. Not that I've had it off with a 17 year old for 30 years, but some things never quite leave you.' She gurgled her best dirty laugh.

'I think they just call it peak because you can do it time and again without much of a rest.'

'Hmm. That sounds like a very typical male definition of "peak" to me. All about amount; quantity rather than quality.'

He laughed. 'Yeah, I'm sure you're right. Talking of panting and dribbling, I've still got one of your pubes stuck somewhere between my teeth. Give us your tweezers.' She passed them to him. He tried to nip it and pull it out but, only succeeded in snapping it, leaving half still buried between two teeth. 'That's going to annoy me all day now. Your pubes are very wiry.'

She pulled a face. 'Well, that's what you get for wearing me like a beard.' She kissed him on the lips. 'You'll have to get something to eat on the train if we're going to get to the station on time.'

Taking one last look in the mirror, she flicked at her hair with her fingertips and then stopped, her attention being caught by something outside.

'There's a bloke out the back, look,' she said.

Nick walked to the window and squinted at the bright morning. A man was squatting on his haunches behind a shrub on the rough ground beyond their garden, as though hiding from someone.

'Weird place to be. Why would you be there?'

'It looks like he's hiding, doesn't it?' she said. 'I think I've seen him before, you know. Do you recognise him?'

'Hard to say. I don't think so. I've seen him out there a couple of times in the last week or so, but just never thought anything of it. Isn't he just a dog walker or something?'

'No, he's not got a pooch. But yeah, he looks vaguely familiar to me. Can't say I've noticed him out there before, but that's not to say he's not been there.'

He was wearing a blue hooded sweatshirt and jeans, had short balding brown hair and a paunchy stomach. Perhaps he was in his late 40s.

'Is he spying on us, or the neighbours?' she said. 'Maybe he's a Peeping Tom. Eee, I was just standing at the window in the nuddy.' She cast him a shocked look.

'Maybe. Aren't you supposed to be better hidden if you're a peeper, though? And anyway, he'd have to hang around for a long time, just for the off-chance of a quick flash of some bare flesh. That seems very hard work when frankly, the internet is full of naked women,' he said.

Julie shook her head. 'Well, I routinely see women whose ex-partners just sit outside of their house or hide in the garden, often for hours at a time, day after day, week after week. It's not that uncommon.'

Nick frowned. 'Why do they do that? What's the point?'

She puffed out her cheeks and blew out air. 'I think they do it to allow themselves to feel part of their ex's life, still. And sometimes they do it out of jealousy that she's seeing someone else and they want to know what she's up to. Others just do it as a form of bullying and enjoy the fact that it makes her uncomfortable. It's...well...it's revenge, I suppose...or a form of revenge, at least. But it's obviously not mentally healthy behaviour.'

'Crazy men, doing crazy things...why am I not surprised? Maybe this bloke out there actually wants to be seen, for some reason. He's certainly not hiding, though he's not even looking up here. He's just sitting staring into the middle distance. Shall I wave at him?'

'Yeah go on, just so he knows, we know he's there.'

Nick did a big arcing comedy wave, but the man took no notice. 'He could be casing the houses, to rob them.'

'Nah, too obvious. I think he's just a trampy homeless bloke or something. Come on, we've got get going.'

As Julie drove them in her blue 1975 Porsche to Darlington along the A66, the white-gold late summer sun cast sharp shadows across the fields.

'Something very, very weird happened last night,' said Nick.

'What? While we were having some naughty?'

'No, when you were asleep.'

She cast him a glance. 'What, like?'

He took a deep breath and explained what had happened with his mother. As he told her, she let out little yelps of disbelief.

'Eee, my god. That must have freaked you out good and proper. And you were crying? Amazing what you can imagine in your dreams. I once imagined I was having it off with Robert Plant in a hotel in Los Angeles in 1973. It was so vivid down to every single detail. So much so that I can still remember some of it. I woke up in a proper lather.'

'I don't think this was a dream, Jules. Not a normal dream, anyway. Time was suspended, I felt the weight of her hand on my foot. I felt totally awake.'

She laughed as she dropped the gears, approaching a roundabout.

'I'm serious. It wasn't a dream. I was sat up in bed. She patted my feet. She was there, Jules. Really, she was. I looked down at you, asleep. I could feel the stubble on my chin. It was as real as sitting here is.'

'Getaway with you,' she said, dismissively.

'She knew about Joni.'

Julie let out a breath of exasperation. 'No, she didn't. You know about Joni. It was your dream. You dreamt it and you put the words into her mouth.'

8

'How did I dream feeling her touch me?'

'I don't know, but it's not impossible. I could feel Robert Plant doing it with me in my dream, to the point where I swear I could feel him inside me. But it was just a dream that I woke up from. The mind is a very powerful thing. It takes our actual experiences and blends them with fantasy or imaginings.'

'She said I always liked passionate girls.'

'So what? Oh, come on, you're not saying she was watching us last night? Come on, Nick, get a grip. She did not see me giving it the old moany-groany as you did your thing. That's too weird. I'm not 'avin' that, me. You're just feeding your own dreams.'

'I don't think she's there watching. She said she just sort of knows, rather than sees. I know it sounds crazy. But I was sitting up in bed, I looked at you asleep, it was 4.27, I looked at my glass of water, I rubbed my own face. I was awake.'

But Julie wasn't convinced. 'OK, so how did this all start?'

'I got shocked by something and I sat bolt upright.'

'What shocked you?'

'I don't know. I seemed to come from sleep to awake in an instant and she was just sitting at the foot of the bed, just like she used to when I was little. In fact, it was like it was still 1970 or 1971. She looked like she did back then, not how she was when she died.'

'See, that's not right. We always wake up bit by bit. No-one just sits up, instantly awake. Look, man, all you did was have a vivid dream. But it was still a dream.'

Nick looked out of the side window of the Porsche. He knew what she said made sense, but even so, couldn't shake the feeling that it had actually happened. But then, this wasn't an argument you could make and win. There was no proof to offer that he'd been talking to his dead mother. But in the bright summer light on a late August day in 2011, he felt it was 100 per cent true, even despite the fact he usually felt a bit cynical about so-called paranormal experiences. Yet when it happens to you, maybe you have to change your mind. None of us can be sure we know everything about such things.

So he went quiet. But even as he went quiet, once again, he could still hear her voice in his head. She felt so near. It was confusing but it wasn't a bad thing. Feeling his mam was still with him in his everyday life was very comforting.

As Julie pulled up at Darlington station, she put a hand on his face and kissed him on the lips.

'Good luck. Remember, you're a great writer. They're bound to want to buy your book. But don't sell yourself too cheaply, right? If it's not a good deal, don't take it.'

He nodded, gave her a quick, tight hug and kissed her goodbye.

There's nothing quite like settling down for a long train journey. Trains allow you to do nothing, whilst simultaneously feeling like you're getting somewhere. It never quite feels like that when driving, not even when being a passenger in a car.

Nick sank into his seat, wondering why the whole carriage smelled of burnt shit. Maybe the toilet was on fire. It was so hit and miss on the trains. Sometimes you got a nice new one, other times one that was like an exhausted insanitary cattle wagon. The fact it wasn't a nationalised service really pissed him off. It made such obvious sense for it to be state run and not fragmented across all sorts of companies, all of whom seemed to need public subsidies, anyway. Bloody idiot Tory idea. Some children started crying, making a noise that felt like a hot needle in his ear. He put his iPod on to block it out, took out his phone and texted Jeff.

'*On the train to London to meet Storyville Publishers about my novel. Will be back by 9.30pm, fancy a late drink in the Royal Oak?*'

Jeff soon texted back. '*Forgot about you doing that. Am in the Newcastle shop with Lukey. Yeah, text me when you're home. Bet you feel like a dirty bit of working class, Northern rough at a London publisher. It'll be all posh people called Jeremy and Clarissa. Hope it goes well. If it doesn't, just shit on someone's desk and tell them it's an artistic statement about decay being at the heart of all existence.*'

Nick grinned. He liked London, or bits of it anyway, but it had always felt like a foreign country from the first time he'd gone there with the school in 1973 to see the Tutankhamen exhibition. Everyone was in such a hurry and so keen to avoid your eye, it made being in such a crowded place, bizarrely isolating. Also it was very noticeable how everyone seemed so uptight, unhappy and stressed out, compared to back home. As a result, it seemed quite a poor quality of life, and when you threw in an incredibly high cost of living, especially housing, he'd never understood why anyone who had the option to live and work somewhere else, didn't do so. Maybe London was addictive and if you left, it'd feel like you were no longer at the epicentre of things.

As he walked out of King's Cross station and down Euston Road, the air felt thick and hot and cars were jammed up as far as you could see. People were absolutely everywhere, crawling over everything like armies of oversized ants. The ceaseless ebbing and flowing tide of humans was almost overwhelming, when you came from a relatively quiet town, which was basically only ever properly busy for an hour or two on a Saturday afternoon, and even then, only around the Pound Pub.

God knows, Teesside wasn't exactly a pretty place, but at least you could see the Cleveland Hills from almost anywhere in the region, so you could see a world beyond wherever you were, but that was something you just couldn't do in London. And that always made it quite claustrophobic, not least because the air felt dirty and used, like it had been through millions of lungs and had had all the goodness extracted out of it. Not just polluted, but exhausted.

Yet the history and architecture and all the stories that went with the capital did make it interesting, fascinating even. When he was a kid, he'd had the notion that you could buy anything in London. Anything at all. London used to have a mystique to it when you lived in the northeast, but it didn't have it for him any more; its streets seemed increasingly paved with misery, as inequality of wealth and opportunity became endemic. Compared to living in the north, it just wasn't as good on almost any level and it had always annoyed him how London had such a self-regard, often despite ignorance of almost anywhere else, yet still tried to pass itself off as cosmopolitan. Then again, maybe he was overthinking it.

He crossed the road and walked down Bloomsbury Street, looking for the offices of Storyville. He'd sent some sample chapters of his novel to them and they'd written back and said they loved it and invited him down to talk about it.

But he hated meetings. Meetings meant you had to pretend to be normal and well adjusted, especially meetings like this where you, at least in theory, had something to gain by saying and doing the right thing, and he could never trust himself to either say or do the right thing in almost any social situation. Also the pressure of trying to be interesting was something he didn't always cope well with. In fact, it tended to have the opposite effect and he ended up defensive and uncommunicative, or just sweating heavily, while desperately trying to think of something to say. If he turned up and the meeting had been cancelled, he'd not mind in the slightest. A meeting where the other guy doesn't show up is always a bonus, because it means you don't have to have a meeting, and not having a meeting beats having one, every day of the week.

The Storyville offices were in what had originally been a Georgian house, set behind a big glossy black door. Feeling nervous and resenting that fact, he rang the bell. A woman's voice spoke out of the small silver intercom.

'Hello!' she said, cheerfully.

'Hi. It's Nick Guymer, I have an 11.30 with Tim Forest.' God, he fancied a drink. Southern men called Tim always made you want to drink.

'Oh, yes. Come in, Nick.'

The door buzzed, he pushed it and walked in. It was air conditioned, which was a relief. As Julie had predicted, his armpits were soaked with sweat, as a result of the combination of physical exertion and nerves. As he entered the building, a droplet of sweat ran down his back. He caught a glimpse of himself in a full-length mirror at the end of a hallway. In the fitted black t-shirt and ecru linen jeans, brown leather boots, and his hair cut shorter and tidier than normal, thanks to Emily's amateur hairdressing abilities, he looked relatively smart, or at least, smart for him. That gave him a little spark of confidence and even if his armpits were sodden, as least you couldn't easily tell.

"Just trust in your instincts, Nick." His mother's voice popped into his head out of nowhere, making him smile. He took a deep breath. C'mon, let's do this.

A woman with chocolate eyes and raven hair smiled up at him from behind a reception desk.

'Hello, Nick, thanks for coming down to see us,' she said, in a voice without an accent. He didn't like voices without accents. Even if he'd wanted to, which he didn't, he could never have stripped himself of his Teesside accent. It was burnt into his DNA like a tattoo. Accentless people felt like they'd been bleached of localness, like they had no roots. Also, people without accents were very middle class and, though he was far from the most working-class Teessider, London's middle class was a breed apart altogether. All of which meant he felt socially out of his depth immediately.

He tried to smile, made the shape with his mouth, but it was fake. He didn't feel happy and he just wanted it to all be over quickly now.

Talking to himself, telling himself to calm down and take it easy because it'd be good if he could get this novel published and potentially

12

start another career, he swallowed hard and wished once again that he had a triple vodka on hand.

She was one of those self-confident, at-ease, middle-class twenty somethings who were professionally pleasant. With a lavender cashmere twinset, a string of pearls around her neck and her straight dark hair pushed back under a black Alice band, she looked almost psychotically straight, like she'd never so much as farted in her life. There was both a weirdly naive and yet hard-eyed look about her, a look which he'd always thought almost unique to London people. Then again, there was a chance, a very good chance, that he was once again totally overthinking things, imposing a lot of preconceived notions onto someone and that she was actually just a perfectly nice, regular person. Her name badge revealed she was called Sophie. She really was such a Sophie.

'Did you have a good journey down?' she said.

'Well, the train smelt of burnt poo. But apart from that, it was OK.' Should he have said that? Bugger, probably shouldn't have.

She pulled a face and wrinkled her nose and turned her mouth down. 'Ooh. Nasty. Can I get you anything to drink? Tim will be with you soon.'

'I'm fine, thanks. Well, actually, I was just thinking how much I'd like a vodka and tonic, but it's probably a bit early for that and you don't keep vodka in your desk, do you?'

She laughed politely. 'Sadly, no.'

He took a seat on a green leather sofa. The whole place looked like it came out of a copy of *World of Interiors*. Plain, airy and tasteful with rich colour accents, it seemed a little over the top for a place which was meant to service authors, most of whom probably lived in messy, scruffy homes. People milled around, coming in and out of other rooms. All of them gave him a quick smile, all were smart but casual, all were very clean and tidy, all very middle class, just as he'd told his mother they would be.

A man wearing a navy blue cardigan and with a receding hairline trotted down some stairs, advancing on Nick with his hand held outstretched. He was in his mid 40s and, by the confident air which swept before him, obviously public school educated. When you come from Teesside and your alma mater is Ian Ramsey School, this stuff is somehow just very obvious.

As the hand came towards him, Nick gripped it, taken with a passive-aggressive notion to grip it as hard as he could, pretty much attempting to

13

break some bones. Let him know who was boss. The man didn't even wince. Disappointing. Bloody hell, what was he thinking? Just be a nice lad. That's what mam had always said. Accidentally, he let out a deep sigh, which probably made him seem a bit odd.

'Hello, Nick. Thanks for coming down to London. Quite a journey for you to make. Let's go up to my office.'

Nick followed him up the stairs. How did they pay for offices like this? By exploiting writers, clearly. Why have it here in north London, why not be in, say, Seaton Carew? Everything was online now. You didn't need to be in primo real estate to talk to writers about books, nor to send pdf files to printers and have middle-class women in expensive twinsets sit and smile at you. It was all bullshit, surely.

He instinctively felt the arsey Teessider stir in him. Who did these people think they were, some sort of arbiters of taste? Yeah, like a public schoolboy in a cardigan in north London would know anything about what a Teessider wanted to read. In a way, it was laughable.

He was shown into a room which had probably been some wealthy Georgian citizen's bedroom and was just as tastefully decorated as downstairs, with a big plaster rose in the centre of the ceiling, from which hung a large chandelier.

'Take a seat, Nick. Coffee?' he pointed at a jug.

'Nah. I'm fine. Thanks. You don't have any vodka, do you?'

'Vodka? Err...no. Sorry.'

'Not to worry.'

Tim sat behind a grand, black oak desk, Nick quite deliberately sat with his legs apart, in the manner of every alpha male footballer on TV. Occupy the space. Be assertive. It didn't come naturally to him normally, but here in London, in front of a middle-class public schoolboy called Tim, it really wasn't as difficult as it would be in the Royal Oak, back home. Back home he was the introspective, beta male who overthought and was over-sensitive. Here in London, he felt more like a dirty Northern sod. And actually, that felt rather good. Maybe taking a shit on the desk, as Jeff had suggested, would be appropriate after all.

'So you liked the book?' said Nick.

'Yes, we all loved it. You've got such a distinctive voice, Nick. The dialogue shows a great ear. It's funny and emotional, too...I really cared what happened to your protagonist, Kidda. And like I say, it's a such a distinctive voice with which you write.'

'What do you mean, exactly?' said Nick, as ever, feeling uncomfortable with praise.

'Well, it evokes the region so well.'

Nick looked out of the window and thought for a moment. 'OK, but how do you actually know? It's a book about a lad from Stockton-on-Tees who, because he is brilliant at football, becomes famous and he can't cope with it and has a complete breakdown. Do you actually know what Stockton is like?'

His tone was aggressive and clearly took Tim by surprise. He was more used to writers being weak at the knees at the prospect of being published, but that was never going to happen today.

'Well, no, I've not been there, but the flavour of the locality really came through. You manifested it so well in your prose.'

'Did it? You're assuming the language I've used is correct for the region. It might not be.'

'It feels very authentic. It's a kind of modern-day *Rake's Progress*, but with added psychological and emotional breakdown, isn't it?'

That annoyed Nick, because it absolutely was that and he wanted Tim to be ignorant of that fact. Then again he'd probably been educated at a cost of 30 grand year so he damn well should know.

'Yeah, well, I wanted to write about how someone from a background similar to mine would react to success.'

Tim nodded. 'It's very funny, too. I'm an Arsenal fan, I loved the section about how Kidda hates Arsenal. '

'Well, you lot need hating. You're the most precious, middle-class poncey football club in England, aren't you?'

Tim laughed and took some papers out of a folder.

'I think you're probably right, certainly compared to Middlesbrough.' He looked up at him. 'Look Nick, you've got a great track record as football writer, established over many years. You've got a good following on social media already, so we'd love to publish *Kidda*. We can offer you an advance of two thousand pounds and a royalty of 7.5 per cent. How does that sound?'

'Predictable.'

CHAPTER 2

He'd said it before he even had time to think. His mother had been right, he'd known exactly what to expect from this meeting. This was exactly what he had told her would happen.

'Not interested, Tim. Sorry, but frankly, that's a bit of an insult. I spent over a year writing that book. If you think you can only sell enough copies to recoup two grand then you might as well not even bother. I want 50 grand or you don't get the book. If you give me a 50 grand advance, it'll make you work hard to make sure you sell some copies to recoup your outlay. Two grand means you won't. That's right, isn't it?'

Tim was clearly shocked by this. He sat back and stared at Nick. Probably no-one had ever turned down his offer to publish a book before, let alone then been told what advance he wanted.

'I'm sorry, Nick, advances like that are rare these days for non-celebrity authors.'

That just annoyed Nick even more. He folded his arms across the chest and sat back in his chair.

'Yeah, yeah. I don't care about that. Can you pay me 50 grand?'

'I'm sorry, no we can't. There's no chance of any publisher paying out that sort of advance on someone like...'

His anger was already locked and loaded. '...like what? On someone like me? Someone not off the telly, you mean. Someone who you've never bloody heard of?'

'It's just economics, Nick.' He said it apologetically. 'It's not a judgement on your quality as a writer. Really, it isn't. This is the world we live in now.'

'With all due respect, Tim, it's the world you live in. Not me. I don't want to live in that world. Well, we're done here. I'm not selling you my art, the art I've lived a lifetime to craft. An art you will treat like so much mince. I'm not that daft, Tim.' He squeezed his bicep and felt like he'd done a good thing. 'You don't get the good shit for nothing, mate, or you shouldn't. Sorry.'

Being Northern in London is a huge asset. For a start, you have the ability to scare the nice people with your accent, secondly, a bit of blunt speaking often catches the Southern middle class off guard because they're so used to being polite but dishonest with each other. It seems to be a social prerequisite when millions of people live on top of and around millions of other people.

Tim looked him in the eye. He'd probably had officer training at public school to deal with stroppy squaddies like Nick. 'That's disappointing, Nick. I was looking forward to working with you on this. I loved the book. I really did. It has humour, pathos and soul. You draw the Northeast almost poetically, and with an obvious passion and affection. And there's a good chance of selling the rights to TV.'

That almost upset Nick. It was a proper compliment. Damn it, he hated it when people he wanted to hate said nice, perceptive things. He took a moment before replying, rubbing at the lines on his forehead.

'Thanks, Tim; well, pay me properly then. I don't even mean the advance. That's irrelevant. I mean give me 25 per cent of every sale. That's not unreasonable. Remember, you don't have a job without me and people like me.'

'I really wish I could do that.'

He did seem genuinely sorry that it wasn't possible. Nick had actually begun to warm to him. Once again his mother's words about being a nice lad and having good manners came back to him, so he took a slow, deep breath and exhaled.

'But Tim, don't you understand? If I publish this myself, I'll make about £4.50 a book, if you pay me a 7.5 per cent royalty, I'll make about 50p, if I'm lucky, by the time all the discounts kick in. How are you going to sell nine times more books than I can sell?'

'Well, we can get it into Waterstones...'

'...so can I, though it's hardly important anymore in terms of sales numbers. You can sit for hours in a bookshop and see only a handful of books sold. There are too many books and not enough punters. Would you spend money on a promotion campaign?'

Tim clicked into auto-reply mode.

'Funds are limited for non-celebrity authors, or for people who are not already best sellers...'

'...so the answer is no.'

'Well...obviously we'd send out a press release and...'

'...so you'd send an email out to reviewers?'

'Yes.'

'I can do that, too. Their email addresses are all publicly available - though we both know that very few people take any notice of them these days, especially if it's not literary fiction, which *Kidda* isn't.'

'Well...yes, that's true.' He was apologetic once more. Again, Nick took a deep breath and tried to be nice.

'OK, so what else could you do for me?'

'Obviously, you'd work with one of our experienced editors.'

'That's great but I can pay an editor to edit my book - in fact I know someone who spent their life being an editor who now works freelance because they can earn more than working for a publisher.'

That was all Tim had. He was out of ammunition.

Nick looked at him squarely and, though he'd won the argument hands down, he felt a wave of guilt for doing so in such a brusque manner. Tim was obviously a nice guy and he hadn't been in the slightest bit arsey with him. Like a lot of Southern middle-class men, compared to their Northern counterparts he was a little insubstantial and without much grit about him, but obviously not a bad person and quite gentle in his own way. Nick knew he'd been too aggressive and harsh with him.

'It's all over this, isn't it?' said Nick, looking around the room, knowing their chat was almost over and feeling relief at that fact.

'What is?'

'You guys. Publishing books in posh places like this. No offence, Tim, but it looks like something from another era. You know you've got nothing to offer over and above what we can do for ourselves, but you're still trying to sell yourself as some sort of gatekeeper to the quality world of letters. It's a bit ridiculous, if you don't mind me saying so. I think you know it, too. You're spending so much money on property like this that you're virtually signing your own financial death warrant, unless you can be propped up by a wealthy benefactor, and it's all to pretend you have status, when really, as you've just illustrated by what you could do for me as a novelist, you don't have any status. Soon you'll be left only with the writers who simply can't be bothered to publish and distribute their own work, or celebrity ghost-written stuff. Anyone with a bit about them will have jumped ship, out of financial necessity, as much as anything.'

Tim nodded. 'I can't really argue against that. The whole industry is in a state of flux right now. Everyone is running around like a headless chicken trying to find a way to make money.'

'I do understand that. See, the problem is, you're asking to make a living from writers, but are unable or unwilling to pay us the same respect, even though you don't have a career without us. Do you see what I'm saying? I know this is how it's always been done, but it's basically unfair. The money is going to the wrong people in the wrong amounts.'

Tim got up and poured himself some coffee into a small white cup. 'Sure you don't want any?' he said.

'Go on then, yeah, black. Thanks.'

Nick took the cup from him, telling himself once again not to be harsh; after all, Tim was just a cog in the machine, not the whole machine. But you had to fight for yourself, didn't you? Nothing was handed to you on a plate when you were from Teesside.

'What you say, in large measure, is correct, of course it is,' said Tim, sitting down again. 'As I said, the publishing industry is in a state of revolution and no-one knows where it's all going to end up. Our model here, and I'll be honest with you about this, is to publish a lot of books, gamble very little money, hope to break even on most of them and occasionally get a hit. It's a low-risk strategy.'

Nick nodded. 'I totally get that. You've got try and survive,' said Nick. 'But the public isn't interested in who publishes a book, they just want a good read and if a writer can put a good book under their nose, then that's the job done.' He sipped at the coffee. It tasted more like some weird sort of Bovril. Christ, they kept up these appearances but couldn't afford decent coffee.

Tim Forest nodded. 'The glory days of publishing are long gone. Authors used to get properly remunerated, along with a publicity campaign et cetera. But now, because we churn out so many books, that's just not possible. We just couldn't risk advancing you 50 thousand because, frankly Nick, it almost certainly wouldn't sell enough copies to recoup that. Almost nothing sells in big numbers. Some weeks you could be in the top 10 best fiction sellers just by selling a few hundred copies. About half of the money earned by writers is earned by the top one per cent.'

Nick nodded again. 'I know. I assume that I'm not going to have a best seller, so I need to make as much as possible from every sale and 7.5 per cent is never going to be enough. Not even near.' He drank the coffee and put the cup on the desk. 'Sorry we couldn't do business, Tim. I'm glad you liked my novel, though. Thanks for that. This whole thing feels weird. A bit like going back in time. It's not a world I feel comfortable in, to be honest with you.'

He stood up and they shook hands.

'I understand that and I'm sorry you've had a wasted trip down,' said Tim. 'I still think you're a talented writer and I wish you all the best of luck. You said my offer was predictable. How come?'

'Well, I dreamed it the other night, actually. I got your offer right, and even your cardigan too.' He laughed a little, but Tim wasn't so amused. Had he offended him? He might have done, but Nick just couldn't tell.

'That's actually very interesting. Tell me, do you believe in precognition?'

'Sounds like a progressive rock band. What's precognition?'

'Being able to see future events, even when you're asleep.'

Nick made a doubtful face at him. 'My mother says I'm special but I don't think I'm that kind of special. I certainly never predict Boro's results correctly.'

'Do you dream them, though?'

'No. Dreaming about the Boro would more typically be a nightmare. Or it was under Strachan, anyway.'

Tim took a book from a shelf and handed it to him. 'I was involved in editing this. It's fascinating stuff. I think so, anyway. She makes a really interesting case for precognition being available to all of us, if we just tune into the right wavelength, so to speak.'

Nick looked at the cover. *Dream Power*. It looked like a self-help book, especially because it had a very long subtitle: *Unlock the power of your subconscious and become at one with the past, present and future*.

Normally, it was the sort of book he'd have dropped like a hot brick, but he took it, just to be polite and also because he'd apparently been talking to his dead mother a few hours earlier and that still echoed powerfully in his mind. Had he been asleep, or in some other strange state of mind? Who the hell knew?

'Thanks. I'll give it a read on the train north.'

'If you do have a change of heart about us publishing *Kidda*, just drop me a line.'

Nick nodded. 'And if you have change of heart about the advance and royalty, get in touch.'

Tim laughed a little. 'Of course. Are you going back straight away?'

'I'm on the 6pm train. Think I'll go for drink. It's so airless down here. I don't know how you stand it in the city.'

'I sometimes wonder that myself.' He smiled nicely and it again made Nick wish he'd been pleasant from the start, instead of fighting a battle that no-one was even fighting with him. God, he'd done that too much in life. It was time to start taking more notice of his mother.

Nick stepped out into the bright summer sunshine and went in search of a drink, finding a rather nice wine bar, which also did food. Was it a restaurant or a bar, then? The lines seemed increasingly blurred these days. It was a long way from getting a toastie and pint of Stones bitter in the Stockton Arms in 1979. How things had changed for his generation. No longer a beer drinker, he ordered a double vodka and tonic and sat down at a pavement table to text Julie about his meeting. As he typed a message he reflected once again on how much easier the meeting had been once he remembered his mother's words. Trusting himself to say and do the right thing was difficult for him and he often ended up being defensive, when there was no need. Maybe his mother *was* trying to help him from beyond the grave.

He was only a couple of hours from home, but it really did feel like he was sitting in a different world, as men and women, seemingly taking half an hour away from the office, dressed in expensive dark suits and crisp white shirts, came and went, mostly staring at their phones for 85 per cent of their existence. They all seemed so busy and there were a lot more frowns than smiles. It was odd, really. You couldn't say this wasn't a massive lifestyle upgrade on sitting outside of the Pound Pub back home, but then people didn't seem any more happy for it; less so if any-thing, and, as he knew only too well, being happy or content in your own mind is pretty much the only thing that matters in life. Without it, you've got nothing. Without it, life is a hollow, empty shell and, as he sat and quietly observed, it looked like there were quite a few of those around.

His phone buzzed. A short text from Julie. '*You did the right thing. 100 per cent. Enjoy your afternoon in London. See you later. Love you. xx*'

As he sipped at the cold drink, he scanned the book that Tim had given him. The author, Sally Mackay, had apparently just made up an idea and then tried to 'prove' it was true, ending by concluding she had, despite having offered no actual proof. She seemed to be saying that when we're asleep we're existing on a different plane of consciousness. There were diagrams of the brain and electrical scans of activity and where it happened in your head when asleep. It appeared that the part of your brain being used was largely only used when asleep. She surmised this was our key to unlocking a non-linear consciousness, which, once we understood it, could allow us to go forward and backwards in time and see our past and our future. She quoted examples of people who had apparently had detailed precognition of famous events, such as the sink-ing of the Titanic. The trouble was, in a world of several billion people, there is probably always a handful dreaming about something happening to a prominent person or object, which then subsequently happens. It's probably just the law of averages mixed with a little knowledge. Did he have precognition of being offered a £2,000 advance or was it just an informed lucky guess? The latter, surely.

Mackay's book read more like science fiction than the serious textbook it purported to be. Naturally, and somewhat inevitably, it contained references to ancient tribes who had words for being able to see into the future through dreams. When in doubt, throw in an obscure tribe or two to add a bit of ethnic credibility to your fabrications. In such books there's often an awful habit of defaulting to the idea that we in the West are dumb saps, but tribes who live up a tree in the Amazon are able to live in ways we can't comprehend because they're so close to nature, even though said tribe being off its face on hallucinogenic herbs and mushrooms seemed to Nick almost certainly to wholly explain their time-travelling ability.

The whole book seemed completely based in supposition. The only plausibility it had was because our experience of dreaming is so unlike anything else we're conscious of, it's easy to assign any amount of theories to it and they can still seem vaguely possible. Even so, it was interesting, after a fashion. He had little doubt the brain had unexplored potential. Or at least his did.

The author reckoned that the déjà vu feeling is actually our conscious and unconscious worlds intertwining briefly, giving our conscious minds access to this subconscious superhighway of non-linear time, and, just for a second or three, you are existing in more than one place simultaneously; both in the then and in the now.

Man, she must have been smoking some good dope when she wrote this. Nick ordered himself another drink along with some poached eggs, avocado and bacon from the light lunch menu at the cost of nearly 20 bloody quid, and wondered if he could travel back through his life, where he'd go.

Back to the happy summer of 1979 aged 18, before leaving for college, for sure, and that last time his mother had been healthy. Back to Alan Fearnley's record shop in 1976 when he'd seen a copy of *Five Live Yardbirds* on the original blue and black Columbia label for £1.00 but for some reason hadn't bought it. That was worth £250 now. Back to meeting Julie for the first time in Jack & Danny's bar in Harrogate, when she turned to him, smiled and made his heart leap. Back to a holiday in Torquay in a hot summer week in 1970, the only really enjoyable holiday his family had ever had. Back to the first blow job he'd ever had when at college and being amazed that a woman would do such a thing without him even asking.

Just sitting watching London go about its frenetic, expensive business and recalling all those times made him feel happy and, in a way, that was like revisiting them; a form of time travel. But what was that process? What is a memory? Where is it until you remember it? How come you can forget almost everything about your life on a day-to-day basis, but a smell, a song, or any amount of random things can suddenly trigger an intense recollection that, until that moment, you didn't seem to have retained any knowledge of?

He had kept diaries during his teenage years and when he read them, he could recall the incidents right away, but without those notes, would never have done so. He knew that was the case because so much had happened and yet he had retained almost none of it. So where did all of that memory go when you couldn't access it? Being human was sometimes an intensely trippy, weird thing when you stopped to think about it.

Something came back to him as he crunched an ice cube. Around the age of 13, as he was in the intense and amazing throes of puberty, something undeniably odd had started to happen to him and even as a young boy, he'd known it was downright strange, even though it had never frightened him.

He'd been walking down Palm Grove, going to school in the morning and as he passed by the last house in the road, the phone in that house, presumably on a hall table by the door, as was traditional back then, rang. He'd thought nothing of it.

But the next day, the exact same thing happened, even though it was five minutes earlier. He noted it, but still thought nothing of it. The following day was a Saturday and, as he often did, he decided to walk into town in the afternoon in the hope of seeing some girls from school. Again, the end house's phone began ringing as he passed the front door, and then stopped as he went beyond the house.

And it kept happening. No matter what time of day he walked past the house, the phone rang. His dad had told him it was just a coincidence, but now that he thought about it, his mother had been much more sympathetic and understanding. She had said that sometimes unusual things like this happened to special boys like him, but not to be scared about it. She'd put her hand on the back of his head and stroked his hair, to reassure him. But he hadn't been scared, just amazed, so much so that he'd 'tested' it by running past the house at pace, setting the phone off for a single ring, and be past the house before it could ring again. Conversely, if he just stood outside the house without moving, the phone just kept ringing and was never answered. However, even more crazy, if he was with anyone else, nothing happened. No ringing, nothing. It only happened when he was on his own. There was no way it could have been a coincidence. No way for it to happen by accident. The ringing was caused by his presence and was stopped by someone else being there.

It had gone on for four weeks when one Wednesday morning, he walked past the house on his own and the phone didn't ring. And it never rang again.

He'd gone to Fairfield branch library to try and find out if this was something which had happened to anyone else and had found a book on the supernatural which said children who were going through puberty were often capable of unconscious, uncontrolled so-called supernatural acts. His natural inclination to not believe himself to be special meant he'd dismissed that as a possibility. But then other stuff happened as puberty progressed and he developed terrible blisters from relentless and overly enthusiastic masturbation.

He could toss a coin and guess which way it'd fall 9 times out of 10. Just as his mother had said, he knew when things would happen just before they happened, whether it was his dad coming home from work, or the milkman arriving. For all he knew, other kids went through the exact same things. It didn't last long, though.

The only time things got scary was when he woke up in the middle of the night with the overpowering sense that someone was in the room, but he was unable to move or even make a noise. It was as if he was being pinned down by an invisible force and, for the first and only time, it felt malevolent and frightening. Then it passed and he went back to sleep. In later years, he was sure it had been a bout of sleep paralysis, where your brain is awake but your body is asleep.

By and large he kept it all to himself, and it had soon all stopped, never to return, and he'd not really thought about it much since. It was all a long time ago. If he had some sort of gift, it hadn't showed itself since.

Julie was surely right, meeting his mam was just a vivid dream drawing on his waking life. Of course it was. Even so, it lingered with him the way a dream just never normally did. Dreams are usually like paintings in the sand that are washed away by the tide of consciousness, but his recollection was as detailed and clear as if it had been a real meeting. That was the really odd thing about it.

Enjoying his food and drink, he felt disinclined to go and do anything cultural. He'd often sat on his own drinking, ever since his first days of underage boozing in the American Tavern at the back of Debenhams in 1976. Other kids sat at home, but he went out and drank quietly on his own and just loved it, even sitting in pubs and reading school set texts. Later in his 20s and 30s he'd liked little more than to stay at home and get pissed. In fact, at one point in Harrogate, he used to go to bed with two bottles of wine and drink until he passed out, in the knowledge he was already in a comfy, safe place.

Of course, drinking on your own could be a lonely, depressing business at times, but mostly it wasn't, or not for him, anyway. Being sober, lonely and depressed was a more familiar experience. There was something undeniably great about drinking on your own. Just you and your mate, the booze. No obligation to talk, be articulate or entertaining. Just you yourself alone, insulated by the double-glazing of intoxication. It was in those moments when alcohol really did feel like a friend who would never let you down, albeit a friend who might trip you up and make you fall through a plate glass window, occasionally.

So he let the hot afternoon slip by on a river of vodka and tonic and then made his way back to King's Cross feeling very mellow indeed, picking up four small cans of vodka and cranberry juice for the journey home. All the previous tension of the day that preceded the meeting had gone.

It was a clean, modern train back to Darlington and it didn't smell of anything that might have come from inside a human body, which was a huge bonus. Better still, it was quite empty. So he put his iPod on, opened a drink and settled down for the ride, tucked into his seat as though it was his own private nest.

It had just left Peterborough station when his phone vibrated in his pocket. It was Jeff calling.

'Hey, big man,' said Nick. 'Mind, I've been drinking all day, so if it sounds like I've had a stroke, I haven't, it's just the booze killing me brain cells.'

'Good lad. Where are you?'

'Just left Peterborough. I'll be back in 90 minutes. It's a fast train.'

'Good. I'll pick you up at Darlo in the van.'

'It's OK, man, Jules is Porsching me home.'

'It's OK, I'll pick you up instead.'

'Err...alright...but why?' He already sensed something odd about Jeff's tone. He was trying to be too casual.

'There's nothing to worry about...'

That always meant there was something to worry about.

'...but something a bit odd has happened.'

Nick closed his eyes and inwardly groaned. Nothing odd had happened for a full year. Not since their honeymoon in Edinburgh, in fact. And he liked nothing odd happening.

'What's wrong?' he said, wearily.

'You won't like it, I'm afraid.'

'Of course I won't like it, I don't like odd things happening. It usually means I have to hit someone in the face and hurt my hand. That's how odd things always seem to end these days.'

'Yeah, I think that might be the case here. Wouldn't surprise me, anyway.'

'Why?'

'Jules has got a stalker.' He said it flatly.

Nick looked at the back of the grey plastic seat. 'What? How? She didn't have a stalker this morning. Is she alright?'

'She's safe. Don't worry about that. She's fine. Everything is cool.'

'Well, why hasn't she called me?'

'She's gone straight down to the Teesside Women offices and is talking to her manager about it. Working out a strategy, like. They deal with this sort of stuff from time to time, apparently, blokes stalking women, I mean. She reckons it might be the ex of someone she's helped at work, who wants some sort of revenge on her, so she called me, told me what was going on and asked if I could pick you up at the station. I think she wanted to get it all sorted in her own mind before she spoke to you.'

Nick stared at the back of the seat in front of him.

'OK. So how's he been stalking her? Was it the bloke we saw out the back of the house this morning?'

'Yeah, she mentioned that, so it probably is him. She reckons someone in a Range Rover followed her into work this morning, then at lunchtime she went into Yarm and they followed her again, then back to work and was waiting to follow her again when she drove home, only she didn't stay at home, she turned around on Oxbridge Lane and went back to her office, after calling her manager and her boss.'

'Did Jules approach the stalker?'

'No. They're told not to. If it persists you have to report it. They take it really seriously. I had a quick word with Mandy about it. Not much the police can do, at least initially. He has to become a real nuisance...but...but that's not everything. There's something else, something worse, like.'

'Bloody hell, Jeff, what now?'

Jeff took a depth breath.

'Someone, probably the same bloke, like, has posted pictures of her on a false Facebook page and on a website in the last day or two.'

'Eh? Photos? Are they photographing her on the street or something?'

'Some are like that, yeah, others are...'

'...are what?'

'Are...' he let out another exhalation of air '...are...well...the fact is...they're pornographic.'

CHAPTER 3

'Pornographic? What? I don't understand. Are they Photoshopped?'

'She reckons not. She said she'd send you the links. I've not looked at them and I don't want to see them. Doesn't seem right. When she called me and told me what was going on, she told me that they were...' he hesitated, struggling to find the words.

'Were what, Jeff?'

'Well...were rude, like. Anyway, it's probably just some nutter. It'll all blow over. I'll see you in a bit in Darlo.'

Nick cursed silently and opened another can of vodka and cranberry. Why couldn't life just go smoothly? Why was someone always stirring the shit, one way or another? He texted Julie to tell her Jeff had called and told him what was going on, determined not to invest his words with any sense of fear or panic. As they pulled out of York station she texted back.

'Hiya. Sorry I couldn't call, I just had to get into work and talk to Hilary, my manager and then to Martha, the boss, too. Get a strategy in place. I don't know who it is and I don't remember the pictures being taken. I had no idea they even existed. They're from the early 90s. We can get the Facebook page taken down, the website might be tougher. They're not very nice, but they are very typical of this sort of perp. He's trying to humiliate and discredit me. I either know him or he knows someone I know or knew. I'm sorry that you've got to see these, luv. But you might as well know what it's all about. He won't win.'

It was typically strong of her. Underneath were two links.

He took a drink and fearfully clicked on the Facebook one.

The page was clearly trying to pretend to be Julie's own page, even though she already had a long-established page. Outwardly it seemed innocent enough. The cover had the same picture of the transporter bridge on it as her own page. But her profile picture was a recent one that he'd never seen before. A close-up head shot of her laughing. All information on it was set to private so only friends could see it. He could see that it already had 11 friends. He clicked the 'Friend Request' button and then went to the website link, www.juliewellsuk.tv

As soon as the front page loaded, his heart sank. Shit. He rubbed his forehead and scrunched his eyes closed. He really didn't want to see this, but he was going to have to see it.

There were four photos in each of three separate blocks of images. Each of them opened to a larger version. The first block had been taken recently in Norton. In two she was mid-step, walking past the library, hands in jeans pockets. In another, she was sitting in the local cafe having coffee, looking at her laptop, and in the fourth unlocking the Porsche outside the house. Underneath was written in block capital letters and, annoyingly, with no apostrophe on the word *she's*, 'SHE LOOKS RE-SPECTABLE BUT SHES A SLUT'.

Another block of four photos was directly below. Clearly, they'd been taken a long time ago. She looked about 20 years younger. Her hair was bleached to almost platinum, centre-parted but raggy and messy in an early Courtney Love sort of style. She wore bright red lipstick and black eyeliner. He'd never seen her looking like this before.

In all four shots, she was lying naked on a bed. White sheets, nothing identifiable. Obviously unconscious, judging by her slack jaw and the almost unnatural angle she was lying at, she was probably drunk or drugged. Shockingly and sickeningly, she had been ejaculated on by more than one man. It was all over her in three distinct streaks and blobs.

The second block of four photos were more of the same, taken from a different angle.

A third block was gynecological, taken at the same time as the previous photos. They'd pushed her legs wide apart and two index fingers, one on either side of her, just pointed to her vagina, in and on which was more semen. It was unmistakably Julie.

You couldn't do this unless you were a misogynist. It was designed to be humiliating and to exert power, to say, 'Look what we did to you'. You couldn't do it unless you were an absolute monster. Men could be bastards, that much was obvious, but surely most men wouldn't do this. Surely almost no men would do this. Surely. Please let that be true.

Underneath the final block of photos were the words, 'See the sort of dirty bitchs that work for Teesside Women. Disgrace!! Sack her now!' They'd spelt 'bitches' wrong. Clever.

His guts felt cold and angry on her behalf. This was, in the modern parlance, 'revenge porn', albeit taken decades ago. Where had it been since then? Why had it emerged now? Who had access to it? What would all her friends think of this when they saw it? Eleven had already got access to the Facebook page and that surely featured a link to these pictures again. As Nick stepped off the train in Darlington, he knew their life was going to be messed up by this. It wasn't happening for no reason. His warm fuzzy feeling had gone. Jeff was waiting for him beside the ticket barrier.

'Now then!' said Jeff, with a slap on the top of Nick's arm. 'Sorry I had to interrupt your drinking session, I bloody love drinking on a train, meself. Now, don't go shatting your nest about this stalker business.'

'She sent me the links. It's some bad shit, Jeff.'

'Really?'

'Yeah.'

'Is Jules with a bloke or what? She never said. She just said it was porn.'

'She's passed out in them. Looks like three blokes have...' he couldn't say the words, instead he made a hand gesture away from his crotch in order to illustrate.

'Bloody hell. Is it, like you said, some sicko using Photoshop?'

Nick grimaced and shook his head. 'It's real, but from about 20 years ago. Judging by what they've written on the website, they're obviously trying to undermine her reputation as a women's support worker at TWC, as well as humiliate her. There's also pictures of her...her downstairs.'

'Christ. Well, everyone is naked on the internet these days,' said Jeff, trying to lightly dismiss the situation. 'Jules was very calm and together on the phone. Some friends had emailed to alert her to the Facebook page and the link on there to the website. I mean, they'll have spotted what was going on right away.'

They got into Jeff's white van.

'It's a bloody horrible thing for you to have to see though, man,' said Jeff.

Nick said, 'Yeah, well, they could be used as evidence for a rape charge, though there's little indication as to who it is, except two index fingers pointing at her. Why they've been published now bothers me more. Someone has had them for a long time and has only decided to use them now, for some reason.'

Jeff started the engine and pulled his seat belt over, clipping it in. 'Maybe they lost them and only just found them?'

'I think it shows she's been raped whilst unconscious. Yes, someone is out to discredit her, but much more than that, they want to humiliate and psychologically torture her. The photos will be all over porn sites, I've no doubt.'

'Bastards,' hissed Jeff.

'Yeah, well, as you well know, this is why I've never liked porn either as magazines or now online. This is the sort of business you get involved in when you buy into it.'

Jeff accelerated away from the station.

'To be honest with you, back in the day, I never really understood or appreciated what you were on about, but I genuinely do get it now. It's took me a long while, but Mandy has told me all sorts of shit about it. They busted some porn racket in Roseworth, of all places, and I won't bore you with the details, but it was horrible from start to end. Drugs, losers, criminals, mentally ill, it was dreadful. Like you always used to say years ago, if you watch it, you're supporting it. I never really got that until now. Sorry, man.'

'Well, I'm glad you're coming round to my point of view, after all these years.'

'Well, Jules sounded in no mood to tolerate it when I spoke to her. She thinks it's one of her punter's exes.'

'Yeah, that occurred to me. Seems very likely. I'll tell you what, she'll fight this for herself but also for other women, and you know how hard-faced she can be when she's got a principle to fight for. This is her thing in life: women's rights. She won't give in to it in any way whatsoever and she'll hunt down whoever's done it.'

'Rightly bloody so.' Jeff changed down gears as he ran into traffic on the A66. 'I really admire her. She's a special woman. Awesome.'

Nick turned to him as Jeff drove.

'I don't think I've *ever* heard you say that before. Not in those words. Cheers, Jeff.'

Jeff said nothing for a minute and looked out of the window as they slowed to a crawl.

'Look, I'll be honest, back in Harrogate, when you first got together, you know I thought she was a right mouthy cow. Great looking, obviously, but a total pain in my arse. Always up my hole about one thing or another - sexist language, sexist assumptions and all of that. It was very annoying, especially as the rest of the time she was such good fun and knew so much about rock music and football. I felt like I was a good bloke but I just couldn't say anything around her, without her getting on my case.'

Nick snorted a laugh. 'Yeah, I remember that. But she was educating both of us, man. We grew up in a sexist culture and we still live in one.'

Jeff held his left index finger aloft, right hand on the wheel. 'Exactly, she was right and I was wrong. She was right about all of it. I just never understood back then. I had a lot of growing up to do but nowadays, I can see it must have been bloody annoying having to put up with a fat sexist idiot, like me.'

Nick, possibly due to being a bit drunk, and the stress of the situation, felt a surge of tearful emotion rise in his throat at Jeff's words.

'That's very big of you say that, man.' He swallowed the tears down.

'It's the truth. Having Argie and thinking about how I want to bring him up and what values to instil in him, as well as going out with Ms Mandy Beale, it's only educated me more. Mandy says, at every level, blokes have almost all the power and until you understand that, you don't understand anything. It took me until being nearly 50 before I properly got that. Shameful, like.'

In the dark of the drive on the A66, Nick, still feeling emotional, squeezed the tears from the corners of his eyes with his thumb and forefinger. Learning stuff in later life can often be hard. We get set in our ways and default to how we've always thought about the world, even though, ironically, having your mind opened to how things really are is always a liberating thing.

'We were talking about this stuff last night actually. We went out to Big Meat,' said Jeff.

'You and Mand?'

'Aye. Had a great night. Cracking it was. Great food and drink, good conversation and a lot of laughs.'

'What did you order?'

'Aw, man. I had the rib of beef served with blue cheese sauce. Mandy went for half a roast chicken. It was a huge old bird, all crispy skin and stuffed with goat's cheese and herbs. That place man, there is no better place to eat on earth, I swear. It should win every award there is. And it was packed to the rafters, as usual. I'd booked it a month ago.'

Nick laughed. 'Mike is King of the roast meats. So simple, but so delicious.'

'Before I forget, we went into the kitchen for a word afterwards. Our boy Mikey is branching out. He's got a brilliant idea and he's starting another place up, funded by Gloria's company.'

'Is he? Doesn't surprise me, that bloke is so talented. Wonderful buttocks on him, as well. I love his arse. I've never seen a man with an arse like it.'

'I agree. I have a so-far unblemished record of heterosexuality, but I know exactly what you mean. It's basically a cracking woman's arse, but on a man. I'm so jealous of him, I could weep. Anyway, you'll like this. He's going to open up a place in the Boro next month called, wait for it, Beef and Vodka. And he reckons all they'll sell is beef and vodka.'

'Nothing else at all?'

Jeff drew a line in the air with the side of his hand.

'Nada.'

'So there's no vegetarian option?'

'Yeah, there is - the vodka.'

The both laughed loudly.

'Ha ha...oh, god, I like the sound of that,' said Nick.

'I know. It's mint. And you know he'll clean up. He's set for big things, is Mike the Meat and his sexy buttocks. He said we'll all get an invite to the opening night as a thank you for being such good customers, which is brill. Oh, and by the way, did I tell you he's been dating a woman?'

'Has he? But he's gay. Isn't he?'

Jeff cocked his index finger. 'Mostly, but not totally. Jo King talks to me about this stuff. She says we're all so keen to box everyone off into straight or gay, but for loads of people it's a lot more fluid than that. Sometimes they like a bit of male, sometimes a bit of female, sometimes a non-binary person. I can't believe I'm even saying non-binary. It's like I'm a PC social worker. Ha...life's for learning, I suppose.' He laughed loudly. 'Who knew life was *this* interesting?'

'I had a short-lived gay phase when I was about 16.'

'Did you now? I don't remember that. Have I erased some sort of gay trauma from my brain? I can't see you as gay.'

'Nah, you're OK, I never fancied you. Oh, it was nowt nor summat. Just curiosity of the male physique more than anything. I'd have had a go if a lad I liked had suggested it, but then Sue Thomas came into my life and she knocked the curiosity out of me with her right hand.'

'Oh, yeah, she was a lot of fun, was Sue. I was in love with her as well.'

'I didn't love her but I very much liked groping her in my bedroom. She taught me how to grope her, in fact, up top and down below. Took my hand and showed me where to put it. Brilliant. It was a biology lesson I badly needed.'

'At that age there is no difference between love and having your hand in someone's pants, it's all happily one and the same thing. Anyway, look, me and Mandy were inhaling our body weight in Mike's roast meat and she was telling me how much of police time is spent attending domestics, right? And it's almost always, drunk or drugged man punches woman in the face, or some variant thereof. The stats are about 90-odd per cent of domestics are violence by men on women, but as soon as they do any campaigns about this stuff, they get complaints from men that they're being ignored and boo hoo, they suffer domestic abuse, too - which is true, like; a few per cent do and that's bad, as well - but it's like 90-odd per cent men battering, abusing and torturing women. She says, even in the abstract, men just hate any power being taken from them, so they complain like they suffer to the same degree as women and by and large, we just don't. We might get punched in a bar fight, or in the street, but we are most unlikely to get tortured at home for years on end. And that's sort of what I was like with Jules. The fact I couldn't say things the way I always had done without her being critical, I was being a typical bloke who felt like he was having his power taken away from him. I couldn't see that the problem was me, not her. I know I'm not explaining this very well.'

'Yeah, but I know what you mean. The sheer volume and degree of abuse of women is misunderstood. The figures beggar belief. Jules has said over 30 per cent of young women report some sort of sexual abuse when they were kids. That's a third...I mean...I can't get my head around it. Then you get situations like this thing with Jules and you can see, there are evil rapey blokes everywhere. I don't mind telling you, Jeff, it scares me to think who we might be rubbing shoulders with, at any given moment. I mean, back in the day, we used to use sexist language, but you're right, we were good blokes. We always respected women and believed in equality. I did, anyway. I know I did. Most of my friends at college and in 6th form were women because I much preferred the company of women. And even back then I used to hear from them how men often behaved towards them and I vowed not to be like that. We'd never have thought of even being rude to a woman would we, let alone anything else?'

He frowned. 'God no. Of course not. But not everyone is as cool as us. Mandy has got a million stories of shit blokes being shit to children

34

and to women. Time and time and time again. She said last night, right, and this is very apposite for what's happened today, she said, "If it wasn't for shit blokes, the world would be pretty brilliant. Shit blokes fuck it up for everyone else, including the decent blokes." And I genuinely think that's true. I remember Lisa Lambert used to say something similar, God rest her soul. Even women who are shitty, are, except for a few rare examples, usually driven to being shitty by some shite bloke, somewhere down the line.'

Nick snorted a laugh. 'You've gone the full feminist, you,' he said, punching him on the arm.

'Aye, I've stopped wearing a bra, haven't shaved me legs and have started listening to Helen Reddy records.' He began singing loudly. ' "I am invincible, I am woman!" Albeit, a bearded woman. Don't judge me.'

They both laughed to try and suppress darker feelings, as they headed into the west of Stockton and drove towards the High Street.

'Come on, I'll buy you a big stiff drink in the Royal Oak,' said Jeff. 'Tell Jules where we are.'

Nick did as he said, texting her as they perched on a stool by the bar. It was quiet, just a couple of skinny grey trackie-wearing losers in one corner spending some ill-gotten gains on lager, and there were a couple of old boys who remembered when things were better than this; a lot better. There always are in Stockton.

'What do you fancy, then?' said Jeff.

'I'll have a large single malt with ice,' said Nick.

'I'll join you.' Jeff blew out air. 'Been bloody hot today.'

'Was roasting down in London. I was sweating like a monkey in Hartlepool.'

'I've not even asked how that went.'

'Oh, it was all bullshit. They wanted the book, but took the piss on the money.'

Jeff sneered. 'That's the modern gig, isn't it?'

'Yeah. Tim Forest, the bloke I met, was alright, though I was probably a bit overly arsey with him.'

'Rightly so, if you ask me. So you turned him down?' said Jeff.

'Yeah.'

'So what'll you do now with the novel?'

'Self-publish it. If it fails, at least it'll fail with me making nine times more per sale.'

Jeff hi-fived him. 'Right on. You're a sodding good writer and the bits you've given me of the book are great. Really Teessidey.'

Nick drank the whisky, ignoring the compliment because he didn't know what to do with it, or how to react to compliments. 'I'll get lovely Sarah Summers to edit it for me. She was my editor on the *Echo* years ago and now freelances her editorial skills.'

'Shortish blonde woman, right? And very lovely in the chestular department.' He made the universal sign for large breasts, scooping out two semicircles of air from his chest.

'Yeah, that's her, well remembered. You've not seen her for about 15 years.'

'I never forget spectacular breasts. I speak as a man who has had spectacular breasts, himself.' He made to push an invisible breast upwards and back into a bra.

'Ha ha...yeah. You did have a good rack on you.'

'You can talk. Your pecs are big enough to qualify as mammary glands, albeit very firm ones.' He reached out, squeezed one, and made a honk-honk noise.

Nick laughed and looked down at himself in the tight t-shirt. 'Yeah, they are. I don't know how, really. It just seemed to happen.'

'Well, I should think lifting very heavy weights for years and eating your fancy high-fat, low-carb diet is something to do with it, soft lad.'

'Aye, but I mean I never did it on purpose. I started exercising to keep the black dog at bay, didn't I?'

'Does that still work for you, then?'

Nick rubbed his biceps 'I still get quite depressed, or just, y'know, just really down sometimes...'

'...Yeah, you do, don't you? I wish you didn't...'

'...so it's not perfect as a cure, but it's definitely a positive thing for me, and also a habit and I need habits to give my life some structure.'

'How much are you lifting now?'

'I can do 35 kilos in each hand, free weights, and I could probably bench press 90 kilos. I say that like I have any idea how to bench press, or even what bench press means.'

'Bench and press are two words that don't even belong together in my world, like banana and wig. Also, I have no idea how heavy a kilo even is and I don't believe anyone over the age of 40 does.'

'I certainly don't, but I know I'm 75 kilos - that's just under 12 stone.'

'That means you could lift yourself.'

'It'd be a bit tricky but aye, I could, if necessary.'

'If anyone can manage it, you can. You, the man who could fellate himself in your teenage years. That still amazes me. Tell us this, could you get it all the way in or just within touching distance?'

'All the way, baby, in the tonsil tickler classic style. It may be my greatest personal achievement to date.' He grinned at him. 'I'm amazed I ever left my bedroom. Fortunately mam or dad never caught me doing it.'

'Ha ha, no it's not something you can easily explain as they open the door. You could have said you were learning tantric yoga. But then again, not sure you're actually supposed to abuse your body while you're doing that. I'm still stupidly impressed. You're so fit these days, I bet you could still do it.'

'Nah, I'm not that flexible any more, and anyway, unlike when I was 17, I've got Jules for that sort of thing, haven't I? And let's face it, she's a bloody expert.'

'Is she? Yeah, I'm sure she is. Actually, speaking of such matters, I wanted to ask you about that...well, not that specifically, I mean...err...'

He looked around himself conspiratorially and moved his bushy eyebrows up and down.

'You know me and Mandy are getting on great, right?'

'Yeah. She's great. You're a great couple, man. You're obviously having a lot of fun.'

'We are. It's great that she's been made Chief of Cleveland Police, now that Colin has retired, and she's great with Argie, having had her kids in her 20s, like. She's an old hand at the gurgling at and bouncing of small human animals. But it's not that, right. Now you're 50, do you...you know...'

'What?'

'How's the...err...you know...' he nodded encouragingly at Nick.

'I take the fact that you're not saying any actual meaningful words means you're talking about sex, in some way,' said Nick rubbing his neck and finishing his drink.

Jeff held up his hands in apology. 'Totally, I am and I'm sorry about that, but you're the only man I can talk to about this sort of stuff, so you're stuck with it. Now, Mandy, in bed, is, err... what's the word...?'

Nick flinched not really wanting to hear what Mandy was in bed.

'...err...vigorous, like,' said Jeff, unable to look him in the eye.

'Vigorous?!' exclaimed Nick. 'In what way?'

Jeff groaned. 'Oh, you know.'

Nick tried to imagine. Mandy was what, if she'd been a footballer, would be called 'a big unit'. She was tall and broad and in the zone between flabby and outright fat. Jeff had, in a drunken moment, earlier in the summer, said it was like making love to a massive blancmange, something which he appeared to enjoy.

'You mean she's rough with you?'

Jeff look incredulous and shook his head. 'No. No. Not rough.'

They were both almost too embarrassed to say anything more.

After a pause, Nick held up his hands and said, 'Just bloody say what you mean.'

He flinched again in anticipation.

Jeff knocked his whisky down. 'Alright. She's a right shagger.'

'Oh, god. Now, I actually feel embarrassed.' Nick shuddered. Jeff nodded.

'Aye, so am I. Let's pretend I never said anything.' He turned to the barman. 'Two more large ones please, Jock.'

Nick felt guilty now. Jeff obviously wanted his help, so he did what men often do to relieve tension, he inflicted a mild act of violence on his friend, kicking him on the shin. 'Owee, you big soft clart, ask us what you wanted to ask us. I won't take the piss, I promise.'

Jeff cleared his throat, and flicked his hair over his shoulders. 'Well, it's just that I can't do it more than once in a night. We go to bed, do some serious jiggy jiggy and then I pretty much need to sleep, but she's not done. She wants some more, but for me, it's like being asked to eat another roast chicken, when I'm already full. I'm just not interested and that makes me I feel like I'm a shit old man. She's four years older than me and, seriously man, could do it for half the night. It makes me feel a bit useless. I mean, she's dead good about it, she's not given me a hard time, but I feel like I'm not doing my duty. I don't know if I'm the normal one, or if she is. What do you reckon?'

Nick pinched his lips together. 'Well, one of the defining things about being male is our massive lust for sex, swiftly followed our massive disinterest in sex, immediately having had sex. That's a common thing for us all, Jeff.'

'Well, I feel bad about it. In fact I don't just feel bad, I feel like I'm not being a good boyfriend, or whatever the word is when it's two old buggers together. Does this ring any bells in your life and if so, how do you deal with it? You've said plenty of times that Jules is...err...oh shit, I'm going to say something inappropriate, I can just feel it.'

'Owee man, we've known each other since 1972. You've been saying inappropriate things for nearly 40 years and I'm still here, aren't I?'

'Is it that long? Jesus, we're so old, Nick. How did that happen? Last time I turned around, me and you were putting records on at lunchtime at Stockton Sixth Form College and drinking Stones Best Bitter in the Stockton Arms every night.'

'Scary, isn't it?'

Jeff took a drink and cleared his throat. 'What I was going to say is you've always said Jules is err...oh god...err, passionate, like, and I was wondering if you've ever been in this situation of having a lass who wants more sex than you can deliver.'

Nick made a decision to be grown up about this, took a drink and said, 'I'll be honest with you, her libido drives our sex life and she proba-bly does want to do it more than I do, actually. Or, at least, I'd not mind if we didn't for a while. When she was upset after losing Joni, we didn't do it for ages and I was fine. I just accept whatever reality comes along. Whatever she wants, I try and comply.'

'That makes it sound like you're a sex slave.'

'It sometimes feels like that.' He groaned a little and tried to work out what to tell Jeff. The fact was, his powers of recovery were unusually rapid, at least according to Julie, if provided with sufficient stimulation. And it had always been like that for him, at least when not depressed. But that was no good for Jeff.

'Everyone is setup differently, man. I don't think there is any normal. The thing is, you've got to pace yourself, haven't you? That's the trick, I reckon.'

Jeff tugged on his beard, staring over Nick's shoulder, still unable to look him in the eye.

'Pace myself? Is that what you do, then?'

Nick hunched up into himself, embarrassed. 'Look, I'm no expert, but this is all I've learned about sex, right?'

'Go on...I'm all ears...and hair...mostly hair, in fact. Sorry...go on.'

'OK, this isn't definitive but here's my thing: It might not be Mandy's thing, but you do lots of foreplay, only put it in when she's well worked up, or asks you to, nip it until she's all done, then and only then, do you blob it.' He held his arms out wide. 'That's my only technique, if it is even a technique. It's worked for me since I was 17. I'll tell you this, Jeff. I could happily just do the foreplay. The sticking it in bit, is fine, and Jules is physically set up to really like it, but I like the fiddling around best. Always have. I've told you before that I'd still be happy dry humping. Anyway, I think sex is all about what the woman wants, not the man. I really believe that. As soon as you accept that, it's better for both of you.'

Jeff nodded. 'This sounds like quality advice, Marg Proops, but I'm not sure I can do that, though. I get a bit carried away. Can't...can't stop it, like.'

'So you mean you just go for it?'

'Yeah, I get overexcited.'

'Aye, well I do as well; sometimes it's a bit overwhelming, isn't it? Jules is...well...I just sort of drown in lust for her, sometimes. It's very intoxicating.'

'It totally is. I totally get that.'

'The thing is, you've just got to learn to nip it most of the time. You know how to nip it, don't you?'

'If I knew how to nip it, I'd not be looking at you with this expression.' He pulled a stupid, open-mouthed cross-eyed face.

Nick blew out air and rubbed his face. 'Talking about this is torture, man.'

'It is, like. I'll be glad when it's over.'

Nick blew out air. 'Look, I'm just going to say this and then we're done, right? OK, you can do pelvic exercises. It's just a muscle thing. You can learn how to control yourself, so you can let her get her rocks off for as long as it takes, and then blob's your uncle, as it were, like. I can't believe I've even said that to you. I hate myself already.'

'Blob's your uncle?! Ha ha, very good. Clever get. Anybody would think you're a writer. You've got to remember I was a fat sexless man for decades so I missed out on all this learning when I was younger.'

Nick blinked slowly. 'I know, it's alright. Just slow it all down and enjoy it and don't worry too much about it. There's nowt wrong with you, man. But now, we must never speak of this again, right?'

Jeff zipped his lips. 'Thanks for the tips. I shan't trouble you again.' He raised his glass. 'By the sound of it, you must be dehydrated most of the time.'

'You're not wrong, but I'm not complaining. Someone lusting after you is just sodding great for your ego.'

'God, yeah. I sort of don't believe it. Do you know what I mean? I look down at myself and think...what? Me? Nah.'

'Totally, and that's what any decent bloke should think. No-one of any quality is taking off their clothes and thinking, I'm bloody gorgeous, me. Cop a load of this, darlin'.'

Jeff laughed. 'No, that's a passion killer, surely. Men who love themselves are always to be distrusted.'

Nick took a drink. 'Sorry I can't be of more help, man. It's just I'm no good talking about this stuff...'

'...I know. It's cool. I like being an emotionally repressed Northerner with my best friend. I only asked 'cos I want to do right by Mand. I want it to work for both of us.' He let out a sigh. 'I'm a bit in love with her, really.'

Nick looked up at him and grinned. That was the first time Jeff had said it.

'You do seem really well-suited. Both me and Jules think it's totally mint that you're getting on so well. And, of course, having a copper in the family is useful for getting off parking tickets.'

'Exactly. And that's my main motivation for the relationship, obviously. That and the free confiscated drugs.'

And, with a joke or two, they were back to their normal mode of communication. Both relaxed instinctively and hi-fived. Nick took another drink, finishing the whisky. They both let out a groan and grinned at each other. You couldn't be friends for 39 years without knowing exactly how the other felt.

'Ah, it's good to be back home. You know, I simply don't like London, but I always feel that makes me seem culturally narrow. Like I'm some sort of hick. But I just don't like how it physically feels to be there, everything is such a hassle,' said Nick. 'The people seem dehumanised by living there, somehow.'

Jeff gave him a withering look. 'I don't trust Southerners, never have, never will. Guilty until proven innocent in my book. Hey, I should've said earlier, There's trouble at t'mill, with our Emily and Matty. I think a break-up might be on the cards. This week and last, there's been frosty looks, suppressed rows and off-hand comments. A distinct lack of either lovey or dovey. It's weird. Matty's a nice guy. He used to write her little notes for her to find around the shop. He'd come in with a single red rose and stuff like that. But she doesn't seem smitten with him the way she once was.'

'Emily is clever, intelligent, funny and, I'd not say this to Jules, but she's sexy, too. He'll never do better than her.'

'I think she's the one who's gone cold. But I agree, she's absolute class. But I'm a bit worried for her. I'm on tears alert at all times, if you know what I mean.'

'Ok, man, but, she's young. She'll get over it, if it happens.'

The doors to the pub opened and Julie came in, bounding up to them in a puppyish fashion, patting Nick on the shoulders with the flat of her hands, kissing him on his neck and giving him a little lick in his ear, as she did so, whispering 'Hiya, gorgeous'. What a woman.

'Now then my lovely hairies, how are we? Oooh, a big single malt, is it? I'll have one of those, Jock, and another two for the lads.'

She pulled up a stool and grinned from one to the other. 'So they only offered you a 7.5 per cent royalty - that's rubbish. Why don't they just have done with it and ask writers to write for free? They'll regret it when it's a best seller. You're such a great writer, and they're idiots.'

Jeff applauded that.

'Never mind me, what about you?' said Nick. 'You've had a helluva day.'

The barman put their drinks in front of them and Julie passed over a £20 note.

'Oh, it's something and nothing,' she said, waving her hand dismissively.

'At the danger of sounding a bit Neanderthal, if someone is stalking or spying on you, why don't we catch him and administer a bit of traditional Teesside persuasion upon his mortal flesh, in order to put a stop to it?' said Jeff.

'I'm not ruling that out - though I'm sure Mandy would disapprove,' said Julie.

'I heard that. What would Mandy disapprove of?' said Mandy Beale, striding into the pub, a whirlwind of raggy brown hair, pink cheeks and baggy lightweight black suit.

'Hello, Mand!' said Julie smiling. 'Have you just knocked off work? You do such long hours.'

'Just paying the cost for being the boss,' she said, in her broad Yorkshire accent, blowing strands of hair off her forehead and then throwing a dance pose in approximation of James Brown, making all her blubber judder. She looked hot and bothered. 'Hold on. I need to have a word with them.' She nodded at the grey trackie men. 'Get us a pint of Stella, will you, Jeff?'

She went over to the two men, who both looked up at her with mock innocence. She pointed a finger at each of them in turn and in a growling, intimidating flat Yorkshire voice said, 'Are you trying to end up in Holme House, Darren? Are you? 'Cos you're going a bloody good way about it. I got a call from your probation officer today. You missed your appointment because you'd rather be drinking in here, wouldn't you? You're a bloody idiot, lad and your brother's no bloody better.'

The other lad made a noise in protest. She put the flat of her hand in his face. 'I don't want to hear it, Dean. I made an excuse for you, Darren. Be at the station 9am and be sober and me and you will be alright. Right? But if you're not there, I'll nick you, and if I do that your mam will give you such a hiding. Won't she? Yes, she bloody will. At least she will if she's not been on the pop 'erself. So think on.' She jabbed her finger into the lad's shoulder. Though both well into their 20s, they reacted like naughty school kids caught smoking by the headmaster. They seemed emotionally stunted at about age 13.

Jeff handed her a pint of lager as she returned to the bar.

'Cheers, luv.' She sank half of it in a few gulps. 'Oh, god, I needed that. How bloody hot has it been today?'

'I love watching you in action,' said Jeff, with a huge grin on his face. 'Who's that?'

She lowered her voice. 'Darren Wassel and his brother, Dean. Not bad lads, not really, just irresponsible and bored.' She took another drink. 'But these kids don't realise that if they don't play the game, they'll get jail, eventually.' She shook her head. 'I wouldn't care if he was a proper villain, but he's just a toe rag who's never done a day's work in his life. I don't know, Jeff. What do we do with kids like him? He's 20-odd, no qualifications. He's no good to anyone really. Thick as pig shit, messed up on drink and cheap drugs. Apart from keeping me and the prison service in work, I don't know what else he's got to offer the world. Can't even put him in the army. You try with these lads, but you know it's only going one way.' She held her hands up at Nick and Julie. 'Sorry kids, sorry. Just pisses me off. So what were you talking about when I came in?'

'As Jeff told you, I've got a stalker, Mand,' said Julie. 'It's like I'm Madonna. Ha! But you might not know that he's posted some old porny pictures of me on the internet.' She was trying to make light of it, but it was just a front.

43

Mandy curled her big pink top lip and, in her broad accent, did what she often did; asked a rhetorical question. ' 'As he now?'

'They were taken while I was passed out drunk or drugged or both, about 20 years ago.'

Mandy sank the rest of the lager with relish and then belched a little. 'Bloody 'ell, lass, you're taking it very well.'

Julie shrugged. 'Well, look, I'm trying sodding hard not to let it upset me. I don't understand how the photos work with being followed. But I do know how this sort of stalking shit goes. I see it at work. They want to upset and undermine me, so I'm going to fight it by not letting it get to me. That's all that I can do. That and find out who it is, of course. And I'm going to do that. They're not getting away with it, if I have any say at all. And I'll be damned if I own one scintilla of guilt or blame for any of it!' Her raised voice indicated the stirred emotions behind her apparently calm exterior.

'So you don't know who it is?' said Mandy.

'No, not yet.'

'We were just saying if we can find him we might just exert a little physical pressure on him,' said Jeff.

Mandy's thick dark eyebrows shot up and she pointed a finger at Jeff.

'I never 'eard that, right. I don't approve of the public playing at being coppers. It's *our* job to twat the general public in a darkened room with no witnesses. Do you feel in danger, Jules?'

She shook her head and explained. 'I feel edgy because I don't know who's done this, or where they are and I don't know why they're doing it now, but no, not in danger as such. Not yet, anyway. Though I must say, being followed by that Range Rover today put the shits up me a bit. You never know how these things are going to go, though. The Teesside Women Centre are aware of it. We do take stalking seriously. These sort of blokes tend to conform to predictable patterns of behaviour. It's something to do with one of my service users, I think. Maybe a woman I've worked with got away from him and he blames me. I'm going to check my records to see if I can narrow it down.'

Mandy nodded. 'So the car following you and the pictures are the same perp, you reckon?'

'If it's not, it's an odd coincidence.'

'And the internet pictures are from years back?'

'They're from the early 90s. I'm naked and clearly unconscious in them.'

44

Mandy's body drooped. 'Scumbags. Any chance of prosecution, you think?'

'Depends. But unlikely. I remember nothing about it. I didn't even know it had happened. I'm clearly in no fit state to have consented to what's happened to me, and I appear to have been penetrated, but how could I prove it at this distance, even if I find out who the perp or perps are?' she said, flatly.

Mandy shrugged. 'Prove it? You don't have to prove it, lady. You just need to suggest it was very likely part of a pattern of behaviour and then get a court to believe you. It'd be a lot of work and hassle and upset for you - but it is possible. Courts are much more sympathetic these days, thank god. And I don't see why nasty sods shouldn't get what's comin' to them, no matter how long it's been, 'cos you know they won't have changed.'

'No, very unlikely to have changed, I'd say.'

'Bloody shite blokes. World would be a lot nicer place without shite blokes, shite-ing things up,' said Mandy, scowling.

Julie nodded and sipped at her drink. And in the plain, undemonstrative understanding between them, Nick saw how they had a female bond of experience which men couldn't really get near - not even empathetic men. It wasn't even something they were necessarily conscious of, but they had all gone through it, to one degree or another; the oppression of men behaving badly towards women. They just understood how the world was for each other, and understood that they were never free from that ever-present threat.

'We'll see how it plays out. Like I say, it's something we often see at work and it tends to follow certain patterns,' said Julie. 'There was someone out the back of our house this morning - don't know if it was the bloke in the car, but someone's obviously taken recent photos of me in Norton village.'

Mandy put her glass down on the bar. 'Thing is, right, he can't be from 'round 'ere, whoever's doing this, can he?'

'Why not?' said Jeff.

'If he was, he'd know about your brothers Ricky and Kev. And he'd know that he'd have seven shades of shite kicked out of him if they found him, not that I approve of such vigilantism, but we all know it'd happen. Everyone on Teesside knows about them. So it must be someone you knew when you lived down in the smoke, Jules. Someone who doesn't realise what they're getting into by doing this. Alright, the gruesome two-some brothers are in Spain at the moment, but the perp can't know you very well. Either that or they're reckless or mad, or both.'

'Hmm, I never thought of that,' said Julie.'

'That's why I'm the Top Copper. It's a Southerner what's doing this, if you ask me. Keep us up to date,' said Mandy. 'I'm not 'avin creepy blokes stalkin' women on my patch. The sooner we get revenge porn legislation on the books, the better, if you ask me. That or legalise castration. Dirty bloody sods. I'll volunteer for that job with my old blunt rusty scissors.'

Julie let out a yelp of a laugh and put her hand up. 'Please miss, can I volunteer for that job. I've got a blunt chisel!'

As had often been the case in the six months since Jeff and Mandy had hooked up, when she and Julie met, Nick and Jeff were left as almost silent bystanders. Jeff had once put it well, saying, 'It's like we're the children at a meeting of the adults.' Nick quite liked it like that. No pressure to talk in a group was always a good thing.

'You're taking it all very calmly, Jules,' said Jeff.

She looked at her phone. 'Ah, the Facebook page has already been taken down. That's a result. Yes. Get in!'

'Should never have allowed the links to be uploaded in the first place,' said Mandy, again silently belching from the lager. 'Another round please Jock,' she said, pointing to their glasses.

'Thanks, Mand. Yeah, well, as I say, I just refuse to get co-opted into his mind games. These types of men want you to feel helpless and bullied and I'm not buying into that. I've had some nice supportive texts from women who thought it was just a new page I'd set up and had sent a friend request only to get an eyeful of me in all my glory when they clicked on the link. Getting the website taken down will be much more difficult, though. Just as well I'm 27 in those photos and don't have any stretch marks or cellulite, because they're probably going to be online forever somewhere in the world.'

Mandy let out a groan of exasperation and shook her head. 'Not right, that. Not right at all. We need to catch these perps before this gets any worse. See, that's what I'm worried about. These things can escalate. Keep me up to date at all times, Jules. Right? I don't bloody like this, it's nasty and I bloody hate nasty.'

CHAPTER 4

When they got home Julie searched her client files on her laptop, using the words 'stalking' and 'stalker' as filters.

'How many has that pulled up?' said Nick.

'Two. Hold on, I'll just read the case notes.' As her eyes scanned to and fro, she bit at her nails, something she never normally did. After a few minutes she looked up at him and took a drink. 'I remember these cases. In each of them it was an ex-partner. This one, John Underwood, was a nasty bit of work. He wrote to us saying that his ex, a woman called Maggie, was a liar and that we'd got her all wrong by believing she was being stalked by him, it was the other way around, she was the stalker. Now, that happens quite a bit - a perp telling us that the woman is the guilty party and he's totally innocent and we've all been conned by her. We've even had letters from prisoners to that effect, even when they've been found guilty and banged up.'

'Getaway. Really? They must take you all for right mugs.'

'They have no fizzin' idea how predictable they are. They don't realise that we deal with men like them every day. There are times when it's quite easy to call what his next move will be.'

'Do any women come to you who are making it all up?'

'Nah. I do see women who are upset and confused and who consequently make mistakes in the wheres, whens and whys of their abuse history and sometimes the perp jumps on that to try and prove she's lying. But I've never even heard of a woman turning up with an agenda against a man and basically busting him for something he didn't do. Why would you come to Teesside Women and do that? I'm not saying it doesn't, in some context, happen once in a blue moon, 'cos I know the police do occasionally get malicious rape or paedophile allegations. That just makes our job harder because when those stories get into the press, it gives licence to every abusive toe rag of a bloke to claim he's also an innocent man and is really the victim of a scheming woman. The way I see it, there's a popular press convention waiting to be deployed at any opportunity: the wronged man. Because life is all about men, all about the exertion of patriarchy. Most things are defined against the male experience, even abuse of women.'

She looked back at her screen. 'So he's an outside possibility because he was very persistent, to the point where he turned up at the office shouting the odds. We had to call the police. Worth bearing in mind that even amongst abusive men, stalking is relatively unusual, so we regard it as sinister, y'know. It rings a lot of warning bells. I mean, stalking and homicide often go together. So we're quick to get the police involved if we can. This Underwood bloke got a police warning and we didn't see him again after that.'

'And what about his ex-partner? What happened to her?'

Julie went back to the notes. 'She moved away and didn't press charges. She was very upset when she first came to us. Felt it was all her fault, poor lass. He hid in her back garden for weeks just spying on her. Very much like our peeper in some regards. Hmm. Yeah.'

'When did that all take place?'

'The police got involved in February, so it was six or more months ago.'

'OK, so why start this campaign against you now? Why wait so long?'

'No idea. Hang on, here's someone else. He's not a stalker, but he totally lost it in a meeting with other partners.'

'Partners?'

'Social services, police and so on.'

She bit her lip as she read her notes. 'Yeah, this was a bad business. God I'm sounding like Colin Harcombe. Bloke called Ron Yeats was up for parole. His ex-wife was afraid of him coming out of jail because she'd essentially turned him in a couple of years earlier. She came to us for help in getting an injunction and the meeting we had with him was part of the parole procedure. It was an attempt to discover how much of a danger he was, if any. I gave his ex-wife's side of things. She wasn't there, obviously. I expressed her fears. And in the middle of it, right on cue, he stood up, pointed at me and said, "If you're not fucking careful, I'll show you what a dangerous man looks like, you fucking bitch".' She chuckled. 'Did my job for me. He didn't get parole but...' she went to Google '...if I remember right, he was on some sort of day release scheme and went then awol. Yeah, here it is, I heard about it. That meeting was in late June and he absconded on 28th July. Weird. He must only have had a few months left to serve.'

'He sounds a bundle of laughs. So would he have known your name?'

'Yeah, we all had to say who we were and where we were from.'

'So he could find us, one way or another if he wanted to.'

'Yeah, but it wasn't like it was just my evidence that tipped the deal against him. It was his own behaviour.'

'Maybe in his mind it did.'

'Well they don't seem to have caught him yet. Doesn't seem to be any more reports about him. But the ex-partner hasn't been back to us and as she'd made such an effort to get him nicked originally, I think she would have, if he reappeared. I hope she's OK. I might check up on her tomorrow. Anyway, he's another who's got grudge potential. And I've just thought of someone else. There's this woman called Aggie Harlow, who hates me. She used to be a friend of mam's and lives on Hardwick Road, right opposite the hospital.'

'Why does she hate you?'

'Because Edie, the wife of her brother, Kenny, came to us. Long story short, we helped her get away from her abusive marriage. She's in her mid 60s and was totally set in her ways and as a result had put up with all sorts off him for years, too afraid to change her life. It's a big ask when you're that age. She came to us many times over three years, I only saw her for the last eight or nine months. Eventually, she got enough confidence to leave him, but Aggie Harlow thinks brother Kenny is great and I'm the bitch who broke up his marriage. I mean, it's pathetic. Mam had it out with her in the Horse and Jockey one night not long since.'

Nick made a short laugh. 'I bet that was worth seeing. Jackie is a force of nature when she's got a cob on.'

'I'm sure I told you about this.'

'If you did, I don't remember.'

'Well, Aggie is flapping her gums about...' she put on a broad Teesside accent to better express it '..."do-gooders like that Julie Wells, breaking up marriages".' Mam hears this, goes over to her and says at full volume, which for mam is like a foghorn put through a 100-watt Marshall stack, "My Jules is a bloody godsend to the likes of Edie, your Kenny is a sodding shitehawk, he always bloody was, and if you dare say anything else about Jules, I'll knock your bloody block off", or words to that effect.'

'God, I wish I'd seen that.'

'Aggie then gets on her hind legs and starts with the "Your Julie is no better than she ought to be" business and how "everyone on the estate had screwed your daughter by the time she was 18", which, to be fair, was factually inaccurate.'

'I'm sure. There were hundreds of men on that estate, there had to be a few blokes you'd not shagged.'

'At least three. Ha ha. So on hearing this, mam lamps her in the mush before Con can stop her. He picks her up like she's a stuffed toy and carries her outside at arm's length, kicking and swearing, to general laughter and cheering. Brilliant. At times like that, I love my mam. I mean, she's an auld shitehawk herself, but you'd not want anyone else to fight your corner when push comes to shove.'

Nick laughed. Jackie was some shade of brilliant, even if she was very, very hard work most of the time.

Julie closed her laptop and rubbed her eyes. 'More seriously, Aggie isn't a nice woman. Her and her brother are cut from the same cloth. I wouldn't put it past her to try and discredit me as a Teesside Women worker. There's nothing she'd like better, in fact. And that's what that shite written on the website is all about.'

'OK, I totally get that. But how could she get those photos from London 20 years ago?'

'I just don't know, but if she did somehow get them, I wouldn't be shocked to find she'd posted them online. Could have been Kenny in the Range Rover for all I know. It was hard to tell and I don't really know what he looks like.'

'Can she make websites?'

'Don't be daft. It'd be her grandson Jason who did that. A young man who I hear has very much taken after his father in being a bully.'

'Really? Interesting. The fruit often doesn't fall far from the tree.'

She yawned, stood up and scratched her arse. 'Bloody internet, it's the wild west. Once something is out there, you can never be sure you've ever got rid of it.'

'Doesn't that bother you?'

'Of course it does...but in a way, it's every woman's story. What happened to me back then has happened, in one way or another, to loads of women. A lot of us have been subjected to unwanted attention, to being groped and all that. A lot of us have slept with the wrong man, or got too drunk to know what we were doing and as a result have been messed around one way or another. And hundreds of thousands of us have been raped. In America a woman is raped every 80 seconds. So to many women, a photo of a drunk or drugged lass in the circumstances they photographed me in, is a case of, there but for the grace of god go I, or, oh yeah, that once happened to me, too. It's so common, but it is as

50

though society has agreed not to talk about it. That's why I'm not going to get my knickers in a twist about it. I bloody well wish it hadn't happened, of course I do, but I don't remember anything about it and it wasn't my fault it happened, so I don't own any sense of guilt about it and I'm certainly not going to be defined by it. Sod them.'

Not for the first, nor surely the last time, he was in awe of her strength of mind. Even so, he worried about her. Like a lot of Northerners, she was good at swallowing emotions down along with her booze, and pretending nothing was wrong.

'I'll give mam a ring and I'll ask her about Aggie. They're a funny family, always were. Aggie had a girl my age called Fiona. She was in my year at Ian Ramsey and because our mams were pally at the time, I'd see her more than most lasses because she'd come round our house with her mother, or I'd have to go with mam to hers.' She sat and thought for a moment. 'I've not thought about this for yonks, but Fiona was, with my 47-year-old women's support worker hat on, obviously a troubled kid.'

'In what way?'

'Well she was one of those girls who'd show boys her knickers. Do you remember that sort?'

'Yeah, there was a male equivalent who would insist on getting his pre-pubescent bits out. It always seemed weird; a bit scarey, even.'

'Yeah, and this was before going through puberty. By 14 or 15 she was very precocious. We all thought she was just more grown up than us; in fact, I sort of looked up to her because she seemed to know a lot about boys. But now I think on, she was behaving in the way a girl who is being sexually abused might.'

'Yeah, well, I doubt any of us even knew that was going on and even if we did, we'd not have had a vocabulary to express it. What happened to her after school?'

'Well, mam and Aggie must have had a falling out when I was about 16 because I never saw Fiona, except in school. Then I went to 6th form and she left to work in Brentford Nylons on Bishopton Lane.'

'God, was there ever anything so 1970s as Brentford Nylons? Home of the brushed nylon bed sheets.'

'Eee, fizz me, aye. I had a brushed nylon nightie and there'd be blue sparks of static electricity flying as you got out of bed.'

'You should have tried wanking in nylon underpants while sandwiched between nylon sheets, I'm amazed there wasn't more fires started in teenage boys' bedrooms in the 70s!'

She hooted a laugh. 'What an appalling thought that is. Anyway, I think Fiona got married, had loads of kids and then got divorced. Mam's probably told me all about it, but it all goes in one ear and out the other.'

'Would it be a massive leap of imagination to think that Fiona was being abused by her uncle Kenny and then Edie, his wife, also abused, eventually comes to you? A fact which annoys Kenny somewhat and he sets about discrediting you with the help of a computer-savvy kid?'

'Not a huge leap, no.' She curled a long strand of blonde hair around her right index finger and thought about it. 'But where did those photos come from, both the old ones and the new ones taken locally? That's what I'd like to know.'

It was just after 1.30am when Nick turned out the bedside lamp and lay down, feeling really tired, dozing off immediately, even as Julie was talking about something.

'...and it's a pity the London trip wasn't more of a positive thing for you.'

He opened his eyes, having been briefly asleep.

'Ah, never mind, it went exactly as I anticipated, right down to the advance they offered. It was just as I'd said to mam it'd be.'

'That's funny. And you got it all right?'

'All of it, yeah. Seven and a half per cent royalty and two grand and a cardigan.'

'You haven't dreamed the lottery numbers, have you?'

'I'll try. I should have a notepad by the bed just in case.'

He got up and went in search of one.

'You're not serious, are you?' said Julie, in the dark.

He came back with a pencil and a white envelope

'Should do this anyway, in case I get ideas for writing.'

'Maybe you can have a word with your mam on the other side. She might be able to tell us the winning numbers.'

He took a quick look between the curtains. It was a still summer night, with a bright silver moon, almost full.

'I don't think they have access to info like that. They're more in an observation mode from what she was saying. It's sort of about knowing things, rather than seeing them.'

'By "they" you mean the dead? You are serious, aren't you? Nick, man, it was just a dream, not a paranormal experience.'

'I know, but what is "just a dream"? What does that actually mean? The only thing we can say for sure is it's not like this, our waking state; apart from that - ' He stopped midsentence.

'What?' said Julie, sensing he was distracted.

'I think there's someone out the back,' he said, looking through a crack in the curtains. 'They're moving around behind that shrubbery on the waste ground again, same as this morning. Shall I go out and have a word? It must be the stalker.'

'Are you sure? It's dark and it's the middle of the night. It'll be a dog walker, if it's anyone at all.'

'Maybe. Yeah. It is very shadowy. Maybe I'm hallucinating.'

'Well, if it is a stalker, he's hardly going to see much, just squatting back there, is he? That makes no sense.'

'That's not the point, is it? Anyway, these blokes often want to just be close to their victim, don't they? It's like a way of keeping in the woman's life. I was reading up on it after I got those links from you. It's partly sexual but mostly because they can't handle rejection. So they hang around their ex-wife or girlfriend's house just to be near them and in that way, it's like they're in her life.'

'That's all textbook stuff, yeah.'

Nick stood and looked at the moving shape. Fuck this.

He ran downstairs, through the kitchen, unlocked the back door and ran down the garden, vaulting over the back wall and running towards the blackthorn bush.

But no-one was there. He stood and looked around in the moonlight. Had he been there at all? Maybe it was just shadows. Or had he made an escape?

He went back to the house feeling jittery but exhausted, got back into bed and took a drink of water.

'This is bloody crazy, Jules. I'm going mental here.'

She let out a sigh and patted at him.

'Are you OK?' she said. 'Not just about this stalking. I mean about the photos. I know it's not exactly a nice thing to see, on any level.'

'At the risk of being incredibly grown up about it, it's the abuse that's really bloody upsetting. And I never knew you went through a Courtney Love phase.'

'Didn't you? I'm sure I must've mentioned it. It didn't last long. I loved that first Hole album, *Pretty on the Inside*. I had their first single on white vinyl, "Retard Girl". It was brilliant and noisy. They were so different after all the big hair rock and I was briefly quite infatuated with her. It all seemed very empowering. But it didn't really suit me as a look. I just ended up looking like a 10-dollar whore, somehow. So I only had that look over Christmas and New Year in 1991 into 1992. And I was never big on wearing a lot of make-up, was I? It was too much of a clart on and you have to keep topping it up all the time. I couldn't be arsed. I liked that idea of scruffy glamour, but it just wasn't me.'

'OK, so you had that look for how long, exactly?'

'About two months probably. December and January. Yeah, then I went a bit Suzanne Vega in the *Solitude Standing* period which was quite smart, involved wearing a black cardigan and seemed more suited to working in a lawyer's office. Eventually, I ended up back at my default low-maintenance, mid-70s Stevie Nicks do.'

'Right, since you can locate it so clearly in time, that means if you get your diaries out, you can find out who you were going out with or seeing at the time.'

'I will do, but I already know I wasn't going out with anyone then. I didn't have steady boyfriends, did I? I didn't have long-term relationships and I wasn't interested in that. I didn't want to settle down and get married. I was a party girl and happily so. I lived for drinking and gigs and mostly had one-night stands or I'd see a bloke for a week or three and then move on to someone else. I liked it that way. It was very liberating, and being down in London was exciting, even though I was living in a shit flat in Hoxton.' She yawned. 'Seems so long ago now.'

'And you were having a good time?'

'Are you kidding me? It was brilliant. I loved it. I felt like I'd really landed on my feet. I was living what I thought was the high life. I had a job paying really good money and flats weren't stupid rents back then. OK, I got burnt out after a few years, and I ended up missing the honesty of Teesside, but it was ace for a while.'

'Were you doing drugs?'

'Nooo, you know I didn't do drugs. Except smoking dope a few times, which I didn't like 'cos it made me dizzy. I had cocaine three times, I think, just so I could keep drinking, but then woke up each time feeling like shit and I also hated having to go to the toilet to take it. Felt seedy and horrible. As a Teesside lass, drink was always going to be my drug of choice. Back then it was red wine. I used to feel so sophisticated drinking wine. It seemed posh.'

'So you could have been passed-out pissed in those photos, as opposed to having had your drink spiked with something like rohypnol - not that I'd even heard of that, until recently.'

She blew out air. 'Pfft, who knows? I wasn't that bad. I didn't get absolutely shit faced that often. Not passed-out shit faced. I'd say I was spiked. But it's 20 years ago, can you remember how pissed you got on any single occasion 20 years ago?'

'Nah, of course not. Not least because you forget everything due to being arseholed.'

'I wouldn't have consented to having my photo taken like that, nor to having group sex, or even a threesome. I was never even curious about that sort of thing. Yuk. So someone has either doped me up or has taken advantage of me when I was vulnerable due to being drunk.'

In the dark, he lay there waiting for his adrenaline levels to drop and thought about it.

'You're dealing with it so well, Jules. Not letting it upset you, like.'

'It does upset me. But being upset isn't going to change anything. And it is a long time ago. Also, I just hear about this sort of thing every week at work. It's a real problem for younger women now - everyone has got a camera on their phone. They have intimate photos taken of them when they're all in love and then later have it used against them when they break up. And women being abused by men whilst drunk or drugged is very common, and often by gangs of men. Vulnerable young girls and women get passed around like cheap meat. So, you know, I'm not exactly shocked. It's horrible, but also it's a standard flavour of shite.' She lapsed into her original Hardwick accent to say it, the way she often did when under stress.

'Jesus Christ', said Nick, under his breath. 'Sometimes the world is just too awful to bear. I just don't understand why people are like that. What makes them think it's OK to do that?'

'That's not a big question for the wee small hours. Oh, and before I forget...'

But he had turned on his side, felt her tuck herself into him, an arm over his waist, relaxed and dropped off immediately, falling into a heavy sleep, totally exhausted.

Soon he was standing in Jeff's shop, looking through an old cardboard box of records that had just been brought from the auction rooms, mostly as a result of house clearances. Jeff got a lot of records this way. Mostly it was junk which he'd take to the council tip - endless Jim

Reeves records along with *The King and I* original soundtracks and dozens of James Last's Non-Stop Dancing albums. It was literally impossible to give it away. In fact, he was fond of saying that people couldn't even be paid to take them.

But occasionally, a dead hippy's collection would turn up and so it was on this occasion. A copy of *Liege and Lief* by Fairport Convention on the pink Island label. A first pressing of John Martyn's debut record, *London Conversation*, a couple of early albums by Audience on the pink Charisma label, which you just didn't see that often, all sitting at the front of the box. Sitting at the back, in a polythene sleeve was a genuine rarity. The original *Glastonbury Fayre - The Electric Score* triple live album from 1972, with all the inserts. Nick lifted it out carefully, never having seen it before.

'Jeff!' He called out. The big man came through from the stock room and gave him an owlish look and waved something at him.

'What is it? I was just about to fire up my pricing gun. You know how I like pricing things.'

Nick turned the record to him. 'Look what was in the auction rooms stuff.'

Recognising it right away, Jeff punched the air and started pogoing around the shop like a lunatic. 'Come to daddy! That is 250 quid's worth of vinyl rarity.'

'There's loads of good stuff in this week. Hippy folk stuff. I wouldn't mind this myself.' He took the triple album from Jeff and inspected the track listing.

But as he was doing so, he woke up. It had been a dream. Bloody hell. It was confusing to emerge from such a vivid dream and actually find himself in bed, with Julie snoring next to him. It was 7.20am. It took a moment to adjust to reality after such a wrench from the dreamworld.

He went downstairs and put the kettle on. It was a clear blue early morning with sun streaming in from the east, quiet except for bird song. Blackbirds clucked and robins chirruped loudly. He opened the back door and sat on the bench that was pushed up against the back wall, face turned up towards the early sun. It felt lovely. Proper summer weather on Teesside, with long sunny warm days, were rare enough for them to feel like a luxurious gift and certainly not something you could take for granted.

Walking across the small patch of grass and a flower border that comprised their garden to a low wall at the back, he peered over it at the

waste ground across which, to the east, was the back of a mid-sized supermarket. Given the desirability of Norton as a place to live, it was surprising that the expanse of land hadn't been built on by now.

Vaulting over the wall, he walked to the big blackthorn shrub that the
man had been hiding behind. It was a tall, dense, sprawling prickly thing.

The grass was flattened all around one side of it. Someone had clearly
been there for a while, or at least for a few times, because the grass was
actually worn away in places, there were fag ends all over the place, a
tissue and some cellophane sweet wrappers. No matches though, so whoever it was smoked, but must have had a lighter with them. Squatting
down on his hunkers he looked for any other indications of who might
have been there. He flicked at some small pieces of flaky pastry from a
sausage roll or a pasty. No cans of pop or coffee shop cups. Maybe they'd
had a flask with them or a bottle of something that they'd taken away.
Whoever it was had, to all intents and purposes, been camped there.
Weird. He must have been there a while before they even noticed him.

He stood up and looked towards their house. Their bedroom window
was in clear view. OK, it wasn't an especially big window but you'd easily see someone standing in front of it or if there was a light on in the
dark. Similarly downstairs. They could see some of the next-door houses,
too, but it was in the perfect place for looking at their house. But this
wear and tear wasn't from one or two sessions. Good grief, it was creepy
to think of them just sitting and watching. Perhaps they were planning a
robbery? Christ, they can't know them well, if so. They had sod all to
steal, apart from records and books.

Returning to the house, he made Sencha green tea and took a mug up
for Julie, who was yawning.

'Morning luv,' she said. 'Ooh lovely, ta. I've got a right gob on us.
Was I snoring? My mouth's so dry.'

'Yeah, you were a bit. It's a beautiful morning. I'll get you some brekkie on. We're a bit late getting started.' She smiled, looking tired around
the eyes, crows feet a little more deeply etched these days, the skin under
her eyes sagging a little as time left its passing on her. 'You alright?'

She nodded. 'Fine. Hungry. I didn't eat properly yesterday, what with
everything.'

'Right, I'll get you sorted.'

He went back down and put the radio onto Planet Rock, put some
dripping in a big pan, and began frying two thick slices of smoked bacon,
halved some cherry tomatoes and cut a thick slice of black pudding and

put it in with the bacon. He peeled a small avocado, chopped it up, squeezed some lemon juice on and added a few chilli flakes, while bringing water to the boil in a saucepan with a splash of vinegar in, to poach an egg. Taking a steel ring from the drawer and putting it at the centre of a warmed plate, he began stacking the breakfast up, starting with black pudding, then avocado, tomatoes, bacon and finally the egg on top, so when she cut into it, the yolk would act like a sauce. A crunch of black pepper, some chopped parsley, and a few flakes of sea salt completed it.

'Brekkie is ready!' He called up the stairs and went back to the kitchen to make coffee.

She came cantering down, sapphire blue eyes bright, throwing a pose as she got into the kitchen.

'Aw, man, this smells great. Hot fat, smokey bacon, phwoarr I've got food horn! Ha ha. And look at this - upmarket, restaurant presentation. Brilliant.' She kissed him on the cheek. 'What a lovely lad you are, eh. A rainbow of protein! Are you not eating?'

'I'll have something when you've got off to work.'

She dug in hungrily, eating big mouthfuls, while he made coffee in a cafetière, pushing down on the plunger and releasing a rich aroma.

She kept making orgasmic faces as she bit into the black pudding and then the bacon. Feeding yourself was simply nowhere near as enjoyable as feeding someone else. Funny that.

He poured the coffee and sipped at his cup. 'Someone has definitely been camped out by that blackthorn bush. I took a look and I think they've been there for a while. I just don't know why, though. It seems really odd.'

'Could they be homeless and are dossing down there?' she said.

'Yeah, maybe.'

She wiped up her egg with the last bit of black pudding. 'That was *so* delish. Thanks, luv. Just what I needed. Right, I've gotta go.' She poured a quick cup of coffee and got her papers and laptop together for her day's work. Nick went up stairs to the toilet. After he was finished, he went back into the bedroom; it smelled like a farmyard. They seemed to give off a lot of weird smells in the night. Part straw, part methane, part damp towel. So he opened the window on the first notch to let some fresh air in and pulled the duvet back to air the bed and laid Julie's pale blue cotton pyjamas on the old wooden chair in the corner.

After watching her drive off and making sure a Range Rover wasn't following her, he made himself some bacon and eggs. By then it was after 10am. He had a couple of newspaper columns to write about the new football season, but they could wait until the evening. It was such a glorious morning and too nice for sitting indoors, so he locked up the house and took a stroll down Norton Road to the town centre, picking up a coffee along the way and heading down to the riverside to watch the water flow, sitting on a wooden park bench. It had all been landscaped since he was a boy, and even though four lanes of traffic on the A135 ran right past, it was about as bucolic as the centre of Stockton got.

A text came in from Jeff just as he finished his coffee.

'Some boxes of new stock just in. If you've nothing urgent to do, you could sort them for me. Am really busy.'

Nick crossed the road and walked up to the High Street, pushing open the door to Jeff's store to be greeted by the smell of coffee, toast and the sound of Jeff Healey playing 'While My Guitar Gently Weeps'.

Emily looked over from behind the counter of the cafe at the back and gave him a little wave but not her usual gap-toothed smile. Regular pensioner punter Tommo was sitting in a corner eating a toasted teacake and reading the paper. Two others chatted over mugs of tea and toast. Jeff came out of the stock room holding his big pricing gun.

'By 'eck, you were quick.'

'I was already in town. You know I can't resist fresh record meat.'

'I've not had a chance to look at it yet. There's two boxes of stuff I've just bought, and another that's just come in from the auction rooms. A whole 30 pounds' worth of Elkie Brooks and *Sound of Music* records, I should think. I shall set the money gun on stun.' He fired it at him, like it was a pistol. As Nick squatted down to look through the cardboard box, a cold, tingling feeling swept through him, making him feel a little nauseous.

Putting his hand to his mouth, he took a moment to compose himself. But he knew what was happening. And what was happening was that he was quite obviously living out the dream he'd just had before waking up.

'Oh, my god...'

CHAPTER 5

Just as in the dream, at the front of the box were the records by Fairport Convention, John Martyn and the two by Audience on the pink Charisma label. Without further hesitation, he flicked to the back of the box. He could already see it in the polythene sleeve; the triple *Glastonbury Fayre* album. With shaking hands he picked it out and stood up, holding it towards Jeff who was fiddling with the pricing gun.

'Jeff! Look!'

The big man looked up, clocked the record, knew exactly what it was in an instant and leapt into the air and did a funny little jig. 'Yes! Get in! Come to daddy, you lovely hippy relic of a bygone age. Whoo hoo! Em! Em!' He went through to the cafe at the back. 'We scored big in this week's auction box.'

'Is it valuable?' she said, as he held it up.

'250 at least. There's other stuff, too.'

She gave him a low-powered smile. 'I'll get it on eBay, when I get a moment.'

Nick had to sit down, resting on a stool by the counter.

'What's up wi' yoor coupon, as our Glaswegian friends might say,' said Jeff, in an approximation of a Scottish accent. 'You look as white as a sheet. Or you would if I had white sheets, which I don't.' He paused and looked at him square in the face. 'Are you alright? Do you want some water or something? You look proper peaky.'

'Yeah, water please.'

Jeff went to the fridge in the cafe and got a bottle of mineral water for him.

Nick took a long drink of the cold water. His mouth was parched dry in the way it is when you're really scared.

Emily came round and stood in front of him, hands on hips. 'You do look rather grey around the gills, as my father used to say.'

'Something weird just happened. Too weird. I don't like it.'

'Did you see a ghost?' she said, wiping her hands on her black Motörhead apron.

'Sort of, yeah. This morning, I had a dream where I was in here looking through a box of records. At the front were the Fairport and John

Martyn albums, and the first two Audience, and at the back was the *Glastonbury Fayre* triple.'

Jeff picked up the box and put it on a stool, flicking through it at speed with the kind of agile, strong fingers every longtime record collector develops over their lifetime. With an open-mouthed look he pulled the other valuable records out.

Emily put her hand to her mouth. 'I don't understand, how did you know they were there to dream about them?'

He shook his head. 'I couldn't have known they were here. I dreamed it exactly as it happened in real life, to the point of knowing where those records were in the box.'

'This is weirdsville, Arizona,' said Jeff.

'He's psychic, Jeff. He must be,' said Emily. She went back to the cafe, calling out to Tommo to see if he wanted more tea. He did.

'It's called precognition,' said Nick. 'I read a book about it.'

'Nah, I could have told you Tommo would want more tea. He's only had two mugs, he always has three. There's nothing psychic about that,' said Jeff, slapping Nick on the back, with a crazy grin.

'Seriously, man. This is too weird. It's scary.'

Jeff just shrugged. 'Alright, alright. I don't know what to say about it. So you can dream things that happen in the future, now what? It's not like it's a superpower you can use for the greater good. It's like when you said you could make a telephone ring, remember that?'

'Yeah, though it never rang when I was with you, only when I was on my own.'

'Aye, you just made all of that up in order to make out you were special, didn't you? I always assumed you did.'

Nick shook his head. 'Nope, I didn't, it was real but only happened for a few weeks. I swear. I don't know if it was all in my head, or if it really happened. Only I could hear it ringing. But it was as real as the smell of toasted teacakes is in here.'

'Puberty makes kids go bonkers. Your brain is practically on fire with hormonal changes. I reckon you'd gone a bit mad and it was all in your head. Audible hallucinations, like.'

'I'm not so sure.' He tugged at the stubble on his chin with forefinger and thumb. 'I think it was some sort of electric or magnetic energy I was giving off.'

Jeff groaned. 'Oh, that's total bollocks, that is,' he said, with a snort of derision.

'Don't bollocks me. What was it, then?' said Nick, a little indignant at being doubted.

'I don't know, but if you were radiating phone-activating energy, why did it only affect one phone, in one house? Eh? If you had some sort of magnetic energy spurting out of you, why didn't the whole of Palm Grove's phones start ringing as you walked past? Why didn't it happen in your own house? If it's a physical phenomenon it has to affect everything. It's not selective, is it?'

It seemed a good point, well made. 'Yeah, well, look, I don't know, do I? All I know is it happened.'

Jeff cocked his right index finger. 'Correction: All you know is you *think* it happened. That's not quite the same thing.'

'No, it definitely happened. Even if it was some weird mental breakdown, it still happened on some level or another. After that phone thing I could predict the spin of a coin to about 90 per cent accuracy. It didn't last long but it was all connected to puberty. My mam said about it the other day.'

Jeff frowned at him, paused and then flicked his long hair over his shoulders.

'Err...your mam is...you know...dead, like.' He cast a look at Nick which suggested he wasn't sure how seriously to take him.

'Yeah, but she visited me yesterday before I went to London. She sat on my bed and talked to me. She said I had always been special and I should trust my instincts, then I went to London and they offered me exactly the deal I told her they'd offer. Right money, right royalty and I even predicted Tim Forest would be wearing a cardigan. She said I'd know and I did.'

Jeff was obviously about to take the piss, but he stopped himself and sat down opposite Nick on a stool by the counter. 'Are you feeling alright, old son?'

Nick knew where he was going. 'I'm not mad, Jeff. Honest. I'm alright.'

'Aye, but that's what your mother used to say, isn't it? Despite being very mad. Are you sure you're feeling OK? If you're not, you can just tell me, right? I'll look after you. It's no big deal. Everyone goes bonkers from time to time. I love a loon, you know that.' He patted him on the shoulder and smiled, looking into Nick's eyes in a kindly way.

'I told you, I'm fine. Just because we don't understand something doesn't make it the product of a diseased mind. Like I said to Jules, what is dreaming? We haven't a clue. It's some sort of existence or reality, but it's just not this type of one. Precognition works on the basis that you slip your moorings and can experience the future before it happens. I read that book about it.'

Emily came through with a white china mug of green tea for him.

'Are you feeling alright now?' she said.

'Yeah. Thanks, Em. That's good of you.'

She squeezed his upper thigh and smiled.

'Well I'd not like to have precognition. I like the future being unknown. It's one thing dreaming about finding records, but what if you dream about something terrible. It'd ruin your life wondering when it was going to happen,' said Jeff.

Nick tugged at his lip. 'Yeah, that's true.' He let out a sigh, unable to work out what was going on, or what any of it meant, if anything. There was no rational explanation to make sense of what had happened. Even if he dreamed of finding records all the time, which he didn't, dreaming of finding those exact ones and then to find them there, in the same order, was all just too improbable. Was it his mother's influence from beyond the grave? Even making the leap of faith that she could do such a thing - why show him some records he was going to see a few hours hence? There's no value in that, really. There was no sense to it. None at all. It was what it was, but who knew what the hell that actually was.

'Don't mention this to Jules, alright? She already thinks I'm mad for talking to my mother. She's got enough to cope with right now without a loony husband.'

'Your secret is safe with me. I shall store it in my impenetrable vault along with everything else immoral, perverted and criminal that you've done in your life, up to and including your brief career as a haloumi and stuffed olive thief.'

'Oh, god, don't remind me. I think I must've been a bit daft in the head when I did that.'

He was just sitting chewing on his bottom lip when Matty, Emily's boyfriend came in, crashing the door on its hinges as he did so, long black hair streaming out behind him. Dressed, as usual, in a tight black t-shirt, very tight black jeans and black pointy boots, he was obviously in a bad mood.

'Yo! Matty!' shouted Jeff, as he put 50p stickers onto John Denver records. But unusually Matty ignored him and stormed into the cafe at pace. Jeff gave Nick a raised eyebrow look and followed him.

'What's this shite?' shouted Matty at Emily, who was cleaning down the sinks. He was holding a sheet of paper.

'You know what it's all about,' she said, quietly, trying to be composed.

Matty was furious, wild even.

'Fuck you!' he yelled.' You know nothing about me and my life. Nothing! Look at you, working in a shitty cafe like a fucking scrubber. Where's your ambition? You're a pathetic bitch!' He literally spat the words out with gobs of saliva. More than furious, he was incandescent. He scrunched up the sheet of paper into a tight ball and threw it at her.

Tommo put his newspaper down. 'Hey, hey! Watch your mouth, son!'

'Fuck off Tommo, you old prick!' shouted Matty.

'Don't be rude to Tommo,' said Emily, indignant.

Nick and Jeff moved towards Matt.

'There's no call for this, son,' said Jeff, putting a hand on his shoulder to halt his advance. Matty shrugged him off.

Nick skipped round in front of him and planted the flat of his hand into Matty's breast plate. He was never like this.

'Calm down, we don't want any trouble in here,' said Nick. Matty was the same height as him, but skinny and lightweight.

Matty stared at him with pure hatred. 'Fuck you, you fucking arse-hole. I'm sick of you and your fucking feminist spunk bucket bitch of a wife!!' He was raging, his eyes burning with fury, pupils dilated into big black circles. It was like he was a different person to the quiet, good-natured lad he was normally. He tried to push Nick out of the way so he could get behind the counter to Emily, who had turned her back and was now just trying to pretend it wasn't even happening. Nick stood his ground.

'I don't know what you're on, son, but I suggest you back off and calm down,' said Nick, trying not to escalate the situation.

Matty stood, panting, looking Nick in the eyes. He looked odd, his skin was damp and he smelled odd; a weird unearthly odour that was a bit sulphurous and a bit kind of vinegary. Out of nowhere, Matty swung a punch at Nick, half-connecting with his cheek bone; but seeing it coming, Nick swayed back and it just clipped him without any power. It was the punch of a man who had never thrown a punch. Matty wasn't a fighter. He'd never been aggressive before.

'What the hell do you think you're doing?' shouted Emily, turning and seeing what had happened.

Jeff got hold of Matty around the neck and dragged him backwards. 'C'mon son, don't get Nick angry, he'll mash you and I don't want to have to wipe your blood off my nice clean floor or off any valuable records.'

'The boy's off 'is 'ead!' yelled Tommo, who had got to his feet.

But Matty wasn't having that, he elbowed Jeff in the belly, winding him, got free and leapt over the counter. Emily screamed and backed away to the sink but he got hold of her and pushed her to the floor. 'If I want you, I'll fucking have you and I'll fucking have you now!' He yelled at her. Emily was clearly terrified and screamed again.

No time for messing around. Nick tackled him from behind, hauling him around and kneed him hard in the balls, then planted a right hander into his cheekbone. Both great hits, but it was like he hadn't even done it. Matty looked stunned but not hurt and, like some sort of terminator, turned back to Emily, pushing her to the floor as she tried to get up, and then straddling her. Grabbing at her t-shirt and jeans, he seemed to be trying to tear them off her. She screamed a third time and started slapping and kicking out at him in a flurry of punches and attempted kicks.

'You're mine. You'll always be mine, remember that,' he screamed at a vicious pitch.

'Right, I'm done messing around, son!' shouted Nick, grabbing Matty by his long black hair. He pulled hard and dragged him off Emily and out from behind the counter, like a sack of carrots, dragged him through the shop and out of the door. All he could think to do was to get him out of the shop and away from Emily. Tommo was shouting, "Go on Nick, 'ave 'im!! The bastard!!"

Matty was screaming and cursing at Nick, now, but there was nothing he could do. The kid probably weighed 60 kilos at most, which was no problem to Nick, and the pain of having his hair pulled seemed to be finally registering in his central nervous system.

Adrenaline raging in his blood and being much more powerful, Nick knew he had control of the situation now, as he pulled Matty out onto the street. He threw him onto the pavement. Blood ran from Matty's nose and he dabbed at it, looking puzzled at the red on his fingers, like he hadn't even realised it was bleeding before then.

'What the fuck has got into you, Matty? You're fucked up on something, aren't you?'

But the fury was still burning in him, despite the blood and despite surely being in pain from the kick to his balls and right hander to his face. Unsteadily, he got to his feet and lashed out at Nick with his right fist; he stepped back, only to have Matty leap at him. Nick held him off at arm's length in an iron grip. Jeff came out of the shop, having got his breath back, pulled Matty away by the shoulders and cast him aside like a rag doll.

'He's raging on something!' shouted Nick.

Jeff turned to Matty. 'Calm. Down!'

But he just wasn't having it.

Matty turned to head back into the shop to get back to Emily. Nick knew there was only one way to sort this out. He leapt through the air and raked his heel down Matty's calf, the way he'd seen Graeme Souness do at Ayresome Park so many times in the 70s. The kid screamed out in pain, just as so many of Souey's victims did. He hit the deck again.

This time Jeff promptly sat on Matty's legs and Nick sat on his back, making it impossible for him to move. They faced each other as their assailant tried and failed to get free.

'He's totally off his face, man,' said Nick. 'I took out his bollocks and twatted him with my best punch and he barely felt it! It's weird. I like the lad, I don't want to be hitting him, but it's like he's gone insane.'

At that point, Matty screamed and his whole body tensed under them.

Jeff raised his eyebrows. 'You know, that was so high-pitched it actually made my balls vibrate, which is always bonus in what is essentially a hostage situation. I think we need medical help here,' he said, taking his phone out of his back pocket and dialling 999 to get an ambulance.

Tommo came out of the shop and looked at them, shaking his head. 'That's right shit, that is. I liked that lad. He used to do my toast. What's up with him? Has he gone tonto?'

'He's on drugs, Tommo,' said Nick.

The old lad just stood there looking at him, shaking his head, then in a quiet sad voice said, 'What a bloody daft bugger,' and walked away.

'Let us up!' demanded Matty.

'No chance. What are you on?' yelled Jeff.

'Fucking nothing!'

'Bollocks,' said Nick.

Matty relaxed a little.

'Look, the bitch drives me crazy. She does it on purpose. This is all her fault. She just doesn't get me. C'mon lads, you know what it's like. Women fuck with your brain! We all know that.'

Jeff looked at Nick and made a loopy gesture towards his head.

'Nothing justifies what you've just done,' said Nick. 'Nothing. You're totally out of order.'

'Screw you, Guymer. You're brainwashed by that feminist slut of a wife of yours.'

'Hey, stop bad-mouthing Jules. She's a good woman and when you're not fuck faced, you know that's true,' said Nick, disturbed to hear him talk like this.

Soon, an ambulance arrived and two female paramedics got out, pulling on blue plastic gloves.

'Alright son. Worravwegorerelike?' said the first, a solid-looking working-class woman, with a Boro accent thicker than gravy from a Newboulds pie.

'We know this lad really well, he's normally a good kid, but he's kicked off and tried to assault his partner and us too,' said Nick. 'We've restrained him for his own good. He's off his head on something.'

Even as he spoke, Matty screamed again and tensed under him.

The second paramedic, an older woman, got on her knees beside Matty's head. 'What 'ave you taken, luv?'

Matty just screamed once more, his whole body rigid, like he was having a fit. It was profoundly horrible to witness.

'If we let him up, he'll just kick off again,' said Jeff. 'He's not feeling any pain. Nick hit him with a big punch to stop him assaulting his girlfriend and it was like he's numb to it.'

'Right. My guess is crystal meth. We've had a few of these recently,' said the older woman, remaining impressively level-headed.

She kneeled beside him.

'Alright lad, we're taking you to North Tees. I know you're not going to be happy about it, but we're doing it anyway.' She was right. He screamed in protest, cursing them in ever more lurid language. Whatever was in his bloodstream seemed to be peaking because his emotions were even more intense. If he hadn't had their collective 27 stone of weight to hold him down, god knows what he'd have done.

'Sorry luv, but I'm going to have to knock you out now. I can't risk you kicking off in my ambulance. This is for your own good.' She turned to her co-worker. 'Get us five milligrams of Midazolam, Sue.' She took a syringe ~~from her co-worker~~the other held out.

Nick and Jeff held his legs and arms down as she jabbed the drug into his thigh. Thank god, it worked almost immediately, and the energy and tension in Matty's body just disappeared as it surrendered to the sedating narcotic. God bless drugs.

They strapped him to a stretcher and lifted him into the ambulance. As they were doing so, Mandy Beale came out of Silver Street and waved at them.

She came up, a little breathless from half-walking, half-jogging, with another copper in tow.

'Someone just told me about this. What's going on with 'im?' she said, nodding at the ambulance, her face set in a scowl.

'He's out of his mind on crystal meth, they reckon,' said Nick.

'He was ready to tear Emily limb from limb, he attacked her in the shop and tried to rip her clothes off,' said Jeff. 'We had to...you know...restrain him, one way or another.'

Mandy shook her head. 'Is she alright?'

'Yeah, we stopped him.'

'Bloody 'ell. He's alright, 'im. Or I thought he was. Who the hell is pushing crystal meth around here? As if we didn't have enough problems with smack, coke and skunk.'

'Someone's probably making it here. Teesside's famous for its toxic chemicals, after all,' said Jeff.

'Not funny, Jeff. Not funny at all. A lot of lives are going to get ruined if that stuff is going to get big here. Sends people off their nut. It's instantly addictive. If it can bend a good lad like Matty Rhodes out of shape then god knows what it'll do to some of the more evil snot goblins we've got 'round 'ere. I don't like this at all.' She turned to the PC she'd come with. 'Get the drug squad in the office for one o'clock. We've got to nip this in the bud.' He nodded. She turned back to them. 'Do you know if he's been on it long?'

'He can't have been. He's worked part time for me for the best part of 18 months or more and he's never been like that. I'll ask Em, though. Maybe it was his first time on it.'

'For 'is sake, I 'ope it's the last.'

Back in the shop, Emily was sipping at some tea. The shop and cafe was empty as Jeff and Nick walked back in. Jeff looked around.

'Funny how having a lunatic man pinned to the ground screaming puts off the punters, eh, Em?'

'Are you alright?' said Nick, going behind the counter.

'Hmm. Is he all right?' said Emily.

'They had to sedate him. They've taken him to hospital. What's he been taking? The paramedic thought it was crystal meth,' said Jeff.

'It's something like that. He got it the other weekend and he was, like, in a state of total ecstasy. It was sooo scary. He was...he was different. It brought something out of him. I wouldn't take it, but he loved it. Then he took it again and he was...' she stopped and shook her head, looking at the wooden floor as she did so. 'I wrote down what he was like on it and I said if he was going to take it, he had to move out because I can't be around him like that and I left this note for him.' She held up the screwed-up sheet of paper. 'That's what made him crazy. I shouldn't have written that.'

'The drug was what made him crazy, Em, not you,' said Jeff. 'Don't blame yourself. You did the right thing. He's obviously taken it again this morning.'

'I know, but if I hadn't been so uncool about it...'

'Not taking mind-destroying drugs isn't uncool, Em. Only losers take that shit,' said Jeff.

Nick took her small hand in his and just held it. 'Has he attacked you before?'

She obviously didn't want to answer that. Instead she just raised her thin little eyebrows a little. 'No comment.' She said it quietly, lingering on the 't' at the end of the word.

He squeezed her hand. 'If you ever want to talk about it, I'm here for you.'

She pulled her hand away and gave him a withering look. 'Oh, shut the fuck up, Nick. You're the least emotionally literate person I know, so why would I do that? You'd make the shittiest agony aunt ever. Just leave me alone. You don't know anything about me and Matty, or what it's been like and I don't want you to. I don't want to talk to you. I don't want your sympathy or some attempt to be touchy feely. You're rubbish at it. So just fuck off and leave me alone.' She pushed past him and marched back into the cafe.

He watched her go feeling like he must have totally misunderstood the situation. He'd just wanted to offer support. He turned to Jeff.

'What did I do wrong there?' he said, quietly.

Jeff pushed up the counter flap and patted him on the back, on the way to the toilet at the back of the stockroom. 'You really don't know, do you?'

'No.'

69

'Think about it, while I go to relieve my bladder of several pints of tea.'

Nick shook his head. He just didn't see it. So he went and picked up the box of auction-room records and began sorting them into Jeff's usual financially defined categories of Lots, Some, Not Much and Bin.

As Jeff returned, Nick held up an early Incredible String Band album, *Wee Tam and the Big Huge*.

'How do you price the ISB? They're in *Record Collector* as valuable but does anybody actually buy them?'

Jeff took it off him and inspected it. 'Five quid at best. We won't sell it for three years but it's booked at about 30. Mad. I hate this sort of twee, whimsical folk music. I'm sure it was great in 1968 when you smoked your first joint, but in 2011 it sounds like it's made by some kids in the remedial class. Can I still say "remedial" or has it gone the way of "retard", "simple" and "slow"?'

'I have no idea. I'm the emotionally illiterate one, remember?'

Jeff laughed loudly. 'I thought that might have touched a raw nerve.'

Four students came in and went through to the cafe, followed by two couples and suddenly the shop had come alive. Jeff took out Mike Oldfield's *Tubular Bells* from its sleeve and showed it to Nick.

'First pressing, black and white Virgin label. Sweet. I'll get £30 for this.'

'I love it. Takes me right back to '73 and '74, sitting in the back room of the house in Palm Grove, beside the rubbish coke Parkray fire and my gran saying, "This is a bit weirdy".'

'Ha ha. Yes, Gran, that's why it's brilliant. Anyway, who invented coke? It was rubbish. I'd have taken the smoky pollution of coal over the soulless glow of coke any day. And don't get me started on electric fires. But to get back to the pixie girl over there...'

Nick glanced at Em. She was chatting to the students and laughing a little as she made coffee for them, which was good to see. Another couple came in and went over to buy coffee and cake, then another group of four, two men from which stopped to look at records, whilst their girlfriends or wives went to get a hot drink. The place hummed with chatter, as Jeff dropped the needle on Spirit's second album, *Clear*, then put his hand on Nick's shoulder. 'Look, obviously, Matty raging on the drugs has probably forced his attentions on Emily and she probably didn't have much choice in accepting those attentions. Yer crystal meth freak isn't a

PC fella, is he? He wants what he wants and he's gonna have it, right? You saw what he was like, and what he said.'

'Well, yeah. That's exactly what I thought. Jules has talked about this sort of thing.'

'Yeah, but it's all too soon for her to talk about. It's just happened. She's losing her boyfriend. She's lived with him for over a year now. They were very lovey dovey, so she's feeling really let down by him, but also defensive towards him. She doesn't want to slag him off because she still probably thinks she loves him and that they can get back together once he's realised that bad drugs are a one-way ticket to loserville.'

'And you think they can't or won't?'

Jeff shook his head. 'Nah. It's been going sour for weeks. Whatever has been going wrong has been going wrong for a while. Not what it once was in the early days, anyway. If you ask me, he's messed up because Metal Road went nowhere and have broke up. Without the band, he's got nothing and that's why he's gone off at the deep end. To be honest, he's not good enough for her. Matty was OK but for all the good-looking, rock 'n' roll posing, he's pretty vanilla and there's not much depth to him. Em needs someone more intelligent and clever, if you ask me, like.'

'So what did I do wrong with her?'

'You treated her like she was a little kid who needed her hand held and to be cooed at. All that does is undermine her sense of self-confidence. It means you're seeing her as a victim and she isn't, or doesn't want, to see herself like that. She's strong enough to deal with this - or she wants to think she is. If she isn't, that's when she'll need us. But not before then. Right?'

Nick looked at him, square on. 'That actually all sounds very plausible.'

'Of course it is. I've told you before, son, if only we'd mixed my emotional literacy with your kick-ass body, we'd have had it off with every good looking lass in this town by now.'

'Should I apologise to her?'

Jeff looked at him like he was stupid.

'Of course not. It's not that big a thing. It's been an upsetting morning for her, so don't go stirring the emotional waters any more. She'll probably make a joke out of it soon enough.'

'You missed your calling as an agony uncle, you know.'

'I know. My life has been full of bloody agony. Boom, bloody boom!!' He held his arms out wide and took a step forward, as though on stage. 'C'mon, I'm selling that one to Big Fish. That's better than his whole act.'

'So is she alright with me? Have we fallen out?'

'Don't be daft. It'll all blow over. She'll have a word with you about it at some point. You know she fancies you.'

'She flirts with me. But that's not the same thing.'

'You can believe that if you want, but I'm here to tell you that if you didn't have Jules in your life, she'd spend all day sitting on your face. You'd be wearing her like a beard.'

'...like a beard? Jules used that expression the other morning. Did she get it from you?'

'Probably, I'm a very influential poet, me, aren't I?' He made a 'the thinker' pose.

'But I'm more than twice her age.'

Jeff shook his head. 'Doesn't matter, does it? You can't control who makes your knicker liver tingle.'

'Your knicker liver? Bloody hell, Jeff. That's gross. When did you make that up?'

'I was pleased with it and I've been waiting for a chance to use it. Anyway, you've seen her naked, remember?'

'How could I forget?'

'Well, she won't have and that's also why she doesn't want your brotherly sympathy. Don't you see that?'

'Sorry, no. I don't. I mean don't get me wrong, I'm not totally stupid, what bloke doesn't like an attractive lass like her flirting with them? But...'

'...but she knows, as well as I do, that you and Jules are forever and ever, amen, like no-one we ever met in our lives. She's tested you out on that front more than once. It's because you wouldn't do anything about her flirting with you that makes her feel safe to do it. It makes her feel good. So she needs you to be the sexy, supportive, strong man in her life, just like she needs me to make her laugh and educate her about the difference between the Peanut Butter Conspiracy and actual peanut butter. The last thing she needs is you cooing over her and being like a sexless, wimpy gay friend who doesn't lust after her. She wants to still be attractive to you, not the subject of your sympathy. It's all to do with self-esteem, innit?'

Nick was amazed to hear this and shook his head.

'How do you know this stuff? How do you discern it all?'

'By keeping my eyes open, sunshine. Look, you just concentrate on looking all moody and gorgeous in your tight t-shirts and bollock-hugging pants and leave the obscure metaphors and being clever to me.' He wafted his hair up and down like a long pair of ears and made a goofy face at him. 'She needs a hand in there, I'll have to do it. Can you hold the fort here until it quiets down?'

'Yeah, of course.'

'I'll have to get a full timer in for the cafe. I need Em on the magic machine to do eBay and stuff and with the club finally ready to go, I'm going to need to be over there a lot.'

'Oh, is it ready to go? Have they finished the bar, then?'

'Didn't I say? All done. I signed off on it yesterday in between all the Jules business. We're ready to open. All we need is some booze delivered, hire some staff and book the first bands. I'm going to sort all of those in the next 24 to 48 hours, I hope.' He shook his head. 'By god, it's been a long, torturous process.'

'Over a year and a half of long torturous process, in fact.'

'If I hadn't had to get a drink licence, and if people hadn't objected to having a live venue in a converted disused church building, and if the council didn't take forever to make decisions, we could have been open within months. Still, what doesn't kill you makes you longer...'

'...you mean stronger.'

'No, I mean longer. Me hair is about four inches longer now! Wish some other bits of me were.'

The shop was busy for an hour. For someone who wasn't that sociable much of the time, Nick liked working behind the counter. All you did was talk to people for a minute or two about music, then they went away. This was pretty much his ideal sort of socialising because it meant he was on home ground, always had something to say, but wasn't required to be entertaining or interesting for any length of time, so it was pretty pressure free.

People asked you all sorts of bizarre things, and you had to know the stock well and where you might be able to lay your hands on a record. So when someone asked if you had a copy of Blackfoot Sue's single, 'Standing In the Road', he knew it'd be in the early 70s rock singles section and could tell a woman who was interested in Odetta albums to look in the blues racks. It played to all of Nick's strengths, or at least it did as long as someone didn't ask about a modern band that he'd never heard of, which as vinyl got more popular with younger people, was happening more often.

Jeff operated on a strict policy that whoever worked in the store had to adhere to; never be critical or sneery of anyone's tastes. He insisted everyone be treated as though they were cool for liking whatever it was, be it Shakin' Stevens, the Chocolate Watchband or Be Bop Deluxe. So when a middle-aged woman bought four Barry Manilow albums for £2.00 he made sure he said something nice to her about his hit song 'Mandy', and how it always put him in mind of Mandy Hilton, a girl he'd once clumsily groped at a party in the 70s. It was funny really, because it was exactly the kind of small talk that he just couldn't do in pretty much any other context of everyday life. Maybe he'd missed his vocation. All those Saturday afternoons as a kid spent in Alan Fearnley's record shop on Linthorpe Road in Middlesbrough must have gone deep into his cultural DNA.

After an hour Emily brought him a mug of tea and left it on the counter without saying anything to him. She was obviously and understandably miserable.

'Thanks, Em,' he said, half wondering if even that was the right thing to say. Luckily, a man came up to the counter at that moment so there was no chance to say anything more to her.

'Are you Nick?' he said, pointing to him.

'That's me.'

'Ah, right, right. So who's that?' He pointed through to the cafe.

'That's the owner, Jeff. Can I help you?'

The man stood and looked at him with watery steel-grey, mottled eyes defined by dark eyelashes which made him look a certain sort of pretty, despite obviously being around Nick's own age. His hair was greying and cut short and he was dressed in a grey sweatshirt and jeans.

'I've just got some records to sell. Someone recommended this place,' he said, in a soft Dublin accent.

'That's what we're all about here - records. Have you got them with you? I can take a look at them.'

'Oh, no, they're at home. I just wondered if you were buying stuff, right now.'

'We always need good stock. Right, well, if you bring them in, we'll have a look and see if there's anything we can sell. Jeff pays good prices for good stock.'

The man was about his own height and lean.

'Fair enough.' He held out his hand. 'What's your name, again?'

Nick shook. 'I'm Nick, I'm just helping him out today 'cos it's got a bit busy. But if I'm not here, and Jeff's not here, Emily will help you. We all know what'll sell and what won't. Is there a lot of records?'

He looked towards the cafe. 'Emily, oh yeah, the little rocker girl, yeah?'

'Yup. We're all experts. Or we like to think we are.'

'Cool. OK.'

As he spoke, a woman interrupted. 'Sorry, but do you mind if I take a photo of that record up there on the wall?' She pointed to the copy of the Mothers of Invention's *Freak Out*. All the very rare stuff was in plastic sleeves on the wall. It was priced at £75. 'I think it's the one my husband wants, but I'll forget what it looks like and I just want to check with him. Is that OK?'

'Yeah, sure. If it is, we can put it to one side for you. Just message the shop on Facebook or Twitter and say "I want this record" if you can't get in for a few days.' He handed her one of the shop's contact cards with Facebook, Twitter, eBay and MusicStack listings urls on.

'Aw, thanks, luv.' She took it and snapped the picture on her phone.

Nick turned back to the man. 'Sorry mate, so there's a lot of records, is there?'

'A fair few, yeah.'

'We can pick them up if you want.'

'No it's OK, I'll bring them down in the Range Rover. Plenty of room in there for them.'

'Alright. No problem.'

'Yeah, thanks for your help, Nick. Nice to have met you.' He winked at him, turned and got to the door of the shop, then stopped, turned to look at Nick, then Jeff and Emily again and with a quick smile, left.

It remained busy all afternoon so Nick wound up doing the full day. By 5pm it had got a lot quieter but Jeff had to go and pick Argie up from nursery, leaving Nick in the shop with Emily.

'We've sold a lot of records today,' he said, as she came over to pick up his empty mug.

'Good.'

'I'll look after everything until Jeff gets back, if you want to get off,' he said.

'I've got nowhere to go except home and I'd rather not be there for long.'

'Aye, I can see why, like. You can come back to our house for the night, if you like. You'll have to kip on the couch because there's no spare bed, but it's easily big enough for you. We can have a few drinks and I'll cook us something. No point in sitting at home stewing things over.'

She sighed and wouldn't look straight at him. 'Would Julie mind?'

'Of course not. It's no big deal. Stay as long as you want while you get everything sorted out.' He tried to be nonchalant about it, in an attempt to be strong and supportive, as Jeff had said. And it seemed to work. She looked up at him and nodded. 'OK, I'll text her, then. She'll be just finishing work.' He tapped at his phone, gave her brief synopsis of the day's events and that he thought Em shouldn't be alone in her flat, in case Matty was released and came back. Julie texted back right away.

'Wow. Of course she can stay with us. I'll give you both a lift home. Will be 20 minutes'.

She was soon walking through the shop door.

'Hello, my lovelies!' she said, as bright as ever.

'Hey, Jules. Did the Range Rover follow you again?'

'Nah. All cool today.' She waved at Emily, who was getting her bag. 'Hi, Em. I just picked up some wine and gin and a roast chicken from Marksies, if you fancy it. Nick tells me you've had one of those fizzin' Shitey Mcshitey from Shiteshire days.'

She almost laughed. 'Yeah, you could say that. Not the most fun I've ever had. Been like that for a while now, Jules.'

Julie shrugged. 'Yeah, well, shit happens, doesn't it? Nothing some food and a skinful of drink won't help repair. C'mon, let's get off.'

CHAPTER 6

Emily locked up the shop and squeezed into the small rear space in the Porsche.

'This is one occasion when being petite is an advantage,' she said, as Julie drove off up Norton Road. 'As opposed to when you have to deal with a raging meth head attacking you. Thank god for Nick and Jeff.'

'That sounds awful. He actually attacked you in the shop?' Julie said, addressing her via the rear-view mirror.

'Yeah, or he would have done, if the lads hadn't been there.'

'He took some decking, I'll tell you that much,' said Nick. 'The boy was raging.'

'Where is he now?' said Julie.

'North Tees,' said Nick. 'They sedated him right on the street outside of the shop. People on the Ingleby Barwick bus were giving us some funny looks.'

'You and Jeff were great.'

Nick turned around and smiled at her.

'We just sat on him until the ambulance came. It's a good pacifist approach, sitting on someone. Worked much better than kicking him in the balls and thumping him in the face. Maybe there's a lesson there.'

'Has he been taking that stuff long, Em?' said Julie, looking in her rear-view mirror at her.

'That was the third time he'd taken it around me. He might have had it somewhere else. I think he has, actually.'

'But you didn't partake?'

'No. I'm so over drugs. Boring. I've even stopped smoking.'

'Really? You didn't say,' said Nick.

'Did I have to? You just didn't notice.'

'Noticing things isn't always Nick's strong point, Em. You know that,' said Julie with a chortle.

Nick didn't say anything, fearing he was about to make a faux pas, whatever he said.

'Here we are,' said Julie pulling up outside the house they'd rented for the past 10 months. 'You've not been here since the Christmas party, slash, housewarming, have you? We've decorated since.'

'I don't remember much, I got so drunk and ended up arguing with Matty. Huh. Irony.'

Nick unlocked the door, feeling a bit stressed by the thought of having to deal with a moody Emily. Still, Julie was the expert at this stuff. She could talk to her, if she wanted to talk. Breaking up from someone is upsetting at the best of times and if you're doing it because they've been crazy with you, it couldn't be easy to cope with.

Once in, Nick put some veg on and made gravy from some stock they had in the fridge, while Julie poured herself and Emily some chilled white wine, and a vodka and tonic for him, chatting away to them both as she did so.

This was a talent he admired in her so much, because she did it so effortlessly. Years as a lawyer's PA, dealing with people in all sorts of legal distress, had made her calm in a crisis, and now her training as a women's support worker had taught her how to listen and respond with positivity, but without being judgemental. She was still learning, still developing her skills, but at least to a civilian like him, it felt like she was some sort of expert in human relations. Everything Jeff had said about being strong and supportive, just came naturally to her. As she asked Emily questions about how she felt about Matty, and how things had been at home, and what she'd like the outcome of all this to be, Nick realised she was doing what she did at work; coaxing out information in order to get a better understanding. It had to be brilliant to have someone like her on your side to help you, when your world was all isolation, nastiness and negativity. When life goes wrong we all need help from sympathetic, non-judgemental people. Not for the first time, he thought Julie and the women she worked with had to be some sort of angels. It was such quietly selfless work and work which took so much out of your emotional psyche, in return for little more than 20 grand a year. It was a poor reward for a bloody tough gig. Many people did much less for much more.

He drained the vegetables, carved the still-warm chicken and served up their food on hot plates, spooning gravy over everything.

'Eee, look at this. What a lad,' said Julie as they sat down.

'Well, the chicken was already cooked,' he said.

'Oh, yeah, ha ha...I withdraw that compliment, you useless get!'

'Does he do a lot of cooking?' said Emily, glancing at her phone, then sitting down and taking a drink of wine.

'He does all of it. I never, ever cook. I've got him well trained.'

'So you don't cook at all?'

'What do I say about cooking, Nick?' said Julie.

'That you don't cook because you don't want to conform to gender stereotyping. Cooking is buying into a core oppressive element of the patriarchy, dear.' He said it in a thin, nerdy voice, pushing up some invisible glasses on his nose.

Julie laughed. 'It's a brilliant excuse to get out of it. Truth is, he's just much better at it than I am and also, right, he thinks he's cool for being a Northern bloke who can cook. He's been using food as a way to seduce women since he was 17, haven't you, luv?'

'My meat and two veg has always been popular with women, aye, and don't get me started on the quality of my gravy.'

Both of them laughed out loud at that, which made him feel good. Making women laugh always had.

'Well, thanks for having me over, this is really nice,' said Emily, cutting her meat.

'It's nice to have you. We don't see enough of you now, since we moved out of Green Dragon Yard.'

She looked around. 'It's much nicer here for you. You've got a bit more room and it just suits you two a lot more, I think.'

After they had eaten, Nick went upstairs to use the toilet. After he'd washed his hands, he went into the bedroom, pushed open the window and leaned out, sucking in some summer air and tried to make sense of the day in the late summer gloaming.

As he did so, he noticed movement by the blackthorn bush. A red glow. A cigarette glow. It was a man, but he ran away towards the far side of the waste ground, climbed over a low fence and was gone. Nick was fairly sure it was the same man they'd seen before. Short brown hair, quite thick set, a beer gut on him. He must have realised that he'd been spotted. It was weird. What did he have to gain by just sitting there, while they had their dinner? There was nothing to even see. No perving to be done. Was he really just hoping that Julie would undress in front of the window and he'd get a flash of nipple for a second or three? If not, why the hell did he just sit there?

He closed the window and sat down on the wooden chair. If it was the ex-partner of one of Julie's service users, were they planning to just sit there on and off for the next few weeks? It can't have been Aggie's brother, Kenny. Kenny was in his 60s, the man outside wasn't that old. So who was he? Their son, maybe? Christ, when would this all end?

A thought occurred to him. Maybe the website pictures were a separate thing. A separate thing which they'd conflated into being all part of the same stalking situation. Maybe this peeper bloke was just someone who was having some sort of breakdown; someone with mental health problems who had decided to set up some sort of base camp there. When you've had someone close to you totally lose their mind, as he had, no amount of odd behaviour was surprising. His mother had once tried to choke the wooden bird in their cuckoo clock, nipping at its throat to kill it, because she thought it was spying on her. Once you've seen that, nothing seems beyond the bounds of possibility.

He put his fingertips together into a pyramid and rested the tips on his lips as he pondered things. It was all very worrying and a brooding sense that things might escalate was hard for him to avoid. No crazy person, whatever their motive, just sits outside a house for a while and then stops doing it, do they? There was bound to be a next step. But what would it be?

They had to get the police involved. All they had to do was to catch them sitting there. It couldn't be that hard. Then again, was it illegal to sit behind a bush on some public land? He hadn't done anything, so, no, it wasn't, and nor should it be. Oh, sod it.

Shutting the bedroom door behind him he went downstairs and into the kitchen. The two women were still sitting at the table with remains of their food on plates still in front of them. Julie, pouring the last of the bottle of wine into Emily's glass, looked up at him and flashed him a smile as she continued to talk.

'You have to look after yourself, Em. Try not to put yourself into a dangerous situation. None of this is your fault, you know that, don't you?'

He poured himself a big vodka and topped it up with some tonic and ice, then set about cleaning the plates away and putting it all in the dishwasher.

'You'll make someone a lovely wife,' said Emily, watching him, much looser and smiley now, as the wine did its job. Heavy drinking is underrated as a temporary cure for life's ills.

'I know, I keep telling Jules this but she won't let me wear her bra and knickers.'

Both the women laughed.

'Feel free, darlin' but they won't cover much of you,' said Julie.

'You've got the slim hips to suit wearing a nice pair of lacy panties, Nick,' said Emily, sticking her tongue between the gap in her front teeth and giggling. 'Just cram in as much of your toilet parts as you can and let the rest hang over the top.'

Julie made a dirty laugh. 'Don't say things like that to him, he goes all weak at the knees at such talk. Look, he's blushing. Aw.'

'Does he now?' Em said, curious.

Julie made her low rumbling laugh again, as she pulled the cork on another bottle of wine. 'Yeah, he loves the dirty talk, don't you, luv?'

'I'm taking both the 5th and the 6th, and quite possibly the 7th on that.'

Emily giggled again. 'That sounded like something Jeff would say. I've started talking like him as well. I even caught myself putting my index finger in the air the other day while I made a point about something.'

'He came up with a strange one earlier: knicker liver. I shall leave that with you.' He put the dishwasher on and turned to face them. 'I've got a couple of pieces that I must write.'

'Knicker liver?!' exclaimed Julie. 'Dear me, that's a bit too graphic!' Both women laughed.

Nick waved at them as he left the room, feeling like he'd played a good gig there, reflecting again that making women laugh is always a brilliant thing, much better than making men laugh. Why was that? Who knows the mystery of the male psyche? Certainly not men.

He went into the music room, full of shelves of records and CDs, took out Paul Kossoff's *Back Street Crawler* solo record, had a long drink and dropped the needle on it and plugged in his headphones.

This was a mental space he loved to live in. A little drink buzz and music in his head, but with nothing to disturb him. All of his life he'd loved to be alone with music and drink, in fact, drinking on his own was probably his preferred option. It allowed you to feel it more deeply and there was no pressure to have to talk to people, or be entertaining and better still, you couldn't make a faux pas and annoy anyone. To the insular person for whom socialising was always a bit fraught, isolated stillness was a blessing.

As he'd got older and understood himself better, he'd learned to find space in life for these moments. It was what kept him sane, along with his daily input of Phenibut. When you're a depressive, you can never take moments of peace and harmony for granted, in fact, you're more aware than most when they're occurring. So when they do happen, however you get them, you do hugely appreciate it.

Quickly, he dropped into his introspective writing mode, a frame of mind he'd had since he was a small boy, where the outside world didn't matter and he felt at home and comfortable in his own psychic landscape. In this frame of mind, half an hour quickly became an hour, became a whole day.

As he tapped away on his laptop, having only got up to put Jeff Beck's *Wired* album on, Julie came in with a big glass of vodka and tonic for him. He slipped off the headphones and took it from her. She'd changed into a t-shirt and sweat pants.

'You look a bit pissed,' he said, as she swayed a little and did her little wriggling, off-beat dance in front of him, a dance he always found a little sexy.

'Aye, I am, like. When a lass goes through the mill, you have to empathise, one way or another, don't you? Emily is in that place where she doesn't need a shoulder to cry on, she just needs someone to be supportive and not judgemental.'

Nick nodded and took a drink. 'Yeah. Jeff said something like that.'

'Jeff's good at this stuff, despite being properly emotionally repressed about himself.'

'Yeah, odd that. Which reminds me I must tell you about the sex tip I gave to him in the Royal Oak.'

'Sex tip? You?!' She laughed.

'Don't be so surprised. I have a tip.'

'I know and it's a very sensitive tip...' she leaned over and kissed him on the lips, while chuckling '...as we'll find out later, if you're a good boy.'

He took her hand. 'You do know that you're brilliant at this, don't you?'

She smiled. 'What? Brilliant at being a bit rude and drinking? I am, like. I've had a load of practice, though, but.'

'You know what I mean. With Emily.'

She let out a long sigh. 'If I am any good, it's only because stories like hers are all too common. I wish I didn't have to be any good.' She perched on the side of the armchair.

'Is she OK, do you think?'

She blew out air from puffed cheeks.

'Well, she's not ready to talk about the specifics, but the questions she's been asking suggest to me that she's been subjected to some sort of abuse in recent weeks.' She raised an eyebrow and turned down her mouth.

He took a drink. 'God, poor lass. You never know what's going on in people's lives, do you? So do you think he was raging on the drugs and attacked her - because, in the cafe, he was trying to rip her clothes off, y'know. He pushed her to the floor and said something like "You're mine and you'll always be mine" and was going on about "having" her.'

She tipped her head. 'Yeah, she said about that. Sorry, but that's a classic power trip, controlling thing.'

'Right. So if he did that at their flat, and followed through on the threat physically, that's rape, isn't it? Being too scared to say no, is rape, isn't it?'

'Very perceptive and yes, you better believe it is. Absolutely. Being coerced into having sex when you don't want to, even if it's done with words and not violence, is still rape.' She lowered her voice to a whisper. 'She's just been doing what so many women do, lying back and thinking of England until it's over. And that is 100 per cent rape.'

Julie ran both hands through her hair and pulled it back behind her head, the drink making her cheeks flushed.

'Like a lot of women in her position, she doesn't really accept, or want to believe that's what it was. She sees it as just one of those awkward relationship things. Like she was accommodating his needs, and I'm not sure, but I think some aggression, at the least, has also been used. A meth head isn't likely to be a sensitive lover.'

'Really? Oh, god. You think you know someone.'

'But she certainly doesn't want to press charges, though she absolutely could and, in my view, she should. No means no. End of story. If a stranger had acted like that towards her, she'd have no doubt it was rape, but because it was her partner, someone she has strong feelings for, in her mind she's excusing it.'

Nick, horrified to hear this, took a big drink. The whole time he'd known Emily, she'd been such a cheeky, effervescent and kind woman. She'd acted like a one-woman social service for Tommo. So often she was a little thread of gold in the grey canvas of life. That someone might bully and abuse her was appalling.

'OK, well, tell her she can stay here for as long as she likes. She's small enough to sleep on the big sofa, or we could get her a camp bed. I don't want her to go back to the flat. Matty will get out of hospital and go right back there and then god knows what will happen. Does she realise the danger she might be in?'

'Not sure. I have told her exactly that, but she's just hoping it all blows over and he'll realise drugs are bad.'

She stood up.

'By the look on your face, you think it won't,' said Nick.

'I think it's unlikely. How do you find a way to patch things up if he's raped her? It's a huge abuse of trust and trust is at the centre of any relationship. Once he breaks that trust, it rarely gets any better, in my experience, no matter how long it goes on for. But then, it's not my place to tell her how to live her life. She's got to make her own choices, all I can do is suggest ways to stay safe and if she wants to make a break from him, how to do it and stay safe then, too.'

Nick took on board more booze. 'For a pissed lass, you're very articulate, Jules.'

'I know, weird huh? I was always good at pretending to mam that I wasn't drunk, when I was a teenager. Speaking of which, I rang the auld shitehawk this lunchtime and told her what's been going on with the photos.'

'How did she take that?'

'Mostly by swearing a lot. But mam is pretty unshockable, as you know. I asked her about Aggie and her brother and what she'd said in the pub.'

'Did she think they might go to these lengths to get revenge?'

Julie shook her head. 'Nah, she thinks Aggie is all wind and piss and, in her words, "too thick to do owt that clever". She still lives near the hospital, though. Fiona had four kids and is, according to mam, "a massive fat slag".'

'At least you're never unsure what Jackie thinks of anyone. By the way, our peeper was out the back again. I saw him from the bedroom window, then he legged it.'

She rolled her eyes. 'God, it's pathetic. I'll text Mandy tomorrow, see if they can't send someone by to try and catch him. Maybe I should show him my stretch marks, that'll put him off peeping forever.'

'I dunno, Jules, they've not put me off. I like 'em. All part of the map that life leaves on your body. We're middle aged, we shouldn't hide from it.'

She made a sympathetic face and stood up. 'Aw, luv. Anyone would think you were a writer or something.' Affectionately, she poked her tongue out at him and, as she was leaving the room, pulled down her navy blue sweatpants and black underwear in one swift motion, bent over and mooned him, wiggling her backside.

He laughed and sat back, feeling a wash of love, and a small thrust of lust. In a way, the easy love he and Julie had for each other made Emily's predicament only more poignant.

After finishing his columns and emailing them in, he went into the living room to find the two women, feet up and watching a documentary about Jimi Hendrix on Sky Arts.

Emily had taken a shower and was now wearing a pair of Julie's pyjama bottoms and one of her baggy t-shirts. She looked up at him as he came in.

'You're the big rock trivia expert, so how big was Jimi's cock, Nick?' said Emily, resting a glass of white wine on her leg and slurring her words. 'Julie says you'll know.'

He flopped into an armchair. 'Ah, we've got to the dirty talking part of the drinking session, have we? A fat eight inches seems to be the commonly agreed dimensions, at least according to the Plastercaster women from Chicago, who preserved his erection in plaster for immortality.'

Emily winced. 'I'm sure that'd bloody well hurt!'

Julie patted Emily on the leg, 'Nah. Don't forget Em, we're designed to push a large animal out of there. It's a very stretchy thing that we've got, fortunately, like.' She gurgled a laugh.

'Well, Matty is nothing like that, thank god.' She squinted at the TV, then her head flopped forward, startling herself by doing so. 'Oh, god, I'm really pissed. I need to lie down.'

Julie stood up so she could lie down full length on the sofa, her head on a big silk cushion. Emily passed out immediately.

'I'll get the spare quilt,' said Nick, going to their airing cupboard where it was kept in a black bin bag.

Julie got her some water, put it by the sofa and laid the quilt on her. She was totally zonked out and lay still, breathing heavily.

'Getting fuck faced is a way of life. It's one of our greatest traditions, but I feel really sorry for her. She's such a nice person. I hate that anything horrible has happened to her,' said Nick.

Julie put her arm around his shoulder. 'That's just life, kidda. It's just the way of the world.' She kissed him on the cheek and slapped his backside. 'C'mon, let's get to bed.'

She went up, while he turned off the TV, locked the doors, got some water for them both and turned out the lights. He had just put a foot on the stairs when he heard a strange noise coming from the living room. He stopped and listened. Was it coughing?

He reversed up and looked in on Emily. As soon as he opened the door, he knew something was badly wrong. She was making an unearthly loud, snorting noise.

'Em! Are you alright?' he said. But she didn't reply.

He put the light on. She was still on the sofa but was now twitching violently. She was having a fit, her mouth open, her jaw slack, thick saliva foam around her lips.

What the bloody hell did you do in a situation like this? He rushed up to her. Her eyes were open and rolled up into her head so only the whites showed. Her whole body kept twitching in an epileptic spasm. It was so shocking and terrifying, that he just didn't know what to do. How do you make it stop?

'Jules!!!' He screamed it at full volume and immediately heard her footsteps coming downstairs.

'What's up?' she said, as she pushed open the living room door. 'Oh, my god. What's wrong with her?'

'She's having an epileptic fit, I think.' As he spoke, Emily reared up from the waist, as though someone had lifted her up, and let out a huge snort, firing spit and snot everywhere, while making a guttural roaring noise.

He held her small frame in his hands, as though wanting to make her safe.

'Em. Emily! Can you hear me?'

No, she couldn't.

She let out a horrible noise, which was part howl in pain and part exhausted bellow. It was deep and visceral and some flavour of terrifying. Was she having a heart attack or something?

'Call 999!' he shouted, terrified that she was going to die. Her whole body seemed to be malfunctioning. Her big gulps of air felt like someone trying to get a breath in order to keep on living.

He heard Julie make the call and describe what was happening, just as the full body spasms Emily had been performing began to ease in frequency. Thank god, she was still breathing. Finally, she gave a really violent and frightening flex of her whole body, seemed to hold herself in a back-arched tensed shape for several seconds, then let out a noise which was part orgasmic moan, part food-poisoned groan, and then the life seemed to pass out of her with a deflating gasp. She lay down, motionless.

'Emily, can you hear me?' he said, shaking her a little, scared she'd died. He put his face up to her mouth to discern her breathing. Small soft breaths came out of her. Thank god.

'They say we've got to keep an eye on her, an ambulance will come soon,' said Julie. 'Is she OK?'

'I don't know. I hope so. She's breathing more normally now.'

Within 10 minutes, the paramedics arrived. Julie led them into the now-peacefully sleeping Emily.

'She was just having a massive fit,' he said. 'But she's calmed down now. Even so, she seems very asleep. I can't wake her up.'

'Is she an epileptic?' said a male paramedic.

'I don't think so, she's never mentioned it, but she did have a lot to drink,' he said.

The paramedic leaned over her and patted her on the arm. 'Are you OK, Emily, luv?' There was no response. She pulled back the quilt and inspected her.

'She's wet herself. Often happens in a fit and especially one that's been brought on by drink. '

'Is that what's caused it? I've never heard of that happening,' said Nick.

'It can do. It's quite rare. People do just have a random fit, occasionally. If she's had a lot to drink, she'll just wake up with a hangover and wouldn't even know what had happened, apart from some muscular pain and being wet, of course. It takes time for the brain to reconnect all its pathways, so she'll sleep solidly now.'

'Well, if she's not in any danger, then we'll look after her,' said Julie. 'It was terrifying to see her like that. I've never seen the like.'

'If you've not seen a proper tonic clonic before, it is scary. She'll be fine now. You did right to call us,' said the paramedic.

After they'd left, Nick and Julie sat in the living room.

'No point in trying to get her cleaned up now,' she said, 'We'll have to get the cushions dry cleaned at that place in town.'

'Yeah, I'll take them in. Poor kid. She'll be really embarrassed and incredibly hung over.'

'At least it happened here where she's safe and we could keep an eye on her. Could have happened while Matty was off his face. C'mon, let's get to bed and get some sleep.'

They went up to the bedroom and closed the door.

Julie pushed her hair off her forehead and looked around the room, eyes squinting.

'Where's my pale blue PJs?'

Nick pulled off his t-shirt. 'I put them on the chair this morning after I turned down the bed. It was stinking like a farmyard in here. We seem to give off some strange smells in the night.'

She looked at the chair. 'Well, they're not there now.' She tipped the chair back to see if they'd fallen on the floor. Nothing. Under the bed? Nothing there either. 'Weird, where've they gone?' She went through to the bathroom and checked there, but returned empty handed. As she did so, Nick sat down on the wooden chair.

'Hang on, I sat here after I'd seen the blackthorn bush peeper. I shut the window and sat down to think about what they were doing out the back and your pyjamas weren't on the chair then, or I'd have sat on them and I didn't. But that's deffo where I had put them and neither of us had been in here since then.'

She gave up and took out a baggy old t-shirt from a drawer and pulled it on instead, removed her underwear and got into bed. 'I'm too fuzzy-headed to think about it. They'll be somewhere, I'm sure.'

Nick took off his pants, got into bed and turned out the light. The darkness brought another thought back to his mind. When he'd come in earlier in the morning, he'd just pushed the window open, but he'd left it on the sneck, so it should still have been on the sneck when he closed it later. But it wasn't.

Oh, shit.

It all fell into place.

'Someone has been in here, Jules. I left the window on the sneck this morning, just to air the room off. But, now I think about it, when I came in this evening, it was off the sneck and just pushed to. That means someone has put a ladder up, flipped the sneck through the gap in the window, got in, taken your PJs and then left, pushing the window so it seemed closed, but they couldn't put it back on the sneck from the outside, could they?'

She groaned and flopped back onto her pillow.

'You're kidding me. Are you sure? Oh, good grief, this is horrible!'

Nick paused, thinking about it.

'This is the next stage in the stalking and it's only going to get worse, if we don't stop him. We have to close this down, as soon as possible. This bloke is dangerous.'

'How are you feeling, now?' Nick pushed a mug of tea across the kitchen table towards Emily. She looked pale and tired.

'I ache all over and I feel like crap, but it's my own fault, so I shouldn't moan. I can't believe I had a fit and I'm totally mortified that I weed all over your sofa. I'm so sorry.'

'You didn't wee all over it. It was just a small pool on one cushion. It wasn't like you were performing handstands and doing an impression of a lawn sprinkler, which, by the way, I'd quite like to see, if you ever fancy trying it.'

She made a weak smile at him. 'Did I do anything else I shouldn't have?'

'No, you're alright. Jules went to work saying you shouldn't worry for a moment about it.'

'I'll pay for the dry cleaning of the cushion.'

'Em, it's not like you did it on purpose. These things happen. I shit all over our bedroom floor, once. I had gastroenteritis and couldn't make it to the bog in time. I went off like a giant crap bomb. Life is just a series of embarrassments connected by mugs of tea and laughter, as someone once said.'

She pushed at her scraggy haircut and pushed her tongue between the gap in her front teeth. 'Was that someone you, by any chance?'

'Well, yeah. I wrote that in my novel, *Kidda*. But it's true.'

'I thought so. Nice. Well, it is all rock 'n' roll, I suppose.'

'Exactly. I'll run you home, we'll pick up some clothes for you and anything else you need.'

'Yeah, OK. Thanks. Feels nice not wearing any underwear, though.' She gave him a weary but still cheeky look.

'That's more like you. Mind, they'll not take much washing. They barely exist.' He held his hands up. 'Sorry, but I do all the washing in this house, so your clothes are my responsibility.'

'I don't mind. It wouldn't be the first time you've seen my underwear.'

'No, indeed.' He moved the conversation on quickly. 'Are you sure you don't want something to eat? You should eat some protein. I'll cook you some bacon and eggs.'

'No, nothing just now. Thanks, Nick. I could really use a cigarette, actually. You've not got any, have you?'

'I thought you'd given up. You know we live a pure, drug-free life in this house. Or we would if we didn't take drugs - well, booze, anyway.'

She groaned. 'Bugger, I need a fag. This is the last hangover I'll ever have. I'm giving up drinking. It makes you feel so shit. I wonder how you-know-who is feeling? He should have come down by now.'

'From what I understand about crystal meth, you feel so bad once you come down, that you want some more to make you feel so good again. Which sounds like a form of torture.'

She looked at her phone. 'Yeah, that's right. He's not texted or phoned.'

'The police will want to speak to him. Mandy saw what he was like. I know you don't want to press any charges, but he can't just go around raging at people. He hit me in the face.'

'I'm so sorry.'

'It's not your fault at all. Not in any way whatsoever.'

'That's what Julie kept saying last night.'

'Right, so you know it's right. She's a professional at this stuff.'

But he wasn't convinced that she was convinced.

'Owee, let's go into town and get your stuff.'

'What time is it?'

'10.30. When do you start work?'

'I'm doing 2 till 10, as it's Friday.'

'We've plenty of time then.' He picked up the cream-coloured chenille cushion cover and the cushion. Emily put her hands over her face.

'Oh, the shame! Don't tell them it's human piss.'

'I might not be emotionally intelligent but I'm not stupid. This is clearly the work of an incontinent puppy.'

They parked on Silver Street near to the police station and walked around to the dry cleaners, then down to Green Dragon Yard, to Emily's flat.

'Do you miss not living here?' she said, unlocking her door.

'Not really. To be honest, I much prefer living in Norton village. We had nothing but hassle one way or another living here. It was a bit jinxed what with us losing Joni and having that lunatic copper's blood on the walls. No, I don't miss it at all. And Jeff is more than happy not to have to go to the flat where the Forever Amber album was snapped in two. He still has nightmares about it.'

'I know, it's like someone killed a kitten, to Jeff.'

She peered around the door and listened and then shouted out, 'Matty! Are you in?'

There was no reply, thankfully. The last thing Nick wanted to have to do was slap a raging druggy down again.

He followed her into the bedroom. She took a hold-all from the top of a wardrobe and passed it to him. 'Open that up and I'll dump some clothes in,' she said. He did as he was told. She took a handful of under-wear from a drawer and tossed it in.

'That looks like a big knot of colourful pasta.'

'If you add your special sauce, you can try eating them, if you want.' She glanced at him and made a cheeky face, then took out t-shirts, tops, two pairs of jeans and a couple of sweatshirts and a jumper. 'That'll do for now. I'll just put together a toilet bag.'

He waited outside of the bathroom as she got some things together and emerged again, taking her contraceptive pill. 'I bloody forgot to take it yesterday. Do you take two at once if you do that?'

'I don't actually know. Google it when you get to the shop.'

'Doesn't Julie take the pill?'

'She used to back in the day, but not since I've known her. She didn't like how it messed up her hormones and she thought it made her put weight on her arse.'

'So what did you use?'

'Rubbers, darling, rubbers,' he said in a faux posh voice.

'Oh, and you were OK with that? A lot of men don't like to use them.'

'Of course. I'm a dab hand with the prophylactic; a rubber master.'

'That's all such a faff on, though, don't you think?'

'Nah. It's not so hard, not unless you're not so hard, anyway. Ha. See what I did there? We always managed, not that we have to worry about such things these days. The key thing is to keep a shoehorn by the bed.'

She let out her high-pitched giggle. 'Is that to get the contraceptive on, or to get your willy in?'

'Get your willy in?! How old are you?' he said, mockingly.

She lapsed into an imitation of a broad Teesside accent. 'Alright son, stick yer big 'ard cock up 'er.' She laughed again in her childish sort of way.

'Thank you, that's much more grown up and polite. Right, are we done? Do you need anything else? A laptop or Kindle?'

She cleared her throat. 'Laptop is at the shop. Don't have a Kindle.' She looked around. 'Yeah, I think that'll be enough for a few days.' She put the bag down. 'Now, I have to give you a hug, just to apologise to you.'

She stood right up to him, took his hands and put them on her small, firm buttocks, as she sometimes did, as though to give him licence to be a little intimate with her, then hugged him tightly. 'Sorry I was a cow towards you. I love who you are, even if you are dysfunctional. And you and Julie have been really kind to me. But you really don't need to fuss over me, you know. I'll be fine. Just leave me to work things out.'

'Don't worry about it. You were understandably upset. All you need to know is I'm on your side, right?' He patted her on the backside.

'Right,' she said, kissing him on the lips.

As he did so, the sound of a key turning the Yale lock was followed by the creak of the door opening. They both turned to see Matty coming in.

CHAPTER 7

'Alright?' he asked, with a nod and a smile, like nothing had happened, a gentle smile on his lips.

Nick looked at him warily. 'Yeah, we're just getting Emily some clothes.'

'I'm staying with Nick and Julie,' she added.

He closed the door and turned to face them. 'Yeah, I can see why. I'm sorry, Em.' He raised his arms and made a helpless gesture. 'I've messed everything up, haven't I? I'm so sorry. Sorry for kicking off on you as well, Nick.'

He ran his hand through his long hair and, shoulders slumped, went into the kitchen, then turned around and walked back to the door, staring at the carpet.

'Hold on. What was going on here?'

'What do you mean?' Said Emily.

'I mean you and him.'

'Don't be daft, Matty. Nothing was going on. I was just apologising to Nick for being rude to him yesterday.'

Nick folded his arms across his chest and stared at Matty. It was as though black shadow was sweeping over him, turning him from the gentle man he'd known to something far darker and nasty.

Glaring at Nick, he said, 'Fucking hell, you didn't take long, did you, Guymer?'

'Don't be stupid. C'mon Matty, she's upset and you should bloody well know why. You were out of order yesterday.'

'Fuck you.' He said it with a bitter, hateful sneer that was so out of character.

'Get out!' said Emily forcefully. 'Don't you dare speak to my friend like that. Go on! Get out! This is my flat, go away and don't come back.'

But he'd crossed to the dark side now. Just like that. The old Matty was gone.

'What have you been saying to her?' said Matty, advancing on Nick. 'You've been turning her against me, haven't you, you and that fucking uptight feminist spunk bucket bitch of yours.'

Emily screamed at him. 'Shut your filthy mouth. Julie is a great woman. You've changed so much. I don't even know you. It's like you're a different person to the man I fell in love with; the man I thought I knew. You need help. The drugs have made you...made you...made you evil!'

Nick jabbed his right index finger at Matty, the urge to batter him not far below the surface. He looked terrible, white-faced with blood-shot eyes. 'I'll discount what you just said as stress. But I won't do it twice. Right? Now, we're leaving, and so are you.'

Julie had said that you have to be calm and authoritative in confrontational situations with jilted partners, but that wasn't something that came naturally to him.

Matty just ignored him. 'Come on Em, we can sort this out between ourselves. Me and you. I know I was out of order but that was just the drugs. I won't do it again. I'm just messed up because the band is over.'

'Yeah, well, forgive me if we're cynical about that,' said Nick.

'This is nothing to do with you, mate.'

'You hit me in the face, son. You attacked my best mate. That made it to do with me. You behaved disgracefully towards Emily. That made it to do with me. Right?'

Matty held his hands up. 'Alright, alright, all fucking right. I hear you. Sorry. I'm a rock 'n' roll guy, right? We don't live like the straight people. We breathe different air. We invent the future.'

Nick looked at him squarely. He was high. Not on crystal meth, coked up, probably. Full of himself. There was no point in trying to make a rational point with him.

'If you say so. But if you want my advice, the only future you're inventing is a one-way ticket to shitsville. We're going now. I suggest you stay away from the shop. Get some of your things together and go and stay with a friend. Because you are that close to getting yourself arrested. I won't hesitate to report you if you make a threat or commit any act of violence or intimidation. You're lucky Emily hasn't pressed charges already. You're that close...right?' He made a small gap between forefinger and thumb.

Nick was giving him a chance. Appealing to his better, nicer nature, which he felt definitely existed, because he'd spent enough time with him in the shop and on occasional nights out to know it existed. But when you feel like you're King of the World because you've got a few grams of Columbian Marching Powder in your bloodstream, such things are irrelevant and are nothing but a tiny speck of dust on your own brilliant view of your own brilliant life.

Matty spread out his arms as though to guard the door. 'No. I'm staying here with Emily.'

'Matty, you don't understand, this is over. You're being horrible,' she said, weary and upset. Clearly, this was just one more battle in a long war for her.

'No, I'm not. I'm being very reasonable to the man who was seducing my missus when I walked in.'

'Oh, for god's sake,' said Emily, and put her head in her hands then looked at him up close, hissing out her words. 'I hate you for being like this. I never thought you could make me hate you, but here and now, I totally hate you. Come on, Nick, we're out of here.' She stood as tall as she could on her tip toes. 'If you damage this flat in any way whatsoever, if you do anything horrible, I will get the police onto you and you will go to jail.'

She picked up the hold-all, pushed past him, opened the door and walked out with Nick in pursuit. He stopped before leaving and grabbed Matty by the collar of his t-shirt, feeling angry and upset on all of their behalf.

'Get your shit together, son. You were a decent lad. Don't fuckin' lose it.'

Matty just looked at him with hard eyes. Then he spat a gob of white spume in his face.

'Why don't you just fuck off, do us all a favour and kill yourself, you depressive shit.'

A hot anger rose up in Nick's chest. He wiped the spit from his cheek, debating with himself what to do. *"Trust your instincts, our Nick."* He wanted to hit him but what did Julie always say? Male violence was at the heart of what was wrong with the world. Yeah. And she was 100 per cent right. Matty was no threat to him. He didn't have to hit him. *"Just be a nice lad, Nick."*

He could walk away from this confrontation.

He should walk away from this confrontation.

And that's what he did.

Emily handed him a tissue to wipe the rest of the saliva from his face, as they went back to the car.

'I'm so sorry about that,' she said.

'Don't be sorry. It's not your fault.'

There was nothing more to be said. They drove home to Norton.

Nick made coffee while she got showered.

'You must be hungry now,' he said as she came out wrapped in one of their big bath towels, rubbing at her wet hair with a smaller towel.

'I am, actually. '

'Right, it's still only just before one, I'll feed you up before you go to work.'

He went to the fridge, took out bacon, a block of dripping, eggs and a ripe Hass avocado. Cutting a chunk of white fat off the block, he put a flame under a frying pan and added the bacon just as it got hot, fried it off until brown, put it onto a plate and put that into the oven on a low heat. He cracked two eggs into the pan and put a lid over it and turned the heat down.

'This is Jules's fave breakfast. Do you like your avocado mashed or sliced?'

She gave him a smile. 'No-one ever asked me that before.'

'Well, I'm not your normal guy.'

'In so many ways, that is true. Mashed please.'

'Mashed it is. Won't be long now. Just waiting on the eggs. You look back to your normal self now.'

'I'm not drunk or hungover any more. As for everything else, I'm in a total fog of confusion.'

'I understand that. My advice, for what it's worth, is don't be in a hurry to sort it out in your mind.'

She pulled her thin brown eyebrows together in a frown. 'What do you mean?'

'I mean, don't feel like you have to sort it all out quickly. You're young, Em. I know you don't feel young, but you are. There are so many years ahead of you. So there's no rush to do anything, or to feel anything. Just let it all play out. Be with people who are nice to you, stay safe and don't be afraid to be on your own. In my experience everyone who appears dangerous and sexy usually turns out to have a very high arsehole content to their character.'

She obviously didn't want to hear that and shrugged off his comments in an off-hand manner. 'Yeah, yeah, whatever.'

He served up the food as she sent a couple of texts.

She ate most of it but he had overestimated the size of portion a petite size 6 woman like Emily might be able to eat compared to what broad 5 foot 10, size 12-14 like Julie could hoover up.

'A bit too much for me, I'm afraid. Thank you, though. That was lovely. Now, I'd better get ready for work.'

'You can get changed in the living room.'

She turned as she left the kitchen and, pulling a silly shocked face, opened up the big bath towel to flash her nakedness at him, wriggling a dance as she did so, as he half expected she would, because she could be quite the exhibitionist when the mood took her.

It was quite a sight. Skinny, with narrow hips, she was extensively and colourfully tattooed over an entire arm, up over her shoulder, across one small breast, down to her hips and round to her buttocks. And she had no pubic hair at all, which immediately caught Nick's eye. But far more shockingly, she was covered in small bruises on her untattooed hip, all around her pelvis, and across the top and inside of her thigh. In the few seconds she exposed herself, he had the distinct impression they were in the pattern of the spread of a hand. The five or more bruises on the top of her thigh and another older, larger dark blueish bruise on the inside of her thigh, looked like pressure points. He glanced at her other hip, but the black, red and green rose tattoos masked any potential bruising, but there was a dark purplish mark at the top of the inside of her thigh.

A picture formed in Nick's mind in an instant. Matty had held her down, had gripped her tightly on her hips and thighs while he forced himself on her. While he raped her. He'd held her down and he'd violently raped her. The bastard.

Perhaps realising what she had accidentally revealed, she covered herself up again and turned around to leave the room.

'Em!' He went after her. She turned around in the living room doorway.

'Are you alright?'

'Yeah, I said I'm not hungover any more.'

'I didn't mean that. I mean those bruises on your hip and thighs.'

She made a dismissive expression. 'Oh, they're nothing, Nick.'

'They're not nothing, Em. Show me them.'

She turned and pushed at the living room door. 'No, you've had your quick flash for the day.'

'Did Matty do that to you?'

'No, I'm just clumsy. Now, I've got to get ready.'

She closed the door behind her.

But she wasn't clumsy, quite the opposite, if anything. And you don't get bruises like that from walking into tables.

She'd said to Julie she'd been passive, but if she'd given in, he probably wouldn't have forced her down so hard. She was probably only eight stone wet through, and even though Matty was hardly a top-notch physical specimen, he was probably 50 pounds heavier and half a foot taller and as such could easily impose himself on her. Even so, she'd fought him.

Bloody hell. This wasn't just having to tolerate having sex when you didn't feel like it, this was a violent assault. He'd pinned her down, forced her legs apart and raped her.

But if she wouldn't report it, what could be done? If he didn't confess to it and she didn't give evidence against him, nothing would happen. Only a small percentage of sexual assaults were even reported, let alone perpetrators getting convicted, and Julie had often told him as much.

She soon emerged dressed in tight black jeans, a capped-sleeve Joan Jett t-shirt and black baseball boots. She'd put on some red lipstick and black mascara, giving her a rather late 70s new wave appearance.

'Hey ho, let's go!' She said in the style of the Ramones song, picking up her shoulder bag.

Momentarily, he thought he should say something more, but then remembered what Jeff had said about her not wanting him to be cooing at her and that she wanted him to be supportive by being strong. Anyway, she'd been through enough in the last day, without having to rake over her emotions about being assaulted. But even so, this wasn't over.

He turned the engine on the old BMW. It coughed into life.

'She doesn't sound very healthy, does she?' said Emily.

'No, Jules keeps the old beast going somehow, but the end is nigh. I'm just reluctant to get rid of her. I've had her 20 years, nearly. The relationship you have with a car isn't like anything else. It's odd. It's only a machine but you get close to them.'

'I'll have to learn to drive. I've been putting it off, but I absolutely must do it. I need to be independent.'

He parked up in his usual spot on Silver Street and walked round to the shop with her. Jeff looked up from the counter as they came in. He was playing some Tangerine Dream.

'Ah, my two favourite people who are standing in front of me at the moment,' he said. 'I have glamorous new staff! That's explosion of colour in the cafe is Alisha Chowdhry and she is making a toastie to a Michelin standard. She can open a tin of beans and put them in the microwave with the highest degree of skill. And you should see her put putting water into a kettle. It's an art form to behold.'

The woman, in her late 20s, looked over and gave them a wave. Of Indian heritage, with long black hair tied back and dressed in turquoise and gold silk, she made a real splash of colour. Emily walked through and shook her hand, exchanging a few words with her.

'Right, I'm off to pick up Lord Argent of Hartburn.'

'I need a quick word,' said Nick. As soon as they were outside, he brought him up to speed with everything that had happened since the previous evening.

'The thing is, Matty Rhodes really hurt her. She's got bruises on her hips and at the top of her thighs.'

'Did she show you?'

'Yes. But she didn't mean to. Maybe in the moment, she'd forgotten about the bruises. She flashed me after she'd had her shower.' He mimed what she'd done. 'You know what she's like, always showing off her ink work and being dirty-flirty with me. I mean, we saw what he was like when he attacked her in the cafe. He was going to tear off her clothes off. To me, it's obvious that, probably more than once, he's pinned her down, pulled her legs apart and...'

Jeff winced and turned away from him, holding up his hand as a psychic defence. Upset and distressed, he interrupted Nick.

'...fucking hell, I really don't want to hear this.' The big man stopped in his tracks and turned to Nick. 'I vote we go and whack the snot out of the twat. I can't believe he's done that. That's just...just...bloody disgusting!' Jeff didn't cry often. He just didn't. But here and now, his eyes had glazed over with tears. 'I'm not 'avin that. No. Not for one minute...how can anyone...'

Nick interrupted him. 'I'd like to hurt him as well, but we've got to be the better men here. We need to get him arrested for what he's done, not least because he might do it to her again, or someone else, the next time he's had a snort of something, or even when sober, we don't know. Us breaking his bones won't necessarily stop that, but him being in jail would.'

'Sorry. I'm sure you're right, but that doesn't matter to me, I just want to hurt him for what he's done to her. It's not right. There should be consequences. There should!! And I'm going administer those fucking consequences next time I see him. It's only right.' He wiped away a small tear from his eyes. 'That girl...' but as soon as he spoke the words, his tears came again. Nick patted him on the back. 'Why hasn't she told anyone that he's been attacking her?'

'There's no easy answer to that, man. Women often suffer in-relationship rape in silence. It's humiliating for them. And sometimes they feel like it's their fault, somehow. Jules tells me some don't even realise it is rape when it's their partner that does it.'

'I don't know how she could stand to even be around him. They've been a bit frosty with each other for weeks now, that must be why. Why didn't she just leave the first time it happened, or kick him out?'

'People want to hang on to their relationships, don't they? They're in love with someone, or they were, and they want to believe it'll all be alright and that it'll be a one-off bad thing. He apologises and says it'll never happen again...until it does.'

They walked on to the white van. Jeff shook his head.

'Christ, you think you know someone...he's worked part-time in the cafe with Em, off and on for ages and I'd never have him down as a bloke who was capable of doing that. He's always fancied himself a bit, but was never aggressive and never even used bad language. I know Emily fell for him because he wasn't a macho bloke, and had bit of the poet about him.'

'Yeah, well, drugs change people. It sounds like crystal meth released his inner devils. I mean, the language he's used about Julie, on two occasions now, has been shocking. And he's always been respectful in the past. It's like he's lost his mind.'

'Shall I talk to Mandy about it?'

'Well, me and Jules will do that. Emily isn't in a place where she'll feel she wants to press charges. I know that. So there's nothing Mandy can do, as regards the rape. Julie texted her this morning. Y'see, there's some other shit going down, right now. We had a visitor yesterday while we were out. I left a window open upstairs, someone got in and took Julie's pyjamas. Nothing else as far as I can tell.' He explained about the window not being on the sneck.

Jeff looked around with astonished owlish eyebrows raised.

'What?! Oh, fucking hell...that's so fucked up. Shit shit shit.' He was exasperated. 'He sounds like a crazy perv. No-one is doing that who isn't seriously messed up. I don't like the sound of it. It's escalating, Nick. He's put those pictures online...'

'We don't know that. It could be a separate thing.'

'Oh, of course it's the same bloke. It's not a coincidence. You're overthinking it.'

'We don't even know for sure whoever took the pyjamas is male. It might not be the peeper out the back. Same goes for the car that followed her.'

But Jeff scowled at him. 'Of course it's a bloke.' He began ranting, talking quickly as the ideas came to him. 'Don't get all PC on me. Only evil blokes do this shit. Women are almost never so stupid, or so horrible. It's some bloke who has taken against Julie, probably because of her work, somehow he's got hold of photos of her from 20 years ago and he's got totally obsessed with her. He's totally glommed on her. So he takes pictures of her on the street and puts them online as well. Then he wants to hang around where she lives, so he feels close to her. That escalates to voyeurism, now he's got something she's worn, but he's not going to be satisfied with that. He's going to want to get really close to her next. That's how this shit works.' He stroked his long beard, a look of real worry on his face. 'He's going to want to have her for himself. He is. He's going to abduct her. This is very, very bad, Nick.'

CHAPTER 8

'The police know about it now, so hopefully they'll catch them. Jules has an idea the pictures might be something to do with a disgruntled ex-husband off the Hardwick estate called Kenny Harlow. It is sodding disturbing knowing someone has been in your house, though. Really bloody creepy.'

Jeff looked at his watch. 'Look, I'm late for picking Argie up from the nursery. I've got to go.'

'Right. When you get back to the shop, don't say anything to Emily about what I've told you about the bruises, right? She'll just get defensive. Maybe when she's got a bit of distance from Matty, it'll help her to see she's got to report him.'

Jeff nodded. 'Yeah, but by then the bruises will have gone and there'll be no proof of anything ever having happened. It'll be her word against his. Even if you gave evidence on her behalf to say you saw the bruises, a good defence would easily dismiss that as circumstantial or at least cast doubt on it. And I can totally see why Em wouldn't want to go through all of that and would prefer to just try and forget about it. Shit, this is just so awful.' He rubbed his face with the palms of both hands. 'Will you stay in the shop until I get back? I don't want Matty coming in and shouting the odds or worse. You have my permission to twat him as often as needed, if he does. There's my old cricket bat in the back if you need a trusty piece of wood to administer justice.'

'Yeah, no worries.'

When Nick got back into the shop, Emily was sitting at the counter, behind her laptop, with a pile of records to one side, the details of which she was uploading to the shop's eBay account whilst playing Mr Big's album, *Lean into It*, one of her favourites.

'You don't have to babysit me, Nick,' she said, without looking up. 'I'll get a cab back to your place at 10.'

'I'm not. Jeff's asked me to help out and I need a mug of tea. Do you want anything?'

She waved a hand to dismiss the idea.

In the cafe, Tommo was sitting in his usual corner, reading the paper and wearing an especially garish Hawaiian shirt. Two other punters were in, both eating coke floats.

'Now then, Nick,' he said, peering over the top of his paper, as Nick sat down opposite him.

'Hello, mister. That is a very vivid shirt, Tommo. I need sunglasses to look at it.'

The old chap picked at it. 'Emily found it for us in a charity shop. She reckons she's my image consultant, you know.' He laughed a little wheezily. 'One in a million is little Em. I hope you sorted that Matty Rhodes out. I never rated him as a bad lad, but he was well out of order yesterday, like. Shockin' what he said. Are you alright? He caught you with a lucky punch, didn't he?'

'It didn't do any damage.'

An idea crossed Nick's mind. 'If Matty comes in when me or Jeff aren't here, will you text me? You've got my number, haven't you?' He lowered his voice so Emily couldn't hear. 'I just want to make sure we keep her safe, right?'

Tommo, who had worked the door of the Fiesta nightclub for decades, nodded. 'Yeah, 'course I will. Used to get toe rags kicking off in the Fiesta and I used to give them what for.' He clenched a surprisingly big fist. 'But I'm too bloody old for that now. Not sure my heart would stand a good scrap nowadays. Back in the day, I'd have smashed that little shit's face in, for what he said to that little lass. She's doesn't deserve that. Little thing 'as been a bloody angel to me, Nick. Got me out of meself. And she's always up there smiling at us, always has me tea and toasted teacake or me beans on toast.'

'I know. She's a good kid. Me and Julie are very fond of her.'

He was glad Tommo didn't know she'd been violently raped and he certainly wasn't about to tell him. That'd only upset him even more. As it was, his heavily sagging, broken-veined jowly face was set in a sorrowful expression. More than anyone, she'd got him out of his house in Bishopton Court, got him washing regularly and wearing clean clothes, at a time when he really needed some help. Jeff's shop, and especially the cafe, had a few Tommo types; older men in their mid or late 60s who had become isolated after retirement or ill health, single or widowed men who stopped looking after themselves and seemed to become invisible to the rest of society. Of course, the more dishevelled and stinky they became, the more everyone gave them a wide berth and the more isolated they then became.

Because Tommo had always loved music, and collected records and memorabilia, he had an excuse to come to the shop and look through the boxes of old 45s in search of the Marty Wilde record he didn't have. He collected Motown singles and at all times kept a grubby list of the ones he needed to complete his collection. That fact alone meant Nick could empathise and relate to him. Lists were a way to hang onto your sanity. They were a life raft on the choppy seas of existence. If you had your list, then you had something. Life had a meaning and there was a direction to go. Lists offered some degree of clarity in the chaos of everyday.

'He probably won't come in, but you never know. He's messed up on drugs, so he might be a bit crazy.'

'That was what I reckoned, like. Terrible what kids do to themselves. Mind, were we any better in the 60s, drinking 12 pints of Strongarm and getting into fights? Not really. And kids these days have it 'ard, I reckon. There used to be loads of work and money around 'ere when I was a kid. I mean, look at Stockton. It used to be right busy all the time. Proper place, it was, but what's 'ere for kids now, eh? No wonder they get out their mind on drugs. I reckon I might if I was 20. Auld buggers these days are too quick to have a go at the young 'uns. We were no better. Not really. Not that it excuses him, mind. Needs a stiff right hander to sort him out, if you ask me.'

Nick patted the old lad on his hand. 'Aye, as the Who once said, "Meet the new boss, same as the old boss".'

'The Who? Never liked them. I've got a High Numbers single, though. That's them before they changed their name, isn't it?'

'Yeah? What's it called, Tommo?'

He frowned for a moment as he went through his mental filing cabinet. 'It's on Fontana. It's called "Zoot Suit". Yeah, bought it when it came out. Never liked it. I reckon Townshend is overrated.'

'Really? That's a valuable record, man.'

'Is it? I reckon I only played it once. It was rubbish.'

'Yeah, hold on.' He got up and went back into the shop, took the *Record Collector* book from under the counter.

'You know what, Em? I reckon Tommo has got a small fortune in his record collection and he doesn't even know it.' He began to flick through the pages.

'He's always talking about records he's got and they're often by loads of really collectible bands. He's got first pressings of all the Small Faces albums. He doesn't even like the Small Faces, so he's never played them much. He even once said to me how he played *Ogdens' Nut Gone Flake* once and hated it. Never played it again. That's £250. Near mint condition.'

Nick found the High Numbers entry. 'Shit, Em, "Zoot Suit" is a £1,000 single.'

She raised her eyebrows. 'Really? He's sitting on a goldmine in that house. I'd love to look through his collection. He should get it insured.'

'Or, sell it and have a nice holiday.'

She looked in a drawer and took out a piece of paper. 'This is his Motown list. From matrix numbers 101 to 1426. That's 1959 to 1994. He's got them all apart from about six. He's got some really rare ones. He's even got singles by the Creation and the Birds and I know they're worth a small fortune. He doesn't seem bothered though, bless him.'

Nick ruffled her scrag cut and went back to the old lad.

'That High Numbers record is worth a grand, Tommo. Did you know that?'

'Is it? But it's shite. Joe Brown was a better guitarist than Townshend. Ah, I don't care. I've got no use for money, me. Youse can have it, if you want.'

'Don't be daft, man.'

'Seriously, Nick. I don't need money. I've got me pension, I've got enough to live off. What's the point in 'avin more than that? There isn't any point, except to buy shite you don't need. People are bloody mad for buying things these days. You know what, right, my mam and dad lived in one of the first council houses they built in Roseworth and they thought they'd died and gone to heaven just to 'ave an indoor bog. But they had nowt by today's standards, like, but I'd bet they were 'appier than most people today are. They appreciated what they 'ad and didn't want for much else.'

'Yeah, well, I've no use for money beyond having somewhere to live and something to eat and drink. You can't buy your way to happiness, that much is for sure.'

He got up and went to the counter, where Alisha was busy making sandwiches.

'Hi Alisha, I'm Nick Guymer, Jeff's oldest mate. Sorry it's taken me a while to say hello.'

She smiled. 'Hiya, Nick. Yeah, Jeff mentioned you. I knew who you were, anyway.'

'He's a good boss, Jeff.'

'I've known him for a while, actually. My mam is Madhur Chopra, that was her maiden name, if you remember her. She remembers you and Jeff at school. Said you were a shy lad who liked records.'

'Oh, god, yeah. She was in our year at Ian Ramsey, wasn't she? I used to sit behind her in history. Well, that makes me feel old. She's right, though. That's exactly what I was like.'

'Well, I'm happy to get a job. There's so little work to be had around here.'

'Well, I hope you like loud rock music because the shop is always blaring out something. And in here it's a funny little community. You get students and kids in but also older blokes who need a bit of mothering via the medium of teacakes and toast, like Tommo.'

She gave him a nice smile. 'That's alright by me. He said it's a bit of community thing. I like that.'

'OK, Alisha, I'll catch you later.'

As he went into the shop, Nick got a text from Jeff saying he was on his way back and would be in the shop in five minutes, so, knowing that she wouldn't be alone for long, he went up to Emily.

'Right, I'm off. I'll see you later.'

'Alright. I'll come straight to yours after we've finished here. Nick, I was thinking, you know those pictures of Julie that are on that website?'

'Yeah, are they still there?'

She glanced at the screen and nodded. 'Yeah, they are. Cowards. But I've just had a quick look at it and I'm fairly sure I can hack it and take it down.'

'Really?'

'Yeah, it's a basic website and hasn't got any high-end security on it.'

Nick tugged at his stubble. 'Hmm, that'd be great. Is there any way you can get into it and find out who set it up?'

'Anything is possible, Nicky boy,' she said, peering at the screen. 'I'll see what I can find out and I'll save a copy of it so we can still use it as evidence against whoever did it, even if I take it offline or delete it.'

He leaned on the counter. 'I forgot that you're a bit of a computer whiz. You hacked Mike Cavani's phone that time. That was ace. You used to do a lot more tech stuff when I first knew you, in fact.'

'Yeah, I've let it slip in the last year or so. I used to really enjoy writing websites and apps. Might get back into it again,' she said. 'I'll wipe their server, don't you worry.'

'Thanks, Em.' He winked at her.

'No worries.' She smiled up at him, but he couldn't help but feel it was a smile that had been dimmed by life, and that she was now living with some terrible hurt that was almost certainly repeatedly playing out in her mind, over and over again, polluting her waking hours, and haunting her subconscious. Yet, the fact she could function in a vaguely normal way was testament to her strength of mind and character. It was as though she wasn't prepared to give into the fear or the hurt that she surely felt. Then again, that all too often seemed to be a woman's lot in the world.

Being a human could be such a shit thing, he reflected, for the millionth time.

Sitting in his car he looked at his phone. There was a text from Julie: *'Mandy is sending two officers to see if they can catch our peeper this evening.'*

He wrote her a message to outline what had happened at the flat and about how he'd seen Emily's bruises. As it was Julie's lunch break, she was able to write back immediately.

'None of this is good. Not happy she's been violently attacked (though thought it was the case). Not happy to let a rapist get away with it. Not happy she's shown herself to you like that. Disrespectful to me, you and her. We need to talk about this before Emily comes home.'

That sounded ominous. She surely knew that he didn't encourage Emily to expose herself, nor exploit the fact she had in any way whatsoever. Maybe he shouldn't have told her. It hadn't crossed his mind not to, after seeing the bruises.

He made himself some tea when he got home and went out into the garden to drink it. After checking that there was no-one hiding behind the blackthorn bush, he sat down to enjoy the warm sunshine, still fretting that Julie was going to come home and give him a bollocking. They had very few rows, largely because he'd long since accepted that Julie was the boss in their relationship.

Every long-term relationship needs a benevolent dictator. If you don't have one who takes the lead, you just keep clashing heads all the time. And he was happy to defer to her judgement on most things, right through all aspects of their life, up to and including sex, which she would almost always initiate. If she wanted them to buy something, go somewhere, or do something, they usually ended up buying, going, or doing it. But if it was something she knew he just really hated, such as going to IKEA, doing DIY or shopping for anything that wasn't records, she'd always give him a get-out, in the same way he didn't expect her to cook, wash, do housework or spend hours looking at records. And it had often seemed to Nick that such accommodations were as much an important part of loving someone, as anything else.

He spent the afternoon researching and emailing people about publishing his novel. First an editor, then a proof reader and finally a couple of printers. He'd need an ISBN number and a bar code and artwork for the cover designing. It was all do-able, but just needed some organisation, and he was rubbish at organisation. Creativity and ideas he could do, getting his shit together in the adult world was far harder.

At five, he heard the distinctive low rumble of the Porsche pull up at the front and Julie walked out of the house into the back garden where he was still sitting.

'Hey, there. Good day at work?'

She flopped into a basket chair in their garden, and dumped her shoulder bag down. 'Oh, just the usual mixture of unpleasantness, with an added dash of misogyny.'

'I'll get you a G & T, eh?' he said, soon returning from the kitchen with a large glass clinking with ice. 'Here's your medicine, lady.'

'Thanks, doctor. Look at all those bees on the lavender. So nice to see a bit of nature after a day's work.' She closed her eyes and took a drink, then rested the glass on her lap.

He couldn't wait, he wanted it all sorted. 'Look, about Emily showing herself to me, Jules. I didn't encourage it, you know. I didn't do anything. I didn't touch her or anything. She just went...' he opened up an imaginary towel for three or four seconds and closed it again '...and that was it. You know what she's like. She's always been prone to a bit of exhibitionism, plus she fancies me and who can blame her for that!' He laughed, a little nervously.

Julie took another drink and snorted. 'Yeah, I can just imagine the situation. Don't get your knickers in a twist, I'm not cross at you.'

He felt instantly relieved. 'Oh, I thought you might be. I mean, it's not like I averted my eyes and I suppose I could have done, if I'm being honest. But...well...it was a freebie, wasn't it? Rude not to look at a naked woman.' He lapsed into a Yorkshire accent. 'That's what me old dad brought me up to believe.'

'Oh, you are a daft bugger,' she breathed out in an exasperated sigh. 'But the fact is, it's disrespectful of her, to me, to you and more than anything, to herself. I'm probably untypical in that it doesn't especially bother me, but most women would be very indignant that a woman was exposing herself to her husband like that. I mean, some would gave her a proper slap for that. Promiscuous behaviour, if it becomes a habit, can draw some unpleasant people towards you. I've been thinking on the way home that it actually explains some things about her.'

'She's not promiscuous, Jules. She was faithful to Matty, I'm pretty sure of that. She wasn't running around shagging people. She's just got this show-off thing going on.'

Julie took another drink and pushed ragged strand of blonde hair off her face. 'No, I don't think it's that simple. By doing something like that, she's blatantly craving approval, attention and admiration. That's the psychology behind it. Like I say, I know how it works. I was just the same in some ways, only without tattoos. It's a subconscious way to get some control or power in your life. However disempowered you are in the rest of your life, you still have control of who you let have sex with you.'

'Except when you're raped, of course.'

'Yeah, exactly, but that's what I'm worried about. You try to regain the control of your sexuality, control that you lost when you were raped, as though to prove to yourself that you're not helpless and as a result, you can get twisted into a knot of thinking that you're in control, when you're actually being very needy and thus very vulnerable. Do you get what I mean?'

He thought about it for a moment. Though Julie hadn't talked about it, she had told him a year or so previously that she'd been raped when she was in her mid 20s, but had 'dealt with it' and he'd not probed further. She'd tell him about it, if she wanted to. Her words now sounded very informed by that experience.

'I totally get that, but she's always been like that with me. She showed me her tattooed breast in the stock room of the shop once. When I went to her house, when she was working at the blues festival, she was quick to try and seduce me. So this isn't out of character.'

'No, it's not. It makes me wonder if she hasn't been assaulted as a kid or as a teenager and that's why it's become part of her typical adult behaviour. Being overly sexual with people is often connected to abuse in childhood. Just like I was saying about Aggie's daughter, Fiona. It's a sad fact that if it looks like you might be up for a good time, all sorts of sleazeball men will appear, as though out of nowhere, sniffing around you. Men who won't think twice about assaulting you and will then blame the woman for leading them on. It's as old as the hills, that. And they usually get away with it, too. Hence why defence lawyers are so keen to bring up the victim's sexual history and what they were wearing. Had a lot of sex? Wearing a short skirt? What do you expect, then? You were asking for it. Even now in the 21st century, that argument is still out there, as though men just can't help themselves from raping someone, like it's the same as tripping over paving stone or...I dunno...the same as breathing.'

She groaned. Nick rubbed his forehead.

'Well, whatever, the long and short of this is that I'm sure Matty raped or at the very least, sexually assaulted her and with some serious degree of violence.' He described where the bruises were. 'I know she sort of hinted at having to put up with his "attentions" in recent weeks. She tried to fight him off, I think, and he had to hold her down to stop her from getting away from him. I mean, she's fought him off as best she could, I reckon and I wouldn't mind betting it's happened more than once.'

'Poor lass. I certainly can't see why else she'd have those sorts of bruises there.'

'So what do we do?'

'Her welfare is our primary concern. She has to decide to prosecute. I can advise her on her options and I can get support for her. But if she doesn't want to take it any further, the bruises will heal and it'll just be her word against his and unless we can show a provable pattern of behaviour, he'll get away with it. All he has to say is she got the bruises in the course of sado-masochistic sex and that she was consenting to him being rough with her. She's covered in tattoos, so plenty on a jury would assume she was a bit of a slut and...'

'...that's so unjust, Jules,' he interrupted.

'Of course it is, and now you can see why Teesside Women and Women's Aid and all the other women's charities exist. This is what we're up against. It's getting better, but there is still a long way to go.'

He let out a low groan. 'You know, I don't think I realised until today just how stacked against the woman these situations are. '

'Well, I looked up the stats before I came home, about 85,000 women in England and Wales alone are raped every year, and 12,000 men. Half a million are sexually assaulted. Only 15 per cent report it and you know how many convictions there are? About 5 per cent of that 15 per cent. So like I say, almost all the men get away with it. That's the scale of what we're up against.'

'I just hope that he doesn't go into the shop when Jeff's not there and kick off again. When we saw him at her flat, he was giving it the "it'll never happen again", "it was just the drugs" routine, but I'm sure he was high, even as he said it. I think he was coked up.'

'Hmm, well, that doesn't bode well. You've got a bloke who has been rejected, feels hard done to, feels like everyone is out to get him, but with his sense of entitlement pumped up on a drug which makes you feel like you're King of the World. Good luck with that.'

'You'll be pleased to know he's referred to you as, err, what was it? Something like an uptight feminist spunk bucket bitch. The feminist thing seems to be an issue for him. He's included that in his insult twice, now. Odd to pick on that.'

She sneered. ' "Feminist Spunk Bucket" sounds like an all-female rock band from Seattle in 1992.'

'I still keep finding myself feeling shocked at him. I mean, we've been out with them about half a dozen times and I've talked to him in the shop a lot. OK, not for long periods of time and not in depth about anything, but even so. And I never got a sense of him being capable of such a thing, even when high. Doesn't it surprise you?'

She shook her head and took another drink. 'As I've said before, one thing I've learned is that you never know what is going on behind closed doors. He might have been horrible to her for months, for all we know. Some women don't tell anyone. They're too embarrassed, or they feel it's their fault, somehow.'

'Hmm, that's what I said to Jeff. He said that they'd had cross words a few times in the last month or so. He thought a break-up was on the cards.'

'Yeah, that's starting to make a picture, I'd say.'

'Talking of pictures. Em reckons she can hack that website and take it down - the one with the pictures of you on. But she'll make a copy of it in case we need it for legal reasons.'

'Really? Good old Em. I forgot she was into all that computer geeking.'

'I think her relationship with Matty made it less of a thing in her life. Not very rock 'n' roll, after all.'

She pursed her lips together. 'See, I don't like that, either. It suggests physical or emotional coercion. She stopped doing something she really liked doing because her boyfriend wasn't interested in it and she didn't want to attract his ire. That's what it sounds like and that's just wrong.

Imagine if I stopped you collecting records, you'd feel like you were being denied a major part of your life. It's a passion for you, so it'd feel oppressive.'

'I wouldn't put up with that, though.'

She cocked an eyebrow at him. 'Wouldn't you? What if I wrapped it all up in a lot of tears and emotional blackmail?' She pouted at him and lightened her voice to pleading whine. 'If you loved me you'd do what I wanted. If you really loved me, you'd want me to be happy. You'd want to spend time with me and not looking at records. You don't want me to be happy, do you? Why don't you care about how I feel?'

She dropped back into her normal voice. 'See, an emotionally manipulative person can turn you into the problem and themselves into the victim. It's so easy to think you'd be strong and fight your corner, but loads of people think that and then, when it happens to them, they just give in and start to think that, well, maybe I am being selfish, when, obviously, we all have a right to pursue the things that we're interested in and any healthy relationship accepts that. But when someone wants to gain control in a relationship, that's the sort of trick they pull and it's a short step from there to controlling other things such as money, who they do and don't see, or whether they're even allowed to work. I've had women who are to all intents and purposes prisoners in their own home, unable to go out until the man lets them.'

He blew out a tense breath of air and pulled at his bottom lip in contemplation.

'Is the fact that she had no pubic hair significant, do you think? That's what caught my eye, if I'm being honest.'

'She didn't have any ink work around that area?'

'I don't think so. But then I only got a quick glimpse.'

Julie didn't reply for a minute, sipping on her gin until it was all gone.

'I don't know. Lasses these days have got it into their head that pubic hair is bad or dirty or something. Almost no woman under 30 has pubes, apparently. It's often said that this is because of exposure to porn, where it's the norm for both men and women not to have any.'

'It's the norm? Why is it the norm?'

She made a helpless gesture at him. 'I really don't know, other than removing it makes every detail of the genitals more exposed.'

'And why would that be a good thing?'

'You're asking the wrong person. There are theories. We've talked about this a lot a work. The concerning thing, for me, is that by removing your pubic hair, you're effectively pretending you're not an adult and I can't see how that's psychologically healthy. And I don't like any notion that suggests something which is entirely natural and normal, is now somehow unacceptable. It's not like women haven't got anything else to worry about.'

'I totally get that. I've no problem with pubes, even if they do get stuck in my teeth.' She aimed a kick at him and snorted a laugh. 'But to play devil's advocate, men shave their faces. That's not natural, it's an affectation. I use a beard trimmer to avoid having an actual beard but also to make sure I don't have to scrape a razor over my face. I like the look that being a little unshaven gives me. That's just a fashion or vanity thing, really. Maybe shaving your pubes off is the same as that.'

She sat forward and put a hand on his face. 'We used to call what you've got "designer stubble" in the 80s. Never knew why. But I also reckon that the hair on your face is different to that in the downstairs department. It's got to be different politics, hasn't it? I'm sure it is. One is literally your public face, the other is intimate and private.'

He nodded. 'Public face versus pubic face. Ha ha. Yeah, you'd think so, but then, humans are very weird. When I hear about this sort of abuse, I often wish I wasn't one.'

'Talking of weird humans, any sign of the peeper pyjama thief?' she said, yawning.

'No sign at all. But then you've not been at home. I don't think he wants to peep at me or steal my bedwear.'

'Mandy said a couple of officers would take a look on their rounds. Don't think they've got the resources to do much more than that. She said they'd do some forensics on the window tomorrow, but obviously those guys are working more on murder and such, less on pyjama thieves.'

'It's so creepy. Aren't you creeped out by it?' said Nick.

'Yeah, of course. Well, sort of. It seems more pathetic than creepy to me. The sort of thing a lovesick teenager might do. '

'Jeff thinks it's an escalating pattern of behaviour.'

'He might be right. The bloke needs stopping. The police will catch him, I'm sure.'

They sat quietly for a minute.

'I like how you deal with all this personal stuff,' said Nick.

'What do you mean?'

'The stalking, the photos and now this intrusion, you're just very cool about it. A lot would be very upset and feel like...I don't know...like it was a form of abuse. Well, it is a form of abuse.'

She pursed her lips together. 'I just hate the idea that someone like this can affect your life, because that's what they want. I won't be bullied and hassled and messed about by some loser. I'm not quitting social media or changing my life in any way, I'm too old and gnarly for that. I obviously don't like it, and it is upsetting, or it would be if I dwelt on it, but I'm not letting them drain any emotion out of me about it. I want to laugh at it and laugh at whoever is responsible for being so pathetic. If they bother me, then they win. And, like I said to you in my first text, they're not going to win. And anyway, I've got you on hand to batter someone if they need a stiff right hander.'

'That's true. I do seem to end up hitting people in the face, every now and then, even though I'm a very peaceful bloke.' He mimed giving someone a right hander.

She smiled. 'On a more light-hearted note, how come you punch with your right hand, but you write with your left?'

He shrugged. 'God knows, some of my wires got crossed at birth. Weirder still, when it comes to throwing a ball, I do that with my left, even though it's basically the same thing as punching.'

She made a rumbling chuckle. 'You're very mixed up. Your preferred wanking hand is your left, as well. So that's hooked up to your writing wires.'

'Technically, I'm ambidextrous at that, and in fairness, it's not much of a skill to boast.'

Flashing bright blue eyes at him, she said, 'Hmm, you do seem very good at it with either hand. Mind, so you should be with the amount of practice you've had. Not sure I could do it with my left.' She put her right hand between her legs and then her left and mimed it with her index and middle fingers. 'No, I'd be useless with my left. Just feels wrong.'

'To complicate matters further, for some reason, I can only administer stimulation to you, with any degree of quality, with my right. It makes no sense. It should be related to my writing hand, surely?'

She gave him a quizzical look. 'Yeah, it's like you're pawing at me with a dead piece of meat if you do it with your left, but your right hand is a proper dancer. Ha, it's so weird, that. I'm right handed for everything. But you're not left footed, are you?'

'Not when it comes to masturbation, no!'

114

They laughed loudly.

And it was good to laugh; it made the worry dissolve for a moment.

It was a still, warm evening, so they ate their tea of pastrami and salad in the garden, listening to football on the radio on 5live. As they did so, they spotted two policemen walking across the patch of waste ground and looking behind the blackthorn bush.

'Someone's obviously spent a bit of time behind there,' said one of them across the wall to Nick. 'Seen them today?'

'No mate, no-one.'

'We'll come by again at around 10...see if we can catch him for you.'

'Alright, lads. Thanks.'

He went back into the house and fixed another couple of drinks.

'You know what we could do? We could set this joker a honey trap,' said Nick, putting a glass of gin and tonic in front of Julie.

'Am I the fizzin' honey?'

'Well, you do smell of honey.'

'Hmm, honey and straw, I know, you've told me often enough. Not sure how I give off that smell, exactly. No-one ever said I smelled of honey and straw until you did.'

'Honey and straw and a musky sort of smell.'

'Alright, alright. I probably just need a shower. It's hot in my office.'

'You know I like it. What do I smell of?'

'You? I've always thought you smelt of black pepper. Definitely spicy. So how am I a honey trap?'

He thought for a moment. 'Actually, it's probably a stupid idea.'

'Why is it stupid?'

'Well, I thought maybe we could lure him in.'

'I know what a honey trap is.'

'But we can't lure him, can we? He's either here or he isn't. I was going to suggest you do something in the bedroom as it gets dark around 10, but have the light on. So whoever is outside can see you easily. I wait out of sight in the shadows and jump on him. If he's local, he might see the light on from a distance and then decide to take up his position, because he might get an eyeful of something. And I reckon he must be living or staying quite locally to keep turning up like he does.'

Julie nodded. 'Aye, I think you're right. Well, let's give it a try. I don't mind, if you don't mind. What should I do? Take my top off? Prance around in a bra and skimpy knickers? Stick my arse up against the window and fart?'

Nick laughed. 'If you did any of those things, you'd distract me too much. *I'd* be behind the blackthorn spying on you, soon enough.'

'Men. You're all so easily distracted by the female form.'

'You can talk, you're the one who notices which way men dress and guesses whether they're well hung or not.'

'That's not voyeurism, it's just a natural talent I've got. I could always tell when I met a bloke if he was going to be small, medium or large.'

'No you couldn't. That's obviously all a myth.'

'Is it now?' She gave him a cheeky look. 'You'd like to think so, wouldn't you? But I can.'

'So did you know with me?'

She nodded dramatically.

'Uh huh, of course I did. You were a dead giveaway. I had you correct, right down to the millimetre.' She put her thumb and forefinger and made a small gap.

'Really? What was the dead giveaway, then?'

'Oooh, that'd be fizzin' telling, kidda.' She tapped her the side of her nose with an index finger and gave him a knowing look.

'Bollocks,' he scoffed.

'No, it's nowt to do with bollocks. I have no interest in them in any way whatsoever, and can never predict their size.'

He laughed and raised his glass. 'Here's to hard-to-predict bollocks.'

A minute or two later, after dwelling on it, he said, 'You didn't know, did you?'

She looked over the top of her glass and, laughing, shook her head. 'Sometimes, you're so gullible. All those clichés about big hands, big noses and big feet...trust me, it's all rubbish. You've only got size eight feet. That shows how inaccurate those old wives tales are.'

As he put his glass down, his phone buzzed with a text. It was from Jeff.

'Just had to "encourage" Matty to leave the shop. Basically said I'd beat him unconscious unless he left on the count of 3. Got to 2 and he was gone. He wanted to speak to Emily. Had been texting her for a couple of hours, apparently. She was OK - no tears - but had the feeling she was prepared to meet with him. Told her not to coz he's dangerous. Not sure she thinks he is, if not doped up. I didn't batter him. Thought you should know.'

Nick read the text out. Julie groaned.

'That's not what I wanted to hear.' She rubbed at her forehead.

'She's a strong-willed person. She won't be told what to do by you, or anyone else,' said Nick. 'When you're her age, you do think you know everything and that people our age are old farts who know nothing about being in your early 20s. When I was her age, I thought I was an experienced man of the world, but really I was still quite childish. You're in a halfway house between being world weary and infantile.'

She turned to look at him. 'Do you think Matty is dangerous?'

He puffed out his cheeks. 'When I saw him in her flat, yeah. No question. Before all of this? No.'

'So is she right? That he's not dangerous unless he's drugged up?'

'Maybe so, but maybe now he's always drugged up, so he's always dangerous. Everything you've told me about how controlling men operate, makes me think, yes, he could have been abusive to her while at the same time putting on a harmless face to the rest of the world.'

She leaned forward. 'I'm going to ask you a question I've never asked you before.'

'Does it involve measuring my bollocks?'

She tapped him with the toe of her slipper.

'This is serious. What's the worst you've ever behaved towards a woman?'

His heart sank. 'Aw, Jules, man...why are you asking that?'

'Settle down. I'll tell you why. From the first day I met knew you, you've never been sexist or aggressive with me, despite growing up in a culture where that was normal. You're the most naturally...I don't know...I suppose the word is feminist...the most feminist man I've known without ever obviously trying to be...but why are you like that and others are just not? You were brought up in a patriarchal, sexist culture, the same as everyone else. Why are you so different to other men?'

Nick adopted a strong Teesside accent. 'Eee, well, show us yer tits, darlin, then get yer knickers off, an' I might tell yer why I'm gorgeous me, like.'

She hooted a yelping laugh. 'Aw, look man, I'm being serious.' She chuckled a bit more.

He exhaled deeply. 'I dunno, Jules, it's hard to say. It's not like it's a role I'm playing, or just following PC rules. I've always been basically like this. But I used to use sexist language back 20 years ago. We all did. I have moved on. I was talking to Jeff about this the other day. I'm far from perfect, but all I know is since I was little, mam always told me to be a nice lad and to not be rude. I had always to be polite and well-mannered with people. She even said that again when she visited me the other night. And that stayed with me once my balls dropped, though in later life I think it got away from me a bit. Also, from about 16 onwards, most of my friends at 6th form were girls. At college, it was the same. So respect for women sort of set in with me early on. And I liked being around women far more than I liked being around men and, as a bonus, it meant you had a lot better chance of getting off with someone. Basically, I never wanted to be horrible to anyone, because I hated people being horrible to me and it upset me so much when they were. I was a very sensitive kid. And also in a vaguely hippy way, I can't help but feel if you're really horrible to someone, you also hurt yourself, in some way.'

'That's all good stuff, but you still haven't answered my question. What's the worst you've behaved towards a woman? Be honest. Ever hit a woman?'

He didn't need to even think about it. 'No. Never.' He exhaled deeply. 'I've turned up drunk to dates and been unsympathetic, cold company because of that. I once, uninvited and drunk, squeezed a girl's right breast at a party when I was 16. Mandy Hilton. She rightly hit me in the face and I felt so bad for so long that it taught me a big lesson about being respectful. But the worst I've been was with you in Harrogate, when I was depressed. I was moody, silent, cold and emotionally withdrawn.'

She drank from her glass. 'You were ill. At the time, I didn't know you were ill, but you were. Very ill, in fact. But even so, you didn't use physical aggression, you didn't try to control me. Mostly you just became unable to communicate. You were just very depressed. So what I take from that in relation to the Matty Rhodes situation is that people who are abusive don't just have a blip of really bad behaviour one Friday night due to drugs or drink. It has deeper roots than that which, if not directly addressed, will continue to feed into the person's behaviour. So if Matty, even when fucked up on drugs, raped Emily, then that's not just a silly mistake, or a one-off, it's part who he is and where his mind is at. And that means it will have manifested itself previously, in one way or another and it will do so again, unless he gets help. The fact that he's been good company with us, the fact he seems to have been a nice lad, is irrelevant. That's just the acceptable public face of private evil.'

Nick nodded. 'That makes sense, but good luck trying to tell her that.'

'No point, but it should inform how we see him, if she does get back together with him which, I have to say, wouldn't be untypical.'

At 9.45pm, they went upstairs and put the bedroom light on. Julie leaned on the window sill and looked out as the shadows fell. 'Right, let's set up the honey trap. I'm going to do a little dance up here.'

'Don't dance, Jules, no-one wants to see you clodhopping around, doing your full body heaves. That'll put him right off.'

She pushed at him. 'Get lost. I'm a good dancer, me. I can hit all the right beats, just not necessarily in the right order, or at the right time.'

Nick went to the back garden and took up a position behind an overgrown rose bush where he couldn't be seen easily.

As the light dropped from the sky, the yellow glow from the bedroom window seemed to radiate out into the gloaming.

Julie stood in the window, and was running a long toothed comb through her hair, as though detangling little knots in the ends. If whoever it was lived locally, and could see a light on, hopefully it'd draw them in.

Breathing in the warm evening air, heart-rate elevated, he stood and waited.

It didn't take long.

CHAPTER 9

A figure in a dark t-shirt and dark pants climbed over the fence on the far side and walked, hands in pockets, towards the dense blackthorn bush, disappeared behind it and didn't re-emerge. Nick was no more than 50 or 60 feet from him. That was far enough for him to get a head start if he saw Nick quickly. He glanced at his watch - 9.53. The police were due around 10 but they could be later, if they'd had a busy night. There was only one way to get to him and that was to jump over the back fence.

As he contemplated what to do, the figure emerged from behind the blackthorn and walked back the way they'd come. Had he seen that he'd been spotted?

Emerging from his hiding place Nick walked very briskly to the fence, jumped it and went after the figure, trying not to make any noise. As he got close, he could see it was a man, with an unshaven appearance.

'Hey!' shouted Nick, now only 10 feet behind him. The man visibly jumped in shock, stopped and spun around.

'Bloody hell, you gave me a shock there,' he said. He was about Nick's age, but a smaller build and with a receding hairline. 'Where did you come from?'

'I live in the house over there with the bedroom light on. What were you doing behind that bush?'

'Err...well...' he hesitated. 'Well...I was having a wee, actually.'

'A wee?' Nick repeated it in surprise as much at a man of his age using the word "wee" as anything.

'Yeah, I had to - I've got this condition, y'see. Sorry, did you think I was up to something?'

Nick looked around to see if the police were nearby. No-one.

'Well...yeah...you never know...I mean there's no reason for anyone to be there normally.'

'Sorry if I shocked you.' He gave him a genuine smile. 'I just saw it from the gate and thought, that'll do for me. Bloody dicky bladder. Scared it's something to do with my prostate at my age.'

Was he genuine or was he spinning him a line? There was no way to tell. Maybe he'd seen him in the garden and abandoned his peeping mission. But he didn't have the beer belly like the man he'd seen from the window, so at least it wasn't him.

'OK, no worries,' said Nick, turning and returning back to the house. Julie was at the back door, arms folded across her chest.

'Well? Was that him? I saw you go after him.'

'It was just a bloke with a weak bladder, having a piss.'

She pulled a face 'Eh? Are you sure?' She was suspicious.

'That's what he said. He seemed genuine and it wasn't the man we've seen before.'

'Well, there's one way to tell if he was telling the truth.'

'What's that?'

'Let's go and inspect the evidence.'

Although the sun was down there was just enough light left to see that, in the worn bit of grass behind the blackthorn bush, was indeed a substantial wet patch.

'Looks like he was telling the truth,' she said. 'Can't have been him. Come on, let's go to bed. I could do with an early night.'

Emily still hadn't come home.

Julie had decorated their bedroom in a lush red-wine and gold scheme with burgundy velvet curtains, a Middle Eastern rug on the polished boards and a dupion silk quilt on the bed. They'd picked up the dark, Indian-wood bedside tables, dressing table and chair up at a car boot for £15. It was a lovely, softly coloured space which, when the farmyard smells had been aired out of it in the mornings, smelt of roses and vanilla from scented candles. With low lamp light and a large soft bed, it was a peaceful environment in which to end each day.

They had a quick shower, and, standing naked at the end of the bed, kissed passionately. She gripped his buttocks and whispered some obscenities into his ear, knowing how it made him feel. Sometimes, his lust for her rose so quickly that it was almost overwhelming and he got carried away with his passion. Julie called it his steam hammer tendency. As they lay on the bed, he was swept up in his lust for her.

From underneath him, she looked up and put her hands on his chest, laughing a little.

'Slow down luv, you'll break the bed and probably have a heart attack, at the speed you're going. It's going to be over in about five seconds and that's no good to me. This is like having it off with a high-performance piston engine.' She gurgled a laugh and pushed at his chest as he slowed down, panting, using his pelvic muscles to stop it being over too quickly, just as he'd told Jeff to do. She held him at arm's length while he did it, laughing a little again.

'I could almost feel you tying a knot in it there. There's a good lad.' She licked her lips, panting a little herself. 'Are you sure you've nipped it?'

'Yeah, just in time. Thanks, Jules. Sometimes it just feels so great I don't ever want it to stop.'

'That's because I have a magic vagina, darlin'. Now, be a good boy and wear me like a beard.'

'Talk to the beard, darlin,' he said, in an imitation of Big Fish, saying his old catchphrase. She cackled a laugh and ruffled his hair as he kissed her from the neck down to her belly. She let out a small gasp as he kissed the inside of the top of her thighs and then between her legs.

Then suddenly, she tensed and let out a cry. Nick looked up at her, sensing this wasn't an orgasmic reaction.

'What's up?' he said.

She pushed at him. 'Gerroffus, man...'

He rolled to his right-hand side of the bed. Her gaze seemed fixed on the opposite wall at the far end of the room.

'What the hell is that tiny red light, at the corner of the mirror?' she said, pulling the bed sheets over her.

He peered at the mirror. And there it was. No bigger than the tip of a ballpoint pen, it was set like a tiny jewel into the edge of the frame of the 3' x 2' antique mirror.

'Surely, it must a reflection or something,' he said, getting off the bed and walking over to it, hesitantly, as though it may be a bomb. Even as he got close, it wasn't clear what it was. He put his right index finger over the light to block it out. It didn't make sense. How was there a glowing red light there?

He put the big light on to get a better look.

'I think I know what it is,' said Julie, getting off the bed and putting her dressing gown on. As she said that, it dawned on Nick exactly what it was. There was a glint of reflection off a small lens set under the red light. He unhooked the mirror from the wall, lay it on the bed, mirror face down and unclipped the hardboard back.

There it was. A tiny camera was wedged into the wooden filigree. He plucked it out. It was about the size of half a betting-shop biro; just big enough for a tiny battery, a lens and the red light which indicated it was working.

He held it up to her. 'I hope they enjoyed the bloody show!'

'Hold it up at me,' she said, a cold look in her eye. He did as she asked. She gave the camera the finger and then made a throat cutting gesture and pointed at the lens.

He took a sock out of a drawer and dropped the device in it. 'We might need that for evidence later. Obviously our intruder left this when they took your pyjamas. This is peeping to a whole new level. This is a new level of weird shit. I never thought I'd appear in amateur porn and, pound to a penny, that's where the footage is headed and there's sod all we can do about it.' He hit a cushion on the bedroom chair; their privacy had been silently abused.

They stood and looked at each other in silence for a moment.

His heart was pounding. 'I'm absolutely fucking furious, Jules. This is another huge intrusion. They've got film of me and you together at our most intimate with each other, and it's going to be broadcast as wanking material for drooling losers!'

She wiped her hand across her face. 'It's not a nice thought. But...but...don't let them take ownership of your peace of mind.'

But that didn't help at all. 'Oh, sod that, Jules, I can't just pretend like some twat hasn't been in here, hasn't taken your clothing, hasn't filmed us together! It's got to intrude on my peace of mind! I'm not about to get all hippy about this. I want to kick this muthafucker's head in and beat seven shades of fucking snot out of him, and I fucking will, given half a chance!' His emotions were running high at the violation. 'We've got to hunt the bastard down who did this and we're going to give him some bloody hell!' He looked around the room for any other red lights. Maybe they'd planted other cameras.

She moved towards him and made a calm-down gesture with the flat of her hands.

'Alright, darlin'. But this is what they want. They want us to be upset and feel violated. That's why they're doing this. Right? The only defence we have, at the moment, is to not feel like that. We deprive them of success if we don't feel hurt and upset. But that doesn't mean we aren't proactive and don't hunt them down and get them banged up, I'm all in favour of that. But don't let them get to you, luv. It'll only cloud your judgement. I'm sure that's what your mother would say, too.'

He climbed into bed and let out a long, low groan, still paranoid they were being filmed, even though there were no other red lights. His brain whirred around and around but eventually he settled a little, relaxing on the soft bed.

Being in bed is a reconnection with being very small. It gives you comfort and security. Everyone wants to die in bed because it completes the circle. Your mother probably gave birth to you in a bed, so to go out the same way seems only right. Sometimes it seems as if every going to bed is just a rehearsal for that last sleep.

Calming down, in the quiet dark, he put his hands together as he lay on his back and let the warmth and internal energy from his own body's circuitry calm and nourish him. As he often did, he recited the Lord's Prayer in his mind, and as often happened, it gave him a sense of having entered a different space.

He prayed to have the strength, intelligence and perception to deal with life. He prayed for Julie, for Emily, for Argie and for Jeff. And for his father and mother.

Amen.

Now, at last, he felt at peace, breathed in, breathed out and felt the velvet softness of sleep wrap him up.

He woke up with a start.

Someone was tapping on his foot.

Through blurry eyes he looked into the darkness.

'Hello, our Nick.'

It was his mother. Dressed exactly as before, hands resting on her lap. She smiled at him with the lovely warmth he remembered clearly from childhood.

He stared, immediately wondering whether he was awake or asleep. He'd felt her tap his foot. This wasn't a dream, or was it?

'Hiya, mam.' He half sat up, resting on his right elbow. 'How are you?'

'Me? I can't answer that, Nick.'

'Why not?'

'Because this doesn't work like that. I'm not well, or unwell. I'm dead. Now, I know you're upset...'

'...I am. Did you see what happened?'

'No, I told you, I don't really see things, I just sort of know things.'

'Can you see me?'

'Of course I can, luv. You're my son. I can see you all the time.'

'No, I mean, can you see me lying here?'

She turned to look at him, staring into his eyes with her pale blue irises, and then waved at him with her right hand.

124

It felt weird. Like she was waving to him from the wrong end of a telescope and couldn't actually focus on him. Oh, god. What the hell was going on? He felt like he wanted to cry like a child, but swallowed it down.

'There's seeing and then there's seeing, isn't there? You understand what I mean. You were always a thoughtful boy. Full of funny, odd ideas.'

'I suppose so. No-one believes I've talked to you, mam. They all think it's just a dream.'

She sat forward a little. 'Do they, now?'

'Yeah. But this feels real to me.' He turned to look at Julie, lying on her back, mouth open, a thin line of drool on her chin, breathing deeply. Yeah, there she was, fast asleep. He turned to look at the clock on their DAB radio. 4.27am again. The same time she'd come before.

'Do you know what's been going on, mam?'

She nodded. 'I understand, yes. You've got to keep your temper, Nick. You were always a nice boy but you would always fly off the handle when you thought something was wrong.'

'Did I?'

'Don't you remember Scarborough in 1968?'

'That holiday we had? They gave us grapefruit juice for breakfast and I said it was horrible and refused to drink it.'

She laughed a little and that made Nick feel good. He'd not seen his mother laugh enough when she'd been alive.

'Aye. That's right. Your dad was horrified. I thought it was funny. But I wasn't thinking of that. Do you remember the fluffy dog?'

Nick sat and thought. 'Oh, god, yeah. The poor thing.'

'Exactly. That man kicked the fluffy little dog in Peasholm Park and you stood up and hit him on the leg and said, "Don't hurt your dog, it's lovely and you're a bully!" Eee, we were shocked, but not as shocked as that man was. But you were in the right, our Nick. And I was right proud of you, even if you shouldn't go around hitting people to make your point.'

'I'd forgotten all about that. It was such a lovely little dog and he really took against it for no good reason. It really upset me. It seemed so unfair.'

'You've always had a strong sense of right and wrong, ever since you were little. But you've got to keep your head. That's why I'm here, to tell you to calm down and trust your instincts.'

'We've been having a lot of trouble mam, I...' She interrupted him.

'...sssh, don't fret. Everything will be alright.' She reached out and touched his hand. He watched as she did so. Her hand felt warm, the blue veins quite visible. She was real, but he just wasn't sure what *real* meant any more.

'Mam, can you see into the future?'

'Don't be daft. Now listen, our Nick. This trouble you've got right now...'

'...Julie's stalker?'

'Yes. They're not right in the head, but you can handle it. It'll be fine.'

'They put a camera in here.'

'Yes, that's terrible.'

'Did you see what it filmed?'

'No. Don't be daft.'

'Me and Julie were making love...'

She held up the flat of her hand at him. 'That's enough of that sort of talk. That's not for me to hear.' She stopped for a few seconds. 'You've always been a passionate lad, I know that much.' She reached out and patted him again. 'But that's who you are and it's good to be who you are and I know Julie loves you exactly as you are. My generation were so inhibited about all that business.'

'But someone filmed us with a secret camera...'

'I'm sure they'll all be jealous of you two. Me and your dad were not like you two, I can assure you of that. But the people who did this are dangerous, our Nick.'

'People? So there are definitely more than one? How do you know?'

'I know because you know. I'm you telling you what you know. All the information to tell you who is doing these things is already available to you. Remember, I'm your mam, I know you better than anyone.'

Nick rubbed his eyes. 'This is just a dream, it must be. It feels too weird to be real.'

She stood up and said, 'Just a dream, luv? Just? What does "just" mean?'

'Can't you tell me who it is?'

'That's not how it works. I can't know unless you know and you won't know unless you let yourself know. You can do that. You've always been able to do it.'

'But how, mam? How?!' He was crying a little now, tears falling down his cheeks.

126

'The only way is to not try. You'll know when you know. Trust your instincts, our Nick.'

He sighed as she turned to leave. 'I wish you'd dispensed these sorts of philosophical aphorisms when I was growing up.'

She stopped at the door, gave him her watery-eyed smile. 'Aye, well, it must be listening to all that hippy music you played in your teens. Look after yourself, Nick. Think about things. Stay calm and everything will be alright. Give my love to Julie.'

'Thanks, mam.'

'Just be a nice lad and remember your manners.'

She went to the door and walked out...or did she just become invisible? The door was open a little way, but she didn't seem to walk through it. He licked his dry lips. Shit, this was so weird. If it had been anyone except his mother, he'd have been terrified, but because it was her, he just wasn't. He looked at the clock. It still said 4.27am. No time had passed again.

He lay down, wiped the last of his tears away and put his finger tips together to try and relax once more.

Opening his eyes, the clock said 7.15am. He yawned, got up and went downstairs to put the kettle on. He hadn't heard Emily coming in, so she must have stayed out late, even though she said she'd come home at 10. The living room door was ajar, so he put his head around to make sure she'd come home.

What he saw made him simultaneously hurt with a massive surge of adrenaline fuelled shock and also feel like vomiting. He couldn't move. He was utterly frozen; paralysed.

'Emily!' he screamed, squeezing the words out of his tightened throat 'Emily!' She was lying face down on the carpet, naked, her lavishly tattooed back towards him. A long, slender knife was buried deep between her shoulder blades. Blood had oozed from the wound and spilled in a river down her spine to her small tattooed buttocks. She was motionless. Lifeless. Dead.

He broke his paralysis and strode towards her, sinking to his knees, he leaned over her body, his hands on her shoulders. She was cold. Cold and dead.

What the hell was this? What had happened? Oh god, oh god, oh my god, Emily. Oh god. What's happened?

He spoke out loud. 'Emily, you poor girl. Oh, Emily, I don't want you to be dead. Please don't be dead. Please.' He hugged her and stroked her

127

head, weeping. It hurt so much, it was unbearable, so unbearable that he let out a loud noise which was part sob, part visceral howl.

'Shhh, there, there. It's alright.'

He opened his eyes and saw Julie, leaning over him, stroking his arm.

'It was just a nightmare. You're alright. Everything is alright.'

She cooed and patted at him, as he swam back up to the surface of the consciousness. His whole body was drenched in sweat, his breath short and panting with fear.

'Emily's been murdered,' he said, loudly, half his brain still locked into the world of sleep.

'Don't be daft, you've just had a nightmare. You were shouting.'

He leapt out of bed, pulled open the bedroom door and ran downstairs to the living room, pushing the door open, expecting to see her body lying there.

And she was.

Of course she was.

It hadn't been a dream at all, it had been precognition.

She was naked and lying on the floor, on her front, on the sofa cushions, eyes closed, the quilt cast to one side.

He went in and knelt next to her, putting a hand on her back. She was warm and stirred a little with his touch.

She was asleep. There was no knife.

Asleep, but not dead.

Asleep, but not dead.

Kissing his hand and placing it on her back, he got up and went back to the bedroom, his mind shredded with confusion.

'Is she alive?' said Julie, eyebrows and tone both arched.

'Yeah, yeah, she is. Thank God.' He squatted down onto his hunkers and held his head in his hands, trying to compose himself. He felt mentally fractured into tiny shards of exhaustion.

'Jules. I've had such a weird night.'

'Alright, go and make tea and then tell me about it. Tea is more important than anything, at this time of the day.'

He did as he was told, bringing up two white china mugs of Sencha green tea.

'Are you OK now?' she said, pushing at her pillows so that they propped her up.

'Yeah.' He gave her the tea and got back into bed. He turned to her. 'Promise you won't be judgemental about what I'm going to tell you.'

She picked at a sleep crust in her eye. 'Of course not.'

'Mam came to see me again and we had a nice chat, she told me to trust in my instincts and then I went back to sleep and...and...and...well, Emily was dead in my dream, with a knife between her shoulder blades. All of that was so real, Jules. So real.' He felt wrung out, shredded.

She patted at him. 'Settle yourself down, then tell me more about it.'

He went over what his mother has said.

'She thinks I know who is responsible for the stalking if I'd just let myself know.'

'That's just silly. You're taking dreams too seriously.'

'I dunno about that. I saw Em, dead.'

'Yeah and that was a dream, luv. She's fine, isn't she? Therefore, you don't have this precognition thing.'

He sat and sipped his tea, still feeling like so much grated cheese.

'Jules, I've never had dreams like this. They're hyper real. I'm worried I've really got some sort of precognition, or that I'm just going mad, the way my mother went mad.'

She didn't respond immediately, continuing to take sips of tea.

'You don't talk about her much, but you really miss your mother, don't you?' she said, with sympathy in her tone.

He sighed. 'Of course I do. She was stolen from me by her mental illness. I wanted to be loved by her, especially when I went to college, but she didn't even write because she was drifting into full-blown paranoid schizophrenia. Soon she was tearing out that bloody cuckoo from the cuckoo clock because it was listening to her and looking at me with that awful stare which was scared, angry and distant, all at the same time.' He turned to look at her. She nodded slowly.

'I understand, luv, everyone wants their mam's support and love, if possible.'

He put his face in his hands. 'I tried to be hard about it, so her being away with the fairies wouldn't hurt me. I shut myself down and pretended I didn't need my parent's love or affection or help. I was 18, but still a boy really. I made out I was fine and never even shed a tear over her and her condition. Not once. I locked all of those feelings away in a dark room and threw the key into a very deep river. I had to learn how to be a man all by myself. And it was harder than I even knew at the time. I had to lose part of myself in order to do it. I had to lose who I was as a boy, because that boy would have been crushed by losing his mother's love. So I think it stunted me, emotionally. The way I was developing up to that point, just sort of came to a halt, I took a detour and I never got back on to the road I'd been on. I left being the nice lad I'd been brought up to be and I became harder and colder. I've always wanted to be able to give her my love, as an adult, and not just as a child. I do feel robbed of that, too, because she didn't know Monday from a banana for decades.'

Tears fell in big, wet drops from his eyes as the words fell from his mouth. 'Mam coming to see me now, like this, even though it's weird, it's still great. I've always wanted it to be possible. Talking to her again, sane and not damaged by the drugs and ECT, it helps fill in a big hole in my soul and...and...and I'm already a bit scared she'll go away again. I was abandoned by her once, I can't face being left again.'

She nodded again and laid her hand on his bare arm.

'I know, luv. I do understand. I think I do, anyway. Maybe she's started talking to you because you need her to talk to you, because of all the stress. Whatever is happening, it's happening because you need it to happen. And you are special. You're a thoughtful, creative, sensitive bloke.' She pushed some hair off his forehead with her fingertips. 'But, let's not get into this precognition thing. It's a bit out there. I'm not pretending I know what on earth our minds can and can't do and I know fizz all about different states of consciousness, but seeing into the future? It seems unlikely.'

'I hope it isn't true. I don't want to see into the future. I can barely cope with the now, sometimes, let alone have to deal with things before they've even happened.'

'Why don't you talk to Marc about it in your next therapy session? These are just vivid dreams, luv, really they are.'

'I'm not mad, you know. I probably sound mad. I think Jeff thinks I'm going the way of my mother. I can tell.' More tears fell in big wet drips.

'You're upset and it's messing with your mind. Just let it all go. Try not to fret.'

As he dressed, he couldn't shake the idea that his dreams were all real. That he was in the middle of some sort of supernatural episode, just as he had been when he was a teenager, making that phone ring and predicting coin tosses. He must be occasionally able see forward in time because, regardless of anything else, how else to explain knowing about the records in Jeff's shop? He contemplated telling Julie about that but decided against it, because it'd just make her think he was even more crazy.

Julie sat at the kitchen table and texted Mandy to tell her about the hidden camera. The degree of invasion was huge and there was no shrugging it off as some eccentric behaviour. Aside from anything else, it was illegal on several levels and a worrying escalation.

'Right. That's that. I daresay she'll be in touch with one or both of us, soon enough. They'll probably send some forensics over.' She pulled her hair back into a pile on the back of her head, held it in place with black plastic clip, and stood in front of the long mirror in the hall, brushing fluff off her loose-fitting black linen trousers. 'OK, I'm out of here.' She kissed him on the cheek. 'Have a nice day, just relax and take it easy. Don't fret about things.'

As the Porsche rumbled into the distance Nick went back into the kitchen and put their breakfast plates into the dishwasher, picked up the dirty clothes from the bedroom and stuck them into the washing machine. That was his work done as a house husband. He made some coffee and perched onto a kitchen stool. Emily came in, now wearing a long baggy black t-shirt and a smile, her hair messy.

'Morning, Nicky boy. Oooh, is that coffee, yes please.' She yawned as he poured her a cup and put a splash of cream in it. 'Those sofa cushions are very comfortable.'

'What time did you get in?'

'Just after midnight. I went out for a drink with a friend.'

He hoped it wasn't Matty, but wasn't about to probe her about it, just as he wasn't about to tell her about his dream.

'Good. I looked in on you on earlier, you were sprawled out. But you look bright-eyed and bushy-tailed this morning.'

She gave him her gap-toothed grin. 'Must be your lovely house. It's very homely here. Thanks for putting me up. I won't be in your hair for long, I promise.'

'You can stay as long as you like. It's been an upsetting time for you.'

'You're both very kind but I'm sure you want to be making noisy passionate love all night and you don't want me to hear you or be peeping through the door.'

'We've certainly had enough of people spying on us,' he said, sitting down opposite her.

'Sorry. That was insensitive of me. Still, at least I got that website down and with Facebook deleting the false page, that's those photos of Julie all gone.'

'Great, thanks for doing that. I'm hoping we've seen the last of those but somehow, I doubt it. Things escalated last night, I'm afraid.'

She knitted her thin eyebrows together. 'What do you mean? Was someone here?'

'Someone planted a hidden camera in the filigree frame of the bedroom mirror. Probably when they broke in and took Julie's pyjamas.'

She pulled a face. 'That's so weird. And so sick. But some people are weird and sick, aren't they?'

'It was really small but had a tiny red light on it - bit of a giveaway.'

'Really? That's odd. They don't need to have a light on them. I've read up on this spy stuff loads. I love hi-tech gadgets and you can get tiny devices which stream live video and run off a miniature battery. No need for a light on them. That's very 2005.'

Nick crossed his arms and thought about it, while she checked her phone and began sending texts, her thumbs tapping out messages at high pace.

'Could it be that whoever put it there, actually wanted us to find it? By finding it, it exerts more stress, paranoia and power over us. If we'd never known it was there, it'd have had no effect in our lives and what's more, they could have kept filming us for as long as the battery lasted. You can only worry about something you know exists. Yeah, that makes sense, it's all part of the torture.'

She stopped texting and looked up at him. 'Sounds likely. So, what would it have filmed?'

'Mostly nothing because we weren't there. But then last night, me and Julie had some, you know, adult fun. In the middle of which, Julie saw the light, as it were.'

'But you had the lights out, surely, so it won't have filmed anything, or not visibly, anyway?' she said.

He scratched his head and gave her a half smile. 'Emily, you surprise me.'

'Why?'

'That's a very conservative assumption about having the lights off. You're always playing the sex kitten.'

She wriggled a little in her seat and mimed licking herself like a cat.

'Actually, we had the lamps on.'

'Nicky boy, you've blushed.'

'It means we were filmed and...well...it'll end up somewhere online, I bet. I was going to look for it, but I lost courage to do so, as I know I'd have to go through a load of porn sites.'

She made a mocking face at him. 'I never, ever met a man who was squeamish about porn, the way you are. You're weird, Nick Guymer. It's just humans having sex.'

'I'm not going over all that again. You know my position on it, well enough,' he said. 'Would you like something to eat?'

She shook her head, staring at her phone, then looked up at him and turned the phone to him. It was the website that Julie's photos had been on. In the centre of the screen was now a video screen. It was titled, 'The Old Slut Julie Wells Being Fucked Again. Sack Her Now!'

She grimaced. 'Right, I'm done with being little miss polite. I'm going to wipe, then break their server. Bastards. Give me your laptop,' said Emily.

He sat back while she went to work.

'I feel like I should feed you for doing this. Let me do some sausages for you.'

'You can sausage me any time you want, you know that,' she said squinting in the glow of the screen.

'Don't be saying that, Em. It's not right,' he said it with a sigh.

'Oh, don't be such a wuss,' she snapped. 'I'm just messing with you.' She tapped at keyboard some more. 'Wow, Julie is one hot chick, isn't she?' Then she paused and put her hand to her mouth. 'Oh, goodness me...look at you...gosh...I've never seen...that's amazing.' Eyes fixed on the screen, she actually blushed pink, swallowed hard and then glanced up at him in embarrassment.

'Don't watch the bloody video. Don't, Em. Please. It's really not funny. Not at all. I'd like your help to get rid of the video but I don't want you going on about what it shows, right? It's incredibly intrusive, I feel quite violated by it to be honest and it most certainly isn't a joke, or something for your titillation. Do you understand? I'm just a slightly weird bloke, not a sodding porn star.' He spoke with a firm jab of his finger.

Responding to his seriousness, she nodded and held both hands up to him. 'Of course, of course...I totally agree. I'm sorry...I'm way too childish, sometimes. Sorry sorry sorry.' She tapped away for a couple of minutes in silence. 'Right, that's the whole server deleted of everything from content to operating system and just to make sure, I've setup a DNS attack on it over the next few days, so it'll make it all a hassle to do anything on it for a while. However, the video is hosted on Pornhub, which is huge, and hacking it off there is above my pay grade, I'm afraid. That place is indestructible. However, I can put in a complaint for you, saying it's video acquired illegally and without permission. Just so you know, they've named you both in the description and tags, so anyone...'

'...anyone searching for either of our names will get the link.'

'Not necessarily. Only if they've got safe search off. But...yeah...most of us who don't have kids, don't have safe search on. I'll put in a request to Google to get the listing removed as well. Might take a while, but I think they'll take it off and I reckon Pornhub will take it down soon enough. It's not like they're short of amateur videos of people having sex.'

'Really? Do they even care?'

'Oh, yeah, they're all too aware that jealous ex-boyfriends clutter the site with revenge porn and they're scared of getting caught up in a court case over that stuff. The law is getting tighter. It won't be long before it's outright illegal and rightly so. It's a terrible thing to do.'

Nick poured more coffee for them, got up and took cream out of the fridge to add to her cup. 'Em? You seem to know a lot about this stuff. Do you have personal experience of it?'

She cleared her throat. 'No comment.' She added, 'and don't go searching for my name to find out.'

'Of course not.' Nick decided to make food instead of sitting in an embarrassing silence. He put a frying pan on, dropped in some lard and when it was hot, some smoked bacon and a pork sausage.

'Oh, god, that smells wonderful,' said Emily.

'Egg?'

'Go on then.' She grinned at him in her almost girlish way. 'I love having someone cooking for me.' She scrunched herself up and grinned at him, tongue pressed between the gap in her front teeth.

'We don't have bread, I'm afraid.'

'Weirdos, the both of you.'

'I know, but we both feel much better for not eating wheat. I've got half a small cold jacket potato, shall I fry that up for you?'

'Yes, please. Well, whatever weird food regime you're on, it really suits you both and no-one could say it didn't, looking at that video. Even if it does lack bread, which, by the way, if you've never tried it, is delicious.'

'You know what?'

'What?'

'You're right. Sometimes the way you talk is *just* like Jeff.'

She made a shocked face. 'Oh, no, is the big man is rubbing off on me?' She held her index finger at 45 degrees and made her voice as low and gruff as she could in an imitation of the big man, 'Which by the way, is against several by-laws and requires a special licence.'

He laughed. 'Perfect.'

'I could do worse than be like Jeff.' She paused. 'He's really great.'

'Jeff? Yeah. Him and Mandy is a great combo too, I reckon.'

'She scares me a bit. Big, busty women always have. They make me feel like I'm not a proper woman, somehow.'

He smiled at her. 'I can totally get that, actually. I'm the same with really macho blokey blokes. Always makes me feel like I'm not sufficiently male.'

'Well you've nothing to worry about on that score. Is Jeff, like, in love with Mandy? You know what he's like, he won't talk about these things at all to me.'

Nick pushed the bacon and sausage around the pan and then put it under the grill to keep warm while he did her eggs and potato.

'He doesn't talk to me about it either, so I have to read between the lines. I think it's quite serious, yeah. They seem to really enjoy each others' company. When me and Jules have gone out with them, they're much more interested in each other than they are in anything we've got to say, which is a good sign.'

'That's so sweet. I'm so happy for him. Does she have any kids?'

'Yeah, two, in their mid to late 20s. She was married for eight or nine years, then got divorced. The way she tells it, the job got in between them.'

'It must be hard to fall in love again at that age.'

'Yeah, I'm not sure "love" is a word they would use yet. They've been a sort of couple for six months, that's all. When you're older, the full flush of love is very tempered by your life experience. The head-over-heels thing doesn't happen so often, from what I can tell. But they're obviously enjoying each other's company and who can ask for more than that?'

She looked up from her phone and cheekily said, 'I hope they've got a massive, heavily reinforced bed!' He raised a disapproving eyebrow at her. 'Ha ha...sorry. I am very childish, I told you. After what happened with Rita, I really hope it works out for Jeff and for Argie. I bet Mandy would be a great mother for him.'

'Me and Jules do, too, but don't tell him that. He'd hate the idea that we're all talking about them.'

He served up her food onto a hot plate.

'Here you go. Would you like any salad leaves?'

'Has anyone ever said yes to that question?'

He pointed at her with his right index finger. 'See, that's 100 per cent Jeff, that is. You're morphing into him.'

She hunched her shoulders and put her right hand to her mouth, as though shocked at her own words.

'This looks super yummy. I'm so hungry.' She ate her food with the speed of someone who was famished but who a few minutes earlier had said she didn't want to eat. That worried him, a little. She was such a skinny, petite lass.

'I'm sure you don't eat properly. You need looking after,' said Nick, pouring more coffee. 'I'm going to start bringing you food into work to make sure you eat. Not eating right leads to loads of other issues, you know.'

'Oh, yeah, like what?' she said, obsessed with her phone again.

'Like getting headaches. Your blood sugar drops really low and makes your emotions veer up and down. And you get big drops in energy, which you then feed with sugar and carbs, perk up for a bit, then crash again. It's a vicious circle. Throw in the monthly vortex of hormones and it can be a volatile mix.'

She ground some black pepper onto the fried egg.

'Huh, well, it's like you're describing a typical day for me. I'm funny about food. Always have been. I like eating when I eat, but it never really occurs to me unless it's put in front of me. I can go 12 hours without eating, easily.'

'My mam always said you should get a good breakfast in you. We had a cooked breakfast every morning before school. That might have been the best bit of growing up, actually. Even aged 18 before going into 6th form, she'd still cook me some eggs and bacon or something. Of course, I totally took it for granted.'

'My mother was never up when I ate breakfast. She was still hungover or whatever and my father wouldn't know what a kitchen was if it fell on his head. So I got used to just grabbing a slice of toast or whatever, before going to my very posh school for Queen Bitches.'

'You weren't a boarder, though, were you?'

'No, thank god. Last thing I needed was to be worn like a beard by some posh girl from the sodding Home Counties.'

'Worn like a beard? How is everyone using that expression now?'

'I think I heard Jeff say it. I am definitely turning into him.'

'And, in fairness, it's not one you could accurately use about yourself now, Em.'

She looked up from her phone again. 'You're very sharp-eyed, aren't you?'

'For some things, aye.'

'I'll show you again if you'd like. I know your generation finds it all a bit exotic.'

He held a hand up and shook his head. 'Thanks, but it would be massively inappropriate. I'm not sure you should make a habit of saying stuff like that, Em. It's just not right.'

That seemed to annoy her and she snapped a little at him. 'Oh, shuttup. You know what I'm like. I'm just a show-off. And I'm only messing about. Don't be so wet.'

'I know. It's just...oh, I can't talk about this stuff, the way Julie can. It's just that being like that, you can pull some dodgy people into your life, even if you don't mean to. Even if to you it's just a bit of harmless fun.'

She put her knife and fork down and glared at him. It wasn't a look he'd seen her make before. 'I know the way the world is, Nick. You don't need to give me a birds and the bees talk. You don't need to tell me anything, about anything, right? And I'd prefer it if you didn't even try. I know all about it, only too well. So spare me the concerned fatherly tone, please. I might be small but trust me, I'm all grown up. More grown up than you'll ever know.'

CHAPTER 10

He just wasn't equipped with the right emotional politics to talk to her.

'I just worry about you. Those bruises on your hip aren't from being clumsy. I know what story they tell, Em. Don't just swallow bad stuff down and try to tough it out. I did that for years and it wasn't healthy. I'm a good listener. Shite at all other human relations, I know, but good at listening. And both me and Jules are on your side. That's all I'm saying.'

But she just wasn't interested, brushing it all off as though it was nothing, speaking in a flippant flat voice. 'Yeah yeah yeah, I'm absolutely fine. Don't worry about me. I'll get through it all on my own, I always have and I always will, so just don't talk any more about it and I promise not to show you my body again, since it's obviously so offensive to you.'

'Oh, don't twist what I'm saying.'

She looked up at him. 'Didn't I say to *stop* talking?'

There was no point in pushing this any more. As long as she knew they would support her, that was much as they could do.

He wiped down the kitchen benches and put clean dishes away from the dishwasher.

'So who did you go for a drink with?' he asked as she continued to take small forks of food and then tap at her phone.

'Do you know Waheeda?'

'Oh, yeah. Isn't she an accountant?'

'She is, yeah. Not exactly rock 'n' roll.'

'Yeah, I've seen her talking to you in the cafe.'

'Most people I know are a bit odd or crazy, or wild. She's my one sensible friend. She's got a good, steady job, married at 21, settled down in a semi-detached house in Hartburn and now they're planning on having children.'

'Sounds frighteningly grown up.'

She looked across the kitchen. 'Yeah, She, totally is. Her life is all about good credit ratings, comprehensive insurance and big knickers. But everyone needs one sensible friend and she's mine.'

'And I'm sure you're her tattooed, freaky, rock 'n' roll friend.'

A slightly exasperated gasp of air came out of her. 'I suppose I must be, for what that's worth.'

'So what does she think of the whole Matty thing?'

'That I should only give him a second chance if he's clean of drugs.' She said it casually.

'Jeff said he came to the shop yesterday evening.'

'Hmm. It was a bit embarrassing, to say the least. He was texting me all day. He's sent me another this morning. I just need time to think about what he's done to me.'

Was that an admission that she'd been raped or assaulted? Or was she just referring to his behaviour in general?

Nick nodded, wondering how to phrase what he wanted to say.

'Do you want to do that? Give him a second chance, I mean.'

She shrugged. Was she not saying anything because the answer was 'yes' and she knew he didn't want to hear that? Or was she genuinely unsure?

'Thank you for breakfast.' She'd cleaned the plate.

'I like feeding people. Not sure why, but it's better to cook for others than it is for yourself.'

'Not if I do it. I can't cook. I'd burn air but leave it raw on the inside, if it was possible.' She stopped and looked quizzical and shook her head. 'That also sounds like something Jeff would say. Talking of which, I'm doing 10 til 6 today, so I'd better get ready.'

After dropping her off at the shop, Nick began to drive just for the sake of driving. Driving randomly around the region was a relaxation therapy he often used. It didn't matter where he went, nor if it was quiet or busy. Just having to drive the car somehow freed him up from fretting quite so much about all the other stuff that seemed to be encroaching his life. He was worried about Julie's stalker and where the hell that was all going to end up. He was pissed off and embarrassed at the photos and video. He was worried about Emily, too. Worried that she was in serious danger from Matty Rhodes. And then there were his mother and all the vivid dreams. It all flew around in his brain like a million fragments of tissue paper in a hurricane. He just couldn't grasp onto anything to form it into a picture, and there seemed no easy way to solve any of these worries.

He did a big loop, going north on the A19, taking the A689 west to the A1, going south and then leaving the A1 on the A167, eventually joining up with the A66, heading back into Stockton and driving to their allotment in Oxbridge.

Parking up outside, he went down to their plot and began weeding their two vegetable beds. At this time of year, it was impossible to keep them clear. He poked around with a hoe and plucked out the worst horse-tails, bugle and ground elder. The outdoor tomatoes were especially looking good due to the warm summer and the courgettes were rampant. It was impossible to eat them all, some would have to be left to grow into marrows. Still, it was very satisfying to grow your own food and he could feed Julie and himself well with what they grew, and that made him feel good.

After an hour of weeding, he sat down for a rest on one of the folding chairs they kept in the shed.

'Sorry to disturb you...' said a woman's voice from behind him. He stood up and turned around. She was probably in her late 30s, with a big moon-shaped face, wild and fuzzy dyed red hair, wearing some sort of tie-dyed smock, black leggings and big boots. She was that rarest of things on Teesside: a hippy. She had to be because, along with the clothes, she smelled strongly of patchouli, a smell which instantly evoked his teenage years. Only hippies wore patchouli, for some reason.

'Hiya.' He thought he'd better try and smile, realised he'd pulled something that was more of a grimace and then stopped and went back to being expressionless. Stop overthinking everything.

She pointed across the allotments. 'I've just taken on that plot at the bottom and it's totally knackered. I mean the soil is in poor condition. I was wondering if you know anywhere I could get some horse muck from, or any rotted manure.'

'Yeah, I don't know where it comes from - well, obviously, it comes from an animal's bum - ha ha - but a big pile of horse muck is often dumped at the top by the gate. I think a farmer brings it down once a month. Should be some more there soon enough. We all just help our-selves.'

She gave him a big pink-cheeked grin. 'Aw, that's great. I'll not get anything grown this year but I just want it get it into good condition for next spring.' She seemed to be good natured and had one of those out-going, open personalities.

'Have you considered a green manure? We planted rye grass, over-wintered it and then dug it in in March. It fixes nitrogen into the soil and apparently this is a very good thing.'

She looked at their plot with admiration.

'Well, you've got proper ace veg beds here. Bursting with life!'

'Or weeds, as they're traditionally called. I've just been trying to get on top of them, but I'm fighting a losing battle. Here, do you want some courgettes? We're overrun with them and have reached our full courgette eating capacity.'

'Ooh, they're lovely. You must be doing something right.'

He squatted down and pulled off three of the biggest ones for her.

'There you go. They're organically grown. That means you have to eat them whilst listening to whale music, and wearing underpants made out of herbs.' That was a Jeff joke, which he'd always liked. She laughed a little.

'Brill. Ta. Oh, I'm Natalie, by the way.' She held out her hand, smiling wide.

'Nick. My missus, Julie, is often down here on evenings and week-ends. If you see her, she's the sweaty-looking blonde woman drinking wine out of the bottle, dancing badly and eating all the cherry tomatoes.'

Natalie laughed. 'I'll look out for her.'

Nick didn't know what else to say now. This was how it usually went for him. He had, at most, five minutes of talk in him, then his chat battery just ran out of power and he stood there silent, unable to think of any-thing else to say, or worse, would start talking nonsense, beginning sen-tences without having any idea what he was going to say.

She smiled warmly at him; her big face had caught the sun, giving her a flushed look. She pointed at him with a forefinger.

'You're a cusp, aren't you?'

'A what?'

'A Cancer/Leo cusp. Born between both star signs.' She narrowed her eyes as though scrutinising something. 22nd of July, I'd say.'

Bloody hell. How on earth did she know that?

'Err...that's very weird, Natalie. The 22nd is my birthday. How did you know?'

'You're an absolute classic Cancer/Leo cusp: the cusp of oscillation.'

'I am? And in what way?'

She waved it away. 'Oh, you don't want to hear about all of that. You're clearly a sceptic.'

'No, I'm interested.'

She looked away down to Oxbridge Lane. 'You're a classic mix of in-troversion and extroversion. The solitude of Cancer and the centre of at-tention of Leo. I bet you're a creative person.'

'I am a writer.'

'Well, that's absolutely classic, too. You're capable of spending a lot of time on your own with your own thoughts, but are motivated by a desire to express yourself, in order to show off your thinking and wit. Cancer/Leo. And I'm sure you struggle with going from highs to lows very quickly.'

'Well, I suffer from depression, which can kick off at any time and drop me down a well of black despair, but on the upside, it makes me appear moody and interesting.'

'And there it is again, vulnerability mixed with the need to make light of it. Classic Cancer/Leo cusp.' She touched him on his arm and gave him her big, warm smile again. Nick didn't know what to say. It was all so weird. How could she know this? Was she some sort of witch?

'And now that I know I'm a massive cusp, what do I do about it?'

'See, that's your emotionally vulnerable Cancer with Leo's upfront bravado.'

'Are you going to do this analysis for every sentence I speak?'

She held up her hands. 'Sorry. I should properly introduce myself. I'm Natalie Townsend.' She gave him a card, which had on it, 'Natalie Townsend: Psychic, Clairvoyant, Angel Light Worker'. 'You might have seen my ads in the *Gazette*.'

'Wow, that's quite a list of...err...I don't actually know what any of them is, but I'm fairly sure the Boro need an angel light worker up front. We're chronically short of goals.'

Her big face broke into a laugh. 'There are some things that are beyond even the help of Archangel Michael, I'm afraid. Anyway, I've taken up too much of your time. Thanks for the courgettes.'

Nick acted on impulse. 'Err...I've got a kettle in there, if you'd like a cup of something. I imagine a psychic drinks, what my mate Jeff would call hippy tea. In other words, Sencha green.'

'That'd be lovely. It's warm again, I'm parched.'

'Right, you take this seat, I'll get the kettle on.'

As he filled it with water he pondered what she'd said. She seemed really nice and a generous sort of person. One of those people you instinctively feel is a good soul. But an angel light worker, huh? It all sounded like utter New Age bollocks. He could just see the sneer on Julie's face, and hear the piss taking Jeff would dish out. But she'd known when he was born and that was impossible for her to know, because she had no idea who he was. And the characteristics she assigned to being a

Cancer/Leo cusp were right on the money, as far as his nature was concerned, but then you could probably find many such astrological descriptions applicable. But recent events had taught him that maybe there are states of being that are outside of our normal perception of life that shouldn't be quickly dismissed, so he held his cynicism in suspension.

He put two mugs down on a wooden crate that they used as an improvised table, then unfolded another chair.

'I sense you have questions,' she said, scratching at her shin. 'Did I shock you?'

'Well, yeah. I mean, you got me dead on with the birthday.' He cleared his throat. 'Tell me this, do you believe precognition is possible?'

She pushed a strand of her dark hair from her eyes, as a breeze blew in.

'Yes. Absolutely. Why do you ask?'

'My mother thinks I have it.'

'Do you think she's right?'

'Well, before I answer that, I need to tell you something. Mam is dead. She comes to me in the night and we talk and she's been telling me that I know what's going to happen in the future. She waves and stares at me like she's a long way away, yet I feel she's close. I did have a few weird psychic experiences as a kid. I'm trying to work out what's going on.'

She rest her chin on an upturned palm. 'That's really interesting. Tell me, when you meet your mother, what age is she?'

'I think she's how she was in the early 1970s. So she'd be in her late 30s. Much younger than me, weirdly, though how I see her is as a person much older than me. As though I'm in my teens again. Yeah, actually, I'd not thought of that. In the visitations, I'm still younger than her.'

'OK, and you say you've had some dreams come true?'

'I dreamed about Jeff, my best mate, buying some records and that came 100 per cent true. They were in a box in the same position I dreamed they'd be in. But last night, I dreamed I saw my friend Emily lying murdered in our living room with a knife in her back. It's really frightened me. She's not dead. She's alive and staying with us. But it wasn't just a dream, it was way more realistic than that. So is talking with mam. I can't shake the worry that mam is right, that I have some sort of special intuition, and that I've seen Emily's murder in the future. I know it sounds loony.'

She shook her head and smiled again. 'Not to me it doesn't. But I think maybe you're taking it all too literally. It's like with Tarot cards. Each one is symbolic and they are not always meant to be taken literally.'

'Sorry, Nat, I dreamed about those records and then there they were in the box, in the right order. The exact same records. That's 100 per cent precognition, isn't it? It's not symbolic of anything.'

She seemed a bit intimidated by his, presumably Leo-like, strident tone.

'These things are not always as straightforward as you might think. Dreams can be a mixture of the literal and the symbolic. That's all I'm saying. Also that dream about records sounds like a different type of experience to the visitations from your mother, which is different again from the dream of the murder. I think you'll find they stem from three different realities; one literal, one supernatural and one symbolic.' She smiled and nodded a little. Until that moment, he hadn't considered how different in their nature those three things were.

They chatted a little more. She knew of Jeff's shop but didn't play vinyl. She had two cats and liked rock and soul music. Nick felt unusually at ease in her company.

'When I was a teenager, I had this phase when it seemed like could make a phone ring at the end of our street. Not an impressive psychic power, I know.' He told her what had happened. 'Do you think that could be true? Have you heard of that before?'

'We all have untapped potential which can manifest itself in many different ways, and that time in a child's life is often assigned special status in some indigenous cultures far less afraid of supernatural occurrences than ours tends to be.'

'Are these actually dreams that I've had with mam in? They don't feel like dreams. They feel more like some sort of alternative reality. I can feel her hand, even though, as I said, she does seem to be looking at me from a distance and isn't quite focused.'

Natalie smiled and nodded. 'It's hard for me to say for sure, but I'd usually call that a supernatural visitation, but not in the sense of seeing a ghost.'

'How do you mean?'

'You're connecting to your mother's spirit and are manifesting her.'

'I'm making her up, you mean?'

She made a quizzical face and tilted her head to one side. 'Sort of. But what does that actually mean, if you think about it? Is it not a reconnection with who she was or is? I'd need to go deeply into this with you in several sessions so that we can get to the bottom of it all.'

That sounded like a pitch for work, but then, if it really was a deep thing, maybe she was just avoiding being flippant or glib and would need more time.

'What exactly is an angel light worker?'

'It's someone who realises they have been sent to heal the world with the pure love of god.'

'Wow. Was that a job advertised in the *Gazette*?'

'It's more something that you come to understand is your calling.'

He grinned at her wryly. 'I had guessed that. I was joking, Natalie. Or, at least the Leo bit of me was. The Cancer part was sneering cynically.' She was interesting and unusual, but his bullshit-o-meter was occasionally twitching.

She smiled, clearly used to people being a bit skeptical. He found himself liking her, and she had identified his star sign, not that he had put any store by astrology in the past, not least because there was obviously nothing to connect random associations of stars and planets which were light years apart. But all the same, she was odd enough to make him think twice about dismissing her completely, especially as life seemed to be in the business of telling him not to take the waking reality as the only reality.

He'd just put the tools away and got into the BMW when a text from Jeff came in.

'*Get your drinking trousers ready, Jeff's Rock Club opens a week today. Come and take a look.*'

Pulling into a space right outside of the club, Nick looked up at it. It had been some sort of Methodist church building at some point, but had been sliced, diced and botched up ever since, spending time as a carpet and a wallpaper warehouse, amongst many other things. A door at each end was shuttered and a tall tower at either end of the building gave it a derelict kind of grandeur. Set on Church Road, with Georgian buildings to one side and a smaller turn-of-the-century terrace on the other, which housed takeaways and a newsagent, it was a great location, close to the town centre. But so many businesses had come and gone, you had to wonder if Jeff's would merely be the latest to fail there.

'Jeff!' Nick ducked under one of the shutters and went in. What greeted him was a remarkable transformation from the first time he'd seen it. Back then it was little more than a big dusty space, with scuffed wooden floors and a couple of old toilets.

It had taken over a year of work and a sum of money that Jeff would only describe as 'trouser browning' to transform it into a concert venue and bar which was licenced to hold 250 people.

Nick stood, slack jawed. It was truly amazing.

Jeff came out onto the stage and stood, arms outstretched, as though the lead singer in a band.

'Good evening, Stockton!' He punched the air and jumped down. 'What do you reckon?'

'It's bloody amazing, Jeff. I've not seen it for, what, about four months? It's transformed. When you kept on going on about how much work was being done, I half thought you were exaggerating. The bar looks amazing. Like something you'd see in New York. Shit, this is so cool.' A prickle of excitement flashed up and down his spine.

'The mirrors behind the bar make the whole place look bigger. I just got all the neon-light beer signs put up as well. They add a bit of colour.'

'Man, the paintings on the walls are brilliant.'

'Yeah, I just got those hung those today. Sodding hard work, that was.'

He pointed at three huge pictures. One was of Jeff Beck with a black Les Paul from the early 70s. Another was a huge landscape painting of Cream onstage in 1968 and a third, a portrait of Stevie Nicks. A large blown-up photo of the Fillmore East in New York in 1969 with people queuing around the block was hung to the side of the bar.

'That's what I want this place to be like. The Fillmore East, even though that was an old theatre and much bigger; I want the JRC to have the same sort of cultural impact on Teesside. That's my inspiration. And in a fit of massive ego-stroking, I'm going to have a huge photo of me here to welcome you, as you come in.'

'It's all so cool. I'm stunned, genuinely stunned. And you've got a bloody jukebox. You never told me that! When did you get that?' He ran up to the huge 1970s machine and hugged it. Jeff laughed. 'It looks like the one that used to be in the Talbot.'

'Yeah, maybe it is! Thought you'd be impressed. Bought it on eBay last week, was just delivered first thing today. Shall we break its virginity?' He held up a 7-inch single by Deep Purple.

146

'Virginity? This old bird was shagged years ago. It looks like it's seen a lot of action.' He leaned over the oblong black, red and gold plastic, metal and glass contraption.

Jeff lifted the glass top off it and put the record onto the deck and then flicked the power on.

'Right, get ready for lift-off.'

There was crackle as the needle hit the run-in groove. Then boom! 'Black Night' kicked off at high volume. The bass sank a punch into Nick's guts. He pulled a face at Jeff.

'This sounds like a jet taking off!!' he yelled. Jeff beamed and played a bit of air guitar. In the empty space, with little furniture and no people to soak it up, it was extremely loud, pounding out of the big speaker in the jukebox but also out of the PA speakers either side of the stage.

Jeff lifted the needle. 'Well that was a success, eh. I wired it up to the PA myself and got Larry the Leckie to check it over. I thought it'd be a nice touch for people to choose the music in between the bands and we can literally coin it. Two plays for a quid. It holds 200 singles. 400 songs. If I change some of them once a month, no-one will get too bored of the same songs.'

'It's brilliant. Just brilliant.' Nick patted Jeff on the back. 'The work you've put into this, big man, it's amazing, especially as you've never done anything like this before. I don't actually know how you've done it.'

'Through being a smart arse with various councillors, using Big Fish's influence and Brian's top-notch lawyers, along with some hard graft and paying immigrants cash to do the grunt labour.'

'It actually puts me in mind of the crypt at Middlesbrough Town Hall.'

'Yeah, well, there's not much natural light in here, so it does have a bit of that about it. The tricky bit will be getting the gear in and out of the back.'

'Got dressing rooms?'

'Room. One. About 10 foot by 10 foot. It was a storage cupboard but I've put a mirror in, what more do they need? Come and see the toilets.'

They went out of the main room to the other side of the building.

'See, this will be the main lobby when people first come in. There's room for a merch stand here so bands can sell t-shirts and records. And through here is the brand-new toilet block. This cost more than anything else. We had to slice and dice the space up, leaving a void behind here, which I'll develop at some point. Once upon a time, it was two rooms, I think it was a verger's office, and the vicar's as well, or one of those sort of religious dudes. We boxed them off and knocked them through, then tiled the whole thing. It's basically one long corridor with eight bogs in.'

In white and black it looked very smart. Two big mirrors and four hand basins completed it.

'So this is the women's then?'

'Nope.'

'So you're not having any urinals for the men?'

'This isn't the gents either.'

Nick looked at him. Jeff was giving him his best cryptic look. 'So whose is it?'

'It's what they call gender neutral, just like your bog at home, anyone of either gender can use it. It's the way forward for bodily functions, brother. It'll have a sign on the door which says 'Toilets For All Humans'.

'Bloody hell. That is very progressive. Will everyone be happy with that? Do women want to piss in a cubicle next to men? Or vice versa.'

'Yeah, it'll be fine. Jo King turned me on to the idea of it. She was saying how if you've got gender-neutral bogs these days, it doesn't single out anyone who's different. I mean, she's totally been through the mill on that stuff while she was transitioning.' He pointed to his own mouth. 'I can't believe I'm saying these words, sometimes, y'know. I sound like a lesbian social worker.'

'We've all come a long way, man. This stuff about men who are women, women who are men, that was unknown to me and thee when we were kids.'

'Unknown to me until last year, really, when you think about it. And I couldn't have faced Jo if I'd not taken what she said on board. I mean, it just makes sense. She's coming to the opening night and is going to do something outrageous to help launch us. It's going to be a glittering affair. You and Jules will get VIP passes, of course.'

'Brilliant, I've never been a VIP.'

Jeff patted him on the back as they left the toilets. 'To me, you've always been a VIP, son: a very impressive prick.' He made a face at him and moved his bushy eyebrows up and down at speed.

'You know what?' said Nick, as they went back into the bar.

'What?'

'This is going to be a huge success. This is the start of something; something big.'

'Is this your precognition kicking in?'

'I have to be asleep for that.'

'Well, I hope you're right. I bloody well need to start getting some money in and quick. So a week today is opening night. I need lots of publicity, to get everyone to know about it. Big Fish is going to get TV here, though I've told him it's not the gig for his, ahem, broad humour. I'll put Jo on to do some butchery. I need to get a band which will not just get punters in but will make a big splash. I would have got Metal Road, if it was a year ago. Can't do that now.'

Nick felt excited and in feeling excited, realised how rarely he actually felt genuinely excited these days. Maybe adults don't. Or maybe it was just him. But this felt so open ended and so full of potential. And it was, when all said and done, an adventure into the arts, into music, comedy and who knew what else? And that was the good stuff about life. The stuff that made life worth living.

Bursting with pride for his oldest and best friend, he went over to the jukebox.

'C'mon let's have the first dance in this fine emporium to the arts,' he said.

'Me and you dancing? We haven't danced together since...'

'...since the Speed King incident, I know. The time we were sent to the headmaster's office for freaking out too much at a school disco. And that was 4th year at Ian Ramsey and if this massive Deep Purple fan is not mistaken, "Speed King" is on the B-side of this copy of "Black Night".' He lifted it off the short spindle and flipped it over and dropped the needle on it. As the music kicked in, they proceeded to not so much dance as go crazy, head shaking, with air guitar, air drums, air keyboards, all fully deployed, whirling around the club in a spasm of let-go freaking.

As the music ended, they came together in the middle of the floor. By instinct, they hugged each other, jumping up and down, just yelling and laughing.

Then they came back to themselves.

'Alright. That was great, but we shall never talk of this moment again,' said Jeff, clearing his throat and pushing his long greying hair behind his ears.

'Never. But it'll always be with me.'

Once home, Nick set about making slow-cooked short beef ribs for Julie and Emily, so there was something hot for them, whenever they came in. After browning the meat, he fried an onion, along with a whole bulb of garlic halved, added half a bottle of red wine, tomato puree and some powerful beef stock he'd made from roasting and boiling beef bones that he'd got from the butchers for free. After seasoning he added in the meat, covered the roasting dish with foil and stuck it in the oven on 170 degrees. It'd take a couple of hours but would only get better the longer it was left. He reflected again on how there was nothing more satisfying than cooking for the women in your life. He still couldn't work out why that was, but it just felt right and it always had done since the first time he'd cooked steak and chips for a girlfriend when he was still just 17, and not just because afterwards they'd spent ages excitedly dry humping in the front room. Maybe it had taught him that cooking for someone was an act of kindness or affection, and an act of basic generosity.

After he'd cleaned down the benches, the kitchen clock said it was 4pm. Late enough for a drink, surely. So he poured himself a vodka, added some fizzy water, lemon juice and ice, raised a silent toast to Jeff's Rock Club, the JRC and, once again felt a surge of pride and excitement. Jeff was amazing. Since his biological mother, Susan, had left him a legacy, he'd blossomed into what business types would call an entrepreneur. He'd pursued his passions. It was so brilliant to see. He felt the cold tingle of the drink on his throat. The opening night was going to be one hell of party. He texted Julie to tell her. She soon replied.

'Whoo! Great news. We're going to party like rock stars, baby!'

There was a knock at the door just before 6pm. Nick opened it to find Mandy Beale standing there in her loose, dark suit.

'Hi Mand...is everything alright?' said Nick, a swell of fear that something had happened to Julie or Emily rising up in his chest in an instant.

She gave a little wave at him. 'Don't panic. That's the trouble with being the filth, everyone thinks you've turned up to tell 'em summat bad. I've just come to collect that camera Julie mentioned in her text. I've also got two of my forensic lads round the back. They're going to the perp's little hideaway to see if we can get anything useful. They'll also dust the upstairs window and the mirror frame for prints. He probably kept gloves on but just in case he didn't, we'd better check, the bloody perv.'

'Yeah, of course. Julie's not back from work yet and we've got Emily staying with us, she'll be back from the shop soon.'

'Yeah, Jeff said. That's a good idea to get her out of that flat.'

He let her in, then went upstairs and got the camera.

'By god, it smells like a restaurant in here, Nick,' said Mandy, as he came back down. 'What's cooking?'

'Just some short beef ribs. I made a lot so you can stay for a plateful if you want.'

'Tempting, 'cos Jeff tells me you're a dab hand in the kitchen, but I'm working, aren't I? So tell me what 'appened wi' this camera business.'

'We just found it. Jules spotted a red light on it.' He gave her the pen-sized camera.

She looked at it in amazement. 'I know nowt about tech, me. I still think a computer is a telly with a typewriter attached. But this thing were filmin' and some 'ow sending it back to a computer?'

'Yeah. Then the video it took was posted onto the website that had had the photos on. Emily is a computer whiz, she hacked the server and wiped it. She kept a copy of it if your mob want to analyse it.'

'We will. I'll get her to send us that info. So what was on the film?'

'Last night me and Jules were...you know, being...' He was too embarrassed to say the words, so made forward and back gesture with his right arm. Mandy didn't seem to do embarrassment.

'OK, I get you, I get you...go on...'

'Well, so, it filmed us doing that. Then it was posted on the website with some obscenities about Julie underneath and saying she should be sacked.'

Mandy had an ability to express thorough disgust with a slightly raised eyebrow and a sneer in the corner of her mouth.

'Dirty bastard. Disgusting. We'll collar 'im, Nick. We will...he'll make a mistake and when he does, we'll 'ave him.'

'I'm worried, Mand. Like you said at the outset, this keeps escalating. It started with following, and peeping, then the photos, then he came in here and took her clothes and planted a camera. The next thing is...'

'...meeting her. I know what you're thinking.' She hissed air through her teeth. 'We need to pull him in, but until we catch him in the act, or get some DNA we can identify, it's not going to be easy. It's not like there's any CCTV we can pull to identify him. Let's see if the lads get anything.' She looked out of the window at two men in white forensic suits combing through the grass and overgrowth behind the bush. 'They might well pick up something which matches someone on our books.'

'I don't know if it's significant, but a bloke had a piss behind there the other night. I caught up with him, but I don't think he was our man. What happened with Matty Rhodes? Did you speak to him?'

'We did. Sent an officer to North Tees. He were all "I bought it in a pub off some bloke, didn't know what it was"...blah blah blah. He took an official warning. We told him to behave or risk being arrested for possession of Class A narcotics and for being a violent twat. We dressed it up in the legalese, but that's what it amounted to. I had a quick word with Emily in the shop and she was sure she didn't want to press charges and neither did Jeff for the ruck in the shop.'

'What would happen if I wanted to bring charges against him for hitting me?'

'Do you want to?'

'I would if it'd help anything.'

She counted her points off on her thick fingers. 'One, he'd get arrested and immediately bailed. Two, it'd eventually go to court and he'd plead guilty, but in mitigating circumstances, i.e., the drugs. It's his first offence, he'd get a fine. It'd take a lot of time up, cost us all money and he'd be fined maybe £500 at most.'

'So what you're telling me is, it's not worth it.'

She looked out the window again. 'No I'm not saying that. I never said that. I'm just telling you 'ow it is. It's not my job to tell civilians what to do. If you want to accuse him of assault you're entitled to do so.'

'Yeah, but what's the point if all that happens is he gets a slap on the wrist, told not to take drugs and has to cough up a few quid?'

'It makes it more likely he'll get put away if he does the same thing again. And he'd know that we've got an eye on him, though he knows that anyway.'

'Hmm. Look, I'm going to tell you something, but it has to be off the record.'

She smiled and revealed her large, wonky yellow teeth, in doing so. 'Funny how many of you lot...'

'...you lot? Who's you lot?'

'Civilians. You trot out stuff you've heard in movies, like it's the same as real life.'

'Well, how else do I say, I'm not telling you something as Mandy the top police dog but as Mandy the woman?'

'Bitch.'

'Eh?'

'I'm a top police bitch, not top police dog!' She bellowed a laugh so loud that it made her whole body shudder. The thick rolls of soft fat on her waist seemed to keep wobbling for a full minute. Sometimes, her degree of bluntness and aggression was surprising. 'So what do you want to tell me?'

'Emily is covered in bruises on her hips and thighs. I've seen them. I think Matty held her down and raped her. Jules has talked to her a lot and even got drunk with her, but she won't admit it; she says he's forced his "attentions" on her, but also says she's clumsy and walks into things, but you don't get bruises like that from walking into a table.' He pointed to his hip and inside of his thigh to indicate where Emily's bruises were located.

The smile slid off Mandy's face in an instant.

'Did he, now? Did this happen when he was drugged up?'

'Yeah, I think so. I'm guessing so. I don't know for sure. He might have been doing it for months for all we know. The bruises were spread out in five patches where he'd gripped her hard, held her down whilst he raped her.'

'The dirty shite.' Her suppressed righteous anger was a comfort, somehow.

'Yeah. I'm worried she's going to go back to him, if he promises to stop the drugs.'

She rolled her eyes. 'He's a good-looking lad. I can see why a lass like Emily would fall in love with him. But we're building quite a picture now. Obviously, she's not for pressing a rape charge.'

'Well, she's not admitted to either of us that she's even been raped. But things haven't been right between them for a month or more, according to Jeff.'

As he spoke, the front door opened and voices came in.

'Hey, here's my favourite policewoman,' said Julie, walking into the room, followed by Emily. 'Are you arresting this fella for being so gorgeous?' She squeezed him around the waist.

'I'm afraid so, it's actually illegal to be as sexy as Nick,' said Mandy, with a hoot. Emily sank to her knees and gripped his leg, kissing him up and down, landing a big one on his balls.

'OK, OK, I'm going into the kitchen. Let me know when the estrogen levels in the room have dropped down to acceptable levels,' he said, really hating being the centre of attention, closing the kitchen door behind him.

He threw some broccoli and carrots into boiling water and then took the ribs out, wrapped them in foil and put them to one side, straining the bits of onion and garlic out of the gravy, putting it in a pan and thickening it with a little flour. As he did so, Julie came in laughing. 'Aw, sorry, love.' She hugged him from behind and nibbled affectionately at his back. 'I know you hate that sort of situation.' She nuzzled into him. 'Smells lovely in here. What are we having?'

'Short rib of beef, slow cooked in red wine and stock.'

'Eee, my god. That's brill. They should call you Nick the Meat. Come here, you.' She spun him around and kissed him on the lips and whispered in his ear, 'I'm going to put your delicious meat in my mouth until all the juices ooze out.' Her sapphire blue eyes had a glint to them, her pupils dilated to a big black circle and maybe she was even breathing a little heavier. Sometimes Nick almost felt like she smelt different in these sex-fuelled moments; that was probably just his over-fertile imagination, though.

Emily came into the kitchen and looked up from her phone. 'Oh, sorry. Were you having an adult moment?' she said, seeing them in each other's arms.

'You're alright. Are you ready to eat?' said Nick.

'Yes, please. I've not had anything since you made me brekkie.'

'Silly girl,' said Julie, reluctantly taking her hands off Nick. 'You've got to look after yourself and eat properly.'

'I said that earlier, didn't I, Em?' said Nick.

'Yes father, yes mother,' said Emily, stroppily sitting down at the table, looking at her phone. 'Mandy is out the back with the forensic dudes. They're coming in here in a bit. Can I cadge a glass of wine, by any chance?' She asked while scrolling down a social media website.

Nick looked in the fridge. 'There's half a bottle of chablis left. You two got through best part of four bottles the other night.' He poured her some. It frosted the glass with condensation.

'Cheers,' said Emily, taking a sip. 'Are you not having one, Jules?'

'I'll wait until I've eaten. Don't want to get too drunk, I've got to go and look through my diaries, which could be a bit traumatic. Last thing I want to do is get all pissed and maudlin.'

'Why do you have to do that?' said Emily, tucking her small feet up into her and sitting cross-legged on the big pine kitchen chair, resting her phone on her lap, constantly checking the screen.

'I'm going to try and narrow down who might have taken those photos of me and exactly when.'

'Can you honestly not remember anything like that happening?' she said.

'Nope. But I only had that Courtney Love look for about six or seven weeks over Christmas and New Year of 1991 and 1992.'

'I thought it suited you, or at least...well...not in those photos, obviously, but you know what I mean,' said Emily, as Nick began to serve the ribs, pouring the thickened gravy over them and then putting buttered vegetables on the plate. She began texting at speed, her little thumbs quickly sending a short message.

'These look amazing, kidda. What a clever boy. No, Em, I just couldn't pull the Courtney haircut off. I also ended up looking a bit of a fan girl for her, and that seemed lame for someone who was 27.'

'Was this when you were living in London?'

'Yeah, I'd just moved down there in the summer. It was really exciting. I shared a cheap shit-hole flat in Hoxton, but got more money in wages than I'd earned before and so I was out every night, virtually.'

'So you could have gone home with someone...'

Julie interrupted Emily '...pissed as a fart, woke up the next day none the wiser about any photos that had been taken of me in any situation at all. That or I was drugged. I suspect the latter. To be honest, I don't think I'll learn much from the diaries, but I've got to do something to try and move this on. I'm not even sure if the photos and break-in are even related. Whatever, the bastards aren't going to get away with it.'

'It might not be just a creepy lone man,' said Emily. 'There were two different hands pointing at you and judging by all the amount of spu...err...you know, stuff, on you, I think it was three men.'

Julie closed her eyes and shuddered.

'They must have cleaned you up, or you would surely have been suspicious,' said Emily, one eye still on her phone.

'Maybe, or I would just have woke up hungover, by which time it'd all have dried. I'd have staggered to the shower and never have known what happened. Well, that's obviously what did happen.'

'Can we not talk about this over food, please,' said Nick, feeling more than a little squeamish.

'Oh, god, this is delish,' said Julie. 'The meat is falling off the bone. So tender. Aw, god it's lush. Honest, Mike the Meat would be happy with this. The sauce is absolutely superb. Honest, I've had expensive meals in London restaurants nowhere as good as this.'

She grinned at him and hunched her shoulders up and down in pleasure.

It was especially delicious. So delicious that he couldn't help but feel a bit proud of himself.

'Yeah, it's very nice. So, do you still keep a diary, Jules?' asked Emily.

'Not everyday, but I don't go more than a week without writing something. I used to be very religious about it. Even when I was out all night, the next day I'd catch up on the entry. Trouble is, there are some things you don't really want to be reminded of. So I never really go through them. But I've got them going back to about 1976 when I'd have been 12.'

'They're very detailed,' said Nick. 'The one I looked at, anyway. There are numbers and codes all over them.'

'Yeah, well, I developed a shorthand for expressing things to speed writing things up, way before LOL and all of that was invented.'

'Like what?' Em said.

'Err...let's see. WTS was went to school. RWM was row with mam. TMK was think mam knows. Later, I had some sexual ones. TDF was too drunk to fuck. CGIU was couldn't get it up. Not complicated stuff.'

Nick grinned. 'You're a texting pioneer, Jules. You didn't invent emoticons as well, did you?'

She put her spoon down while she chewed. 'Not exactly. I did go through a phase when I was 17 or 18 of drawing penises in my diary to remind me of what the latest one I'd seen was like.'

Emily giggled, but was distracted again by an urgent need to text someone on her phone. After every fork full, she'd stop and send another one or flick at the screen. It was as though she kept leaving the room, so absorbed was she in the phone. Like a frustrated parent, Nick found himself getting narked by her inability to stop using the damn thing for five minutes. It actually felt like an insult to the time, effort and skill he'd put into the meal.

'Who are you talking to?' he said.

'Oh, no-one you know,' she said.

He glanced at Julie, she twitched an eyebrow ever so slightly, clearly also thinking what Nick was thinking. He contemplated snatching it off her, but that would only mean confrontation and he really didn't want that and it'd do no good anyway.

There was a knock at the back door and Mandy put her head around. 'Sorry to interrupt, just need to dust in the bedroom for prints.'

'Sure. I'll show you where the camera was,' said Julie.

They trooped off upstairs.

'Have you heard from Matty today?' said Nick as Em began tapping at the phone again.

'Uh huh.'

'Was he saying sorry for being a bastard?'

'Uh huh.'

'That's usually what bastards do.'

'Uh huh.'

She just tapped away and didn't even look up at him, playing a straight bat that Geoff Boycott would have been proud of.

'I know you're looking at me disapprovingly,' she said, head still tilted to the screen. 'But I told you, I don't need looking after by you or anyone else. I don't know how many times I have to say that. It's getting very, very annoying.'

Soon enough they all came back downstairs and the two forensic men took Nick and Julie's prints to rule them out.

'Right kids, that's us done,' said Mandy. 'We'll let these lads get off and do their jiggery-pokery and see what they come up with.'

'Sure you won't stay for a beef rib?' said Nick. 'There's two left. They're really good.'

The two men left.

Mandy licked her lips. 'Sod it, I've not had a decent meal for a few days. Go on then. Cheers, Nick.

She pulled up a chair while he got the last two ribs out and slathered them in sauce. 'There's not a lot of veg left, I'm afraid,' he said.

'Thank god for that,' said Mandy and bellowed a laugh.

He put the plate of meat and veg in front of her. 'There you go.'

'Cheers, Nick. Must be great having a fella who can cook, Jules,' said Mandy slicing into the meat.

'Aye, you're not wrong there. I'm fed like a queen. Honest, he amazes me. Just does simple stuff, but does it perfectly. Everything from fish to liver to this hot and spicy Vietnamese rice noodle broth he does.'

Mandy put a huge fork full of the soft meat into her capacious mouth. 'Bloody hell, this is delicious.' She put a thumb up at Nick. Within two or three minutes she'd eaten the whole lot.

'Well, I'm glad I stayed now. Excellent. Thanks, Nick.'

'No worries. Glad you liked it.'

Mandy then turned to Emily.

'Emily, while I've got you here, I need a word about Matty. I can do it in private, if you want.'

Emily looked up from her phone with a wide-eyed sneer. 'Not you as well! Everyone wants to tell me things about him and about me.' She snapped at the police chief. 'Go on then. What? What is it? You can say anything you want in front of Nick and Julie. I don't give a shit. But, y'know, don't feel obliged. I'm fine and I'll deal with everything on my own without all you lot sticking your unwanted oars in!'

Mandy, raised her eyebrows, unimpressed.

'Nice little speech. Now listen to me, madam,' She leaned over the table. 'He's been buying crystal meth for quite a while. He might not have used it around you, but we pulled in his dealer this morning, with a little help from Hair Bear's inside knowledge. Long story short, he described Matty to a tee as one of his regulars. He's not a big dealer, he's little more than a gofer for some proper big dealer in the area. Probably sells in return for a free supply of whatever he wants. Anyway, he said he'd started topping up his usual cocaine order - which I'm not happy to hear about, either - with meth and other pills, such as rohypnol. And I'm sure you know why men buy that. Now, I'm not accusing you of nowt, Emily, but we've got a bloody cocaine epidemic on Teesside.'

Emily sat sullenly staring at the policewoman, as she went on. 'Every bloody scumbag here is using the bloody stuff. There's more cocaine in the water here than anywhere else in Europe, because so many people take it and are pissing it out. I know it might seem all bloody rock 'n' roll, but it's not. It messes people up and I can't tell you how many heart attacks I've seen induced by it. You're a good kid, with some solid mates around you, don't end up being a druggie and don't get mixed up again with that lad again. I'm telling you, he's riding the sodding crazy train, that one, and sooner or later he'll be trouble.'

Emily stood up, now red-faced and indignant, her voice at high pitch. Leaning over the table she fearlessly stared Mandy down.

'Are you done lecturing me? Done telling me how to live my life? Are you?!' She was shouting now. 'Anyone else want to tell me who I should see and who I shouldn't see? Everyone seems to want to do that these days.' She leaned forward again and jabbed a small finger at Mandy. 'You do know you're treating me like I'm 12 years old, don't you? Like I don't know anything. You haven't a clue what it's like to be me and you've haven't a clue what I've been through or what I'm going through, but you're all quick enough to tell me what to do. Well, fuck you all! I'll do what I want. I always have and I always will.' She spun around and marched out, with her bag on her shoulder. The front door slammed behind her.

CHAPTER 11

They all looked at each other in a silent moment. 'Did I make a total balls of that?' said Mandy.

'Yeah, you totally did,' said Julie. 'That was the absolute wrong way to handle her. You should've asked me or Nick to say something.'

'I'm not sure that'd have helped, actually,' said Nick. 'She was very narky earlier. She's been building up to that.'

Mandy was unsympathetic. 'She's been living with a man who is buying a fairly large amount of cocaine - which I assume she's also been using - and he's now moved on to meth. He's also bought date rape drugs on at least one occasion. She's got no parental influence here, so she needs warning, 'cos pound to a penny, he'll get her on the meth soon enough. You mark my words. And if what Nick says about those bruises is right, my guess is he's got rohypnol so he can rape her all the more easily because she's fought back. In other words, the boy is a total scummer and needs locking up!'

Nick didn't say anything but he knew for a fact Emily had used cocaine quite a bit.

'Alright, but you don't know her like we do. She's a strong-willed lass. And she's right, just because she's petite, we do treat her like she's a kid. She's 24. When I was 24 I wouldn't have taken a lecture like that from you, I'd have given you two fingers,' said Julie.

'I suspect she's been texting Matty today and that she's now gone to meet him, almost as a rebellion against you. Which worries the shite out of me,' said Nick.

Mandy shook her head and swore under her breath. 'I'm not exactly a bloody mother hen. And after what you'd told me about those bruises I just wanted to warn her off him...'

'...that's not how it works. I have women who are abused by their partners and husbands for literally years. It's very hard for some of them to leave. Some do leave and then they go back, time and again...it's complex, Mandy.'

That infuriated Mandy. 'Well they bloody shouldn't! I've only got so much sympathy. There comes a time when you owe it to yourself to do the right bloody thing and if you won't, then don't ask me to cry for you when my lot 'ave to scrape you off the bloody wall.' She was furious now, shouting loudly. 'I'll bloody tell you this, I sodding well know what's going to happen to that lass. She likes the bad boys. And 'e's one of those. He's a wrong' un. And it's sodding fatal. One day I'm going find her half dead somewhere. Beaten up, doped up and raped. I've seen it time and time and time again. Nice lassy, gets in wi' the wrong bloke. He corrupts her, she becomes dependent on him for everything and it all ends up down the bloody pan and a good woman's life gets ruined.' She was ranting at a fast pace.

'She's not that stupid,' said Nick, while privately worrying she was right. His dream came back to him powerfully, once again. He could still clearly see her lying there, the knife between her shoulder blades, the river of blood down her back.

Mandy yelled him down. 'The 'ell she isn't! She's got a big decision to make soon, that one. Take the wrong choice and in six months 'er life will be ruined by the meth and by god knows what else. I fear for 'er, I bloody do.' She got up and marched through the house to the front door. 'Now excuse me while I go round to her flat, see if I can find her doped-up boyfriend and get 'im off the bloody streets before he starts raping people again!' She slammed the front door behind her.

Nick turned to Julie. 'Bloody hell, I've never seen Mandy like that. She was steaming mad.'

'Urghh. I had hoped she'd be a bit more understanding about why abused women don't leave. But the worse thing is, I think she's right. Well, about Emily being on a slippery slope, anyway. I think she has been all the time we've known her. I think she's very vulnerable and she's got abuse issues that she's just not addressed and won't face.'

'I have wondered if the amount of tattoos she's got in the last year, is in inverse proportion to her amount of self-respect or self-belief. I know our generation sees tattoos differently but she's taken it to something of an extreme. And it pretty much all coincides with her relationship with him. Maybe it's been a bad relationship from the start. Like you said, you never know what goes on behind closed doors.'

'Hmm, mind, they are lovely tats, though. I mean, the colours are amazing. The rainbow that circles around the top of her arm is great,' said Julie.

'The red and black roses and thorns that are on her arse and thighs are really works of gothic art,' he said.

'Well, I've not seen them, largely because she's not interested in showing me that area of her body, because to do so wouldn't be sexual and I think she's always trying to assert her sexuality. It's one thing to be mildly flirtatious, it's another to show yourself naked to someone, or to expose your tits or whatever. The more I've thought about it, the more it worries me, because one day, she'll do it to someone less morally upstanding than you, they'll say it's a huge come-on, will grab her, rape her and then will get other sleazeball mates in to do likewise and they'll get away with it, because all a bastard lawyer has to do is point to her behaviour. She's insecure and drugs can get you over that. And we know she's used cocaine, which is ideal in those circumstances. You fall in love with a man, he moves in and then you're hooked into that relationship and will do anything to keep it going, because if it fails, then you fail and you live down to your self-identity as a loser. The more I think of it, the more we should have picked up on this much earlier. Christ, it's hard trying to look after someone's best interests. This is what we missed out on by not having kids.'

'True. It must be very stressful, like, I'm worried all the time.' He ran his hands through his hair. Right, I'll get us drinks and then we'll go through your diaries and look for names.'

She puffed out her cheeks. 'OK, the future's in the past, as Sammy Hagar once said.'

He patted her on the backside. 'A woman who quotes Chickenfoot songs. This is why I love you.'

'You might not love me quite so much when you see the diaries.'

'Don't be daft. If they're not full of drinking tales and wild sex with rampant stallion-like men, I'll be disappointed.'

'Pah. Don't judge men by your own standards, lad. There are very few of them around, I can tell you that for nowt.'

He fixed them both a drink and then went up to the bedroom. Julie had taken a trunk out from under the bed. It was full of old notebooks. On the front of each in black felt pen were the dates it covered.

She took a long drink. 'Think I'm going to need a couple of these to cope with the sins of my past.'

'Oh, don't be daft. It is the trunk of your life, though.'

'I'm looking for late 1991...and here we are. December 1991 to April 1992. Luckily it was on the top.'

'Huh. What are the odds? There must be hundreds of notebooks in here.'

It was a red ring-binder book. She took another drink, sat on the bed and flicked through the pages.

'I'll have noted when I got my hair done. I always do, even now.'

Nick stood at the window and looked out. No-one was behind the bush. He rolled the gin and tonic around his mouth, feeling worried, a gnawing edge in his guts. He kept thinking of the man coming into their nice bedroom. He shivered. No-one who was right in the head would do that.

"Just trust your instincts, Nick."

He shook his head as though to dislodge his mother's advice.

'Here we are. "Went to Toni & Guy's and got the Courtney haircut. Not really sure it suits me. I look more like a druggy hooker. Gina says I look like a rock star. Hmmm." Gina was a very strait-laced woman I worked with. She thought tight jeans were virtually obscene.'

She sat, eyes flicking from side to side, reading her neat handwriting.

'Anything significant?' said Nick.

'It's funny, life seems very flat and boring when laid out in a diary. Listen to this. "Went to work, argument about north/south divide with Alan D. Had chicken salad for dinner. Went to Silver's for drinks after work. Had cranberry and vodka. Delish. Cab home. HAW"...that means, had a wank. Ha ha...I was going through a loveless phase.'

She kept skimming pages.

'I wasn't even going out with anyone in December 1991 or in January 1992. At first, I really didn't like Southern blokes, Sounds shallow, I know, but I really didn't. They didn't sit right with me. Seemed all mouth and trousers.'

'Every Northerner that goes to the south, finds their Northern voice more strongly, I think.'

She didn't respond and was pulling at her bottom lip a little, then tapped at the book with her nail.

'I went to a Christmas party on 21st December, which was our last day at work for two weeks. Then the next day, the 22nd...yes...I remember this, it says, "Met a bloke called Tommy Green in the Red Admiral. Works in publishing. Had a nice smile. WMAF." Which means...'

'...wouldn't mind a fuck?' interrupted Nick.

'Exactly. I don't know why I've stuck with the acronym thing. I only invented it to hide stuff from mam, as I knew she'd read my diary.'

'Do you still do it?'

She looked up at him and grinned. 'Yeah, it's totally a habit now.'

She turned over a page. 'Yes, here we go. I do remember this. On the 23rd it says, "Went to Oregano Wine Bar with Yvonne and Celia. TG was in. They had to catch a train, so I stayed and talked to him again. He was quite intense and went on about his work at lot. But he is very, very cute. He works at a publishers called Storyville." Hey that's funny, that's who you went to. I wonder if he still works there? Wouldn't it be funny if you'd met him?'

'Not just funny, it'd have been weird. But I didn't. The bloke I met was Tim Forest. Anyway, there's no way he'd still work there after 20 years. I bet they've shed loads of staff in the last five years alone. Publishing is going down the pan.'

'Yeah, you're probably right.' She found her place again. 'Err...ah, right, here we get some rudeness. Are your loins girded?'

'At all times.'

'It says, "Went back to mine. Drank vodka and wine. Urgh. Why? Asked him if he wanted to get in my knickers. He was surprised and said something patronising about 'northern girls being forward' which nearly put me off him. Wish now it had. At first I panicked as I'd forgotten I had put big Period Pants on by accident due to being hungover in the morning. Changed into little sex pants in the bathroom. Got down to it. Average size. He said he hadn't done it for ages. Got hold of him and he came almost immediately. Couldn't stop himself. Didn't even get it in. Oops. He was embarrassed and almost sort of angry. I said it didn't matter and that we could do it in the morning, which I thought was v good of me. Was a bit relieved as I felt a bit sick and dizzy from mixing drinks. In the morning there was no foreplay, in case he came too quickly. Boring. He lasted about minute. Didn't even touch the sides. Was all about him. Paid no attention to me at all. I tried to be nice about it, but he seemed annoyed at me again. Said something pathetic like it was my fault for being so sexy. It's not my fault you can't control yourself, son. All a bloody waste of time. Worried he's a clingy sort. Had that intense thing about him. Think he'll be sniffing around me now. Will have to give him the hard word if he does. Why don't I make better choices?" '

'In a way, that's a bit sad,' said Nick.

But she just shrugged. 'Nah, not really. It was just normal life and I wasn't so bothered about it at the time. You're throwing the dice, aren't you? You fancy someone, but it turns out you're not compatible sexually, or in any other way. I do remember Tommy Green quite clearly, now. He was nice looking and quite clever, but he got really defensive with me because he couldn't hold back. I mean, I wasn't a kid and it had happened

164

to another bloke I'd been with and we just laughed about it. It's not the be all and end all.'

She thought about it a bit more.

'As far as I recall, he seemed to treat sex like it was a competition and felt that he'd failed the test.' She chewed on her bottom lip, staring into the middle distance. 'In the morning, it was like he wanted to prove to me he could actually do it, y'know, like I even cared, but it was still over really quickly. Then he repeated the whole, "well what do you expect, you're too sexy" thing, but not in a fun way, in a defensive, angry way, like it really was all my fault. I should've left my big knickers on, might have put him off. Ha! He was making a fuss over nothing. Being able to laugh at yourself and your body's failings is one of the first rules of being a decent human, I reckon.'

'So did you run across him again?'

She frowned, trying to recollect, counting days off on her fingers. 'Well that morning was Christmas Eve. I got the train to Teesside later in the day and was there until the New Year. After that, I saw him around for a week or two or maybe more, but then he must have moved or something, as I never saw him again, thankfully.'

'So he didn't get clingy, as you thought?'

She shook her head. 'No, I must've scared him off with the Hardwick hard stare.'

'Your hard stare scares me.'

'So it bloody should.'

'Ok, so given this happened just before Christmas when you had the haircut, it can't have been long before the photos were taken. Do you think this bloke Tommy Green was capable of being part of that?'

She scrunched her face up, making deep crow's feet appear at the corner of her eyes.

'God, it's impossible to say. But how could he have done that without me meeting him again?'

'Easy. He's mates with someone else you met, who drugs you, then he calls Tommy up and they do the deed. For Tommy it was a kind of act of revenge on you.'

She bit her bottom lip, thinking. 'Yeah, he definitely felt humiliated, though I gave him no reason to feel like that. I've never done that with a bloke, not even the worst shaggers. It's just a no-no. Same as being disparaging about their dangly bits, even if it looks like a tiny mutant worm, it's not like he had a choice in it, so you can't have a pop at him for that.

Also, I figured out early that you're in a vulnerable position on those occasions, so you're best not winding a bloke up, in case he turns nasty.'

'Did you tell any girlfriends about him popping his cork at top speed? Maybe word got around and that angered him.'

'I probably told Angie, who was my best mate at work. But only in a quick jokey way. It just wasn't that big a deal. It really wasn't. I didn't have those sorts of friends who sit around in the pub swapping tales of Men I Have Slept With, like a vulgar hen night. I got over all of that sort of showing off by the time I went to college.' She gave him a flat smile and patted his leg. 'Are you sure you're OK about this talk of my old lovers?'

'I'm just being grown up, Jules. It's all in the past and it's actually quite inspiring for writing. OK, so there's no-one else you had a one-night stand with before you got rid of the Courtney hair?'

'No-one, no.' She went through the diary and pointed at an entry marked 29th January 1992. 'Here it is. "Went to Toni & Guy. New hairdo is straight and a bit shorter, a bit like Suzanne Vega a couple of years ago. Feels a bit sensible, but prefer it. Don't look like a smack head, at least! Bye bye black mascara." '

He took the book from her and turned over the pages going back through January.

'You're very thorough. There's an entry on every day.'

'It was quite therapeutic. Felt like I put the day to bed each day by writing about it.'

'What happened here then?' He pointed at the pages. The left was dated 5th January, the next, 7th January. 'Where's the 6th gone?'

She took it off him and, frowning, inspected the ring binding on the notebook. 'It's been sodding well torn out! I wouldn't have torn it out. And I *would* have made an entry.'

'Would you have written the 6th entry on the 7th?'

'I would have if I was out on the 6th.' She read the next day's short entry. 'Hmm, this is interesting. All it says is, "Woke up feeling knackered. Must've drank a lot again. Starting a three day detox. Been too heavily on the piss, I think. Got to stop drinking for a bit. Exhausted from it." Now, I'd have written that on 7th, probably after I'd written the 6th entry. As I don't refer to anything that happened on the 6th on subsequent days, I can't have had any memory of anything weird happening. So the 6th must have said something like, "Did shopping, was cold weather, went for a drink in Oregano wine bar." So why it was torn out must be

166

because of where it located me, or because it was a note of who I saw, not because it stated I'd been assaulted or raped. If I knew anything about it at all, there'd be other mentions on other pages, but there isn't.'

'Any other memories from early 1992?'

She shook her head. 'Could you remember how much you were drinking in any given week nearly 20 years ago?'

'I can't remember anything from a week ago.'

'Like I said, I was on Teesside from Christmas Eve to the New Year and then gone back to London on the 2nd. I always did that.'

'So it seems likely, after over a week away, you'd have got back to London, met up with friends and had a bit of a night out to catch up.' He looked back two pages. 'Yeah, you got the train on the 2nd. Home at 10pm. You met someone called Ruth on the 3rd, went out for pizza.'

'Ruth Hamer. I lost touch with her. She was a teacher, married a Kiwi and moved to New Zealand. Loved the Byrds.'

'Classy. You went back to work on the 4th. There's some stuff about a case FBJ has taken. Who's that?'

'Frank Borthwick-Jones. I was his PA.'

'What was he like?'

'Old school. He was about 60. He'd been a Communist in the 70s and was still very left wing, very anti-establishment, even though he was quite posh.'

'Sounds interesting.'

A warm smile broke across her face. 'Yeah, I loved him. He was a father figure to me and taught me a lot. I was 27 when I went down there and he seemed so old and wise and had such a powerful sense of right and wrong. He hated people with money and power being sneery about the poor and the working class. We did a lot of employment tribunals and such. Famously, he once suggested that anyone who was poor that didn't steal from a multinational employer was an idiot because, the company was, in effect, stealing their labour from them, by paying low wages.'

'I like the sound of him.'

'Yeah, died in 1999. I went to his funeral. We were all in bits.'

Nick read on. 'On the 5th you talk about the case again, you were also worried you were getting fat...'

'...I was. I remember that. I thought all the boozing was putting weight on my belly and thighs, but it was more likely to have been all the bloody pasta I was eating. I still thought eating pasta was quite posh back

167

then, especially fresh pasta. Thought I was a bit of a foodie 'cos I knew what pesto was. Seriously.'

'Oh, we were all like that. I went out with a girl who thought that because I could cook a chickpea stew, that I was a Michelin-starred chef.'

'Oh, god, chickpeas!' She made a rasping noise. 'They make me fart like nothing else. Virtually gassed myself first time I ate them. Dreadful things.'

'They do bloat you up.' He finished reading the 5th entry, skipped forward to the 7th, 8th and 9th. She was right. There was no mention of all of what had happened on the 6th.

'You've documented every day you had the Courtney Love haircut other than 6th January, so I think we have to assume that's the day the photos were taken on. And that in turn means that someone has removed the page in this to protect themselves, and they did it when they broke in here. That's why the diary was on the top of the pile, obviously.'

They sat in silence, pondering this new horrible intrusion.

'Actually if you think about it, this is good to know because it once and for all ties the photos to the current stalking. The same person was responsible or involved in both. We weren't sure if the two things were connected, but there can't be any doubt about it now and you know what, that almost certainly rules out it being a disgruntled ex of someone local, at least not unless they're local now, but weren't back then,' said Nick. 'Mandy said it was Londoner, remember. That's why they didn't know about your brothers.'

'But taking a page out of the diary makes little sense. How could they know I just wouldn't remember whatever it was, regardless of the diary. I mean, I can't, but they don't know that.'

'Yeah, but if there was a court case, a credible contemporaneous account might be enough to help convict them, even if it was just to locate you somewhere where they were, or even a half-remembered incident might jog a bigger memory. I bet you that on the 7th when you wrote the 6th entry, you remembered something you'd done and seen that connects you to the men who abused you and took the photos, even though you thought nothing of it, due to having no recollection of anything. As far as you knew, you just had a hangover. No need to take it out otherwise. And they must have known you'd likely have recorded it in the diary.'

She rubbed her eyes. 'OK, but how did they know I even kept a diary, and more than that, how did they know I would still have them and then where they would be in the house?'

Nick let some thoughts coalesce in his brain. It returned to him that his mother had said he knew who was responsible if he would only let himself realise it.

'You know, this really narrows down who it was who broke in here, because it has to be someone who knew you quite well, at some point. Well enough to tell them you kept a diary. You'd not do that with a one-night stand would you?'

'Seems unlikely, but you never know. I might have done.'

'No, this can't be a stranger. It's not some random pervert. They knew back then that you kept a diary and that you had done so for years, so it was probable that you still did and that you'd have kept them all. No-one who religiously keeps a diary for a long time wants to throw out their diaries at any point, because it'd be like throwing away your life. You've never considered throwing them away, them have you?'

'No, of course not.'

'OK and this is a smallish house, so finding them wouldn't have taken long and they had all day anyway. Under the bed or top of the wardrobe would be the first two places I'd look. Diaries belong in a bedroom. People don't keep their diary in the living room or spare bedroom, it's too open to public scrutiny. Everyone keeps them in the bedroom because visitors don't go into the bedroom.'

'That's good thinking. The gin must be making you brainy, lad.'

They sat in silence again for some time, thinking it over, both taking a big drink.

His mother was so sure he knew who was responsible. Maybe, if he could just trust his instincts, he really did. He tried to let the information come to him, rather than think it up. Maybe this was like trying to lose your ego by meditation; the same process of disengagement from the everyday waking reality of physical existence.

So he let his mind go as blank as possible by closing his eyes and breathing slowly and deeply. After a minute he opened them. It was impossible to stop thinking. Impossible to become a blank vessel. There was too much consciousness to get in the way, everything from an itch on his foot to the damp sweat patches on his t-shirt armpits.

But even so...something occurred to him, not in a blinding flash as such, but more of a tide of realisation.

'I think all of this is down to the exact same people. I'm sure it is, in fact. It's the same people then and now. And I think there are three of them.'

169

She clinked ice in her glass, frowning as she did so. He went on.

'We know those photos date from 6th January. Something happened to you on that day which you've got no memory of and after which you must have woken up and just thought you'd been drunk, hence your 7th January pledge to detox. That means it must have happened in your flat, so when you woke up, you just thought you'd passed out after a drinking session, or whatever. You weren't suspicious at all. It also means there were no witnesses who could have said something about it to you. You shared a house, didn't you?'

'Yeah it was a four-bedroomed flat in Hoxton. The other three girls were LSE students.'

'Right, actually that explains why there were no witnesses who might have seen you being brought home unconscious or wrecked. No-one to ask, "Were you OK last night?" It was the first week of January, students were probably still away, term wouldn't start until the following week. So you were alone in the flat.'

She pointed and nodded at him. 'You're right. I was. I remember I liked it because it was quiet for a change. The three girls were all hand-bags, dance music and short skirts. Not really my sort.'

He got up and walked around the bedroom in contemplation, standing at the window.

'OK, so that means, at least one of the three men knew where you lived. And that means it was someone you knew, or someone you'd already had around your flat. So here's a theory, right? We've got one person who has created the website and uploaded the old photos, one who has taken the new photos up here and we've got the peeper who broke in, took your clothes and planted the camera. How many people is that? Three. Alright, it *might* just be one person, but it's three different sorts of commitment. And taking on board what Mandy said, the other day, they're all from London - or at least not from around here, because if they were, they'd be afraid of your brothers. After what they did at MIMA everyone in this area knows about them. Right? Now, I know this is nasty, but the reason I think it's three people that abused you in 1992 is evidenced on the pictures, just as Emily said.'

Getting out his phone and loading the photos that had been on the website, he sat beside her on the edge of the bed. 'Looking at these...and I'm just going to say this, Jules, as horrible as it is...there are clearly three lines of ejaculation.' He pointed at the screen. 'There's one from the left over your breasts, one from the right doing likewise, and one between

170

your legs and up your belly, where all three trails meet. You can see that must have been intentional. It's like a brotherhood thing. It's quite clear. You can see the direction they've each done it. So there's no way one or two people could have done that. Two were standing either side of you, one between your legs. They've done it together and at the same time. A team sport, if you like. Being a rapist team is part of the thing they like. All getting off on it together. And the photo of your vagina features two different index fingers pointing to you, so the third must have taken the shot. Yeah, there was definitely three people involved in this. And now, there's three people doing your stalking. It all makes sense. Now we're getting somewhere.'

'Why couldn't the peeper also be taking new photos of me and uploading them?'

'He could be. Yeah. It could be a solo job, but it was a collective effort in 1992 and to me, for whatever reason, this looks like three old friends getting back together to do what they did before.'

She looked doubtful.

'If that's true, there has to be something which provoked them to do it now, doesn't there? I'm still sure it's something to do with my work because of what was written on the website about me. It even said "sack her now". Why would it say that if it was the same three people as before? They wouldn't care what my job was. Those words are part of a grudge.'

Nick nodded. That was certainly true. She went on.

'At work, we know that perps always look for a woman's vulnerabilities, in order to exert power over her. They'll pick on something she's insecure about. It could be her appearance or just the fact she likes doing a hobby. He'll make her feel bad and then stop her doing something she likes to do. Now, to me, this looks like they think my sex life is that vulnerability. They think they can paint me as some sort of loose woman and thus discredit me in my job. To such men, women are often seen as either madonnas or whores and I'm no madonna, thank god, not least because I'd look rubbish in one of those pointy bra things.' But neither of them felt like laughing at her joke.

'Maybe the partner of a woman you've worked with was one of the original bad guys in 1992 in London. Or maybe the original three know someone up here with a grudge against you?'

She took a drink. 'I see women who've moved to the area from all over the place, so that's not totally impossible, but it is an unlikely coincidence.'

'OK, so look through your last couple of months' case notes and find someone who is from London. There can't be many. What about Hardwick Aggie's brother, Kenny? Did he move down there, by any chance?'

She stopped and looked up at him, eyes wide. 'I think he did, yeah! Oh shit. He worked at Barclaycard in Stockton and then got transferred down south for some reason. I don't remember the details but mam definitely said something about it.'

Picking up her phone, she called Jackie immediately.

'Mam. Did Kenny Harlow move down to London in the early 90s?' She sat and listened, making little agreement noises. 'So it was like some sort of short-term secondment? A temporary transfer? Right. So Edie wouldn't have gone with him? Right...Ok, thanks, mam. No, no...I'll tell you later. No, they've been taken off. Aye. Alright. Ta-ra.'

She looked over to him. 'He was down there over Christmas and New Year 91 into 92. Came back at Easter 1992! How about that?! He must be involved.'

'Are you sure Jackie is remembering that correctly? I'm hopeless at dates. Seems odd she'd remember it that precisely.'

'She seemed sure.'

'But Jackie doesn't do doubt or nuance. Her world is black and white. Right or wrong.'

'She said he was sent down there by Barclaycard but Edie stayed up here as they didn't want to take the kids out of school.'

They went downstairs. Nick poured them another drink and joined her on the sofa with his laptop, putting a pile of cushions in place of the one which was at the dry cleaners.

'This room smells of Emily,' he said, sniffing the cushion. 'What is that smell?'

'She wears that Kiss, perfume, doesn't she?'

'Kiss? As in the band, Kiss?'

'Yeah, it's quite nice, actually.'

'It is quite nice. Unlike Kiss, ironically enough.'

'No, I never got into them. Put your tongue away, Gene, lad. We're not impressed.' She spoke almost under her breath, as she flicked through information on her laptop.

Nick went to Julie's Facebook page, logged out so he wouldn't be recognised as a friend of hers and then viewed what was publicly available to see. There wasn't much. Just a profile picture of her that he'd taken outside of Middlesbrough Town Hall before a Joe Bonamassa gig earlier in the year. It wasn't even a close up, just a shot from the knees upwards, hands in old jeans pockets, looking scruffy in a loose, green and blue plaid shirt, head slightly to one side, relaxed and grinning in a silly, toothy way and clearly having a good time. He looked at it for a few moments, wondering how anyone could look at that photo and take against someone with a such a nice, fun nature? Maybe that was exactly why.

'Why did you choose that picture for your profile?'

She leaned over and took a look. 'I don't know. I thought I looked OK in it, I suppose. And we had a great night, didn't we? We'd had a few by then and the gig was magic. It's a nice memory.'

He went back to her Facebook page. 'You've got this pretty much all locked down as far as privacy goes. There's nothing to see unless you accept someone as a friend and even then, it's not like you've posted much.'

'Well, that's how we're advised to run our social media at work and I'm careful which friend requests I accept. I mean, I can't accept them from service users or family. I've got it set so you can't find me by searching on Facebook for my name. But if someone wants to find you, they can still do it via other people's Friends list, if it's left on a public setting. It's not that hard. I don't even click "like" on any public posts because my name could be found by a search that way.'

'Really? I didn't know about any of that.'

'You can't stop service users posting something that might compromise you, though obviously, we give advice on that sort of thing. But it's all a bit of a minefield and operates on common sense, as much as anything. At the end of the day, it's only as secure as the weakest link in the chain. Anyone determined enough and with a little bit of info on you could find out where you live or work.'

He went to his own page and viewed what was publicly visible. He had been far less careful and a lot of what he had posted over the past year was public. While he didn't use it a lot, there was a picture that Jeff had taken of him and Julie outside the house in Norton, the day they'd moved in. Innocuous enough, it was just a portrait of them both, his arm over her shoulder, hers around his waist. Underneath a few people had wished them luck in their new house. There was a picture of Jeff's shop, and of Emily behind the counter. Another of Jeff pulling a crazy face while he was holding Argie on his head. Nothing special really, but if you were trying to find where Julie was and who she might be with, this was all the info you needed and anyone looking for Julie could have found it sooner or later. There was a link to the shop's Facebook page, too. He clicked on it. It had over 13,000 'likes' and as a business page was all available for anyone to see. There were more pictures of them doing silly things on it. Basically, an active social media life was incompatible with having a totally private life and you had to accept that to one degree or another, if you were going to use it.

'Making your own page secure is a bit pointless to an extent. You're all over Jeff's shop's page. There are photos of us all going back to the opening day,' Nick said.

She kept looking through her work records. 'It's hard to be anonymous these days, but I made sure our names were kept off the publicly available version of the electoral roll.'

'Eh? I don't get you. I thought the electoral roll was available for anyone to look at.'

'You can opt out of your name being publicly listed. So if someone wanted to find where we lived and searched for our names online, nothing would come up because I excluded us from the Open Directory. You just tick the relevant box on the electoral register form. So no-one can get it online on one of those people finder websites.'

'I had no idea that was even something you could do.'

'It's there so that people in sensitive positions can't easily be found.' She leaned over. 'Give us a look at the shop photos.'

He turned the screen towards her and she scudded the page down.

'Oh, my god!' Her hand was over her mouth, she visibly jumped and went really pale in an instant. 'Oh, god. Oh, no. No no no no!!'

'What's wrong?' he said, looking at her and then to the screen.

She pointed, unable to say anything. Her face set in a wide-eyed, shocked expression. He looked at what she was pointing at.

'Oh, I was there when this was taken. A woman thought that Mothers of Invention record was the one her husband wanted. She took a picture. Yeah, look, she's posted it on the shop's wall and said, "Can you reserve this for me, please?" That's what I'd said she should do. And Jeff or Emily has put a thumbs up, underneath.'

She shook her head. 'It's not the sodding record, man. You were there when this was taken?'

'Yeah, I was helping out because it got really busy.'

'Did you see that man, to the left of the record?'

Nick looked at it again. The photo had captured the record in the plastic sleeve on the wall, and to the left it had also accidentally captured the Irishman who he'd been talking to at the time.

'Oh, yeah, I was speaking to him. He had some records he wanted to sell and was asking how to go about it.'

'Was he local?'

'Err...no, he was Irish. Soft lilting voice.'

She closed her eyes slowly and swallowed. 'Did he tell you his name?'

'No, he was going to come back with the records at some point. What's wrong? Do you know him?'

Swallowing her gin, she cleared her throat.

'He's Sean O'Connor.'

'And how do you know him?'

'We used to go out in 1989.' She glanced at the screen and flinched again. 'Shit, he's hardly changed at all.'

'OK, but why have you gone so pale?'

She turned to look him eye to eye. 'Because he was the man who raped me.'

She'd told him the previous year that she'd been raped in 1989, but had dealt with it and didn't want to talk about it. He'd always respected that and hadn't raised it since.

He reached for her hand to squeeze it, but she drew it away. She stood up and left the room to go to the toilet. Nick waited for her, his mind racing to make sense of this news. When she returned, she had obviously shed a few tears.

'Don't try and sympathise with me, or pat me better. I don't want that,' she said, firmly.

'OK. So you've never seen him since?'

Sucking in a deep breath of air through her nose, she composed herself and set her jaw defiantly. 'No. He moved back to Dublin. Or that's what he said.'

'But he lived in Stockton?'

'No, he lived in Middlesbrough. He had a short-term contract at Teesside Polytechnic, as it was called back then. He worked for a term lecturing in Irish poetry.'

'Yeah, you said he was a poet.'

He sat and waited for her to compose herself again, knowing this wasn't something she wanted to talk about and that it would hurt her to do so. She was pale and upset and he hated that.

A dark scowl spread across her face at the memory of the man.

'I suppose I'll have to tell you all about it.' She sighed. 'When it happened, I didn't fight back. And I felt so guilty about that for so long, like as if I'd let myself down. But I was scared of him. Really scared and really shocked.'

'Were you going out with him at the time?'

'We'd gone out half a dozen times. And I really liked him. He was different and interesting and quite a pretty man, with long eyelashes. He had the same birthday as Pat Benatar, and I stupidly thought that was a good omen.'

'I noticed that thing about his eyelashes myself, actually. It emphasised his watery greyish eyes.'

'That's him. He was on a short-term contract and was due to go back to Dublin the following day. We went out for a meal and then went back to his flat in Middlesbrough, near the Poly. We'd not had any sort of sex before, except kissing and I sort of thought that night, we probably would, as he was leaving for Dublin the following day. I thought I liked him a lot, but I knew there was no future in it, really.' She finished her gin. 'Anyway, we got back there and were messing around on the settee. Just kissing and that...the usual stuff.'

Nick nodded, but fearing what he was about to hear and how, once he'd heard it, he couldn't ever unhear it.

'I mean, I was 25 then and I was far from an innocent girl. Things were going as things always tended to go. A bit of fondling. Hands down pants, y'know. And I just didn't see it coming. Until it happened, I hadn't picked up any hint of violence or aggression or anything horrible. It was as if someone pulled a lever and changed him into another man.'

'So you hadn't been scared of him before in any way?'

'Nope. Not at all. I wouldn't have been there if I had. It wasn't even as if I was going to deny him sex. In fact, when he changed, I was probably on verge of the "shall we go to bed?" moment. Out of nowhere, he started getting rough with me. Grabbing at my breasts and saying I was a dirty bitch, saying he was going to give it to me hard and all this crap. For a moment, I thought he was joking, until he began pulling at my jeans and virtually tore them off me. Then did the same with my underwear. I let out some sort of noise at first but then I was frozen. My mind was telling my body to protest but my body couldn't respond. He threw me on the floor and pushed my legs apart. I remember thinking how weird it was that he already had a full erection as he took it out. The aggression, power and control was obviously a big turn-on for him. And he proceeded to furiously, and I do mean furiously, rape me. That was another reason I just lay there and let him do it without any real protest. I was scared shitless. It was as if he was really angry at me, like he was stabbing me with his penis. And he made sure he was as removed from me as possible, suspending himself over me, arms either side, as though not to touch me with any other part of himself. He didn't even pull his own pants down, just got it out through his flies. There was some psychological shit going on about that. And as it happened, it was as though I was watching it from the outside, as an observer. It seemed to go on forever, but it was probably only a minute or two at most. As he ejaculated, I can still hear him saying in a soft Irish growl, "Look what you made me do to you, I'll fill you up with my muck, you dirty fucking whore". Charming, eh? He said some other horrible stuff but I sort of stopped listening. I just wanted to get away.'

Nick knocked back his drink. It was difficult to listen to, but now wasn't the time to be squeamish, or even think about his own feelings. Even so, as he heard her say those words, he resolved to make sure Sean O'Connor got what was coming to him, whether it was jail or the kicking of his bloody life, or preferably both.

'See, that's significant, what he said.'

'How?'

'Look, words are my thing. We don't use specific words for no reason. You don't call your semen "muck" for no reason. It's as though it's dirty to him, it's part of a self-loathing mindset and he's infecting you with what he feels he's polluted with. He wants to make you dirty. He walks around feeling like he's a dispenser of dirt. To say it's a sick mentality is to massively understate it. You didn't get VD or anything, did you?'

She shook her head.

'Hmm, that "look what you made me do" thing is also revealing. He's absolving himself of blame and putting it on you.'

'Yeah, not untypical of rapists. Like he couldn't help himself. Rape is about power, not sex. He could have had consensual sex with me, but obviously didn't want that.'

'And isn't that exactly what those photos were also all about? You were powerless and they covered you in their "muck". And I'll tell you something else, Tommy Green was quick to blame his inability to control himself on you, as well.'

'Like I say, it's a common attitude. Why me, though? What is it about me both then and now? I'm just a normal lass.'

'I don't think it's about you as a person. I think it's about what you represent to them; an independent, strong, intelligent, sexually liberated and confident woman. That's a threat to men like them. I think they love it and hate it at the same time. They find you sexually attractive but that makes them hate themselves for being so weak as to be attracted to the sort of woman they dislike most. You don't buy their whole male power trip. And they'll have done it to other women, I'm sure. So, when he'd finished, did he say anything else?'

'He got off me and went somewhere. The bathroom maybe. I was shaking and totally in shock and I didn't know what to do or say. I mean, back then, no-one had talked to me about what to do if you're raped, in terms of evidence. He didn't use a condom, so thank god I was on the pill. All I could think to do was to get out of there. I just got dressed as quick as I could and ran for it. As I opened the door, he came out of the other room and actually said goodbye to me, like he hadn't just done what he'd done. He said he'd write and what a nice time he'd had with me. The rage had apparently gone and he was back to who I thought he was before. I mean, that was very weird. I don't think I said anything, I just fled.'

'And you didn't think of going to the police?'

'I did by the time I got back to my place. But all I could think was that I hadn't said no. It all happened so quickly and I hadn't really resisted. I was so shocked and frightened that I had barely even protested. I didn't even try and push him away. So I didn't see how I could prove he'd raped me. He hadn't hit me, as such and though I was sore because he'd forced himself in me and been so rough, it wasn't anything you could have seen in terms of cuts and bruises. He'd just have said it was consensual. These days, maybe I'd have a bit better chance of being believed, but in 1989, there was no way that'd have happened. I went over and over it in my mind. I wondered for a long time if it had been my fault, somehow.'

Nick shook his head. 'Obviously, no rape is ever the fault of the victim. By definition, it's the fault of the rapist. You know that, Jules.'

'Of course I do and I did then, too, but you look for reasons it's happened, don't you? As I say, he must have known we were going to have consensual sex, but he didn't want that. He wanted it to be rape. Even now, as a 47-year-old who understands this behaviour much better than I did back then, and who listens to not dissimilar stories from women most weeks, I couldn't tell you why he suddenly went from being an apparently normal and rather nice man, to being a vile rapist, other than to say he was psychotic and something triggered a psychotic episode. Maybe I failed to pick up on warning signs, but I did what women all too often do, I put it down to experience, was glad I didn't get beaten up or worse, and then tried to forget about it.'

'Didn't you get counselling?'

'Nah. In 1989 help wasn't nearly so easy to get. And anyway, I just didn't want to go over it. I just wanted to forget it had happened. I tried to tell myself it was just some sort of bad sex and I'd had bad sex with men before, so it was no different to that. That's how I dealt with it. But I have talked to Linda, my counsellor, about it since, because 20 years on, I know it's had a profound effect on me. In some ways, it eventually made me decide to be a women's support worker.'

'Is Linda the person you talk to about all the horrible stuff you hear about at work?'

'Yeah, as part of the job, TW have independent, external counsellors who act like blotting paper for all your vicarious trauma. We all have them. You'd go daft if you didn't. You have to let all the anger and frustration and upset out somewhere. I can't come home and do that, it'd not be fair on you.'

'Yeah, you don't talk much about your work when you come home, do you?'

'This is my refuge from it all. I don't want to bring it home unless I can avoid it.'

'I'm all for people being paid to listen to you talk. Having Marc as my therapist all these years has been...well...it's been invaluable to me. The fact he annoys me a bit has made it even better, somehow. It makes me less bothered about boring him or saying something offensive or shocking.'

'Even now, it's still upsetting to talk about it, but I have dealt with it, by and large. But it never leaves you. I can still hear his voice.'

'But he got away with it, didn't he? I wonder how many more times he's got away with it? Let's face it, you don't have that sort of behaviour in you, just the once.'

'Yes, well, it was that thought which put the seeds of working for Teesside Women or maybe Women's Aid in my mind, eventually. I never told you all this because I don't want to make a big deal out of it, because if I do that, he wins all over again. I'm not a victim of it, I won't let myself be a victim of it. I've tried to use all my experiences, not just that one, to help other women, and to turn a bad thing into a good thing. That's the best revenge available to me. It's all a long time ago, it could really upset me if I let it, but I'm not letting him upset me again. I'm just not. I won't do it. That's why when I said to you about not letting the intruder steal your peace of mind, I really knew what I was talking about.' She folded her arms across her chest and let out a tense breath.

'But if we could somehow prosecute him for it now, would you want to? Even if it involved dragging it all out again?'

'I don't know how we could, but yeah, absolutely, I'd take that bastard down in a heartbeat.'

CHAPTER 12

As she went to get more drinks, Nick took out an A4 notepad and began to make notes of everything that had happened to them in relation to the stalking, the photos and the break-in, then put the names of Tommy Green and Sean O'Connor under the diagram.

"Trust your instincts, our Nick."

She put the glasses down and sat down on the armchair across from him.

'That looks complex,' she said, pointing to his doodlings. 'Any ideas?'

'It's just occurred to me that you were followed by a Range Rover, weren't you?'

'Yeah, a silver one.'

'When I met O'Connor in the shop he said he had a Range Rover and there was plenty of room in it to bring records down. Coincidence?'

'There are a lot of them around.'

'True. Is it possible that somehow Tommy Green or Sean O'Connor knew each other in London and are involved in what's been happening with the stalking and the photos? I mean, we know O'Connor is up here, but that doesn't prove anything. He may have contacts up here, or whatever. He was quite nosy in the shop, but perhaps not untypically so.'

'Green was a Londoner and one of those Londoners who think the north is a foreign country. He'd never even been up here. It was over two years after the O'Connor incident that I met him. I simply don't see how we can tie them together. O'Connor being here is just muddying the water; it's just a coincidence. Even if he's visiting the area or even lives here, and has checked out old girlfriends on Facebook and thought he'd go to the shop to see his old girlfriend's husband - it still doesn't have to be connected to the peeper and everything else. Remember Kenny was in London back in 91 to 92. He must be our main suspect for what's happening now, at least. I'm going to tell Mandy about him and she can send someone round to question him.'

'Yeah. Good idea. You're right. The only thing I'd say is that I've looked up old girlfriends on Facebook. Everybody does it. But I've not gone to the shop where their husband's mates work. Still, we don't know O'Connor consciously did that, I suppose.'

'Maybe he really does have records for sale. He looked up the shop online. That's all it is.' She took a drink, relishing the alcohol the way we all do when under stress.

Hearing his mother's voice to trust his instinct, once again, he didn't know why or how but Nick felt strongly that somehow, in some way, O'Connor and Green *were* involved in the abuse both then and now, it was just a matter of proving it.

He put his laptop aside. 'Come on, let's forget about it for a bit. It's been a tough evening, one way or another.'

She closed her computer, too. 'Yeah, I hope Emily comes back in a decent mood.'

'I just hope she comes back at all and isn't with Matty somewhere. When I told you I thought she'd been raped, you must have got some sort of flashback.'

She shook her head. 'I told you, I don't let myself get bothered by it. It's just a bad movie I don't ever want to see again.' She got up. 'I'm going to put a record on, let's cheer the hell up. What shall I get?'

'*Dreamboat Annie* by Heart?'

She pointed at him. 'I like your thinking. Love "Crazy On You"; hold on...' she went to the smaller second room, initially intended as a dining room, but which now housed 4,000 vinyl albums, 2,500 CDs and over 1,000 singles, all alphabetically ordered, returning with the Heart record and a couple of others, Stevie Nicks's *Bella Donna* and Pat Benatar's *Precious Time*. She dropped the needle on *Dreamboat Annie* and sank down into the armchair, blowing out air as she did so.

'OK, let's talk about something else. So the big JRC opening night is a week today?'

'Yup. Jules, man, it's amazing in there. I just feel like it's going to be really successful.'

'What Jeff's done with Susan's money, opening two more record stores and now the club, it's nothing short of amazing. I'm such a fan of his, and all the while bringing up little Argie.'

'I know, and he does it all with such a laid-back attitude. The hoops he's had to jump through to get the club open would have put most people off. Oh, and we're getting VIP guest passes, you know.'

'Cool. I'll wear those distressed black jeans I got from English Laundry in Los Angeles with studs on and that faux leather fitted shirt.'

'Those jeans are impressively tight, so I'll look forward to you cramming yourself into those. What does the 50-year-old rocker gentleman wear for such an occasion?'

She looked at him and grinned. 'You wear your tight Tommy Hilfiger jeans, you'll have to stuff your tackle all down one leg though, in the traditional rock stylee...ha ha...and you've hardly ever worn that tailored Fender shirt with the guitar embroidered on the back we bought in that Santa Monica store. Add in your leather boots and that's you sorted.'

'Pity I can't grow long hair any more. My follicles don't seem to have the energy, though weirdly I have acquired the ability to sprout hair from everywhere else. What's that all about?"

'Aw, never mind, love. I like the haircut Emily did for you. You look sexy and rugged.'

'Get away with you, I do not.'

She looked at him squarely. 'You totally do to me.'

'I'm sure I don't. You're the good-looking one in our team. I'm the interesting weirdo, if I'm anything.'

She put her glass down, got up and came over to him, sitting on his lap, arms around his shoulders and hugged him, sinking her head into his neck, kissing him with wet lips. 'And I love my interesting weirdo, so much.'

He held her close and tried to let his love infuse into her. Sometimes, those who have felt the weakest, know how to be the most strong.

The following morning at 7.30am, Nick stood in the living room doorway, looking at an Emily-free sofa. She hadn't come home. He texted her, just to ask if she was alright. Groaning to himself, he went to the kitchen to make coffee and get Julie some breakfast.

'Smoked haddock and scrambled eggs OK?' he said, as she came in, fixing up her hair.

'Have I ever said no to anything you've cooked before?'

'You once rejected some hummus I made for you.'

'Aye and for very good pollution reasons. I'd have punched a hole in the ozone layer if I'd eaten chickpeas in any format and probably burnt a hole in the arse of my pants.'

He grinned as he whisked some eggs in a bowl, added a bit of cream and seasoning. 'I'm afraid Emily didn't come home.'

'Y'know, I had a feeling she might not. God, I hope she's safe and not holed up with Matty getting fuck faced on drugs.'

'Aye, I can't help but worry about her, though I'm not sure how you stop a grown woman making bad decisions. It seems so obvious to me that she should stay away from Matty, but I bet she spent the night with him.'

'Emotions, relationships, self-identity are all complex things that don't always surrender to logic. I bet Matty is being nice to her, is deeply apologetic for what he did and is swearing it won't happen again. And when the man you love or loved is being that nice person again, in a way, why wouldn't you believe him? We have a natural instinct to give everyone a second chance.'

'Yeah, well maybe we've got her all wrong, and she's not with him. Does it ever work out after someone has done what he's done?'

She put both thumbs down. 'It usually goes the opposite way. You get a respite for a week or two or longer, then it happens again, and again and again, more and more frequently. Rapists can re-educate themselves and I'm not saying he couldn't rehabilitate himself, but he needs to take responsibility for his actions and actively seek help. If he doesn't, then I don't see it ending well at all.'

He piled some rocket on a warm plate, put a chunk of butter into a hot frying pan and added the fillet of fish in at full heat for 10 seconds, flipped it over, turned it off and put a lid on the pan to cook the fish in the residual heat while he made the scrambled eggs.

'Seeing you cooking is like watching a dancer. I've no idea how you keep it all together and get the timings right.'

'I don't always, do I? Fish is so hard to get spot on. A minute too long and it's awful.' He took the lid off the pan and nipped at it to see if it was cooked. It yielded nicely. 'Think I got it just right.'

He sat down to have coffee while she ate.

'Aw, this is delish, as per usual,' she said. 'You get better and better, you know. You could be a chef, if you wanted to give up the writing.'

'I like cooking for you and you're always appreciative but I'd bloody hate working in a restaurant with fussy punters who don't like celery, or won't eat liver, or whatever it is. Getting requests for a vegan option would drive me crazy, as well.'

'Is Jeff doing food at the club?'

'No, except crisps, nuts and maybe some wasabi peas.'

She pointed at him. 'There's another thing that turns my arse into a bunsen burner. Bloody wasabi peas. I can feel a wind egg forming just talking about them. Ha. But I can't wait to see the finished club. It was still getting done out last time I was in there.'

'It's really impressive. Jeff will be running around like a blue-arsed fly this coming week.'

'Will you give him a hand?'

'Yeah. When I can. What time are you working to today?'

'I'm only doing a half day, I'm finished at 1pm, so if there's anything he needs doing that I can help with, I can always pitch in.'

'OK, I'll text you later. There was no peeper again this morning.'

'No, I noticed that. Maybe he's given that up, whoever he is.'

'What do we do if Sean O'Connor comes back in the shop?'

'Well, don't just twat him in the face. You'll get arrested. See if you can find out where he lives and what he's doing here. Does he live here, or is he visiting?' She finished her coffee. 'That was ace, kidda. Got to go. I'll see you later.'

He stood at the door, hands in his jeans pockets, as she got into her blue 1975 Porsche parked out the front. It coughed as she turned the ignition and then died. She tried it again, to the same result.

Nick walked up to the car as she got out and peered into the engine. 'What's up?'

'Spark plugs, I think. Manky.' She pulled on some neoprene gloves, got a can of WD40 out and began to quickly clean them with a rag. 'She needs a proper service. I never seem to get the time.'

It started next turn of the key. She ripped off the gloves and drove away, already late for work. Nick gave her a wave and watched her go.

Almost directly across Norton High Street was the Highland Lad pub, or at least that's how they knew it from their youth, and still called it, despite it actually being called the Highland Laddie, these days.

It had benches and tables outside, so people could drink al fresco in the nice weather and also have a smoke. Sitting at one of the picnic-style tables was a thick-set man with a sunburnt pink, bald head. On the table was a 35mm camera. He was sitting legs crossed, looking at his phone. Nick's instinct was to run over the road and take the camera to see if he'd been taking photos of Julie, because he'd have been in a perfect position to do so. But he didn't. Instead, he sat down on the small park bench-style seat that was against their front wall and also took out his phone to pretend to be distracted.

As secretly as he could, he took several pictures of the man. In a black polo shirt and grey tracksuit bottoms, when he stood up to go, Nick could see he was a very big unit. Over six foot and broad in the shoulder, he was probably 16 stone. A classic Teesside thug, he had tattoos up his arm, a spider's web on the left side of his neck and a roll of fat at the base of his skull. In short, he looked the sort of man who was unemployable and had probably been in jail most of his adult life. No-one has to look that intimidating. It wasn't a fashion or style choice, it was an expression of a dissolute life and the desire to fight everything and everyone.

As he watched the man get up and go, apparently without even noticing Nick, he was glad he hadn't acted on impulse. Unless he got a lucky punch in, he was no match for someone of that size and power, not without a bat, some sort of stun gun, or possibly a cannon. Whatever he was doing there, one thing was for sure, he hadn't been the peeper at the back. That man had a paunch, had hair and was more average height.

After a half hour lifting his weights, he had a shower and had just got out when his phone rang.

'Hey, Jeff.'

'Now then. Is Emily with you?'

'Nope. She didn't come back last night. She stormed out after Mandy had a go at her.'

'Yeah, she said what had happened.' Jeff distorted the phone with a groan. 'Well, Em's not come in and she should have been here at nine. She's not texted or called either, and she always does if she's going to be late. I've called her and texted her but got no reply.'

'Bloody hell. She's left her stuff here, including her flat keys. Shall we go round and see if she's there and if she's not, let ourselves in?'

'I can't. I'm on my own, except for Alisha. You'll have to go alone. I hope to god she's alright.'

'Right, I'll go down there now.'

Nick parked up in Silver Street and walked around to Green Dragon Yard with a knot of worry in his guts. The horrible image of her lying with a knife between her shoulder blades kept haunting him and as he walked, his mother's voice returned to him once more telling him to trust himself. But that was just a dream. Stop thinking about it. His subconscious was messing with his mind. It was just a vivid dream. Precognition was nonsense. Even so, his mouth was dry as he rang her buzzer and listened at the intercom. No reply. He buzzed again. Still nothing. He called her on his phone. It went to voicemail.

Letting himself in, he climbed the stairs to her flat on the top floor. Putting an ear to the door he listened, intently focused on even the slightest noise. All was silent, so he unlocked it, fearing what he was, with every step, increasingly certain he was going to see.

'Emily!' he called out.

Nothing.

The flat smelt of stale cigarette smoke and cannabis, as well as something unpleasantly sour and burnt.

With a shaking hand he pushed at the ajar living-room door which led off the hallway. The white plywood door creaked a little as it opened.

Nick's heart leapt into his mouth.

Oh, god, there she was.

Face down on the blue carpet.

Naked from the waist upwards. Tattooed back. Motionless. Dead. Dead. Dead. The dream had been right. He had it. He had precognition. Oh god! This wasn't a dream. He wasn't dreaming. He was awake. And she was dead.

It was only three strides from the door to her body, but by the time he'd taken the second, he realised, that no, it wasn't her at all. He let out a primal noise of relief. He was so certain the dream would come true that he'd virtually hallucinated her being there. But this was a man. A man with similar coloured and length hair and some sort of dragon tattoo down his back, nothing like Emily's inkwork.

Nick got onto his knees and shook him.

'Are you OK, mate?'

But no, he wasn't OK. He wasn't breathing and he felt oddly cold.

Nick called 999 and described the man's condition. They dispatched an ambulance.

'They're on their way now, mate. They'll see you're alright,' Nick said, to the body.

It felt wrong not to talk to the man, even though he was dead. Despite this fact, he felt OK about it because the dead human is a lot less dangerous, difficult or depressing than the alive one often is. He opened the blinds and looked around the room. That was when he saw the pieces of aluminium foil on the sofa. By no means was he an expert in drug paraphernalia, but was fairly sure that you used foil to warm up and inhale heroin; chasing the dragon.

There was nothing to do but wait for the paramedics to come. Wandering around the small one-bedroomed flat, it was in a right state, with rubbish strewn around the place and something going off in the kitchen bin. Who was the dead bloke? A dealer and a doper? Matty had been there, surely, perhaps with Emily. He went into her bedroom. The white cotton quilt was hanging off the bed but it didn't look like she'd slept there the previous night. There was none of her clothes out and nothing in the wash basket.

When the paramedics arrived, they confirmed the death and even tried the defibrillator on him. Nick watched them try to put life back into the slab of meat that had been a human. But it was no use. He was an ex-life.

'What has he actually died of?' asked Nick.

'My guess is a heart attack or he just passed out and forgot to breathe,' said the paramedic, a woman in her early 40s. 'Heroin relaxes you so much, you get respiratory failure. The system that normally keeps you alive while you're sleeping, just shuts down.' She shook her head and looked down at him. 'He's no age. Shitting drugs. I'm sure he didn't want to die. Such a waste.'

Two police officers soon arrived to take a statement. As he waited for them to talk to the paramedics he texted Jeff and told him what he'd found. He then texted Emily.

'Em. There's a dead man in your flat with a dragon tattoo on his back. He'd been smoking heroin. A friend? A dealer? Please get in touch, if only to tell me you're alright.'

One statement to the police later, he walked down to Jeff's shop.

'Ah, there you are. I've got to go, can you fill in for me until about three?' said Jeff. 'I've got to be at the club. What the hell happened?'

'I think he was Matty's drug dealer, or maybe I should say Matty and Emily. The police have put out an alert for Emily. I've got her keys so Matty must have let him in with his set.'

Jeff cast him a stressed look. 'Where the hell is she? Why isn't she answering her phone?'

'Maybe she's lost it. I've lost mine before now.'

'Hmm, or maybe Matty has confiscated it and is holding her captive somewhere.' Jeff shook his head and gave Nick a weary look. 'I've gotta go, the brewery people will be waiting for me.'

Nick went over to Alisha, had a quick chat, got some tea, then perched behind the counter and looked at his phone, hoping Emily would have been in touch, but she hadn't. It was all very stressful, but at least the shop was quiet, so he took the opportunity to upload the photo of the thug he'd taken to Jeff's big screen.

Christ, he was a mean-looking sod. Why would he be there with a camera at that time of day, opposite their house? Who was he? He wasn't some kind of amateur photographer. He was just a hard-faced bugger, the sort of which you saw a lot of Teesside. Born out of strong, steel industry labouring stock, but after a largely workless life on the drink, had totally gone to seed. Still big and meaty, but also flabby, beery and really un-healthy-looking. By any definition, he looked like A Bad Man.

Nick sipped at his tea, looking up as Tommo came into the shop.

'Hey, Tommo. How are you today?'

'I'm maftin' me, like. It's too bloody hot. Emily was going to get us some of them army shorts. Is she in?'

'Not just yet, no.'

Tommo was a bit of a loner, and from a different era really, but he was nobody's fool.

He stood and frowned at Nick. 'Is she alright, like?'

Nick sighed. 'I hope so. She's not come in and we can't get hold of her.'

Tommo raised his greying eyebrows and rubbed at what hair he had left. 'Is it that bloody Matty?'

'We just don't know.'

'I tell you what, Nick. If that lad hurts a hair on that lass's head, I'll kill him. So help us, I will.'

'She'll be fine, don't worry, Tommo. Hey, do you by any chance know who this character is?'

He turned the screen so that the old lad could see it.

Without missing a beat, the old lad replied, 'Oh, aye, that's Boz Bai-ley, that is. I heard he was back up here, like.'

'You know him?' said Nick, shocked.

'Aye, he used to drink in the Rimswell 20 years ago when he was a kid. He's just back up here from London. Why've you got a photo of him, Nick?'

From London? Oh, fuckety fuck fuck, to use Lisa Lambert's old ex-pression. It was all falling into place now. 'He was taking photos of Julie getting into her car this morning. Or I think he was.'

'Was he? Your Julie? Bloody hell, Nick.'

Tommo's purple-ish, broken-veined face flushed a little.

'What's up?' said Nick.

'He only got out of prison few weeks ago. Got out early for good behaviour, didn't he?'

'Did he? What was he inside for?'

Tommo puffed out his cheeks and blushed a bit. 'I can't say them sort of words, Nick.'

'Eh? What words?' Nick frowned.

Tommo wouldn't look him in the eyes. 'Dirty words. Me mam and dad brought me up right, y'know. Swearing, I'm alright with, but dirty stuff isn't right.'

He shuffled off to get his usual mug of tea and toasted teacake. Nick's heart rate had increased by 50 per cent. Up from London. Been in jail. Dirty stuff. Bloody hell. This did not sound good at all.

Nick put 'Boz Bailey' into Google. Nothing.

'Tommo, what's Boz's first name, his proper name, like?'

'Err...it's Raymond, isn't it?' He nodded in agreement with himself.

'How do you get from Raymond to Boz?'

But Tommo now had a buttery teacake in his mouth. He seemed to chew it with his entire face. As it disappeared, he wiped his mouth on his big baggy army shirt, another of Emily's fashion choices. 'It's the Bad Company bass player.'

Nick squinted at him. 'Boz Burrell? His real name was Raymond, yeah, but so what?'

'Boz's dad was a big Bad Company fan. Saw them at the City Hall a few times, met Rodgers and Ralphs. When he had his first son, he'd always liked Boz as a name. So he followed yer man, didn't he, named him Raymond but everyone called him Boz?'

'Could he not have just gone for Paul, Mick or Simon?'

'His old fella was a bloody nutcase. Always was. Got sacked from Head Wrightsons for putting a molten rivet up some bloke's arse.'

'What? Literally?'

'Aye. Well, I say he got sacked, that was mostly because he was sent down for 12 years for GBH, or whatever putting a rivet up someone's jacksie is.' The old lad shook his head.

'Setting a good example to his son, there. So Boz is a bad man, right?'

'Very bad. Don't ask us. Look it up on your computer.'

Nick turned back to the screen and continued his search but nothing came up for Raymond Bailey that seemed relevant.

Nick gave Alisha his mug for a refill of green tea and then went to sit next to Tommo, who was now reading one of the copies of *Classic Rock* that Jeff kept in a big magazine rack.

'Tommo, I can't find anything about this Boz bloke. Give us a clue what he did.'

'Nick, I told you...'

'...I know. It was dirty. But I need to know, for Julie's sake. If he's after her for some reason, I've got to protect her. You like Julie, don't you?'

'Yeah, 'course I do. She's a right proper sight for sore eyes is your Julie. And she's daft about you.'

Nick laughed a little. 'Why do you say that?'

'Whenever she comes in here and you're in, she's all goo-goo-gah-gah over you. Can't keep 'er 'ands off you. You're lucky lad, for an ugly get, like.' Tommo gave him a look, sort of halfway between a grin and a sneer.

Nick smiled. Tommo saw more than you thought he did.

'Well, then, what's this Boz bloke done? Just tell me in words you're comfortable with.'

Tommo hissed some air between his teeth. 'He was, like, not nice...err...like...err...to women. They sent him away for it.'

He nodded. 'Did he rape them, Tommo?'

The word *rape* made Tommo visibly wince.

'Aye, aye, nasty like. Bloody sod.' He began chuntering to himself. 'Don't need his sort...rotten get...poor lasses, like...should've stayed in that there London...twat...why couldn't he be a good lad?'

Nick leaned over and put his hand on Tommo's arm. 'So he's from round here, but he lived in London?'

Tommo nodded. 'Like I said, he's a Rimswell lad, isn't he? But he were living down south when they caught him.'

'Would you know if Boz knows a bloke called Kenny Harlow? Who worked for Barclaycard?'

'Kenny Harlow, him what was married to Edie?'

'Yeah, that's him.'

'Aye, he was no better, 'im. Nasty sod. He was always in the Rimswell an' all, years ago. Got barred eventually for causing fights. Couldn't keep his fists to himself that one, especially with a drink on 'im.'

'Right, so he could have known Boz Bailey from back in the day?'

'I suppose so, aye. But Boz 'as been in jail for years.'

'And Boz was arrested In London?'

'Aye. Proper bad sod.'

'When was this?'

'Early 90s or mid 90s, summat like that. He went down for 15 years. When they let him out, he came straight back up 'ere.'

'15 years. Bloody hell. That means he must have got 25 or 30 years, if he got out with good behaviour. What did he do to get that sort of stretch?'

'It were disgustin', Nick.'

'I need to know, Tommo. Jules could be in danger.'

Tommo stopped and went quiet, as though summoning up the courage to say the words. 'He killed a lassie while he was...while he was...while he was...doing sex with her, like. Suffocated her, like. He went down for manslaughter, said he never meant to do it.' He spoke in a barely audible whisper.

'Jesus, really?'

'Aye, it were all over the *Gazette* back in about 94 or 95.'

'I was living in Harrogate by then, so I don't remember it.'

Nick sent an email with the photo attached to Mandy, with Tommo's info about Bailey's crimes.

While these things were big issues in their lives, he knew Mandy had hundreds of ongoing crimes and operations to oversee. The fact she'd treated their problems so personally was as much a favour to friends as it was a desire to exercise the law. But she had so much on her plate as Chief of Cleveland Police, that he didn't expect to hear from her too soon. He then texted Julie with the same info, telling her to be vigilant.

The stress of it all was leaving him feeling exhausted. He'd seen a dead bloke already today, he was really worried about Emily, and very scared for Julie. It was alright her saying that you couldn't let them win by letting them worry you, but being bloody worried when a bloke like Bailey was apparently taking photos of your wife, was surely the correct response.

He went back to his page of notes, drinking tea while he thought it over. Kenny Harlow was in London for a few months in late 1991, early 1992. Tommy Green was in London when Julie was there, but then disappeared early in 1992. This Boz character was busted in London in 1995, so could have been living there for a few years. If he could locate Sean O'Connor in London around late 1991, then they really were onto something.

He did a search for 'Sean O'Connor Teesside Poly' but it didn't produce anything. He looked for him as a poet. Trouble was it was such a common name. There was a poet in Seattle by that name, another in Cork. Neither were him. Maybe he hadn't even been a poet for 20-odd years. Then again, if he'd been published, his books must still be around somewhere. Going onto Amazon he did a search for the name.

Scanning the results he found a listing on the marketplace for a small volume called New Irish Poets, published in 1988. Sean O'Connor was one of the 12 names in the volume. On the next page was another volume, this time under his own name, *Green on Red on Green*. Nick copied it and pasted it into Google, and found it was reviewed positively on an Irish literature website.

'Still only 30, O'Connor is one to watch. A powerful voice that deals with powerful issues. Published by Storyville Verse £4.99'

His heart leapt into his throat. Bloody shitting hell. He was published by Storyville! Their poetry imprint went back to the 1920s and was quite well renowned. This had been published in March 1992. That meant he had to have been in London in the preceding month or three, if only for publisher's meetings. And who also worked there? Tommy Green. Julie had documented that in her diary. Oh, god. That's how they knew each other. His instinct had been right. He knew they were related somehow and this was how. Mam was right. Trust your instincts. He'd always known Julie had been raped. Why wouldn't it be that man back again for some more?

Nick sat and tried to relax and take it easy, but he couldn't settle. He was nervous and he knew bad things lay ahead. He just knew. His mother's advice to trust himself had now opened a door in his psyche. Who knew how it worked? Who knew why you knew what you knew and when you knew it, but you knew it all the same?

He found himself sweating heavily with the stress, and wanting to drink something cold and alcoholic, and then just before 1pm, Mandy Beale put her head around the door.

'Now, then. Jeff said you were on duty. This isn't a social visit this time, I'm afraid,' she said, all pink cheeks and messy hair. She turned her watch around on her wrist and looked intently at him.

'Did you get my text?' he said.

'Yeah. Bailey is very much on my radar, believe me.'

'Is he?'

'Yeah. Very much so. Don't like him taking photos of Jules.' She pushed her right fist into her left palm. 'Not one bit.'

'What about the bloke in Emily's flat?'

'Sam Wallace. He was the dealer we pulled in. He supplied the crystal meth to Matty. Seems to have been sampling the produce. Any news of Emily? Jeff told me she'd not come home.'

'Nothing.'

'Bugger. And how are you? You're really going through the wringer, lad.'

'Honestly? I'm feeling stressed out beyond belief.'

Mandy rubbed at her eyes and let out a heavy breath. 'I understand that. Nick, look, things are getting serious.' She came behind the counter so she could speak quietly with him and avoid being overheard. She looked him square in the eyes; her breath smelled coffee sour as she stood close to him. 'Bailey is a proper evil sod. Do you know what he did?'

'He killed a woman.'

Mandy blinked slowly and then stared at him. 'He killed a woman whilst having sex with her. He put his hand over her mouth, leaned on her and suffocated her. By the time he was done, she was dead. He went down for aggravated manslaughter, saying it was a sex game that went too far. Got lucky on that, in my view, simply because the woman was an S&M sex worker. He did 11 years of 22 for it, but was rearrested and found guilty whilst still inside, on a historical rape charge, and had another four years added on. So he did 15 in total.'

'He should never have been let out at all. I mean, he's obviously a bloody monster.'

'I know, but I can't control that. Look, that's not all. I'm here because I think we've got to take Julie into protective custody. Put her in a safe house.'

His heart began to pound hard again. 'What? Eh? Why?'

She looked around herself and spoke in a low voice. 'Because forensics have found DNA behind that bush out the back of your house. Semen was found on several tissues and we've just had a match come through.'

Nick felt physically sick. 'The DNA is on the police database?'

She nodded and blinked slowly. 'And it's another potentially very dangerous man called Thomas Green...'

CHAPTER 13

'...Tommy Green? He's here? Oh, my good god.' He grabbed her by her jacket lapel and hissed into her face, on his tip toes. 'Fucking hell, Mandy. Shitting hell. Julie went out with him, well, she slept with him about 20 years ago. He was weird with her because he had premature ejaculation and sort of blamed it on her.' He was shaking a little now. 'She only knew him for a week or two in 1991, then never saw him around.' His mind had reached top speed now as all the locks dropped and the whole thing fell into place. Green was the peeper. He broke in, took the pyjamas and installed the camera.

Mandy pulled his hand off her lapel and looked at him with a clear, focused brown-eyed stare.

'What you're telling me only makes this more urgent. Green did 18 years for an especially violent rape of a woman that he had stalked for some time, in exactly the same sort of way as is happening to Julie. He was obsessed with her, followed her, then kept a vigil outside her house, then he broke in and stole her pyjamas, then he abducted her, and conducted a horribly violent rape which he actually filmed. When did you say she knew him?'

'December 1991, but he disappeared soon after.'

'He was arrested and on remand by late January 1992. That's why he wasn't around any more. I've got officers looking for him. He's only been out for about six months.'

'Yeah, but Mandy, have you looked closely at the photos that were posted of Julie?'

'I saw them, yes.'

'How many people were involved in that, do you think?'

'Two. The photo pointing to 'er vagina, is two different 'ands.'

Nick shook his head and took out his phone, showing her the photos. 'No, there were three.'

He explained why. 'Three. Green, O'Connor and Bailey. I think they were all in London in early 1992. We've narrowed it down using her diaries, and we think they were taken on 6th January 1992. There's a page missing from her diary on that day and it was torn out by the man who got into the bedroom, probably because it had something incriminating on it, which was probably Green. Now, you don't know this, but this bloke called Sean O'Connor raped Julie a little over two years earlier. Raped her in Middlesbrough. They went out half a dozen times. These men all met up in London, probably at Storyville Publishing and on 6th January 1992 conspired to drug and rape Julie.'

Mandy was used to hearing about depravity. It didn't shock her. All she wanted to do was arrest the guilty. She didn't get distracted by her own emotions. 'This O'Connor man, I don't suppose there's any chance of knowing his birthday? If so, I'll get the PNC onto it.'

'Yeah, I know his birthday, it's the same as Pat Benatar's.'

'Who's she?'

'One of Julie's favourite singers. She thought it was a good omen. It wasn't.'

'Right, well, when's that?'

'I'll have to look it up.' He went to the computer and found her wiki page. 'Here we go, 10th January. She said he was two years younger than she is. So he was born in 1966.'

Mandy wasn't prone to panicking. Keeping a calm head was essential. She nodded, twitched her lips and went outside to make the call to pull up information from the police computer, returning a couple of minutes later. Her face was set in a look somewhere between thunder and lightning.

She jabbed a finger at him. 'Right, I don't care that you're looking after the shop, I'll give Jeff a call, you've got to come with me and see Jules at her work, now. I can't make her go into hiding, but I will strongly suggest she does and so should you, until we've got these three bloody perverts under lock and key.'

'What? Is O'Connor on the PNC?'

'Yes. And I'll give you one guess why. He was released five weeks ago from Wormwood Scrubs after a nine-year stretch for a violent rape. His fourth conviction in 20 years.'

His legs felt on the verge of collapse.

'Oh, god. And I bet that he was in the same jail as Green and Bailey were sent to.'

She nodded, 'Of course he was, for a while anyway. They move the pervs around quite a bit, but they all did time in the Scrubs together. O'Connor's was aggravated rape and involved two others. He had a knife. Held it to her throat throughout.'

Nick winced. 'Jesus, Mand, these are three serious headcases. And they've all come here at the same time and one of them is wanking outside of our house and breaking in, another is taking photos of Jules and the third came into the shop a few days ago.'

'Right, right, I 'ear you. That's why we need to go and see Julie and quick. I think we've enough cause to believe that these three all being back in Stockton at the same time is not a coincidence at all. That they're planning something. Green is already 75 per cent down a road he's walked before. I'm not 'avin scummers like these three violating women on my patch. I'm going to take them down and take them down as quickly as I can. Two have done nowt so far, but if I can find Green I can have 'im on summat, I'm sure, even if it's public indecency. No mercy. I'm 'avin these. They're mine.'

'They can sod right off! They don't scare me. I'm not changing my life because of them!' Julie folded her arms across her chest and jutted her jaw out, her mother's jaw. Hard and defiant, her eyes scowled.

Mandy Beale wasn't impressed. She leaned forward and jabbed her head at Julie, in order to make her point, her voice raised in Yorkshire indignation.

'Don't be bloody stupid, woman. It's quite clear from the PNC info. They were all in London when you lived there. They were all in Wormwood Scrubs together at one point from 1996 to 2000. O'Connor, Green, Bailey. All for sex crimes with additional violence. One of 'em, Green, were also a stalker, a stalker that did what he's now doin' to you. They spent years banged up together. Now they've all met up again on Teesside. I believe they've done this specifically to torture you and quite possibly some other women. I reckon back in 1992, it was Green and the other two who drugged you and took the photos. I also reckon there's something to Nick's idea that Kenny Harlow knows Bailey from back in the day, and has a grudge against you, so he's told them where you live and has added the stuff on the website about you being unfit for your job and all of that. Wake up and smell the coffee, Jules. They're planning something. One has already raped you, another is obsessed with you, another has a grudge against you and the fourth probably hates you just because his mates do and because you're a woman and he bloody hates women! They've drugged and raped you before and they want to do it again. That's my professional view. These sort of men seek out other men

197

who feel like they do. They gang together. That's what they did back then, and it's what they're doing now they're all out of jail.'

Julie jabbed her finger at Mandy. 'Well you've got to stop them, then. You've got to pick them up! Why should I have to be the one to change my life? That invests them with power.'

But Mandy was relentless.

'And I will pick them up if we can find them. I've got enough of Green's DNA to hold and charge him with something. We got a partial print on the outside window sill. If it matches him, I'm nicking him as soon as I find the sod. But I can't bust the others for just being here, not until they do something and in this case "do something" probably means abduction and rape and even murder. I've got someone going round to interview Kenny Harlow. He's a mean sod, he is. I remember 'im from back in the day. Always fighting. He won't give us anything, but 'opefully it'll put the wind up 'im.'

'Well, then. If I'm out and about and they threaten me, or whatever, you can nick them for that.'

Mandy was exasperated. She gasped out impatient air. 'Yes yes yes, I can if we're right on hand, but I can't have an officer follow you around, Jules. I can't do that. It'd take them no time to drive up, bundle you in a car, drive you away to some sordid hideaway, they'll dope you up, wait 30 minutes and then they will takes turns raping you and probably film themselves doing it and once they're done, they'll probably choke you to death. These are evil bastards, Jules. They drugged you once and abused you 20 years ago, and probably look back on it as a great old time. Probably did it to several women. You can't just tough this out. We need to keep you safe.'

Julie leaned forward and shouted. 'But that's just what they want! They want to destroy my life!'

Mandy wasn't having it and shouted full blast at her. 'For a clever lass, you're a bloody stupid woman! I repeat, what they want to do is abuse you and maybe even kill you. Do you want to be killed, just to uphold some sort of feminist principle? Eh? Do you? 'Cos that's what'll bloody happen. You're bloody mad. You're a clever woman, take a bloody telling off me!' She swung around and gestured at him. 'Tell 'er, Nick!'

'She's right, Jules. You know she is. You're just digging your heels in and I totally understand why. But it's too risky. If they can at least arrest Green, it'll probably scare the others off...but until that...'

'What do you think, Martha?' said Julie, turning to her boss, in her office.

She was unequivocal. 'I'm with Mandy on this. I understand your resistance, but it's far too risky. If you had a service user who presented us with this scenario, we'd be all in favour of her leaving for a safe house or a refuge, wouldn't we? It doesn't have to be forever. Just give Mandy time to do some work. We can give you a week off work. It's no problem. These men might get scared that they'll be arrested and leave the area.'

She spoke with a calm rationality that had been absent until that moment. It was an irresistible argument.

Julie looked at them all, let out a groaning sigh, swore and slumped her shoulders. 'OK, I give in, where do we go?'

'We've got a safe house out in Great Ayton, right on the edge of the Cleveland Hills. Nice little cottage on its own. As far as anyone knows, it's a holiday cottage that's rented out to tourists. Just make sure you don't put anything about where you are on Facebook, or anywhere else. Tell no-one where you've gone, right?'

'Ok, so do we go now?' said Nick.

'Go home and pack a bag for a week. I'll have the address and key brought round for you. I've got your numbers, I'll call or text you with any developments.'

'What about finding Emily?' said Julie.

'We've got an eye out for her and Matty Rhodes. If you want my view, they're holed up at a mutual friend's place taking drugs.'

Julie closed her eyes and shook her head. 'Shit, don't say that, Mand, I love that little lass.' She rubbed at her face with her hands, as though to wake herself up from this nightmare.

Mandy was resolute. 'The world is shit. No point in dressing it up as anything else. Look after yourself first, let us worry about everything else,' she said. 'Think about it as a free holiday. I wish I could have a week off in the countryside.'

'Alright, but I'm not missing the opening night of Jeff's club. No way. We're coming back for that, whatever! Right?!' said Julie.

'Yeah, that's a line in the sand,' said Nick.

'Fine. Give me a week to find these men and nick 'em or make them leave under fear of arrest. I'll also kneel on Kenny Harlow's neck and find out what the hell he's been up to. If I remember right, he's not long since got a suspended sentence for beating his wife.'

'That's right. He'd hit her for years. Decades, in fact,' said Julie. 'She told me all about it.'

'Bloody toe rag. If there's so much as a hint of him committing a crime, any crime, I can get him sent down like that.' She clicked her fingers. 'That should sharpen his focus and get him to cough up anything we need to know.'

They got back to Norton, put some clothes into two rucksacks, along with walking boots, and made sure the house was secure with all windows and doors locked. As they were doing so, two Cleveland Police officers arrived and gave them the address and keys for the house.

Nick stood on the doorstep and looked up and down the street for Bailey and his camera, but there was no-one around. He packed Emily's stuff into her bag and dropped it off at the shop, in case she reappeared.

'I got your text,' said Jeff, taking it off him. 'Just take it easy and have a break. For a few days you're no-one, you're anonymous.' He gripped Nick's hand in the rock 'n' roll clench.

'Don't tell anyone where we've gone.'

'I can't because I don't know where you're going. And don't tell me,' said Jeff, putting his fingers in his ears.

'We'll be back for the opening night.'

'OK. Look, Nick, have a good time wherever you're going. Disconnect from the day-to-day shite. Relax. You look super stressed, old son.' Jeff patted him on his neck and smiled.

'I will. We will. Cheers. Sorry I can't be here for the shop.'

'Don't worry, Lukey is coming down. He's got good cover up in Newcastle. We'll be fine.'

'Good. Sorry, man, it feels like Julie is being hunted down by these pervs.'

Jeff put a big fist into his chest, gently. 'You'll be fine. Mandy will sort it. I just hope Emily is...well...to be honest, I just hope she's alive. I'm starting to try and get used to idea that she's not here and that's because she's...' he took a breath '...because she's dead. It happens, you hear about this sort of shit and maybe, this is one of those times.'

'You know, it's funny how we take people for granted. And then shit happens and we're robbed of them. I hope she's OK. But I have to say, I'm not optimistic, either. I'm just preparing myself for the worst and I can't believe I'm even saying that. Makes me feel sick to my stomach.'

'Yeah, me, too. Right, get yourself away. I'll see you in a week.'

They stopped at a supermarket to pick up food, tea, coffee and booze and then drove in the BMW in silence, wrapped up in their own thoughts, as he took the A19 south and the A174 east. The sun dipped in and out of big clouds over the Cleveland Hills.

He looked at her, her blonde hair blushed golden with late afternoon sun.

'I can hardly believe this is happening,' he said. 'How have our lives ended up like this?'

She snorted air out of her nose. 'I feel bullied by those men and I hate feeling bullied. I resent it on absolutely every level,' she said.

'Yeah, I do, too. Instinctively I want to fight them, not hide from them, but it makes sense to dip out for a short while. Things have escalated and they're no ordinary peepers or voyeurs or whatever...these are evil, vicious and disturbed people. We've totally underestimated them, if you ask me.' He took the A172 towards Great Ayton, then continued. 'Clearly, back in the day, you didn't hear of the conviction of Tommy Green or of Sean O'Connor, or Bailey.'

She looked out of the side window. 'No, even though I was in London, it's such a big place and all sorts of shit is going on all the time, you can't keep up with it all. Also, it wasn't like I lived in a community which knew me well and who could have spotted a news report and told me about it. I'd never even heard of Bailey anyway. Those LSE girls I lived with, they moved out after their term finished. Another three student lasses came in, then I was tired of sharing and as soon as I got my next pay rise, I moved out to a one-bedroom flat above a Greek restaurant on Farringdon Road. It was stupidly expensive and tiny but I was independent. There was a high turnover of staff at work and outside of grafting, I was only interested in drinking, seeing the Boro, and going to see bands. Local news just passed me by. I suppose all three cases were reported, but I just never saw anything about it. Eventually, what sent me back to Teesside was that lack of community in London. All the years I lived there, it always felt cold and uncaring and that was fine for a while, liberating even, but it's a soulless way to spend your life once you get a bit older.'

She directed him into Great Ayton, one of those places that's too small to call a town, but too big to call a village. Set against the hills, and with a lot of bungalows which Nick had always assumed were for the retired gentlefolk of Teesside: a place to die within earshot of birdsong. You could do worse.

'It's just beyond the station, on Dikes Lane. On the left, a white cottage,' she said, reading from Mandy's directions.

He slowed down. 'Is that it? Aw, Jules, look at it, it's lovely.'

He turned off the narrow road onto a small gravel drive. The small, pretty cottage was painted white and had borders of flowers all around it, mostly marigolds. It really did look like a holiday cottage. Set right on the edge of Great Ayton, with open countryside to the east, it was idyllic and was so quiet as he unlocked the front door, with just the sounds of birds and the breeze in the trees. Inside it smelled of potpourri and clean linen. It was plain and simple.

They had a little hug in the small kitchen.

'We'll be nice and snug in here, Jules. The forecast is good, we can go walking up in the Cleveland hills. We've not had a break for yonks. Let's just pretend this is a romantic holiday. No-one will know we're here. Just me and you together, with each other. I can't think of anything better.'

She sighed. 'Yeah...yeah...it will be nice. Really nice. Let's sit in the sun, have a drink and relax. It's been a very stressful day and my head's splitting again.'

Nick unpacked the shopping, put a bag of ice in the freezer, ripped it open and poured them each a large gin and tonic. Julie had set up two loungers on a patio on the south-facing wall. Beyond were fields and in the distance the green hills which ran up to Roseberry Topping.

'Cheers, luv.' She took the glass from him, along with two Ibuprofen. 'Oh, it is bloody lovely here. I wonder how long Cleveland Police have owned this for?'

'Aye, at last we're getting something in return for all the council tax we pay. It's spotless inside. Doesn't look like it's used that much. It feels like we've gone back in time by about 60 years. We might have got privileged treatment by Mandy, you know.'

She took his hand as he sat down and gave it a squeeze.

'I've been thinking, this must be all very difficult for you,' she said.

'Well, it's not the most fun I've ever had, that's for sure.'

'You've found a dead man. You've had the vivid dreams. You've had to see your missus in those photos, and I've had to tell you about the rape and about Green and all of that. Not many blokes would like to hear about their wife in those sorts of situations. I hope it doesn't fizzin' well put you off us, physically, I mean.'

'You're not really worried about that, are you?'

'Yeah, of course I am.'

He squeezed her hand. 'Owee, man, don't be daft. You know that's not how my brain works.'

The sun was hot on their faces. Nick closed his eyes and soaked up the heat.

'No, it's not, is it?' she said. 'I don't recall you ever being jealous or possessive or being hung up about the love life that I had before we met. In fact, when we first started going out, that used to annoy me a bit. It felt like you couldn't care much for me if you weren't jealous of my old lovers.'

'Well, you weren't like that about my old girlfriends, either.'

'I was a bit. I still am, a bit. When you say how good an old girlfriend was in bed, I do feel something. I feel sort of jealous or...no...it's not that...I don't know what it is. I'm realistic about it, but if our positions in this business were reversed, I'm not sure I'd be anywhere nearly as cool about this business as you're being.'

'I have mulled it over quite a lot.'

He tried to focus his thoughts, eyes closed, absorbing the hot sun.

'See, the whole sex with other people thing just doesn't bother me at all. Sex makes the world go round and I loved it when the chance came along. Alright, occasionally it was embarrassing or awkward, but life is like that to me anyway, and pretty much on a day-to-day basis. I'd rather have awkward and embarrassed, but with the added bonus of some naked flesh and physical pleasure. And when I met you, from the first time, it was obvious that we were so good together - physically, like - that it never felt I was competing to match your previous conquests. It was obviously special.'

'We just clicked, like that. From that first night together, even if you had been competing, you'd have won. I even told you that early on, as I recall.'

'Aye you did sing "you're simply the best" to me, after one especially good session. Obviously, I didn't let myself believe it.'

'I know you didn't. That's you all over. Ironically, it's probably why you're so good in bed.' She squeezed his hand. 'But don't the photos bother you at all?'

He didn't respond immediately.

'Yeah, of course. You were abused. It's disgusting. But I look at it like this; who you are, how you are and what makes you the woman I love so much, is all a product of everything that happened to you before we ever met. So despite being disgusted and furious about it, the way I deal with this and everything else bad that happened to you, is by accepting it made you into this bloody fantastic lass that I fell head over heels in love with, from the first time I saw you. We just have to catch them and get them to pay for their crimes...and we will...or Mandy will, anyway.'

She looked over to him, her face desperate and upset at his loving words.

'Oh, come on, luv. Don't cry. Please. You'll set me off,' said Nick, seeing her expression.

'Well stop being so sodding lovely, you git! You're so nice. Sometimes I feel like I don't deserve you,' she said, squeezing tears from her eyes with forefinger and thumb.

'Don't be daft. I am lovely though, as long as you ignore all of the distinctly unlovely things.'

She put her hands on his cheeks and looked at him with reddened, bloodshot eyes. 'You're joking, but it's true, you're so lovely and I love you so much that it almost physically hurts. Your mam was right, you are special.'

That did it. He had only one emotional response available to him; he burst into tears. All of the tension and psychic upset flooded out of him uncontrollably.

The hot, sunny, late summer weather didn't break for three days, allowing them to go walking all over the hills each day, arriving back at the cottage each evening, feeling pleasurably exhausted. There was no word from Mandy.

On the Tuesday evening, a storm got up and blew in from the North Sea, making the temperature drop considerably. They sat in the small living room, either side of an open fire which they'd managed to light with some dry sticks picked up on their walk. There was a small bag of coal at the back. Nick dropped a couple of lumps on the burning wood.

'It's funny how nice an open fire is; almost like having something living in the room,' said Julie, sipping at some green tea. 'It was such a normal part of life when we were little, lighting and maintaining a fire. And the smell of the coal smoke hanging in the air on a still, frosty cold day is the smell of being little, to me.' She sighed heavily. 'Oh, god, where's all that time gone? How did we end up middle aged, we were only kids not long since? I really miss being young and having my whole life ahead of me. I always thought there was so much time for everything and anything to happen. Now there feels so much less time and every day seems to pass faster than the last.'

'I was saying to Jeff the other day how I miss the smog of our childhood. Even now, when I smell coal burning, it takes me back to being a little boy. It's actually almost a comforting smell.'

She nodded and grinned. 'I know just what you mean.' She yawned. 'God, I'm knackered again. My thighs are feeling strained and not for the usual mister thrusty reasons.'

'I'm not at home to mister thrusty, today. I'm ready for bed and it's only eight. We must have walked at least 12 miles today.'

'12.6 to be exact, according to my phone's GPS.'

'I hope Jeff is managing to get the club sorted out without Emily to help in the shop.'

'Lukey will be down from Newcastle, I should think. Why hasn't she been in touch with him or us? Surely she would have been if she could. I'm so concerned about her. I hate to say it but it really does look bad. Matty Rhodes has turned evil and I'm sure he's done something to her.'

'Yeah, Jeff said the same thing and it's hard not to think that her just falling off the radar is a bad sign. My dream of her having been stabbed keeps coming back to me, you know. But what can anyone do? It was like when Rita went missing, hunting for someone is hard, especially if they don't want to be found. You can't just go around the region knocking on doors. She might not even be around here. She might be anywhere.'

'But she left her stuff at ours,' she said.

'It was just clothes and the keys to the flat. There was no money or debit cards. She must have had those on her.'

'But she must know we'll be worried about her.' Julie yawned.

'She will, but maybe she wants us to be worried. She's using her disappearance as a weapon against everyone she feels was telling her what to do. Maybe it's even some sort of empowering thing for her.'

'Or she's being held against her will by Matty, or...or worse,' said Julie.

He didn't want to think about 'worse'. He went to Emily's Facebook page. It hadn't been updated since she'd left. Neither had Matty's. 'You know how you have your Facebook page unavailable to be found if someone searches for your name and it won't come up either on Facebook or Google?'

'Yeah. That's what we're advised to do. But if someone knows one of your friends, they can find your page via their list of friends, if they don't make their lists private. It only takes one person in your network to not have everything locked down to be able to find you, in theory at least.'

'Hmm, see, I can't find either Boz Bailey, or the right Tommy Green or Sean O'Connor using Facebook's search options, but if we knew the name of one of their friends, we might be able to find their pages and see if they've accidentally made a recent post public, sometimes that happens and you don't realise. And that way we can probably get a current profile photo of Green and maybe even find out where they are. Any ideas of names that Green or O'Connor was friends with?'

The fire crackled as she tried to recall. 'God, it's so long ago. And who wants to be friends with a convicted rapist?'

'Other rapists, maybe? Who did Green work for?'

She clapped her hands together. 'Storyville Publishing! Remember?'

'Of course. O'Connor was published by Storyville's poetry arm and that was where they must have first met. Right, I'm going to write to Tim Forest and ask him if anyone remembers Green before he was hauled off to jail.'

'Are you going to tell him why?'

'Yeah, I see no reason, not to. This is serious stuff.'

Julie held the mug to her mouth, inhaling the steam from the tea.

Nick wrote the email to Tim Forest, then got up and went to the toilet, returning to find Julie dozing off.

'Come on, Jules, let's hit the hay.'

He hauled her up to her feet and was just about to shut his laptop when he noticed an email had come in immediately from Tim Forest.

'What's he say?' said Julie, scratching her left buttock, farting and yawning.

'Err...that he remembers him. He joined the company in 1990 and Green was working there when he started. Was a popular worker. Everyone was shocked when he was sent to jail. No-one suspected him of anything at all, let alone something so serious.'

'I didn't suspect him until going to bed with him. And even then, I wouldn't have said he was a rapist. I didn't write that I was scared of him, only that I thought he might be bit clingy. I mean, for whatever reason, he didn't rape or assault me, but was arrested for that only a few weeks later. That's almost as weird as anything else. You're in bed with rapist who doesn't rape you.'

'Tim says he remembers Green was friends with someone called Leo Ulloa. That's all he remembers. Ulloa left before Green was arrested. Right, let's find Ulloa. Odd name...'

'It's Argentinian or Uruguayan, I think.'

Nick typed the name into the Facebook search bar. There was only one Leo Ulloa.

'Is that him?' said Julie, looking over his shoulder.

'Yeah, look, in previous employers he's listed Storyville. So it's deffo him.'

He looked in his mid or late 40s. High cheekbones and light brown skin. Nick clicked on his friends list. 'Excellent. He's left his friends open to the public. Let's see now. There's 598. Ridiculous. Scrolling down the page slowly, he got half way down when Julie yelped and pointed.

'Tommy Green!'

'Got him!' Clicking on the image revealed a profile picture of a man standing, arms folded outside of what looked like a pub.

'Is that him Jules? It is, isn't it? He's our peeper. Same short brown hair and the same pot belly.'

She nodded. 'I honestly wouldn't have recognised him as Tommy Green, if I'd passed him in the street. He's changed a lot. God almighty, he looks much older and he's totally gone to seed. The gut on him. But it is definitely him. You can actually see the cute man he once was under the jowelly fat face, and he's the same build as the peeper. Even if we didn't have the DNA on tissues, this proves it's him.'

Nick saved the picture, attached it to an email and sent it to Mandy and Jeff. In a way, he didn't want to linger on the man's face. He'd done extraordinary, terrible things and yet he appeared so ordinary. At least Boz Bailey looked like a thug. This man looked like so many ordinary men. Did that mean everyone was capable of being a violent rapist? Surely not. He knew he couldn't be.

'It is hard to look at him and believe he's done what he's done. Even harder to think that you once shared a bed with him.'

'Hmm, well, if he had raped me, at least it wouldn't have lasted long, huh?!' She snorted a bitter laugh and flicked the V's at the screen, jaw jutting out, in defiance of the man looking back at them.

'Right, well, now we've got into their circle, let's look on Green's friends list.' A few clicks later he'd found Sean O'Connor.

She stood, hands on hips and fearlessly peered at the screen. 'Good grief, he's hardly changed. That photo on the shop's Facebook page didn't really do him justice. He's 45 but he looks about 30 or 31.'

'Considering he's spent years in Wormwood Scrubs, he doesn't look bad at all. Not like Green. This is exactly how he looked like when he was in the shop, so it's a recent photo. He was very personable. That's the worst thing about it. Remember Jimmy Repp, the goalkeeper? He was like that. Such a nice man, but a nice man who did terrible things.' He went to O'Connor's page and looked at the posts. The latest one was of him with his arm around a blonde woman, posted a month ago.

She let out a sigh and shook her head. 'There's always a new woman. A new victim.'

There wasn't a lot to be gleaned from either of their Facebook pages. They'd not made any public postings. Boz Bailey wasn't on either of their friends lists. Bailey looked like the sort of man that would think Facebook was shite. Jail was his social network. Nick sent Mandy O'Connor's Facebook photo, too.

'Well, at least Mandy's got current photos of them to circulate. Should make things easier for them,' said Nick, taking off his clothes in the small, warm bedroom. Julie pulled off her t-shirt and sniffed at her armpits.

'Dear me, I stink. But can't be arsed to have a shower.'

'Yeah, me, too.'

She sniffed at him.

'Oooh, you are a bit tangy but it's such a warm night, we'll get in a right lather, anyway. Get a shower in the morning.'

'Yeah, it's roasting in here. No need for pyjamas tonight.'

'God, no. I need some air around my sweaty parts, even if I am a bit cheesy. It must be 10 degrees hotter in here than downstairs.'

'Warm air rises, doesn't it?'

'I'm not complaining. We get so much cold weather that sleeping in the nuddy feels quite daring.'

Nick turned out the light and they lay on top of the duvet.

'Night night, mister,' she said, kissing him on the neck and giving his balls a light squeeze.

He put his fingertips together and breathed slow and deep, reciting the Lord's Prayer in his head and then praying for Julie, for Jeff and Argie and for the strength of mind to cope with whatever life might throw at him. Amen. Praying didn't feel like it was anything to do with the church or religion in the conventional sense, that all felt too earthly, too made up by humans. The space he went to in these moments was above and beyond all of that nonsense.

'There's a good lad. It's nice to pray, I think. I'm no fan of the church but I always liked Jesus, not that he's made an appearance since I've been dead, so I'm not sure what all that means.'

Nick sat up, feeling hot and his skin a little damp. He was less shocked this time when he saw his mother sitting on the chair in the corner of the room. She was dressed in the same clothes as before. She smiled warmly at him. Glancing at the clock it said 4.27am, as usual.

'Now then, our Nick,' she said in her distinctive Hull accent, an accent that sounded like a close cousin of his own Teesside voice.

'Hello, mam.' He smiled, happy to meet her again. 'Yeah, you always said I should feel like Jesus was my friend. I'd forgotten about that until the last year or two. I do find it comforting, though I've no interest in religion really.'

He turned to look at Julie, lying on her side, the round curve of her bare backside towards him. She was breathing heavily. For a moment he felt like he should cover himself up in front of his mother and toyed with the idea of putting his hands over his bollocks.

'It's hot in here,' he said. 'Sorry, I've not got any pyjamas on.'

'Oh, don't worry about that. I'm your mam.' She said it with a flat certainty, as though it explained everything.

'It feels a bit weird, though.'

She smiled at him in that distant sort of way which suggested maybe she couldn't really see him clearly.

'Eee, you really take after your dad.'

'In what way?'

'In the downstairs department.'

'Well I couldn't take after you, could I?' He covered himself up by throwing the edge of the duvet across his midriff.

She laughed a lovely warm, rolling laugh. 'Oh, you were always such a funny and cheeky and rude lad. Eee, you made me laugh so much, when you were little. The way you went on. Eee, I miss those days, holding your hand as we walked around town. You'd look up at me with bright eyes, all happy and I thought you were the most beautiful, special boy in the world.'

'Do you remember what you used to always tell me?'

'To just be a nice lad and have good manners. And if you can't say anything nice, don't say anything at all.'

'That's it. I've been thinking about that quite often these days. I never realised what simple but good advice it was. For years and years, I'd forgotten it, or didn't appreciate it. But now I try to remember it when I get cross or impatient.'

'Good lad. I'm glad about that.'

'Do you know what's going on with those horrible men, mam?'

'Of course I do. I told you that you knew who it was, didn't I? Julie had told you about the man who attacked her. So you knew who it was, but you didn't let yourself tell yourself.'

'I know, you were right. But how was I supposed to know it was him again?'

'All I'm saying, our Nick, is trust your instincts. That's all, luv. You do know what's going to happen. In your heart you do, just like you knew what the publisher would offer you. You're a special lad, but don't overthink things, just act on your instincts.'

'You keep saying that, mam, but...'

She interrupted him and shook her head. 'Listen to me. Listen now. Are you listening?'

'Yes, mam.'

'When I say you're special, I really mean it. You've got to believe in yourself and your own special qualities, that's all it is. You've always lacked self-confidence, despite being funny and clever and a lovely boy. You've always thought you weren't quite up to things, even though it's not true. It's probably me and your dad's fault. I never told you how talented and special you were, not enough anyway. And then I went daft and I couldn't help you. And your dad was no good when it came to feelings. I'm so sorry. I'm sorry you had to grow up on your own, we should have been there for you, Nick.' She got up from the chair and sat down on the edge of the bed, right beside him. The bed creaked as she sat down.

Nick propped himself up. He could feel her weight on the bed, it pulled the quilt a little. Does any dream do that?

'Do you understand me?' she said, leaning forward, putting her hand to his cheek.

Could he feel her touch? He could. Or could he? She looked into his eyes again with her watery stare, unfocused and, you had to say it, ghostly.

'Are you real, mam? I find all of this so weird.'

She smiled and it really did feel like he was about nine and she'd come into his bedroom, the way she always used to do. 'What does "real" mean, luv?'

'I mean, am I making this up in my sleep?'

His mother looked at him up and down, from his eyes to his toes.

'You're my Nick, you're real to me. Whatever I am to you, I don't know. It's not like it was, though. This is something else. I don't know what is, no-one gives you a rule book. It is what it is. But I can tell you this. I'm here with you. I am. Not like when I was alive. But in some of the important ways. But you have to listen to me. Whatever happens, trust your instincts.'

'You keep saying that over and over. What does that mean, mam?'

'It means, don't doubt yourself. The answer to anything is always in your head. You knew how much the publisher was going to offer you, you knew about those records, you knew about Emily...'

'...I didn't know about Emily. She was alive, not dead. Unless you're saying she's dead now.'

'Don't take everything so literally. Sometimes we tell ourselves truths through symbols.'

'She had a knife in her back. How should I not take that literally?'

'For a bright lad, sometimes you're a bit slow, our Nick. Just think about it. Let yourself understand yourself, luv. You've already been told about dreams being symbolic, by someone who understands what this is all about.'

He let out a sigh. 'Oh, mam, I don't know what that even means.' He was exasperated by the vague way she was speaking.

She stood up and smiled at him. 'Life isn't easy. I can tell you this, being dead is much easier.' She laughed happily, in a way that he hadn't seen for so long. She looked over to Julie, still sleeping on her side. 'Eee, she's got a lovely bum, that girl. Must be nice for you. Your girlfriends always had nice bums, didn't they? I know you've always been that way inclined. Funny that. Your dad wasn't fussed.'

She walked around the bed, pulled open the bedroom door. 'Ta ra, then. Think on about what I've said. Give Julie my love. And give her your love, too.' She paused. 'I know you know how to do that. It's alright, I won't look while you're doing your business.' She'd always been good at not saying rude words or talking about anything sexual, but letting you know exactly what she meant all the same.

With another laugh she left...or did she leave...wasn't it more like she faded?

Nick got the small glass of water from the bedside table and drank it all, noted it was still 4.27am, closed his eyes, put his fingertips together to try and get off to sleep again.

'Look at the state of you.' He opened his eyes and squinted into the sunlight coming through the window. The yellow-white light backlit Julie, making her look like an angel in a religious painting. Then again, angels were never naked, didn't smell a bit sweaty and they certainly didn't bend over and let fly with noisy farts, either. 'What have you been dreaming about?' She lifted up his erection between thumb and forefinger and inspected it, like it was a specimen in a laboratory, then leant over and lightly kissed it on the tip. 'And good morning to you, too.'

Nick laughed, feeling nice. 'Amazing what needing a pish does to a chap's priapic tendencies,' he said, getting off the bed to go to the toilet. As he did so, he glanced at the bedside table. The glass of water he'd drank from, was now full again. He'd only dreamed he'd drank it.

'What are you looking at?' said Julie,

'Oh, nothing. It doesn't matter.'

'Put the kettle on before you go to the bog, there's a luv, it'll be five minutes before that thing softens enough for you to pass water,' she said, getting back under the duvet.

He turned at the door. 'Mam came to me last night, again.'

'That's not why you've got a massive bonk on is it? Ha ha, I've not used that expression since about 1978. "He's got a big bonk on". Ha ha...eee, that takes me back. So what was she saying?'

'Aw, she was being really nice. And told me again to trust in my instincts and that Emily having a knife in her back was symbolic. What do you reckon?'

'I reckon I need a brew. That's what I reckon.' She paused. 'You're just trying to work stuff out when you're asleep. If it doesn't always make sense, that's why.'

'I keep thinking that. But when she's here, it's so real. Though she is sort of...'

'...what?'

'Sort of - and don't skit me for this - she's sort of ghostly. Here, but not here. She looks at me, but not in a way which is quite right; like I'm a long way in the distance to her. But she sat on the bed and I could feel it move. Then again, I drank from that glass and emptied it and now it's full. So I must have been asleep and just dreamed that I drank it.'

'Yes, of course you were. Don't fret yourself about it.'

'And she admired your bare arse. Said you have a lovely bum.'

She laughed. 'Well, that just proves it's the product of your imagination, doesn't it? That's totally your thing. And anyway, no-one's mother would admire their son's wife's arse, would they? That'd be proper weird. Your mother wasn't like that.'

He looked at the plain cream-coloured carpet. 'Maybe, yeah. She said to give you her love. And that I was to do the same to you, but she wouldn't look while I did, what she euphemistically called "your business".'

'She said you should do "your business" to my arse? Now, that's definitely you making it up in a dream.' She gurgled a laugh.

'She didn't specify where my love should go, Jules.'

He made a duck face at her and looked down at his softened erection.

She feigned indignation, arched eyebrows raised. 'Well, unless you get the bloody kettle on, there'll be no business for her to not look at!'

Nick put two green tea bags into mugs, went to the toilet, then waited for the kettle to boil, watching a blackbird hacking at some moss on the lawn, reflecting on his latest meeting with his mother. After each one, even though it was a bit confusing, he found himself feeling happy to have met her. It lifted his spirits.

'Thanks, luv,' Julie said, as he put the mugs down and got back in bed.

'That storm seems to have passed and it's sunny again,' he said, looking out of the window. 'Shall we have a lazy day? I'm still sore from all the walking.'

'Fine by me. It really does feel like the sort of holiday we always say we should have but never get round to.'

He got back into bed. 'Yeah, it's an odd situation, but I don't want it to end. I like being away from the day-to-day grind and all that horribleness. And it's so nice to spend so much time together, as well. I love just being with you all day.'

She smiled, stroked his arm and drank tea. 'What else did your mam talk to you about, then? Apart from believing in yourself and rather improbably suggesting some arse-based business.'

'She said she was always with me in all the important ways, but couldn't really explain why or how, only that this was how it was. She was quite chatty. It's funny because I didn't really have a normal chat with her for literally decades. She was always doped up or fried, one way or another, so it's really odd talking to her now. But I really love it, Jules. I hope she doesn't stop coming to see me.'

Julie turned to him. 'Aw that's quite sweet, in a way. Freaky, but sweet. I think she'll keep coming for as long as you need her to.'

'Oh, and I was lying there with nothing on and she said I took after my dad in what she of course called "the downstairs department".'

'Ha ha. That's such a nice polite term for it. Did she mean in shape or size, I wonder? Or rather, what you meant by creating it in your dream?'

'It made me feel awkward, so I covered up.'

'Being embarrassed in a dream by the ghost of your own mother's comments about your wedding tackle being like your dad's, is some serious psychological stuff, man. Don't go too deep into that. You can't afford that much therapy.' She chuckled just as Nick's phone buzzed to tell him a text had arrived. The joy dropped out of him. That was the modern world calling. He looked at her, dread suddenly heavy and leaden in his guts. It was going to be bad news. It was going to be awful news.

CHAPTER 14

'I'm scared of what that says, Jules.'

With the kind of fearlessness that an upbringing in Hardwick had tattooed on her DNA, she got out of bed and picked the device up from the dressing table, skimming the screen.

'It's from Jeff. Oh, my god!' She held her hand to her mouth.

'What? What is it?' He leapt out and took it from her.

'Double Good news: Emily is back, safe and sound this morning. Says she was at her dad's country pile in Lincolnshire "sorting shit out" but is keeping quiet about everything. Also Mandy says the 3 Evils were spotted together leaving the region yesterday and heading south. Been scared off by her mob, she reckons. Woo! She'll be in touch later. Hope you're having a good time wherever you are - I imagine you're in an underground Teletubby-style house. Everything is fine here. Nothing left for you to worry about. See you Friday.'

'Oh, thank god,' said Nick, suddenly really emotional. 'Shitting hell, that's such brilliant news...I never thought it'd say that. I was sure it was bad news.'

She hugged him and they shook each other up and down and side to side, laughing.

'As soon as those blokes knew that Cleveland Police were onto them, they must have legged it,' she said. 'Mandy could easily have arrested Green for what he's been doing out the back.'

'Yeah, well, they've already spent years in jail, they don't want to go down for another long stretch, at least not so soon, so they took evasive action.'

'I'm so glad Em's alright...so glad...oh, bloody hell.' She filled up with tears and that set Nick off too as the pent-up tension and worry was released from their bodies.

'God, I've not cried so much in my whole life as I've cried this week,' said Nick. 'And I hope I never do again.'

They got home on Thursday afternoon. The house was still locked up safely. No-one had broken in and there was no sign of Bailey and his camera, O'Connor or Green. Early in the evening Jeff called by.

'Now then, big man,' said Nick, opening the door and gripping hands with him. 'How goes everything?'

'It goes like a blue-arsed fly riding a bike on speed. I'll be up all night at the club getting it ready for tomorrow's opening.'

'Hi, Jeff,' said Julie, 'do you want a drink?'

'I'd love one but can't risk it just now. I'm driving a van full of booze, plastic glasses, chairs, mops, bleach and an almost unfeasible amount of toilet paper.'

'And that's just to get you through the night,' said Nick.

'Exactly. I do feel a degree of incontinence, actually.'

'Any excuse to wear a nappy,' said Nick.

'You know me too well, old son.'

'Do you want some tea, then?' said Julie, filling the kettle.

'Aye, great. So how are youse two? You've both come back tanned. Was this mystery hideaway on the Algarve?'

'Not exactly. Didn't Mandy tell you where?'

Jeff shook his head. 'Nope. I never even heard of them having safe houses, but I suppose that's why they're safe.'

'It was a nice few days away, as it turned out. Lovely weather. It was on the edge of the countryside so we did a lot of walking and drinking...' said Nick.

'...as well as a lot of crying and some quality downstairs business,' interrupted Julie, winking at Nick.

'Bloody hell. I'll have go into hiding if that's all being provided by Cleveland Police free of charge. State-funded sex is the way ahead for civilisation.'

'So, what's the situation with Emily? She's still not been in touch with us,' said Julie.

Jeff sat down on one of their kitchen stools while Julie put the kettle on.

'She just strolled into work at 9am on Wednesday, as cool as you like. As though nothing had happened.'

'What did you say?'

'Tommo was in, he was first up to her. "Where've you been, little Emily? We were worried about you", he goes. She just says, "Oh I had to sort some things out at my dad's house in Lincolnshire". But Tommo wasn't having that and you know how he is, he gets quite indignant if he thinks someone has behaved badly. "You might have rang in, lass. You knew we'd all be worried about you", he says.'

'What did she say to that?' said Nick.

'She just apologised and said that she'd lost her phone, but obviously other phones exist and she could have called from her dad's. So she'd definitely decided to disappear and not tell us.'

'And was she OK, physically?' asked Julie.

'As far as I could tell, she was more like her old self than at any time in recent weeks. She was clean and sober with no cuts or bruises visible. I haven't probed her any more because she's not a kid. If she wants to go awol, she can. It made life difficult in the shop and I told her that. She said sorry again and that she'd work overtime to make up for it.'

'So, did you believe her?' said Julie. 'Had she really gone to Lincolnshire?'

Jeff shrugged. 'I don't know. I could ring her dad up, I suppose, but I'm not her carer, am I? She's gone down in my estimation, though.'

'She was very pissed off when she left here. She felt like she was being lectured and hectored by the grown ups and I can see why. I think she's tried to punish us by not getting in touch,' said Julie.

'Aw, diddums. Someone looking out for you, how bloody terrible. Sorry, I've no sympathy, you don't do that to your mates,' said Jeff, flicking his long hair over his shoulders. 'She could have just told us she was OK. She did it to punish us. Still, for what it's worth, it feels like she's made some sort of decision. There's been no talk of Matty, no frantic messaging on her phone. And he's not been around at all. So maybe she's drawn a line under him.'

'Maybe she went away to get some thinking time, to get time to sort out what she wants to do. Sometimes you need to get away to do that. So where's she staying now?' asked Julie.

'Back at the flat, or that's where she said she was going last night. I've started to not believe her, though. Don't like that at all. She was always so reliable. To be honest, Jeffrey's Psychic Arial is twitching. I don't think this is going to end well and I don't even have precognition, unlike some.'

'But she's going to the big opening, isn't she?' said Nick.

'As far as I know, yeah. Talking of which...' he took out four black laminated cards with the letters JRC intertwined in a gothic font in metallic silver. 'VIP' was written underneath in red. 'These will get you in tomorrow night. Thought I'd give them to you now because I'll be so busy tomorrow that I might not see you. The first door is for the public, second door is for VIPs. There's two for you and two for your mam and

Con, Jules. Don't pull a face, those two will put me in profit from their drinks bill alone. Con likes his music and your mam knows everyone, so it's like getting an advert on national TV. Once she knows about something she'll tell everyone.'

'That is true. I'll drop them in before work tomorrow. Is Mandy going?'

'She most certainly is. And you better watch out when she starts dancing, it's like an explosion at an overstocked butchers. There's meat everywhere!'

They both laughed.

'This is all brilliant,' said Nick. 'So who've you booked to play?'

'We kick off with Status No, a Quo tribute band. Really good, I've seen them before. Double denim all the way. Then I've got Jo King on. She's doing a 30-minute set of some of her most gross acts of self-mutilation, whilst telling jokes. I think it'll really appeal to a rock audience, but she's not sure. What do you reckon?'

'I think it will. Yer rocker loves a bit of shock and gore,' said Julie, pushing a mug in front of him.

'Well, we'll soon see. Headline act is Hurricaine, Alison Caine's new band. Have you heard them?'

'Ali Caine's mam, Heather, was in my year at Ian Ramsey,' said Julie. 'She looked like a glamorous Romany lass, with gorgeous, thick, wavy black hair. Always loved swimming. In fact, didn't she become a swimming instructor at the baths?'

'Yeah, she did. I saw her this week, actually. Had a quick word. Still a lovely lass. I went to see the band earlier in the week playing Fibbers in York. Amazing. They'll blow you away. She's got a voice like Beth Hart, the guitarist puts me in mind of Paul Gilbert. In fact, they do a few Mr Big and Heart covers in their set. Think they'll go down well.'

'Brilliant!' Julie clapped. 'Ali is amazing. Huge voice on her. I saw her old band a few times, what were they called, again...oh aye, Raw Blues,' said Julie. 'Hurricaine sound great.'

'Yeah, they're very upbeat. Sort of heavy, poppy and shreddy all at once. I've told them, no ballads. All balls-to-the-wall rock.'

'Or fanny-to-the-wall in Ali's case,' said Julie, admonishing him with an accusatory finger.

Jeff held his hands up. 'Hey, sister, you can't get me on a sexist charge anymore, the JRC is the only club in the northeast to have gender-neutral bogs. Thus I am cool and thus when I say I admire Ali Caine's melonic tits, it's not sexist, right?'

'Melonic? Having the properties of melons!' said Nick. 'Actually, you're right, they do.'

'I tell you what, I wouldn't mind being reincarnated as her bra,' said Jeff, conspiratorially.

'Alright boys, put your willies away,' laughed Julie. 'Her mam was the same. We were all jealous of them. We had bee stings in the second year, she had a proper booby cleavage. They must be around her waist by now, poor lass. There was always one lass in every year at school that gets the big knockers early.'

'They were still quite firm by the look of it, actually. Well upholstered, obviously. Anyway, we've got the jukebox hooked up to the sound system and I've loaded it with 200 of my favourite singles.'

'So there's 25 Uriah Heep on there, then,' said Nick.

'Only two, actually. "Gypsy" and "Easy Livin'". I think you'll approve of the selection.'

'I'm sure we will. Jeff, man. I'm so excited. This is amazing,' said Julie, bouncing in her seat.

'So is the amount of money it's cost me. I went in thinking 100 grand would do it, but we topped out at 155k!' They both looked shocked. 'I know, it's trouser wetting. I'm totally skint. So I really need to coin some money quickly if I'm going to be able to fund it ongoing.'

'So how are you selling tickets for tomorrow at such short notice?'

'Local radio, the *Gazette* and I've got *Look North* coming to the shop later to interview me. We'll sell some through the shop and the rest on the night, first come first served.' He puffed out his cheeks. 'I should have had a month to prepare for opening, but needs must.'

'It'll be a huge success, man. You know it, I know it, everyone knows it,' said Nick, kicking Jeff on his boot.

'I wish I had your confidence. All I see right now is a giant hole into which, like a lunatic, I am hosing money, money which mostly isn't even mine.'

'Yeah, well, if it all goes tits up, Barclays can take the hit. Fuckers,' said Nick.

'Aye, fuck 'em. Justin, from their lending department, was about 24 and knew the square root of fuck all about rock 'n' roll. The whole thing was phoney bullshit. They pretend they know about business but they've never even run a fucking business, let alone a rock club. At the end of the

219

day, they gave me the money because I own a house they could sell if I don't pay them. I secured the loan on the house. And that's the start and end of it all. The rest of it is just window dressing and the funny thing is, they think we don't know. It was embarrassing for me and this twat in his cheap Burton's suit with his degree in Being A Git in his back pocket. They sent him to look around what was, at the time, a total shit hole, with me telling him how it's going to be a great club. He's nodding and trying to pretend he's a professional when he's just a corporate drone who ticks boxes. I had ticked the box marked "has a house worth three times what he's borrowing", that's all it was. It's not like the old days when a bank manager would assess your worth as a man and as a business. No words could express the contempt I have for Barclays and their blank-eyed drones.'

Nick and Julie stood up in unison and applauded.

Jeff laughed. 'Aye, and you two can sod off as well.'

Julie opened the fridge, took out a bottle of tonic water and began to make herself and Nick G & Ts.

'So what's the future plan for JRC?'

'I'm going to try opening every night as a bar, bands on Friday, Saturday and Wednesday. comedy on Sunday nights. I'm booking acts in now. I literally have no time to even think about the shops. Do you fancy working for me? I need someone I can trust to run the shop. Lukey and Harrogate Harry already run the other two shops virtually autonomously, so there's just Stockton to keep ticking along.'

'I don't know. I have to write. Writing is my thing, not retail.'

'I know, but I'm knackered in the short term, man. I can sort it out in the long term, but for the next few weeks I need a responsible adult in charge. I would have been happy to leave Emily in charge until this past week but now, I'm not so sure. She'll have to prove herself all over again, I think.'

'Yeah, well, of course if I can help, I will. But I'm not a natural salesman.'

'You don't have to be, you just need to know where everything is and have the patience of a saint when someone tells you a record is too expensive, or another who returns a £1.00 record because it's got a scratch. The rest of it is just talking to over-focused people about music, and I know you can do that.'

'That's about the only thing I can do.'

'We're getting dressed up to the nines for tomorrow night,' said Julie. 'Full rock 'n' roll garb.'

Jeff stood up and finished his tea. 'Well, I look forward to seeing both of you in your finery. I'm determined it will be a night no-one will forget, one way or another. Ta for the tea. I'd better get off. I've got bar staff coming in this evening for training.'

'Training? Do you need a lot of training to pour drinks?' said Nick.

'My bar staff will be part of the entertainment. All will be revealed!' He moved his eyebrows up and down in a cryptic manner. 'I'll see youse both tomorrow. Kick off is 7pm, but you can get in with your passes from 6.30. Let's hope someone turns up, eh.'

Julie finished work early and got in just after 5pm on Friday. Nick was ironing his shirt and jeans.

'Need anything doing?' he said, as she bounded in, doing one of her excitable impromptu dances that looked like a cross between an epileptic fit and someone being tasered.

'No, thanks, I'm all sorted with the distressed tight black jeans with silver studs on, my faux leather shirt and the pointy pointy boots.'

'The ones with the Cuban heels?'

'Aye, so you've got to wear your leather boots with a heel, or I'll be taller than you.'

'Would that matter?'

'It shouldn't matter, but it does. Dunno why and now is not the time to have a philosophic discussion about gender, height and shoes; I need to get a shower. Make us a brew, will you, luv?'

She ran upstairs while he put the kettle on. He was looking forward to the gig, but being in a hot, noisy club with a lot of Friday night pissheads - and Stockton did Friday night pissheads very well - was much less his idea of a good time. Maybe it's an age thing, but just before you're due to go out, staying in always feels like a more attractive option.

He prepared some strips of beef and finely chopped some vegetables and ginger for a stir-fry, then took her tea up to the bedroom.

'Thanks, luv,' she rubbed at her hair. 'Do you think I can get my hair to look like that?' She pointed to a picture of Kate Moss on her laptop, wearing her blonde hair centre-parted, but sort of messy, like she'd just got out of bed.

'Well, I'm no hairdresser but I reckon so, aye. Bed hair is easy enough to achieve with the judicious use of a bed...god, *that* sounded just like Jeff.'

'Yeah, well, there's no time for bed-based activity.'

Nick looked at the clothes she'd got out. 'Blimey, Jules, did Emily leave these?'

She glanced over at him as he held up a small pair of black knickers. 'Emily's pants wouldn't get past my knees, she's so petite. I just got those on my way home. Those jeans sit quite low on my hips, so I don't want a big wad of knicker hanging out the back, do I? So I had to get something the *Daily Mail* would certainly call "skimpy". And you can put your tongue back in lad, there's no time for any of that business, thank you very much.'

'Spoilsport.' He pulled them over his head. 'I'll go and make our tea.'

'You daft bugger, give us them back. Not too much food, though, I'll never get them jeans on, if my belly is full.'

After they'd eaten, he had a shower and dressed. As he fastened his tight, fitted white shirt, embroidered front and back with the outline of a Fender Stratocaster, and rolled up the sleeves, he looked at himself in the long mirror in the hall. It was right up his armpits and that meant he'd be wringing wet with sweat soon enough, but it wouldn't show too much on white. Did he look any good? He had no idea. How could you tell?

'How do I look?' said Julie, coming downstairs and posing hand on hip in front of him. 'Is the make-up too much?'

She'd put on a little mascara and deep pink lipstick. Her hair was now very rocky Kate Moss-ish.

'You look amazing. Those jeans looked almost sprayed on. Turn around.'

She did so. 'Any good?'

'Aye, you'll do.'

She looked down at her crotch. 'No camel toe?'

'Nope, they fit really well.'

'The jeans are digging into my hip bones a bit. Don't normally wear them this low.'

'Yeah, but you've still got a flat belly, so you can pull it off and I love that leather-look shirt. You look very glam, Jules. Very late 80s rock 'n' roll.' He put his hand up, in the manner of a kid in class.

She pointed at him like a posh, stern school teacher. 'Yes, Guymer?'

'Can I call you sexy, miss?'

'Go on then, just this once, Guymer and be quick about it, please.'

'You look very sexy, miss.'

'Thank you, Guymer. Do want some sort of sexual activity in return for that compliment?'

'No, miss.'

'Are you sure, Guymer?'

'Yes, miss.'

'Oh, that's a pity. I was hoping for a damn good rodgering. Any reason why not?'

'My mam might be watching, miss!'

They both laughed and pushed at each other playfully.

'I'll tell you something for nowt, I'll need to be cut out of these pants. Once I get a sweat on, they'll stick to me like glue. God knows how I'm going to go for a piss in Jeff's gender-neutral bogs.'

'I'll crowbar you out of them later,' said Nick.

'You and that crowbar of yours, I don't know. Now, give us a look at you.' She eyed him up and down. 'Alright! I see you're at home to Mr Sexy. Obviously, dressing to the left I see. Ha ha.' She grabbed at him.

'They don't leave much to the imagination, do they?'

'Almost nothing.'

'I think it's because it's a lightweight denim. Shall I change into my old ones?'

'No no no. You look really good and your bits aren't that obvious. I'm just kidding you.' She gave him a squeeze. 'Oooh, if I had a spoon, I'd eat you.' She rubbed his belly and slipped her fingers playfully down his pants, pulling a lusty face at him.

'Don't do that, man. If I get a hard on in these, they'll probably split in two. There's no room for any expansion.'

'Ha ha, I'd pay to see that. It'd be like the Alien bursting out of the bloke and looking around. Ha ha. Very similar-looking thing, in so many ways.'

She squirted a little Calvin Klein's Escape for Women onto her neck and wrists and messed with her hair in the mirror. 'I feel weird in make-up. I wear it so rarely, I'd almost forgotten how to put it on.'

'Aye, you do suit it for a special occasion, though.'

He nuzzled her neck from behind her, squeezed her backside and whispered an affectionate obscenity in her ear about what they might get up to in bed later.

She spun around and held him around the waist, pecking him on the lips. 'Oooh, you sexy old dog.' She laughed, took another quick look at herself. 'Right, come on then. Are you ready? Have you got your phone?'

'Yup. Have you?'

'Nah, I'll leave it at home. There's no way I can get it in these jeans pockets and I'm not taking a shoulder bag, like I'm a good little girl.'

'Hang on, I've left my cash in the bedroom,' he said patting at his pockets.

'And there was me thinking that bulge in your pants was a roll of money,' she said, making a goofy face at him.

Sprinting upstairs, he went into their bedroom and picked up the money from the bedside table. He counted it. £150. That should be enough. He jammed it into his pocket, took a quick look out of the window to check on the weather. The sky was blue, a few white clouds. No chance of rain. Warm. Ideal. Check the window is locked shut. Yes. Right, let's rock 'n' roll.

He turned to go downstairs, but as he did so, something caught his eye outside. Movement. He froze and stared at the blackthorn bush. Someone was there. He dropped to his knees, so he wasn't so visible. Whoever it was, was obscured now. Was it that bloke who had used the bush as cover for a piss? Or was it Tommy Green back for another wanking session? Surely not. They'd left the region.

Julie's voice came up the stairs. 'Owee, man, I'm gagging for a drink!'

He squinted but couldn't see any more movement. If anyone was there, they were hiding in the dense part of the bush. Had he imagined it? Maybe it had been a bird or something. A fox, maybe. Yeah, that's what it had been.

'Right, Jules, come on, let's rock it,' he said, running downstairs, grabbing her around the waist and planting a kiss on her lips. He called a Norton-based cab. No point in walking and getting a massive sweat on. It turned up in five minutes and took them down to the JRC on Church Road.

Nick paid the driver and got out, amazed at what he was seeing.

Julie looked at him, eyes wide. 'I do not believe this! I just don't believe it,' she said, as the cab pulled away.

There was a huge queue of people standing in line, stretching back beyond the swimming baths.

'Bloody hell, Jules!'

She looked at him, astonished. 'There's hundreds in this queue. Hundreds! Look at them all. They'll not all get in, surely.'

'Nick! Nick! Here!' A woman standing in the line was waving at him. It was Natalie Townsend standing alongside a man with long hair.

'Oh, hello, Natalie. Jules this is Natalie, we met at the allotments. She's taken that one on the far side.'

'Hiya. Looking forward to a night of rock 'n' roll?' said Julie, holding out her hand.

'Yeah. Me and Rob love a bit of rock.' She jerked a thumb at him.

'Isn't it amazing there's so many here?' said Julie.

But Natalie seemed distracted, staring into her eyes. 'Yeah, great, err, let me see, you're a Leo. 26th or 27th July...26th, yeah, 26th,' she said, and smiled.

Julie laughed. 'How did you know that? It is the 26th.'

'She did that to me, too,' said Nick. 'Apparently I'm a classic cusp.'

'I've been saying that for years,' said Julie, making a haw-haw face.

'You ooze Leo passion,' said Natalie.

'I do feel a bit oozy. Probably due to wearing these tight pants. Ha ha.' Julie laughed and made a shape and threw her head back. 'It's our mate who's set the place up. We're very excited for him,' she said, bending a little at the knees and doing a little wriggling dance on the spot.

'Aye, we've got VIP passes, so we'd better get in and a get a drink before they let the punters in. Nice to see you again,' said Nick.

They'd taken one step away from Natalie, when she grabbed at Julie's arm. Julie jumped, shocked to feel her firm grip. 'Be very careful, Julie. Right? Just be careful.' Her big face was set in a deep frown.

Julie shook herself free of her grip. 'What? Why are you saying that?'

'I'm just feeling negative energy around you.'

'Eh? I don't get what you mean?' said Julie.

Her words instantly worried Nick. She'd got the birthdays spot on. She had some talent or wisdom or whatever it was. What did she mean?

"Trust your instincts, our Nick." His mother's words rebounded around his brain once again. But what were his instincts? His instinct was that she had some sort of psychic power or understanding.

'What do you mean, Nat?' said Nick. 'Don't sugar coat it.'

She wouldn't look at him. 'I...I don't know. Some people give off a sense of danger...or...or...or doom. I can't say more than that. It maybe nothing. I'm sorry, I shouldn't have said anything.'

Was she for real, or a fake? He didn't know and couldn't tell.

'Natalie is a psychic,' said Nick. 'I forgot to tell you about her.'

Julie snorted and look from him to her. 'Seriously? It's all rubb...I'm sorry Natalie, I'm not a believer in any of that.'

'I'm sorry. I shouldn't have said anything,' said Natalie. 'It's probably nothing. I am probably projecting something onto you. Just have a great night.'

'She was a bit of a freaky hippy,' said Julie as they walked past the queue to the second door marked VIPs.

'Yeah, she's an angel light worker or something.'

'Is she? Well, aren't we all? Weird she knew my birthday, though.' She glanced at him a little nervously.

'And mine too. How could she know that?'

'Oh, there'll be a rational explanation.'

'I'm not so sure,' he said, a knot of worry forming in his guts as they walked up to the VIP entrance, where stood a big fat man with a shaven head.

'Evening madam, evening sir,' he said in a Brummie accent so thick you could have cut it with a knife and crafted it into a primitive form of origami. Nick produced the two black, silver and red passes.

'Alright, man. Quite a crowd, eh,' said Nick, casting a glance back to Natalie.

The big man inspected the cards like they were passports.

'Oh, yeah. Way more than 250 in the line, I reckon. Right this way, sir.' He ushered them through the door onto a red carpet.

'Bloody hell!' they said in unison, looking up at the wall in front of them.

They were staring at a huge, artistically lit black-and-white photo of Jeff, long hair framing his face, wearing an old denim shirt, arms outstretched in an embrace, a huge grin on his face. Underneath it said, 'Earth. Soul. Rock 'n' roll & Jeff.' He must have had it put up earlier in the day. It looked brilliant. Like he was a movie star or something.

'I can't take all of this in,' said Julie, looking up at the 10-foot-high, 5-foot-wide picture. 'Is that really our old mate?'

'Yeah, well, it's Jeff's Rock Club, so he's selling it on his own image. I think it's brilliant and, if you think about it, it makes commercial sense. Everyone knows Jeff.' A shiver went up and down Nick's spine. This was like something they'd have dreamed up at school.

The long bar had five bartenders, all dressed in black t-shirts with the JRC logo on the front. They were juggling bottles and doing tricks with glasses, bouncing them off their arms and pouring drinks behind their back. Tommo was standing holding a pint of bitter, looking at the juke-box.

'Alright, Tommo!' shouted Nick. The old lad turned and raised his glass to them, a big smile on his face.

'He put some Joe Brown on the jukey just for me!'

'Ah, here they are, Teesside's rock 'n' roll answer to Hart to Hart,' said Jeff, striding in. 'You two look very glamorous. Love your hair, Jules, looks like Kate Moss. What do you reckon, then?'

'It's bloody brilliant, Jeff. I can't believe it's the manky, damp place I saw a few months ago,' said Julie, raising herself on her tiptoes and kissing him on the cheek.

'Have you had a glass of bubbly yet?' He took them each a flute off a tray on the bar.

'Cheers, man. Here's to massive success,' said Nick.

'Yeah, well done, Jeffrey,' said Julie, sipping at the wine. 'Oof, that's not actually champagne, is it?'

'Of course not, it's white cider! Haha. This is a rock club, we don't serve champagne! Aye aye, here comes trouble.'

They turned to see Jackie Wells and Con coming in. With jet-black dyed hair, heavily made-up face, lots of blue eye shadow and pencilled-in eyebrows, she looked like a startled budgie. She was wearing a bright cerise blouse and black slacks, a black leather handbag over her shoulder. He was in a black v-necked t-shirt and blue jeans. With skin as tanned, creased and leathery as an old suitcase, the big Geordie looked like a cross between Brian Johnson and Johnny Cash.

'Alright, our Jules, hello, Nick. By god, Jeff, this place is a bit flash,' Jackie said.

'You look a bit flash yourself, Jackie,' said Jeff. 'New hair-do, is it?'

'Me and Sandra just did each other's hair. I totally butchered her, couldn't stop cutting it with me long hairdressing scissors. Just kept hacking away. She's virtually a skinhead. Ha ha.'

Con looked around. 'Must be some money been spent on fixtures and fittings here, Jeff. By god. That bar alone must've cost you a fortune.'

'I don't want to think how much it cost,' said Jeff, as someone came to him and shook his hand.

Jackie had already found the tray of glasses of white cider. 'Are these for us, like, Jeff? Eee, I'm bloody parched. Me throat's coated with hair

227

spray.' She took a flute and necked it in down one, before he had time to reply. 'Oh that's a canny drop, is that. What is it?'

'It's battery acid and lemonade, mam,' laughed Julie.

'What's that? A cocktail, like?' Sometimes you couldn't tell if Jackie was serious or was just making a very dry joke.

'It's gut rot cider isn't it?' said Con, taking a drink. 'Aye, it is a canny drop, if you ask me.'

'Eee, my god, look at you, Jules. You look like a million dollars, kidda,' said Jackie.

'Aw, thanks, mam, you're never nice to me. Are you on drugs?' said Julie, looking her up and down.

'You've always had a bit of flash in you. Nowt wrong with it. How much did those jeans cost?' said Jackie.

'150 dollars in America.'

'Bloody hell, and by the look of it you've got 100 dollars of them up your fanny.'

Con burst out laughing.

Julie rolled her eyes. 'I have not, mam. Don't bloody start. I like them.'

'I'm just kiddin' you, aren't I? You look lovely, doesn't she, Con?'

'Aye, you've got a lovely figure for a lass of your age, Jules. Take after your mam in that, like. Everything in the right place. All the right curves an' that, like a proper dolly bird.'

Despite his gnawing sense of worry, Nick couldn't help but laugh. It was so funny how a bloke like Con, as unreconstructed working class and Geordie as they came, broad of beam, six foot something and fore-arms like a pit pony's leg, still talked like it was 1975. He meant no harm by it, but it sounded very out of date, and the look on Julie's face as he said it was a mixture of amazement and humour.

'You can't say "dolly bird" anymore, Con,' she said. 'It's sexist.'

'Can I not? What's wrong with being sexy, like? I divvant knaw what ye can say these days, an' what ye' can't. Apparently "darkie" is wrong, so is "chinky" and I cannot say "gypo" anymore, either, and someone had a go at us for saying "spaz". And I'm certainly not allowed to say "cunt".'

'No. You're not,' said Julie. 'It's very much not allowed.'

'Right, well I'll not say it, then. Last thing I want to do is upset some cunt.' He winked at Jackie and Jackie laughed and raised a toast to him, emptied another flute of awful cider and picked up a third.

'It's nice to see you in a bit of make-up for a change, Jules. She looks proper classy tonight, doesn't she, Nick?' said Jackie.

'She looks amazing, yeah.'

Jackie stood in front of Nick, looked him up and down. 'Mind, son, them pants are so tight, I'm surprised you've not turned into a soprano. He fills his pants well, doesn't he Con? Aye, plenty of meat for dinner there, eh.'

What the hell did that mean? It seemed to be an in-joke between the two of them, as they both laughed.

'Aye, you're in good shape, Nick, I'll give you that,' said Con, who drank the acrid white cider down like it was water, reached for another one, sinking that in two gulps, and picking up a fourth and then a fifth in the space of a few seconds. Free drink was not to be ignored.

'You can talk, you're built like a brick shit house and you're in your mid 60s,' said Nick.

'Eee, he is well built, isn't he?' said Jackie who, it seemed likely, had been drinking before she'd even come out. 'In all departments, I can tell you that Jules. You should see the size of his bloody co...'

Julie held up her hand, turned her head away and interrupted her loudly '...Alright, mam! That's enough of that, thank you! Are you trying to be obnoxious, or does it just come naturally?'

'Oh, shut up. Sex makes the world go round, you know that as well as I do. Nowt wrong with a bit of nookie. Is it a free bar tonight, Jeff?'

Jeff turned round from talking to a journalist. 'I'm trying to make money Jackie, so no. Only the VIP cider is free and you've nearly had all of that.'

'Eee, no free drink. What sort of a launch party doesn't have a free bar?'

Julie looked at her mother in astonishment. 'Mam, how would you know? You've never been to a launch party for anything in your life.'

Jeff had given passes to a few of the shop regulars, a handful of old friends. They stood around, some managing to swallow the remaining cider, most opting for lager instead. Notable by her absence was Emily.

Nick was still nervous and he sensed Julie was as well. Natalie's words were haunting him and, looking at Julie, he knew she was feeling a bit edgy, but was putting a brave face on.

At two minutes to seven, Jeff stood in the middle of the club's floor and clapped his hands.

229

'Can I have some quiet please? Thank you. Don't worry, I'm not going to do a long speech. Just before we let the punters in, just wanted to say thanks to everyone who made this all possible, whether through hard graft or emotional support, and to tell you that my need for profit means I have to encourage you to have a long bout of thoroughly irresponsible drinking. It just remains for me to put the inaugural record on the juke-box and to declare Jeff's Rock Club officially open!'

They all cheered and clapped as he dropped the coin into the 1970s machine and selected Uriah Heep's 'Easy Livin'. It burst out of the PA system at volume. All the VIPs cheered, some started dancing. The line of people outside began to file in and head straight to the bar. Jeff went to deal with Status No.

'Hey, Julie.' A woman with neat, bobbed hair came up to them. Nick recognised her as one of Julie's co-workers at Teesside Women.

'Eee, hello, Yvonne. I didn't know you were coming.'

'Me and Dave just decided at tea time to come down 'cos he loves Status Quo, doesn't he? I thought it'd be quiet but it's packed out. We only just got in before it was full. It's brill in here, isn't it?' She looked around.

'Yeah, it's really impressive, posher than I thought.'

She looked her up and down. 'You've got all dressed up. Very nice, Jules. I don't know how you keep the weight off when all we do all day is sit on our arses.'

'Low-carb, high-fat diet, man. I keep telling you it's the way to go. Works for me anyway. But then I've got my own personal chef looking after my diet.' She patted Nick on the backside.

'Aye, but my life would be significantly more shit without chips, beer and toast, though. Hey, did Martha tell you what happened late this after-noon?'

'Tell me what?'

'About Emily Davids?'

'Emily? I'm sorry, what about her?' Julie shook her head, frowning.

'She came into TW this afternoon.'

They both stared at her. 'Are you sure?'

'Yeah, you left an hour early, so you must have missed her. She was assigned Karen Simmons as a support worker. She's coming back on Monday.'

'Did Martha say why she came in?' said Julie.

'She just said one word.'

'What word was that?' said Julie.

Yvonne cast a quick glance at Nick, turned back to Julie and silently but clearly mouthed the word 'rape'.

CHAPTER 15

Julie closed her eyes for a couple of seconds. 'Oh, god. Poor lass, but that's not actually a surprise. It's a positive thing that she's getting some help. I think she's got a lot of baggage that she needs to sort out. I'm sure Karen can help her.'

The two women talked, leaning into each other's ear, to make themselves heard over the sound of Deep Purple's 'Never Before', a record that Nick had always loved and still had his original copy of. This wasn't his conversation to have, so he happily ducked out of it.

The club was full now, the bar two deep with the five bar staff performing all sorts of tricks with bottles. It was amazing entertainment. One of them, a woman in a black vest who was covered in tattoos of skulls, flicked a glass down from the rack, bounced it off her shoulder, grabbed it and pushed it under the Stella Artois tap all in one move, then grabbed a bottle of Budweiser from a fridge, threw it 10 feet in the air caught it by the neck, whipped off the cap and scudded it across the bar. Very classy. How had Jeff found these people? Were they in the Yellow Pages under 'juggling bar staff'?

All the while, the jukebox had people pumping money into it, like it was a fruit machine; a great way to make money without anyone even realising it. One brilliant classic rock track after another blasted out of the speakers. Quite a few were dancing down by the stage. It was weird how if you make up something, people would flock to it. What would all these people be doing tonight if Jeff hadn't opened the club?

Nick went to the bar and got himself and Julie some vodka and tonic. The dude spun the measure on the bar, then poured the vodka from an arm's length into it and tipped it into glasses. It was all Las Vegas impressive.

He went back with their drinks. Julie was still talking to Karen, so he gave her the glasses and took the opportunity to go to the toilet.

Pushing open the door of any facility is always a tense, worrying thing to have to do; he peered inside. The line of stalls was pristine and clean. He took the first one, had a piss, washed his hands and dried them under the power dryer. As he was doing that, the door opened and two men came in.

A life of not looking at men in toilets meant that he didn't even think to look at either of them. Not until he heard an Irish voice say, "Did you see her? She looks fuckin' amazin' in those jeans. Always had a great arse. Can't wait to rip into that. Yeah, we'll bloody well have her.' They both laughed.

The two men went into stalls.

Nick left and stood opposite the toilet door, just waiting to see the two men come out, worried about the Irish accent. Was that Sean O'Connor? Was the other man Tommy Green? Come on, it can't be. There are plenty of Irish people around.

The man that opened the toilet door had a big, loose fitting t-shirt on and low slung, ill-fitting jeans. Short dark hair. Was that Green? Did he have the beer belly? It was hard to tell under the big shirt. Maybe. The other was wearing sunglasses, was lean and had a baseball cap on. Was that O'Connor? Shit. It was impossible to tell. They walked outside quickly, pulling out cigarettes, as they laughed at another joke.

He leaned against the wall, feeling paranoid and worried. An Irishman. Surely it couldn't have been them. They'd left the area, supposedly. But what if they *had* come back? Oh god, the stress of this was fucking destroying him. How long was this going to go on? It was torture.

As he stood mulling it over, he suddenly saw Matty Rhodes showing a VIP pass to the doormen and coming in. Oh, good god. What now? Jesus, the state of him. He looked wasted.

Should he confront him? There was no way Jeff would have given him a VIP pass. No way on earth. But he would have given one to Emily, and Emily wasn't there. He must have taken it from her. She wasn't going to miss this opening night, but she wasn't here. This was bad. Something was really wrong.

"Trust your instincts, our Nick."

Rhodes was a scumbag and had done something terrible. Nick felt it in his bones.

'I don't think it's a good idea that you're here,' said Nick, intercepting him, pushing him backwards.

Matty looked at him expressionless; his long hair past his shoulders was lank and greasy. Even though he wore black eyeliner to try and look a bit elegantly wasted, he just didn't look well.

Nick put an arm across him to prevent him walking on. There was a weird sickly, cheese and vinegar smell coming off him. The same smell that had been in the flat. Was it from smoking heroin? Yeah, it was. He was very double-glazed.

'And who the fuck do you think you are?' said Matty, staring right into his face with the look of a man who had lost his mind somewhere and was never going to find it again.

'Come on, Matty. Don't do this. Jeff will just have you thrown out. Why not just go now before Emily gets here?'

He gave Nick a look that was part sneer and part smile. 'Oh, she's not coming, Guymer. She's going nowhere. Not now, not ever.' He reached over to Nick, and patted him on his cheek with the flat of his hand. 'And your nightmare is just beginning, you fucking prick.'

Nick grabbed him by his t-shirt. 'What have you done to her? Where is she? Where's Emily?'

He just got a silent, sneery smile.

'Alright lads, that'll do,' said a big bouncer, coming over, hearing Nick's raised voice.

Nick let go of him. He was fucked up. There was no point in trying to beat it out of him, even if the bouncer would let him, which he wouldn't. Nick cast a glance back into the club, it was packed. There was no time to lose. He sprinted out of the club down Church Road to the High Street and then left.

The image in his brain returned.

The image of Emily lying dead with a knife between her shoulders.

This was the moment it was going to come true. He just knew it. That was his instinct. 'She's going nowhere. Not now, not ever' - that meant Matty had murdered her. He was sure beyond sure. Mouth dry, panting for breath on the warm evening, he sprinted down the High Street to Green Dragon Yard.

Gasping for air, and wishing he'd remembered to bring out the keys to the flat that he'd used previously, he pressed the buzzer. Come on Em, come on...answer...please answer. There was no answer. Of course not. Fuck it. He pushed at the door. Locked. Not for bloody long.

He took a few steps back, took a run and jumped fully off the ground, both feet in the air and slammed into the Yale lock, splintering the wood on the door where the catch was. As he clattered to the ground and got to his feet, a couple of drinkers standing outside the Green Dragon pub raised their pint glasses in salute, possibly used to seeing criminality occurring and rather enjoying it.

'Emily!' he yelled as he ascended the stairs to the top floor and beat on her door with his fists. There was no need, the door was on the latch and creaked open as he leant on it.

'Emily!' Still no response. The bedroom door was open.

Even as he noted that fact, he could see the side of a leg, lying on the bed.

This was it. Oh, god.

It was all leading to this. He was in the bedroom in three strides.

And this time, this time it really was her.

There was no knife in her back, but her naked body lay diagonally across the bed from corner to corner. She was face down and as motionless as the drug dealer he'd found in this flat of death.

'Emily?' He put his hand on her back. She wasn't breathing. She was still. She was dead.

With shaking hands he called 999, trying to keep calm as his mind raced.

'I've found a dead body. It's Emily Davids.'

'Are you sure she's dead? Is she not breathing?' said the operator.

He got on his knees, putting his hand on her back. 'No.'

'An ambulance has been dispatched. Does she feel cold?'

'No. She's no clothes on but she's not cold. She feels warm.'

'Is there any sign of drugs being taken? Any bottles or packs of pills?'

He stood up and looked around the bedroom. 'I can't see anything.'

'Any weapons?'

'Nothing.'

He put his hands under her left-hand side, lifted her up and turned her onto her back. She was floppy, like a dead cat. Her face as pale as putty, her eyes closed, her mouth slack. Now he could see all the bruises on her hips and thighs, and for the first time he could see there were at least three generations of them on each side, some masked by tattoos. She also had a big blotch on her rib cage. It looked like someone had punched her there recently.

'She's not breathing. I can't hear or see her breathing.' He tried to keep on top of his shock and fear.

'OK, I want you to attempt CPR. If she's still warm she might not be deceased. Do you know how to do CPR?'

'Yeah, two breaths, then 30 compressions, isn't it?'

'Yes, pinch her nose and put your mouth to hers, so it forms a tight seal and then blow as hard as you can to inflate her chest.'

He put the speakerphone on.

Her lips were bone dry as he placed his on hers, nipped her nose and exhaled into her, hoping his breath would bring her back to life. After doing it two times, he interlocked his hands over her breastplate and pressed down firmly, releasing the pressure and repeating the process to the rhythm of 'Stayin' Alive' by the Bee Gees.

'Come on, Emily, come back to me. Come on lady, you can do this. You can come back to the surface and embarrass me by being naked. Come on. We all love you. We want you to come home. Come on, come back. It's not your time, Emily. You're young and healthy and a good soul and it'll be such a waste of money on all these amazing tattoos if you die now. Don't die. There's no need to die. Whatever has happened, you can get over it.'

'You're doing well. The ambulance is nearly with you.'

He nipped her nose again, took as deep a breath as he could and exhaled into her mouth. Her chest rose significantly and then fell as he took his lips away, inhaled deeply again and once more breathed his life into her. Again, her chest rose and her small breasts moved a little. But it was all an imitation of being alive.

Voices downstairs told him the ambulance had arrived. He shouted out and the exact same two paramedics that had come when he'd found the drug dealer the other day entered.

'Not another one,' said the older woman.

'I've been giving her CPR but it doesn't seem to have made any difference. She's still warm but her skin feels clammy and sticky, like she's been sweating a lot.'

'Right, we'll defib her...see if we can get her going again and then we can work out why she's like this, though I think I can make a guess.'

The sight of a naked woman as slight in stature as Emily being blasted with jolts of electricity was almost a surreal thing, as her lifeless body juddered and spasmed. And every time they did it, just for a split second it looked like it had worked, then she went still again.

'Come on Emily. This time,' said the paramedic.

She sent another bolt of volts in to her, but to no avail. The woman looked at him with a shake of the head.

'One more go,' said Nick. 'Please.'

It was unbearable to see her like this. Nick turned away, still hardly able to believe what was happening. He heard the defibrillator discharge its electricity for the last time. There was silence. He closed his eyes and said a prayer for her. C'mon lady, not now, come back, please come back.

'Here we go! Yes, I've got a pulse. Come on, Emily, focus now. Come on, girl,' said the second paramedic.

Nick turned around just as Emily made a noise, a gasp and cough and then began taking shallow shuddering breaths. He cried silent, dry tears.

'Right, her heart rate is erratic and weak, we need to get some adrenaline into her and we need to get her to hospital asap to get her stablised.'

'Has she tried to kill herself, do you think?' said Nick.

'My guess is she's done just what the man we found here did; smoked some unusually pure heroin and suffered a respiratory collapse.'

'My god, but she's not like that. And it doesn't smell like it did when we found the bloke. It must be something else. She's not that sort of girl.'

'She wasn't that sort of girl, but now she is,' said the woman, weary from having to say this to too many people, too often. 'And, I'm no expert, but I'd say, looking at how she is, she's not long since had aggressive sex, or rather, someone or some people have had sex with her.'

'What? How do you know that?'

She looked at him witheringly. 'Mr Guymer, she's naked and she's red raw. Get me?' Her eyes looked at him, black and unyielding.

Nick put his hands over his face, unable to deal with this news and unwilling to check the evidence for himself.

'Has she been raped?'

She nodded, solemnly. 'Almost certainly. I'll report that when we get to North Tees.'

The other paramedic left the room to get a stretcher to take her downstairs.

The paramedic looked around the bedroom. 'There's no drug paraphernalia in here which means she was here with someone who took it away with them and left her here in this state or, at least in a bad way. I would suggest that she was raped after, or while she was becoming unconscious.'

'I've a good idea who was responsible for that,' said Nick.

'Well, I suggest telling the police, then. This poor lass only just made it; next time she won't be so lucky, and she's not out of the woods yet.'

They took her away to North Tees hospital. After they'd gone, Nick took a good look around. There wasn't so much as a packet of cigarettes in the place. No booze in the fridge. Since he'd found the man dead, she had totally tidied up and cleaned the place from top to bottom. The small bedroom was neat and tidy, without as much as a speck of dust. He pulled open a chest of drawers to find all her clothes neatly ironed and folded. The only exception was the clothes she had to have been wearing. Black leggings, underwear, t-shirt and socks were scattered apparently randomly all over the room. Hang on, hang on. Why the hell was she naked? Nobody takes drugs naked, do they? And no-one would take their clothes off and just throw them to four corners of the room. No.

Standing back in the doorway he looked around the room for clues as to what had happened in there. She'd been at Teesside Women between 4 and 5pm, it was now just after 8.30pm. He walked into the kitchen. There was a empty mug on the drainer. A single mug. He looked in the bin. It was empty except for a plastic tray. He fished it out, along with a card wrapper: 'Chicken and vegetables in white wine and tarragon cream sauce'. It was a microwaveable meal for one from Marks and Spencer. Sounded nice. She'd eaten a decent meal for herself, as he'd said she should. Good girl. She must have eaten that when she got in, 5.15 to 5.30pm.

What had happened? When he'd been here the last time, the place was in a terrible mess, but she'd transformed it since. She'd had a major clean-up, as though maybe drawing a line under a time in her life, having finally decided to seek help at Teesside Women. That's probably what he'd have done, too. You made a physical change in your surroundings to mark a big change in your life. It was the end of a relationship, so you made it a physical bookmark in your life by changing your surroundings. Jeff had said she was her old self. Making a big decision can lift your spirits. It ends the doubt and confusion.

Back in the kitchen, he rested on a stool and looked at his phone, going to Matty's Facebook page to see if there was any clue as to where he was staying. The place was too clean and tidy for it to have housed a wasted druggie for any length of time.

In his profile photo, he looked healthy, but it'd been taken a year ago. He had to be staying with a friend, dossing on someone's floor, someone local. He went to his friends list and looked at the photos and names. Everything was on a public setting.

What he saw made Nick's brain freeze.

What?

Fucking what?!

Recently added friends: Sean O'Connor and Tommy Green.

No, no, no. His brain just couldn't compute it for a second or three. He hadn't been a friend of theirs when he and Julie had found Green and O'Connor on Facebook. That meant it had to have happened in the last couple of days.

They all knew each other.

Two worlds that, until that very moment, were entirely separate in his mind, were being stitched together.

He just stared at the phone as his mind clicked into gear. Hold on, hold on. Boz Bailey had been a drug dealer in the past, Tommo had said that. So maybe he was again, now that he was out of jail. Mandy had said the now-dead dealer was just a gofer for a bigger dealer, and had told her that Matty had bought cocaine, crystal meth and rohypnol. Could that dealer have been hooked up with Bailey? Very probably. That dealer knew Matty. So Matty and Bailey met and when Matty wanted revenge on Emily for throwing him out, he'd found the right three amoral, evil bastards to do that. They were here. Here. In the flat. And not long ago.

Sickeningly, it all fell into place in his mind. Yes.

When he'd turned Emily over, she'd been clammy or sticky but only on her front, not on her back. He'd touched her belly to feel if she was breathing. Then pressed on her breast plate giving her CPR. Both areas had that same sticky, clammy feel to them.

Nick closed his eyes as the realisation of what had happened bore into his consciousness.

They'd done to Emily what they'd done to Julie, all of those years ago. Doing what they'd used to do, before they'd all been jailed, but with a new fourth member. They had gang raped her.

A wave of nausea crashed over him. Oh, god. This was a place of utter depravity. Suddenly, their evil seemed to ooze from the walls.

He ran to the bathroom and dry-retched into the sink, the thought of their rape and abuse of Emily making his stomach vomit, as though to both literally and symbolically expunge their evil. Afterwards, he washed his hands thoroughly, trying to not to think of what had been on them.

The fact she was still sticky meant it hadn't been long since they'd done their party trick. It would have dried had it been a few hours previously. And that meant one thing: they were back in town, here and now. They'd been here in this space not long ago.

As he dried his hands on a towel, he heard his mother again. *"You're special. Believe in yourself. Trust your instincts."*

He slapped himself in the face. Right. Come on. Get your shit together. Was that O'Connor and Green in the toilets, after all? Yes. Yes, more than likely, it was. The boys were back in town and they'd be after Julie. Call the police first. With shaking hands he wrote an email to Mandy, tried to explain what he'd found here and what he thought had happened. He texted it to her as well, just to make sure she'd see it. After a quick re-edit, he sent it to Julie - told her to stay in the club and not to do anything alone, took the keys for the flat from the door-side table and closed it behind him.

'Who broke this?' said a woman, pointing at the splintered front door, as he left.

'I don't know. Some lunatic, probably,' he said, on his way out. That much was true.

He ran as fast as he could back to club, showed his stamped hand to the bouncers and went back in.

Status No were in full flight, playing a heads-down-no-nonsense-boogie version of 'Mean Girl.'

People were head-banging everywhere, like it was 1972. Even Tommo, in his Hawaiian shirt, pint in hand, was bobbing his head up and down. That was a brilliant thing to see. But where was Julie?

Nick stood and looked into the crowd for her.

Where was she?

Where was she?!

With rising panic, he just couldn't see her anywhere. His breathing began to increase. Julie where are the hell are you? Oh god, oh god, they've got her.

He was on the verge of losing it and began pushing through crowds at the perimeter of the club, desperately looking for her. Julie. Oh, my god. Julie where are you?

'This is the last song.' There were loud boos. 'A little song called "Roll Over Lay Down".'

The crowd erupted in appreciation.

Status No were brilliant at being Status Quo. All in their late 20s, it was like seeing the real thing in the mid 70s, everyone in double denim, hair and head banging.

And then...there she was. Front and centre, blonde hair bobbing up and down, on and off the beat at random, as ever. Oh, thank you, god.

Fucking hell. That was a relief. His heart was pounding. Sucking in the hot, damp air, he tried to get himself together.

240

Right. Stay calm, stay calm. Nick sucked in air through his nose and looked around for Rhodes, Bailey, O'Connor or Green. They were no-where to be seen. Thank fuck for that.

He went to the bar, ordered a triple vodka and tonic and, as it was pushed across the bar to him by a hipster, sank it in one and pointed at his glass for another. The music was superb, and if he hadn't been through what he'd just been through, he'd have loved it, too. But it was all too much to cope with. Emily was in hospital and three vicious rapists were on the loose, not to mention Matty Rhodes or Kenny Harlow. God almighty, what sort of world where they all living in when this sort of thing happened? It was beyond sickening.

Status No left the stage to huge acclaim.

He waved at Julie as the crowd dissolved towards the bar.

'They were brill!' she said, excitedly bounding up to him. 'Where did you get to?'

Taking her by the hand he led her outside, walking her down the road.

'OK, listen to me, Jules. O'Connor, Green and Bailey are back on Teesside. They know Matty, right?' He held a hand up at her. 'No, don't say anything...they know Matty...early this evening, they drugged and raped Emily. Just as they did to you 20 years ago. She's alive, but only just...I found her in her flat...Matty was here, I confronted him, but it looks like he's gone now...I knew something was wrong.'

'What? What? You're talking too fast. I can't understand you.' She was a bit drunk and not grasping what he said. 'I...I...I can't understand what you're saying.'

'There's too much to tell you. Didn't you get my text?'

She shook her head. 'I haven't got my phone, have I? Is Emily al-right?'

She looked at him with her mouth open, trying to grasp what he was saying.

'She's in North Tees. She was dead, Jules. I gave her CPR and then the paramedics got her back. As I just said...' he spoke slower so she could understand more easily '...she'd been drugged and raped and then had some sort of respiratory attack from the dope they'd given her.'

She looked at him with a degree of incomprehension and reached to hold his hands for reassurance. 'Bloody hell. That's disgusting. Fucking hell. Are you sure? But she's alive, right?'

'Yeah, or at least she was when the ambulance took her away. You've got to be careful, Jules. Those three men are back. We should go home until they've been caught. Matty's involved as well. They're bloody crazy.'

Her eyes, glazed from the booze were now distressed and scared.

'Are they really going to attack me here? I'd like to stay. The music is great.'

'Obviously, I don't know what they've got planned. But my instincts say that they're coming for you and that's why they've come back today.'

Jutting her chin out, she shook her head. 'No bloody chance, I'm going nowhere. I've run away from them once and I'm not doing it again. Mandy will hunt them down and arrest them soon enough. Have you told her?'

He didn't need precognition to tell him she'd say that. The Hardwick fight was never far below the surface.

'Yeah, Mandy knows.' They hugged tightly. 'Well, just be careful, stay close to me, right?' he said.

'That's not a problem.' She put a hand to his neck and kissed him properly with a wet, boozy tongue, as though to physically bind themselves together in that moment in defiance of the evil in their midst. The warm summer Stockton air blew around them. He breathed her breath, felt the heat from her body, felt his love pour into her.

'Can't you two keep your hands off each other for more than a few minutes? I never saw the like.' Nick turned to his right to see Jo King standing there in a single-breasted metallic silver suit, with flame-red, lopsided, asymmetrical hair and broad, wonky-toothed smile.

'Hiya, Jo. Good to see you again,' he said.

'That's a top-notch suit, luv,' said Julie, giving her a quick hug. 'How's things going?'

'Alright. Just about paying the bills, which is all I want, really. From what Jeff's told me, you've been having a bit of a rough time, Jules. Some stalker shit?'

Julie, not wanting to let out the bad vibes, made light of it. 'Ah, it's something and nothing. Just some losers. It'll all blow over.'

'Well, remember, if you need a severed limb or some offal, I'm your girl.'

'Have you played a rock club before?' said Nick.

'Yeah, a couple of times. It'll bomb or it'll be loved. There's never an inbetween.' She looked at a large blue watch on her wrist. 'Gotta go and get ready. Catch you later.'

She strutted into the club with her usual confident stride.

'I love her style,' said Julie, watching her go. 'She's a big star just waiting to be a big star.'

'Yeah, one day, she's going to get a big break. I totally believe in her.'

They went back into the club, his arm around her shoulder, her arm around his waist. He didn't want to let her go. His instinct was that this wasn't over. She went to the bar while Nick stood to one side, keeping an eye on her at all times. The place was jumping, almost literally, bouncing up and down to UFO's 'Only You Can Rock Me', another old classic he and Jeff had loved back in the late 70s and on clear vinyl, too, which had seemed very exotic at the time.

'So tell me about Emily, again,' she said.

He went over what had happened and showed her Matty's Facebook page on his phone.

'They're listed as recently added friends. The thing is, when we found the other two on Facebook, Matty wasn't on their friends list. So he's literally only just been added. Now, Bailey was a drug dealer back in the day. Tommo told us that. Once a dealer, always a dealer. I reckon that's how he met Matty. The dead bloke we found in the flat was probably dealing for Bailey. He has to have been there with Matty, smoking heroin. The paramedic thought Em had gone the same way as the other bloke, but I don't think she did. The flat didn't smell the same as it did previously.'

'So they've given Emily a date rape drug and she's had some sort of reaction to it?'

'Exactly. Maybe respiratory or heart failure, poor lass. The paramedic thought she'd been raped, judging by how she looked down there. And she was sticky on her front. If you ask me, they've done that group wank thing again. I've told Mandy all of this by text and email. Not heard from her. I thought she was going to be here.' He looked around, hoping to see her.

Julie shook her head in disgust and disbelief. 'Oh, god, poor Em. Oh, god...the bastards. The absolute bastards.'

'I know, they're sickos, man. I mean, evil sickos.'

'Mandy is probably busy on a bust. You know what she's like, she works all hours. But, let's calm down. No-one is going to do anything here. The place is guarded by bouncers for a start. If anyone grabbed me, I'd just scream the shitting place down. They'd not get away with it.'

'Yeah, but I think they like the danger. I think it turns them on. It's all part of the challenge. Remember, you said when O'Connor raped you, he was really turned on by the aggression and the power he had over you? That's not going to have gone away over the years. Look, I heard an Irish bloke in the toilets talking about a woman's great arse and what they were going to do to it later. I now think it was O'Connor and Green.'

'Nick, man, there's loads of Irish people on Teesside. Always has been. And isn't that sort of talk, just how men go on, all the time? They're always going on about wanting to stick it in some poor lass, aren't they?'

'I suppose so. It wasn't like normal bawdy talk, though, it was nastier than that.'

She glanced at him and sipped at her vodka. 'Shit. You're getting me scared now.' She gripped his arm.

The music stopped and Jeff strode out onto the stage and took the microphone. It was weird to hear people cheering him. He really was the biggest star of the night.

'Now then, my lovelies. We've got the amazing Hurricaine in about an hour. They'll rock your socks off...' he raised his right index finger to 45 degrees '...which I suppose means, they'll rock your footwear off as well, because you can't rock socks off without first removing the shoes, can you?' He pulled a mock puzzled face.

Everyone laughed and laughed loudly. Maybe he had some of his brother, Big Fish's, stand-up comedian genes.

'But now, for your amazement, for your horror and for your funny bone, a very good friend of mine, a local lass who is making it big in that there London. Please welcome the very special talent that is Jo King.'

There was cheering and applause from the 250. Jo ran out to the microphone and into a single spotlight.

Julie looked at Nick, still gripping his arm. 'She's so cool. I love that we know her. I just wish I could get the Emily business out of my mind. I'm so worried about her.' She rubbed a finger across her forehead.

'Thank you, thank you. You're all rock 'n' roll people, aren't you?' She raised her hands to elicit a response.

The crowd yelled in the affirmative.

'Yeah, me, too. I like the music so loud it makes my ears bleed.'

More cheers.

'Yeah, so they bleed like this...'

As she spoke, she took a small hammer from her pocket along with a huge, thick nail. It was brilliant. Nick knew what she was going to do, but even so, it was still so shocking to see a woman apparently hit a nail into her ear and see blood running down her cheek and neck as a result. What made her so great was she let out a howl of pain that seemed so genuine that you believed, for a split second, it was for real.

The crowd groaned, there was an audible gasp, along with laughter, as Jo cupped her bleeding ear to the audience, as though to hear them better. 'Eh? What? I can't hear a bloody thing now.' The spotlight was turned off for three seconds. When it came back on, she was standing, blood free and arms outstretched.

'Sorry about that. It's the only way to get the wax out of my ears.'

There was applause, laughter and a few cheers. For half an hour it was an arms race of gross-out illusions with a doomy, riffy, heavy metal music soundtrack to punctuate proceedings. By the time she ended the show, leaning over a chair, facing the audience, slowly pulling a cheese wire across her neck, blood leaking, then oozing, the spurting from the wound, then yanking it hard and in doing so, apparently decapitating herself, the crowd were in the palm of her hand.

Her head fell off and rolled under the chair. It was a bit like watching Alice Cooper's early 70s shows, only without skewering babies with swords. That might be a bit hard to get away with in the 21st century.

But the crowd loved her. The lights went out for 10 seconds and she reappeared to take her bow, head now back on her shoulders.

'Thank you. Thanks to Jeff for getting me here. Rest assured, I shall be keeping my eye on you all.' As she spoke, she jabbed her index finger into the corner of her eye and apparently prised the eye right out of its socket, holding it up to the crowd, blood dripping from it. The crowd broke out into football crowd-style chants of 'You're Jo King, you're Jo King, you're Jo King!' She was a huge rock 'n' roll hit.

As she took her applause, Nick looked around the room.

His heart leapt.

Boz Bailey! Oh, shit. Oh, fucking hell. How did he get in? Using Emily's VIP pass that Matty had taken?

He was standing by the door, his pink shaven head almost iridescent. He was chewing gum, distractedly.

'Look, by the door. That's Boz Bailey,' said Nick into Julie's ear.

She leaned over and took a quick glance.

245

'Bloody hell, he's massive. Why is he here? This is wrong. I don't like it at all.'

'I want us to go home. There's some shit going to go down here, Jules. I'm sure of it.'

She squeezed into him. 'I'm scared too, but let's not be daft about it. I want to see Ali Caine. I love her. Like I said before, the place is packed with bouncers and they're all looking for anyone who's causing trouble. So no-one can just grab me. I'd scream the roof off if they did. And I'm going to stick right by you. It'll be alright.'

'Will it, Jules?' He searched for peace of mind in her eyes, but saw only the fear in her stare.

'Yes, it bloody will.'

As the roadies began to prepare the stage for Hurricaine, Jeff emerged from the crowd.

'Am I crazy, or is tonight going really well?'

'It's amazing. I can't believe all of this,' said Nick, even though his mind was shredded. He wanted to tell Jeff about Emily, but the big man was totally hyped up, looking around with wild, excited eyes at what he'd created.

'I have no idea what's going on, or if I'm doing this whole thing right, but it feels bloody good. I just hope we're making money.'

'It's three deep at the bar, man, of course you are,' said Julie.

'Right, I've got gotta go and find Ali Caine. When this is all over, stay at the bar and we'll toast my hairy brilliance.'

He wafted his long hair up and down.

There was no time to talk to him properly. 'Jeff...look, Boz Bailey is here,' said Nick, nodding in the big man's direction, who was now drinking a pint of lager. But Jeff was too distracted by what he had to do.

'Oh, yeah. Big sod, isn't he?' he said, as he walked away backstage in a hurry.

'This is a bloody good night, like,' said Con, sidling over from his residence, three steps from the bar; like all classic old-school drinkers, he didn't stray far from the pumps. 'I think I saw Status Quo in the early 70s, y'knaw, because my mate was in that group called Geordie, if you remember them. Had a couple of hits and they supported them on a tour.'

'Their biggest hit was "All Because of You",' said Nick. 'Which one was your mate?'

'The singer, Brian. Aye, Jonno went on to sing for ACDC. Lives in Florida now, lucky get.'

'Why didn't you tell me this before now? This is brilliant, man,' said Nick. 'You know Brian Johnson?!' he said, incredulous, but unable to stop glancing at the big bastard by the door, his stomach churning all the while.

'I did do, aye. Not any more, more's the pity, like.'

'You actually look like him, only bigger,' said Nick, sweating heavily now, with nerves.

'Is mam alright?' said Julie, chewing at a nail.

'Aye she's alright, hinny. She's a bit pissed, but that's how she likes it. She's just gone to the bogs.'

Nick couldn't stop himself looking at Bailey again. Why was he here? Was he dealing drugs? Had he really just been at Emily's and do-ing...that? It was hard to believe simply because it beggared belief that any human would do such a thing. Instinctively, you want to think it's not possible. But he had to say something to someone; his fear was over-whelming him, to the point where it almost physically hurt.

"Trust your instincts, our Nick."

'Con, see that big bald bloke over by the doors?'

He glanced and narrowed his eyes.

'Oh, aye, what about him?'

'I think he's a drug dealer and a rapist.'

'Bloody 'ell...but apart from that, he's a canny lad, eh. He's a size, like. Soft as shite, though, obviously.' Con sniffed, rubbed his big nose, and looked away dismissively.

'You're kidding me, he's a six-foot-four monster,' said Nick.

'Nah, he's a flabby get. Is he causing any trouble? Shall I get the lads on the door?'

'Doesn't seem to be,' said Julie. 'Nick's worried that him and two other blokes are after me. It's a bit complicated. Don't say anything to mam.'

'After you? In what way, like?'

'All three of them are rapists - so, after Jules in that way, Con. The other two know Julie from back in the day.' said Nick, glancing at Bailey again. He wasn't looking at them, in fact he was staring at his phone.

'Bloody 'ell. Here's your mother, Jules. Well, lerrus knaw if you need any help, Nick.' He made a forearm smash gesture, and Con's forearm was like a pit pony's leg.

'Eee, them toilets are weird,' said Jackie. 'There's no ladies or gents. It's everyone together. I don't like having a slash when there's blokes hav-ing one next door to us.'

'What difference does it make, like?' said Con. 'It's all piss.'

'I know, but it comes out of different places, doesn't it?'

'Technically, it all comes out of the bladder,' said Julie. 'I know what you mean, though, it's a big cultural leap for us all to make.'

'You can say that again, Jules. Blokes piss all over the seats. I don't want to have to mop up a man's piss when I'm out for a night. If I want to do that I can just stay at home!' As she spoke she took two vape pens out of her pocket and began sucking on them furiously, releasing clouds of steam.

'Well, I'm going to have to go and use them, if I can actually get these jeans down to do it. They're sticking to me something rotten,' said Julie, pink in the face, fanning herself with her hand. 'Mam! Do you need two of those things?'

'They're weak as water. I'm a 60-a-day woman, these things don't do nowt for us. I've got two nicotine patches on an' all!"

Nick squeezed out a tight, nervous laugh. 'It looks like you're on fire, Jackie.'

'Right, I'm off for a gender-neutral wee,' said Julie.

'I'll come with you,' said Nick, looking around, feeling paranoid, but now noticing that Boz Bailey had gone.

'There's no need,' she said. 'It's less than a 15 seconds' walk.'

'Humour me. A lot can happen in 15 seconds. I'll just wait for you outside.'

She linked his arm and they walked through the lobby area to the toilets. Quite a few people were milling around outside, smoking. A stall selling Hurricaine CDs and t-shirts was doing a bit of business.

'I'll be alright on my own in the toilets. Just wait for me outside. I'll just piss on anyone who comes near me.' He let go of her and she pushed open the wide black door. Nick leaned against the wall and waited for her. It was an amazing building. There had to be a lot of space above the false ceiling to expand into. Maybe when Jeff had made some money, he could open a separate, smaller acoustic club up there, or a comedy club. There was plenty of room to expand. Yeah, this was all very positive. A sold-out opening night; you can't do better than that. And people seemed to be drinking a lot - no surprise there, the north is built on booze and plenty of it. The spirit of 'drink today for tomorrow we may die' had always played well in industrial towns that spent more time in recession and decline than they ever did on the lush uplands pastures of economic riches. Having a good time now, because you never knew how long you had left, was a mindset he totally understood. The future? Who knew what the future held? It was the reason he'd kept drinking in recent times, when he knew it sometimes provoked his depressive moods. You ended up trading off the good times against the bad times, and that's what the oppressed, the beat-down, the poor, the working class and now, the underclass did and had always done. The only thing you knew how to do was, like Dylan said, "to keep on keeping on, like a bird that flew." He blew out air. Yeah, 'Tangled Up in Blue', that could be his autobiography title.

A couple of people went into the toilet and then came out. No sign of Julie. She must be struggling with those jeans. They were tight, like. It was so much easier being a bloke when it came to toilets. He'd always thought that from the day he learned how girls did it. And lads didn't even have to deal with all that monthly shedding of the womb. He'd learned about that in biology class in second year at Ian Ramsey Comprehensive. The shock of finding out that girls were actually bleeding to the left and right of him was profound. It seemed brutal and not a little bit unfair. Maybe that was why women were less squeamish in an accident; they are used to regularly dealing with big globs of blood and tissue.

There was still no sign of Boz Bailey, nor of sunglasses man, his mate or indeed, Matty. It was an obvious place to sell drugs, but maybe he'd just been checking it out. He could hear Jeff again, at the microphone.

'Ladels and gentlespoons, please put your hands together for the awesome Hurricaine.'

Cheers and whistles raised the roof as the band launched into a frantic version of 'Shy Boy', a song originally on Talas's debut album, later recorded by Mr Big. Bloody hell, it was awesome. Ali Caine was a great singer, full of power and range. The band also had a guitar whiz, slamming out the riffs in the style of Paul Gilbert.

Nick looked at his watch. She'd been in there for nearly eight minutes. Everyone was watching the band.

He pushed open the door to the toilet and shouted. 'Jules! The band is on. They sound amazing! Are you alright?'

Expecting her to call out, he wasn't worried, at least not for a few seconds. 'Jules!'

No reply.

He walked into the toilet and walked the line of cubicles, shouting her name.

They were all empty, the doors on all 10 ajar.

For a split second, it felt like seeing one of Jo King's tricks. It was an illusion, surely. She couldn't just vanish.

But vanish is exactly what she had done.

CHAPTER 16

Unable to comprehend what had happened, he called out plaintively, like someone calling the name of their cat at the back door. 'Julie! Where are you?'

She wasn't there.

He was worried, but not too worried. She must have walked out past him...or something. Was there any other exit? No. No windows. Well, that's what must have happened, then. She hadn't been abducted by some invisible people.

Going back into the noisy gig, he looked around, expecting to see her give him one of her nice smiles.

No. She was nowhere to be seen. A panic was starting to rise in him now. Where the hell had she gone? Boz and his sickos couldn't have got her. They couldn't. Even if they'd waited in there for her to come in, there was no way out other than past him. It was OK, surely it was OK.

"Trust your instincts, our Nick."

As he desperately searched the crowd for Julie, Natalie Townsend came walking towards him. He grabbed her by the arm

'Julie's disappeared.'

'What?'

'She's gone. I can't find her.'

'Are you alright, Nick?'

'You said there was negative energy around her. I'm scared something has happened to her. There are three rapists in town who want to attack her.'

She looked at him with understandably confused eyes.

'What? Are you OK?'

He gripped her more tightly. 'Please, use your powers to find out where she is...'

She looked at him wildly. '...My powers? I don't have any powers, Nick. I'm not a superhero.'

'You do, you do...you knew our birthdays...where's Julie gone?'

But it was no good. Obviously scared by his wild demeanor, she pulled away and went outside.

Nick looked back into the club.

'Jeff! Jeff!' Thank god. The big man was edging around from back-stage to stand at the back to get a drink and watch the band. He made a goofy face at Nick and put his thumbs up.

He leaned into Nick's ear and shouted. 'Everything's coming up Jeff's Rock Club tonight. They are brilliant. Like a cross between Heart and Mr Big... the second Mr Big, obviously, not the 70s Brits who had a number four hit with a dreadful song called "Romeo".'

Nick pulled him out through the doors as the band launched into a raucous version of Heart's 'Crazy on You.'

'Jeff, listen to me, right. Julie has disappeared. She went to the toilets, I waited outside, she never came out. I went in and it was empty. I'm shit scared that they've got her. They're all here...you don't know what's happened to Emily...'

'Em? What's happened? She was supposed to be here. Where is she?'

'I think Green, O'Connor, Bailey and Matty first raped her and then did what they did to Julie 20 years ago. I only just got there in time to save her. She was dead on her bed.'

Jeff was staring, not comprehending what he was telling him. 'Eh? What? I can't believe it...where is she now?'

'Hospital. I think she'll be alright. Jeff, there's no time! Julie's missing! We have to find her, man! Something bad has happened, trust me, my instinct is that something very fucking bad has happened and I'm going with my instincts.' Nick grabbed him by his damp, sweaty t-shirt.

Jeff shook his head as though to shake the shock out of himself. 'OK, OK, so she went for a piss, and never came back? That's not possible.'

'I know. There's only one door in and out of the toilets. But she's not around. She's not here.'

'Have you called her?'

'She's not got her phone with her. Nowhere to put it in those jeans.'

Jeff stood and stared into the middle distance, thinking, then a look of horror spread over his face like a rain cloud over the sun. 'Bloody hell, I've got it. Where's Con?' He swivelled around looking for him.

'Con? What's it to do with him?'

'We need muscle, there's four of them, isn't there? And Bailey is a beast.' He raced back into the club, got hold of the big Geordie who, as ever, was no more than three paces from the bar.

'What's gannin' on, like?' he said as Jeff pulled him towards the toilets. Jackie watched on as he did so.

'Are you up for a serious fucking ruck?' said Jeff, eye to eye with the old fella.

'Jeff, man, I'm a Geordie, and it's Friday neet, of course I'm up for a ruck.'

As they walked to the toilets, Jeff quickly explained the situation to Con, pulling out a massive tangle of keys as he did so.

'Aye, Nick was saying about that big get with the bald heed. Rapists. Bloody twats. They hurt a hair on that lass's head and there'll be bloody hell to pay, I'll fucking tell you that for nowt.'

Nick followed them as he strode past the toilet stalls. For the first time, he noticed there was a handleless door right at the back corner, set flush into the wall. Jeff put a key in, turned it and pulled it open with the key.

The noise of the band playing a blues song blared out as he opened the door onto a space that had been part of the original church building. The air felt colder, smelt damp and mouldy.

'This is part of the old church,' said Jeff. 'It was all sliced up and this part left unused. All the workers had access to it when we put the bogs in. Jules!!!' He yelled like a bear and ran to the back of the space.

'Up here,' he said, pointing to a decrepit set of wooden stairs that led up to another level. The first one broke and shattered into dust and splinters as soon as Jeff put his foot on it. 'Watch these, they're rotten,' he said, quickly getting to top of the them, a couple more cracking under their collective weight.

They clattered up behind him. It was dark, but some light was coming in from old skylights in the sloping roof. Nick looked around. It was a wide balcony that ran around the perimeter of the building. Originally a chapel gallery, it had obviously just been used as a dumping space for all sort of packaging and other crap over the years. Thick with dust and rubbish, it hadn't been touched in a long time.

'Jules! Are you here?' shouted Nick, just as Boz Bailey appeared from behind one of the central iron pillars which held the place up. There was no need to ask why he was here. No need to doubt the evil that was happening.

He spoke in a classic Stockton accent. Unfussed, he held his big hands wide. 'Alright lads, somehow you've ended up in the wrong place. Nowt to see up here. Away you go, eh.'

'You don't tell me what to do, you big arsehole,' said Jeff, indignantly. 'This is my bloody club, son!' Jeff gave the big man a push in the chest and went toe to toe with him, staring him down. 'What the fuck are you doing up here? Eh?' Again, Jeff pushed him hard, making Bailey stagger backwards. 'I note you're not telling me. I've got the police coming, son. We know all about you.'

Bailey laughed bitterly in Jeff's face. 'I'm going break you into pieces, you long-haired fuck knuckle!'

But Con stepped in front of Jeff. 'Howay, Jeff, stop fucking stroking him. We both know you're a total cunt, Bailey.' Con pushed him backwards with a violent shove. 'Now, I'm really sodding going to hurt you, just so's you knaw, like.'

Bailey was a lifelong thug, and knew when someone threatening violence was serious and when they weren't. Con was old-school hard. You didn't mess with him, so Bailey lashed out while backing off. Con ducked his punch, went on the front foot and leathered Bailey in the face, once, twice and got a third in, even as Bailey was staggering back and turning to get away, but Con, lighter on his feet than any man of his age had any right to be, took a couple of skips forward and buried a low punch into Bailey's kidneys and that was what did for him. It was a boxer's punch, perfectly placed to cause maximum damage. Bailey shuddered like he was a stinking, massive pink jelly, let out an involuntary groan and slumped to the floor. One punch had robbed him of energy and sent him into a world of pain.

Con stepped forward, paused, weighed up the fallen Bailey, and then mercilessly and with huge power, volleyed him in the face, breaking his nose, inflicting a lot of blood and snot damage. Just for good measure, he kicked him again to make sure he was out of action. Whether Bailey was incapacitated through pain, or was just semi-conscious, wasn't clear but he was slumped on the floor and was unable to move, making noises which suggested something had burst inside him.

At that moment, there was a choked scream from somewhere, a scream so-piercing that it cut through the sounds of the rock music below.

It was Julie. He knew it. With hot fury and fear burning through his body from his soul to his arteries, he yelled back 'Julie!! We're coming!!' but the band was so loud, it was unlikely she could have heard him.

'They've got her hidden somewhere,' shouted Con, above the din of the band, looking around the roof space. 'Where could she be, Jeff? Think, man.'

With panic in his eyes, Jeff tried to think, knowing every second that passed was crucial.

'I just don't know, Con. I've not explored up here much."

Nick said, 'OK, let's just consider this. We know what their modus operandi is. They'll want to film or photograph what they're doing. It's too dark in here. They can't be in here, there's another space somewhere. They want to do it collectively. Bailey was on guard, so that leaves Green and O'Connor and Rhodes. They won't need a lot of space.' He looked around again. The band below was now playing an original instrumental with some incredible guitar sounds.

'What's up there, Jeff?' said Con, pointing to a small wooden door set at the back of the balcony.

'Bloody hell, I never saw that. It's just a broom cupboard, though, I reckon.'

Con, who had worked as a builder all his life, was dismissive. 'Is it bollocks? That's access to a roof space, man. The water tank will be up there. Howay, bonnie lad, let's get it open.'

Running up to it, there was no handle, only a lock. He ran at it to try and kick it in, but it was solidly locked.

Nick turned to Jeff. 'Have you got a...' but he was interrupted by another strangulated yelp from somewhere above them '... that's her! Bloody hell, man...have you got a key for this?' He was shaking now, fearing what was happening to Julie at that very moment.

Con wasn't going to wait to find out and he began kicking at the door, like a kung fu expert. One kick, two kicks, and it broke open on the third, snapping the lock casing and swinging back on its rotten hinges.

Nick was first through. It led into a small dark passage way, off which a spiral staircase ran upwards into the old loft of the building.

'I never even knew this was here!' shouted Jeff as they went up the wooden steps. Yellow light flooded down, so there had to be electricity up there.

They had to go up single file.

As soon as Nick got to the top of the steps, he looked into the loft space. It spread out across most of one half of the building's floor plan. Hurricaine's music still pounded from down below, the bass vibrating through the whole building.

Strip lights illuminated the whole space.

What the hell was going on?

The scene playing out before them was vile and disgusting; like something from hell.

Nick took it all in a millisecond as he took off towards Julie. She was lying on her back on a ripped and stained old mattress, at the far side of the roof space. Her leatherette shirt was torn open revealing her breasts, her jeans and underwear pulled down beyond her hips. She looked dazed and seemed to be trying to get up but was unable to do so.

Three men were on three sides of that mattress. Each of them turned towards Nick, Jeff and Con as they ran towards them, shouting. It was obvious what they were doing. Tommy Green, Sean O'Connor and a stoned-looking Matty Rhodes had all unbuttoned their pants and were ready for action, penises in hand.

'You dirty fucking bastards!!' yelled Con.

Nick didn't waste energy on words. He'd known all along that this was where the whole thing was headed and so with the power of his mother's love and the power of his love for Julie, he flew into the nearest of them, Rhodes, taking him down with a rugby tackle, picking up his head by the hair and slamming it into the old wooden floorboards. Rhodes left consciousness behind with a groan.

Getting to his feet, Nick turned to see Con booting Green in the balls, followed by a knee to the face. That was him done. But O'Connor was quicker on his feet, he evaded Jeff's grasp, side-stepped him and sprinted for the stairs down. Nick took off after him.

This was his moment, the moment to avenge the sins this man had committed.

No retreat, no surrender.

He went clattering down the steps, trying to not break his neck by falling head over heels, only to be met, as he emerged onto the old balcony, by a red-faced Mandy Beale and what looked like half of the constabulary of Cleveland Police, two of whom had already got hold of a panting O'Connor, had pushed him up against a wall and were in the process of handcuffing his hands behind his back. Gasping for breath, Mandy pushed Nick to a halt.

'You know who he is, don't you?' said Nick, his brain in a whirr.

'Of course. What's up there?' she shouted, pointing through the door.

'It's an attic. Julie's up there. They've drugged her. Jeff and Con are up there with Green and Rhodes, beating the crap out of them, I hope.'

Mandy turned to give O'Connor a furious look, turning back to Nick. 'Scum. Have they...'

'I don't know what they've done.'

She turned and shouted to her officers, 'Robert, Harriet, Dilip, up-stairs, and seal it all off. This is a crime scene. Do not put your size 12s in any evidence. Forensics are on their way.' She turned back to Nick. 'Anyone hurt up there?'

'Rhodes and Green. We battered them. And Bailey downstairs...'

'...yeah, we've got him and Mr Scumbag, there, ran right into us.'

'He got away. I was just after him. He's an evil twat. I was looking forward to beating the snot out of him, Mand. God knows how many other women they've attacked since they got out of jail.'

She turned and looked at O'Connor. He seemed unperturbed by it all, maybe even expecting it. Mandy walked past him and said something into the ear of one of the officers, then leaned into O'Connor's face, jabbed a finger at him but said nothing. She walked back to Nick, and led him by an arm along the balcony, well away from everyone else. The music had stopped now. The police must have pulled the plug.

Mandy rested a hand on his shoulder and looked in his eyes. 'Look, I'm not Colin Harcombe, right? Now for all we know O'Connor got hurt in the fight. That could have happened, right? You've got to stop a rapist any way you can, right? And we've got medics on the way, anyway. So if I put O'Connor in that side room there...' she pointed to a small space be-hind an open door, in which was a lot of rubbish and leftover junk '...and later, when we find him with a few bruises and a broken nose, we will as-sume he was hurt in the struggle, right? After all, a shit like him...well...he's got it coming, hasn't he? I think most women would want him seeing to, wouldn't they? Dirty scum like him. It's the only thing he understands.'

For all that he wanted to get back to see how Julie was, it was a shock to hear what Mandy was saying; that she was giving him licence to beat the shit out of that man. But this was the only chance he'd have and it was too good an opportunity to pass up. He nodded. 'Please get someone to look after Julie, while I do this.'

Mandy nodded and pointed to officers piling up the stairs. 'It's being sorted. Got to protect evidence. DNA and such. Get me?'

Signalling to the officer she'd spoken to, he led O'Connor to the room. O'Connor just stared at Nick in silence as he passed by, surely knowing what was happening.

Nick followed, his heart pounding, closing the door behind him, sweat running down his back. It was dusty and damp in the old room.

O'Connor stood and looked at him without fear in his watery blue eyes. He knew there was no escape and with his hands cuffed at his back, no way to really defend himself. He spoke in his soft Irish lilt.

'So, now what, Guymer? Did she tell you where to hit me so it doesn't leave a mark? Feckin' police are worse than the people they arrest.'

For a moment, Nick just couldn't get any words out and could barely even look at him. The man was so despicable, it was, even now, still hard to believe he'd done what he'd done. He was furious at what he'd done to Julie, back in 1989 and again today. Absolutely bloody furious.

But did you avenge it by breaking someone's face?

From the first moment he'd heard about the old photos, he'd known it'd end in him having to hurt his hand by hitting someone in the face. Mam had been right, he did know what was going to happen when he trusted his instincts.

Or was she? Was it really so inevitable?

'I've pretty much got a licence to accidentally kill you, O'Connor.'

'Ah yer bollocks, you wouldn't kill me. You wouldn't know how.'

Nick licked his lips. It was always good to be underestimated. O'Connor was defenceless. It was a free hit. A completely free hit. There was a lot of revenge to be exacted upon this man, for Julie and for all the women he'd abused over the years. He'd vowed to visit some bloody hell upon him. But now, standing in front of him, he felt reluctant to do it. It's one thing to fight, it's another to beat up someone who is powerless to resist. That's the sort of thing a man like O'Connor does - assault the defenceless.

'Why are you a rapist? You're not stupid, you know it's horrible abuse. But you don't care. Tell me why.'

'Why shouldn't I be?'

'You know why. Everyone knows why. Were you abused as a kid? Is that it?'

O'Connor laughed. 'You'd love to think that, wouldn't you? No.'

'I don't believe in evil, but I do believe in insanity. I think you're insane. You're psychotic.'

O'Connor laughed a proper, genuinely amused laugh.

'Ye can call it what you like. I don't give a fuck. I've seen enough shrinks to know that whatever I am, it is the way I was made, son.'

But Nick couldn't let it drop. 'Julie is a lovely person and I think you know that. So why hurt her back in 1989 and why today? Why? There must be a reason.'

O'Connor just pulled a face. A silly face, mocking Nick's concern.

'Exactly because she is a lovely person, obviously, plus she's beautiful and she's got a fuckin' great body. Always did have. Fuckin' magnificent. When I saw her on Facebook again I couldn't believe it. What a looker. I had to get a piece of her cunt again. Had to.'

It was the fact that he said it in his soft, rounded accent with such a lack of malice or self-consciousness that made him so unnerving. It was as though he was talking about something innocuous.

'I said to Greeny, we had to get her and do it somewhere good, and he was all for it. He's still in love wi' her 20 years on. Stupid eejit. He's loopy. He gets obsessed. Sitting there knocking one out into a hanky at the back of yer house. Sniffing the crotch of her pyjamas. He's fucked up. But we talked about her when we were inside and what an amazin' fuck she was, so when Kenny tells Bailey about her and that fucking bitch palace, Teesside Women, and told us where you lived, it was all perfect. I followed her in the Range Rover. It was all a piece of piss.'

'Kenny Harlow told you where we lived?'

'Yeah, he's Boz's mate, isn't he? He told me what to write on the website to let the world know what a slut she is. Kenny's another man who doesn't like her. A lot of men don't like your missus, Guymer, but they all want to fuck her brains out. How d'ya feel about that?'

Nick flinched a little at his language, and seeing that, O'Connor made a mocking noise.

'Does it bother you that I fucked your wife, Guymer? That I filled her up?' He looked at Nick almost blankly but with a hint of a smile on his lips.

Nick didn't flinch this time. 'What bothers me is you did it against her will.'

'Oh, come on, Nick. Every man hates the fact that his wife has been fucked by other men; that she's had their sticky muck inside her. That she's lay there, legs apart and loved getting fucked.'

Nick folded his arms across his chest and shook his head.

'No, you're wrong. Every man doesn't hate the idea that their wife has had a sex life before they met. You've just made that up in your own mind, but I see something about you now. Yeah, yeah, alright, I've got you now, O'Connor. I know what you're all about.' Nick leaned back against the old wooden door. 'You think you're somehow spoiling women don't you? Ruining them for other men. Ruining them with your so-called "muck". That's it, isn't it? Yeah, it's all about power, not just

259

over the women, but over everyone else connected to them into the future. On the inside, you hate yourself, you feel small, powerless and weak, so you're trying to bring Julie down to your level. To make her feel as corrupted and damaged as you feel inside. You want to co-opt me into your perverted world view. But you haven't. You've lost.'

His words clearly touched a nerve, and a flicker of anger registered on O'Connor's face.

'Spare me the therapy session, Guymer. You know fuck all.'

'You've failed, O'Connor. You've lost. You're just a loser. She doesn't feel like that. I don't feel like that. All you ever did was in the long run to make Julie stronger and give her energy and power to fight other men like you. She took your evil and turned it into good. You can't even admit to yourself what the reason for all of this is. You're lying to yourself even now. Your whole life is a lie. You're pretending it's all a bit of game but it's all about your own inadequacy, misery and self-loathing.'

'Are we going to stand here all day while you figure out why I held your wife down and fucked her to within an inch of her life?'

'See, you're lying again. You didn't do that. You've told yourself a story. In 1989 you did it quickly and aggressively and it was soon over. That's not "to within an inch" of her life. It's like you don't want to know the truth, you even started to drug women in order to rape them, so they're not witness to it. And without a witness, you can make up anything you like. You keep the control and that's the most important thing to you, isn't it?'

O'Connor sneered and him and kicked fresh air with his foot. 'Ah, screw you and your half-baked theories. People like you always want a reason. There is no reason. I like raping women, preferably with my mates, or even with strangers. It makes me feel good. And that's the whole thing. End of. We planned this for weeks. It was brilliant. Wouldn't have changed any of it. It was a great game for Tommy, Boz and me. Finding the roof space, setting all that up so we fucked her on your mate's big night...brilliant.'

'How did you get access to that roof space?'

O'Connor sighed wearily. 'Through Kenny. He was an electrician contracted to do wiring. He told Boz, Boz thought it sounded like an ace place for our little adventure and he was right. I've got to say, Guymer, your missus is still a great fuck. She fucking loves cock. Loves my cock. We all went through her cunt.'

260

Nick ignored his horrible words, instinctively feeling they were not true. 'But you must have known you'd get caught.'

'Maybe. I knew that Rhodes was a druggie liability. But he was another bloke who was pissed off at your missus, very pissed off and it was worth getting him involved just get into that wee tattooed slut of his as well, what a bonus. We took a good old go on her, I can tell you. She was so tight, at least at the start...ha ha ha. We literally fucked her to death.' He began laughing. Nick gripped his right fist tightly.

This seemed to be the real Sean O'Connor, the one that lay underneath the calm, intelligent, rational exterior. This was the cold, black-hearted, vicious rapist.

Nick found it hard to look at him, staring at the wooden floor, instead. 'You didn't. But she nearly died, man. She nearly died. And all so you could just use and abuse her like she wasn't even a human being. You're a disgrace, man.' He didn't raise his voice. There didn't seem any point.

But O'Connor just shrugged.

'I don't care. That's what you and your sort can't get your head around, isn't it? Just. Don't. Care. All I came here to do was choke Julie Wells with my cock.' He started to use more and more violent, vulgar language, but Nick stopped listening.

There was no point in this conversation. No point at all. He had tried to reach the human in O'Connor but there was no human left, if indeed there had ever been any. Whether he was some flavour of insane, or really was possessed by some elemental force that we usually call evil, was impossible to say.

'I thought you were going to kill me, but you're not, are ye? I told you you wouldn't. You've had your chance and you've not took it. Yer a fuckin' shite. No guts to ye. I was gonna ride yer wife, I was gonna shoot my load in her face, and you can't even bring yourself to hit me. We were going to ruin the bitch. If you were a real man, you'd knock the feckin' shite out of me. Green is weak and fucked up, Boz is just a head case, I'm the really evil cunt. I planned all of this, go on son, fucking hit me. I deserve it.' He jutted his jaw out, as though to make a better target.

"Trust your instincts, our Nick."

Nick shook his head. 'I don't want to even touch you. My revenge is to deprive you of the punishment you seem to think you need. This ends now.'

'Ah, ye fuckin' prick!' shouted O'Connor as Nick turned his back on him, pulled open the door and left the room, shutting the door behind him.

Mandy turned around. 'What the hell have you been doing for so long? I 'ope you've not made too much of a mess of 'im. He's not dead, is he? I don't mind if he is, but it's a lot more difficult to explain to the people who think men like 'im should be alive.'

'I was talking to him, but I never touched him.'

'What?' She was surprised. 'Why not?'

'He almost seemed to want me to do it to him. So I deprived him of that pleasure. I'm not some avenging angel, I just want to be a nice lad, like my mam always told me to be. She said to trust my instinct and my instincts say that if I batter him, I somehow get co-opted into his evil.'

Mandy raised her eyebrows and puffed out her cheeks and gestured to three officers gathered behind her to get the Irishman out of the room.

'Well, I might struggle to match your standards, I'm afraid. I might have to accidentally tread painfully on some bit of him. He'll go down for a long time, but I wish we had the bloody death penalty for scum like him.' She put her large fleshy hand on his arm. 'Now, listen, I've taken a look at Julie, she's disorientated by the rohypnol, but the paramedics will take care of her. She's not had the reaction to it that Emily Davids had. More crucially, they didn't rape her, Nick. They made her swallow the dope but it takes time to work and they don't do it to women who are fully conscious. They tore her shirt open and seem to have pulled her jeans down and they'd decided to wank off over her. There's nothing on her, though. Nothing. Alright? You got there just in time.'

Nick nodded. He began to walk away to go and see Julie.

Mandy called out, 'Nick!'

He turned around.

'When I took over from Colin Harcombe in June, he told us what a good fella you are. These were seriously bad people and whether by intuition or instinct, you saved Emily's life and probably saved Julie's as well. Good work, lad. I wouldn't have got here when I did without your texts, without you doing what you did.'

'Well, I've probably got my mam to thank for being able to trust my instincts. But, bloody hell, as Col would say, this really was a bad business.'

As he spoke there was a commotion on the stairs. 'Get your bloody hands off of us. It's my daughter and my bloke up there.'

It could only be Jackie Wells. She pushed her way through.

'What the hell is going on? Where's Jules?' she demanded, hands on her hips in indignation. 'Where's Con? Will someone tell us what the bloody hell is happening here?!'

Mandy stepped forward and put her arm around Jackie's shoulder.

'Julie's upstairs, she's OK. Paramedics are looking after her. Four men drugged her and were about to rape her when Nick, Jeff and Con stopped them.'

'Is that right, Nick?' said Jackie, who was as unshockable as any human that ever lived. She just seemed to be able to absorb any information with a calm sort of rationality.

He nodded.

'And is he one of them and did he do them photos?' she nodded toward O'Connor, who was being led away.

'Yeah. He...he actually raped Jules back in 1989,' said Nick. 'I know she never told you about it.'

O'Connor turned and shouted, 'And she was tremendous fuck, missus, let me tell you that. Lovely juicy cunt on her. You should be very proud.'

The look that went across Jackie's face was like none Nick had ever seen her make before, combining the fiercest aspects of both fury and disgust.

'You think you're clever, son, don't yer? Eh? You do, don't yer?'

'I know I fuckin' filled your daughter with a load of my muck, missus, that's all I know.'

'You dirty bastard!' yelled Jackie. Mandy made a gesture to her officers to take O'Connor away, but Jackie was a couple of strides ahead of them. She pulled a long, sharp pair of hairdressing scissors out of her shoulder purse, ran in front of O'Connor and lashed out at him, making an uppercut movement, sinking the blades between O'Connor's legs, pulling out the scissors, blood smeared and sinking them into what had to be his balls, once again. He screamed like a stuck pig.

The police showed no inclination to stop her. So, with a face like a storm, she reversed her grip and, like fast bowler in a cricket match, brought the scissors down in a plunging overarm move, once, twice, surely skewering his penis like a prawn. She left the scissors buried into him. It was all over in perhaps five seconds. O'Connor sank the floor whimpering, with blood leaking through his jeans.

'Is that our Jackie?' came Con's booming voice as he came down the stairs.

'Aye, I've just been sorting out this shite,' said Jackie, poking at O'Connor with her foot.

'I wish you'd not done that, Jackie,' said Mandy, wearily. 'I'm going to have to arrest you now. As if I don't have enough on my plate with four bloody rapists.'

'I don't give a bloody shite, Mandy. We both bloody know he had it comin', dirty bloody sod. Nobody does that to one of my kids and gets away with it. He's sodding lucky I've not killed him. D'ya hear me, son? I hope I've cut your sodding balls off and if I haven't by the way, my Ricky and my Kev will make sure someone does that to you, in whatever jail it is you go to. This isn't the end son, this is just the start. You don't cross the Wells family and not suffer the bloody consequences. Right?! I'm your worst nightmare and it's a nightmare you're never going to wake up from! Do you hear me?' She screamed it out at a vicious, high-pitch. She was the very definition of a banshee. Everyone was at least a little bit afraid.

'He is a shite, like,' said Con, walking past O'Connor, quickly kneeing him in the side of the head, as though accidentally.

'Alright, let's all calm down now. Get a paramedic, Dilip and let's see if Mister Rapey has got any balls left. Alison, take Jackie and Con down the station and wait for me.'

Nick turned his back on the scene. O'Connor was clearly losing significant blood. Jeff came down the stairs and looked at the Irishman on the floor, looked around at them all and shook his head. 'Well I said I wanted an opening night to remember, didn't I? And no-one is ever going to forget this. More's the bloody pity.'

CHAPTER 17

'Eee, fizz me, look at this place, it's total class, like,' said Julie, as they walked into Beef and Vodka at the top of Albert Road, in the centre of Middlesbrough. It was a large red-brick Victorian building with big arched windows. Black and white tiles on the floor, large impressionist paintings on the exposed brick walls and dark wood furniture. 'I'm glad I got dressed up now.' She smoothed out her vintage 1920s black silk lace and embroidery dress and pushed a set of fine silver bangles around her left wrist.

'We've got a table for five booked under the name Guymer,' said Nick, to the maître d', a tall, elegant woman in her 30s dressed in a black suit.

'Gloria has spent some big bucks on this project,' said Jeff. 'Speaking as a man who knows how expensive it is to make a place look half decent, she's got to have put 300k into this, easy. Yeah, I'm glad I put my best pants on, now.'

He hitched up a capacious pair of black linen trousers, adjusted his loose, collarless blue shirt, flicked his hair over his shoulders and stroked his long beard. 'What do you reckon, Em?'

'It's great. The smell of hot fat and meat is already making me hungry.'

'Yeah, sorry about that, my thighs have been rubbing together,' said Jeff, slapping at his legs.

She giggled and hit him on the arm.

'I hope we get a chance to see Mike the Meat,' said Julie, as they waited to be shown to their table. 'Have you met him before, Em?'

'I've not, no. But I've heard a lot about him, or at least about his buttocks, mostly from you, to be fair, Jules.'

'I am moderately obsessed with his bum. He's got the best arse on Teesside,' said Julie. 'Honest, it's two perfect handfuls.'

'I do hate this sort of objectification of men, don't you, Nick?' said Jeff, adopting the voice of a posh old lady. 'All this talk of bums is absolutely shocking. Personally, I find it hard to be taken seriously due to being so physically attractive to ladies. They can't see past the glamour, you know.'

They all laughed.

'Is he being silly again?' said Mandy, coming in and giving Jeff a little hug of his arm and kissing him on the cheek, grinning at him. ' 'Ello, kids. Sorry, I was a bit behind schedule. Bloody hell, it's a palace in here, isn't it? Nice to get an invite to a posh opening night. I knew being mates with you lot would pay off eventually.'

'To be fair, me and you have put a fair few hundred quid into Big Meat in Hartburn Village. We must be some of his best customers,' said Jeff as they were shown to a table.

'So 'ow are we all?' said Mandy as they sat down. 'You're all looking very smart, I must say. That's a posh frock, Jules. I've never seen you in a dress.'

'I've started calling it my Lady Mary dress. You know, like in Downton Abbey. It's a vintage 1920s thing. It's literally the only dress I've got, it only gets an airing every two or three years.'

'It's proper classy. You look like Lady Muck in it, and I've never seen you in a suit, Nick.'

'This is my wedding suit. I also only get it out for special occasions like...well...weddings.'

'And you're looking expensively dressed, Em,' said Mandy, pushing raggy curls off her forehead. 'Not the usual rock star garb, though.'

'Yeah, I'm having a bit of a change of image. Bit fed up of the rock chick thing. Might go a bit more baggy and arty farty, I think. Thinking of getting a loose perm.'

'Well, what you've got on really suits you, lady,' said Mandy, smiling widely.

Emily wore a silk blouse and loose harem pants made from a multi-coloured Indian print cotton fabric. It was almost exactly the opposite of what she'd normally wear, which had all been tight and black.

'I love that shot silk top, sometimes it looks cerise and other times purple,' said Julie.

'Well, they're much more comfortable clothes to wear on a humid summer night than tight jeans.'

'Aye, as my mam used to say, it's absolutely maftin' today,' said Nick.

'Right, let's have a look at this menu,' said Jeff, holding an A3-sized laminated card. The others did likewise and began to laugh.

'Hang on, there's only two things on it. Ha ha...beef and vodka,' said Nick, pointing to it. On the left side was three beef-based starters and three beef main courses. On the right, an extensive list of vodkas.

'Well, he wasn't lying by calling the place Beef and Vodka,' said Jeff.

'Brilliant. I love lack of choice,' said Nick. 'If there's one thing that has ruined the quality of life in the modern world it's having too much choice.'

'Amen, brother...except when it comes to vinyl records, of course,' said Jeff.

'I absolutely sodding love both beef and vodka,' said Julie. 'C'mon, how about we get a bottle of crystal skull, and five T-Bone steaks. Job done.'

'Two bottles, I think,' said Mandy. 'We don't want a thimble full each.'

'I can't eat a whole T-Bone,' said Emily.

'Don't worry, luv, we will dispose of any unwanted meat you have about your person,' said Mandy. 'Won't we, Jeff?'

The big man cocked his index finger and looked around the table. 'The Cult had a song called "Love Removal Machine", but I am the more rare form, a Meat Removal Machine. And a damn fine one, at that, as I intend to prove tonight.'

They all laughed again. Nick glanced around the table. It was good to see everyone smiling after everything they had all been through.

The waitress brought two of the skull-shaped vodka bottles, a large ice bucket, some bottles of tonic and fizzy water, slices of lime and lemon and five glasses. Classy. Julie did the honours.

'OK. First toast of the night. Here's to these three fantastic women, Nick,' said Jeff. 'Clever, beautiful and fun.'

'Aye aye, what are you after?' said Mandy, with a laugh, pushing at him.

'Aw, Jeff. You're a big soft clart, you,' said Julie. 'I thought you were the emotionally repressed one.'

'I am, but I can't admit it, due to being emotionally repressed.' He moved his eyebrows up and down.

'Well, I shall also propose a toast as well, then,' said Emily, as they all clinked glasses. 'Here's to you two wonderful men. Men who are loving and funny and kind and god knows, we should celebrate that after what we've been through, Jules.' There was a sudden hint of tears in her voice as she spoke, but she didn't let it come too far forward. It was still only six weeks after they'd both been attacked. Far too soon to have got over it.

They clinked glasses with each other again and took a drink.

267

'Ooh, that hits the spot,' said Julie. 'I fancy a good drink up. Can you get a cop car to take us home, Mandy?' She laughed.

'Of course, and I'll tell them to put their woo-woos on, as well, eh. Actually, I don't want to talk shop, but I had some very good news today, which was why I was a bit late. It seems that our gruesome foursome, currently on remand in four different jails, over two hundred miles apart to prevent them conspiring, are all planning to plead guilty.'

'Good. And I hope when they're sent down, they throw away the key,' said Julie, sipping at her vodka.

'Do we have to talk about them?' said Emily, looking into her glass.

'No, of course not, but it's good news for all of you,' said Mandy. 'It means you won't have to give evidence in court. With Kenny Harlow fessin' up to conspiracy 'an all, the whole thing won't need to be raked over any more, so you can just get on with your lives in the knowledge that they'll all be behind lock and key for a hell of a long time. There's nowt I like better than locking up dirty bastard villains.' She beamed around at all of them, the copper's instinct to celebrate this fact overriding any other sensitivities.

Emily nodded. 'That is good news. I was not looking forward to having to say what happened to me.'

'You and me both,' said Julie, patting her on the arm.

'If you had needed to, though, would you have?' said Mandy, who wasn't the most delicate person; but then, when you had her job, it mitigated against it.

'Well, we don't need to consider that, thankfully,' said Julie, trying to move the conversation on.

'I'm not sure.' Emily paused and then nodded. 'Yes. Yes, I would. Of course I would. It'd be the right thing to do. I'd hate every minute of it, even giving the statements was very upsetting, but I'd still do it.'

Julie patted her on the arm again, and gave her a wink.

'Top lass,' said Mandy, raising her glass. 'Can't let scum win. I'm totally anti-scum.'

'It's a shame your big opening night ended the way it did,' said Nick, looking at Jeff.

Jeff waved away his comment. 'It's turned out fine, hasn't it? Big police raid on your first night, evil blokes nicked, and a virtual cockectomy courtesy of Jackie's scissors, I mean, you can't buy publicity like that. People have been coming just to see if anything like that happens again. It's been packed every night.'

'What'll happen to mam, Mandy?' said Julie. 'I mean, OK, she's out on police bail, will that end up going to court, do you think?'

'I was looking at your mam's record today, actually. Or rather, I wasn't. She's never been arrested. Nothing as much as a speeding fine.'

Julie pulled a face. 'Are you sure? I'm sure she must have been nicked for something at some point. She's such a narky auld shitehawk.'

'Nope. Whatever laws she's broken, she's got away with. Point is, this will work in her favour, if she pleads guilty to assault...'

'...which she will. She can hardly do anything else,' said Julie. 'Gaunty will tell her as much.'

'Jon Gaunt? Aye, good lad, is Gaunty, one of the few lawyers I see with any integrity. So if she pleads guilty and Gaunty presents the judge with the proper context to the attack, she's got a good chance of a suspended sentence. Judges tend not to want to send down women in their late 60s without a previous record, especially for an assault on one of the most vicious rapists I hope I'm ever going to have to deal with. I mean, the press would have a field day with that. Ninety-nine per cent of the public would be on her side and would probably like to think they'd have sunk a pair of scissors into the man's danglies, too.'

'He was horrible, that man, O'Connor,' said Emily. 'The fat one was mentally ill, I think, Matty was insane on drugs, Bailey is a psychotic thug, but I think O'Connor is sane. He's just full of evil. The words he used to me, the way he said things, it was...y'know...I'm so grateful to Jackie, Jules.'

'Why's that?'

'Because he's going to suffer for the rest of his life with the injuries she inflicted on him. So at least he has to live with what he did, the way we have to live with it.'

Julie nodded. 'Yeah. In a way it's as well she avoided the artery in his groin, that might just have killed him and that would have been too easy a way out.'

Mandy poured them all another shot of vodka. 'Yeah, it was fortunate, but all the same, stabbing a man four times and through clothing and managing to sever enough blood vessels and muscle to give him a strong likelihood of being impotent for the rest of his life, was quite brilliant. Good use of hairdressing scissors. I've seen his medical report. First strike went in his prostate. Second in his balls, third ripped off the top of his cock, the fourth lanced it like a prawn. Went all the way through. Doctors reckon none of it will work again. He needs to piss into some sort of bag. Jackie couldn't have designed a better punishment for a rapist.'

'Maybe I should have beaten the crap out of him when you gave me the chance,' said Nick, who had felt, ever since, that maybe he'd let himself, Julie and everyone else down by not doing what he'd been invited to do.

'No, you did the right thing,' said Julie.

'Definitely,' added Emily quickly. 'In a way, it was better that a woman ended up hurting him. More just, somehow. And I wouldn't have wanted you to hurt yourself on him.'

'Hurting myself wasn't a consideration,' said Nick. 'I think he really wanted me to hurt him. And I couldn't help but feel that since assaulting someone who is powerless was what he did, I'd have been as bad as him, in a way.'

Mandy, not one of life's philosophers, made a "pfft" noise. 'With all due respect, that's rubbish. That man has violently raped a lot of women in his life, you breaking his face with a couple of right-handers is nowt compared to that. You're overthinking it.'

'No, I'm not,' said Nick. 'I just didn't want to do what he wanted.' But he sensed his reluctance had disappointed Mandy, ever since. She'd gone out of her way to allow retribution and he'd passed up the chance. Even though she'd been good enough to say what a good bloke he was, he'd subsequently felt a degree of quiet disappointment from her. It brought back a feeling he'd had at school of not feeling like he was man enough to play his part in the roister doister of alpha male life. His reluctance to join in had often left him outside of the mainstream and a propensity to overthink everything hadn't exactly helped.

But even so, he still felt in his heart that he'd done the right thing. Mam had said he should be a nice lad. Beating up a rapist, when he'd already been arrested, wasn't the act of a nice lad and he felt sure his mother would agree. It's one thing to defend yourself and those you love, quite another to just assault the defenceless. Then you really did get sucked into their evil.

They all went quiet, all thinking over for the thousandth time what had happened.

'The meetings I've had at Teesside Women Centre have been great,' said Emily to Julie. 'So supportive and just...just nice and down to earth. Helping me sort it all out in my head.'

270

'Oh, I didn't know you'd been to Julie's gaff,' said Mandy, now hammering the vodka heavily, pouring herself another big one.

'You've got a great support worker in Karen. She's very experienced and pretty unshockable.'

Nick smiled at Emily. Since the attack, quite understandably, she hadn't quite been the same person that he'd known before. All the flirty thing had stopped. She'd been staying in Jeff's spare room ever since. There'd been a lot of tears and a lot of late-night talking over drinks. She'd apologised, and they'd all forgiven her for going away down to Lincolnshire without telling any of them.

When she'd been raped, the drugs hadn't rendered her totally unconscious, so she'd been semi-awake throughout the whole terrible thing, as the four of them had taken turns in raping her, only passing out when her respiratory system had begun to fail in response to whatever was in the pills.

She'd talked about it; the bewilderment, the horror, the fear, the physical pain. You read about attacks like this with disgust, but when it happens to someone you know and care for, it's beyond horrific. All you could do was to be there for them and listen when they wanted you to listen. But at least the men were all arrested and would not be coming out of jail soon. This was not typical. And how much worse must it be to have gone through this and the men responsible not be held to account.

It was clear that, at least for a while, Emily had given up being the rock 'n' roll sex kitten. That was all too connected to her life with Matty and the attack. And tonight, dressed as she was, with no make-up and in loose colourful clothing, she was clearly taking the first steps in a new phase of her life. The fact she was still working in the shop and able to come out for a night, Nick felt, showed just how strong she was. But then, what choice did she have?

Her sessions at TW had revealed an upbringing that, as Julie had speculated, had some incidents of sexual assault. Her uncle had abused her by putting his hands where he shouldn't have, when she was just 11 years old. In Lincolnshire, she'd finally confronted her father about what his brother had done to her and had finally made up her mind to go to Teesside Women and begin her recovery, only to subsequently be attacked by the four men in her own flat while getting ready for the opening night. The terror of that was never going to go away.

Nick felt instinctively protective towards her, but you had to be a grown up about this shit. You had to be strong. You were no use being

271

drippy or weak or overly emotional, just as Jeff had said after the first Matty incident. Oh, god, life was nothing if not a learning process.

The T-Bone steaks were brought to the table, wonderfully medium rare, served with four different sauces and a rocket-based bowl of salad. It was delicious.

While Emily was a decent boozer for a small woman and Nick, and Julie and Jeff were all excellent drinkers of long standing, Mandy was something else. It was very impressive. She seemed to be able to knock back an almost infinite amount of vodka without ever appearing to get drunk. She ordered a third skull of vodka and poured herself half a glass and added ice and proceeded to demolish it.

As they finished their meals, a voice shouted across the restaurant.

'Hey, you guys!' It was Mike the Meat.

Julie stood up and gave him a hug, letting one hand stray to his backside. Jeff and Nick shook his big, strong hand.

'So what do you reckon? Is this place going to work?' He said, holding out his arms wide.

'It's brilliant, Mike,' said Nick. 'Beef and vodka. It's all anyone needs.'

'It was all cooked to perfection,' said Emily, offering her hand. 'We've never met. I'm Emily Davids. You're a very talented chef. It was all absolutely delish.'

'Aw, thanks, Emily. What a nice thing to say.' For a moment, they stared at each other, he held her hand for one, two, three seconds, then kissed the back of her small paw. 'I'm so happy you enjoyed it.'

'It was meatylicious,' said Jeff.

'Well, thanks for supporting me. I really appreciate it. I hope I see you all again soon.' And with a last glance at Emily, he left them.

Jeff began clapping. The rest of the table did likewise and within a few seconds the whole restaurant was doing it. A chant of "Mike the Meat, Mike the Meat" started up. The chef looked elated and embarrassed by the attention, in equal measure, clapping his hands above his head in front of the kitchen doors.

'Aw, he's *really* nice, and very, very talented,' said Emily, as Mike disappeared back into the kitchen. 'How wonderful this must be for him. Having your own place and everyone loving the thing you've invented, that must be brilliant.' She watched him go. 'And you're right about his bum, Jules. Gosh, it's totally lush.'

'Told you, didn't I?' said Julie, making a nice face at her.

'How old is he?' said Emily.

'It was his 30th the other week,' said Jeff. 'The boy's got a big future ahead of him, I reckon. He'll be on the cooking programmes on TV soon.'

'And you said he's gay, right?' said Emily.

'Yeah. Well, that's what he told us once, but it's not like he chats to us about it,' said Julie. 'Maybe I should try and seduce him just to make sure, purely as a public service to all the straight women of Teesside, like. It'd be a selfless act of humanity to have it off with him, really.'

'Don't you mind her saying that?' said Emily to Nick.

'Nah, her lust for Mike is an open secret. I quite fancy him myself. I could definitely have sex with him, it'd be the hugging and kissing after-wards that I couldn't do.'

Everyone laughed at that.

Jeff had his index finger cocked at 45 degrees. 'Listen to your uncle Jeffrey. Mike is not exclusively gay. He's been going out with a human female. I met them in the village, so there's hope for you yet, Jules...and you, too, Mister Muscle.'

At this point, Emily would normally have chimed in with some sexual comment or other, but not now. Funny how life changes you.

'Well, this place is a big hit, isn't it?' said Mandy, looking around the packed restaurant at all the clean plates. 'Seems such a simple idea, but then all the best ideas are simple, I suppose.'

'He's a beef visionary,' said Jeff. 'Maybe he dreamed it. He might have your precognition thing, Nick.'

'Precog-what?' said Mandy.

'Nick thinks he can see the future, in his dreams,' said Jeff.

'Bloody hell. You don't, do you?' said Mandy.

'I dunno. Something weird has been going on in the last couple of months.'

'His mam keeps visiting him,' said Julie.

'But she's dead, isn't she?' said Mandy.

'Yeah. I don't really know what's going on with all of that,' said Nick, feeling awkward and not really wanting to discuss it because every week or two she'd come to see him and it felt like a quiet, private thing.

'Too much cheese before bed, if you ask me,' said Jeff.

'You say that, but I dreamt about those records didn't I? I got those 100 per cent right,' said Nick. 'That was seriously weird. You can't say that wasn't supernatural. It totally was.'

Julie frowned. 'What are you talking about? Which records are those?'

'I never told you about them.' Nick explained about the auction room box and what was in it. 'It was too weird, I didn't tell you because I knew you'd just laugh at me. But it did happen.'

'I think you are psychic, or something,' said Emily. 'You must be. That's the only explanation. There's no way you could have known what records were there and what order they were in. No way at all.'

'Maybe I should set up in business like Natalie Townsend, on our allotment. She says she's a psychic, a clairvoyant and an angel light worker,' said Nick.

Mandy burst out laughing. ' 'As she got wings? What the 'ell is one of them when it's at 'ome?'

'God knows, but she was able to tell what our birthday's were, though, wasn't she, Jules? She must have some sort of insight,' said Nick.

'She did, like and she said there was negative energy around me just before I was attacked. I'm as down to earth as anyone, but even I think she had something about her.'

Mandy took another big drink. 'Excuse me for being a cynical old cow, but I'll tell you 'ow she knew your birthday's, shall I?'

'How could she know both of our birthdays?' said Nick.

'Easy. I'm not even an Angel Shite Grafter, I know 'cos I bet you've both got the dates publically visible on your Facebook pages, 'aven't you? Pound to a penny, she finds out your name from someone on the allotments, looks you up and then pulls her little trick. Easy. And as for negative energy, that's the sort of thing that you can never be wrong on, because every single day, something goes wrong, big or small. So she can go, oh see, I was right, that's your negative energy kicking in. It's perfect. You can't lose.'

Jeff laughed and pointed at Mandy. 'You should take up working stuff out for a living.'

'God, I'll feel a proper mug if you're right,' said Nick, head in his hands, then checking his and Julie's Facebook pages on his phone.

But she wasn't right. They'd both hidden their birthdays. Natalie couldn't have known them. Somehow, that was a relief.

'Nope. She didn't know via Facebook, Mandy. I think she's got something about her, I really do. We shouldn't be too cynical, I reckon,' said Nick.

'Aye, we should. There'll be a rational explanation,' said Mandy, bluntly.

'Well there certainly is for how you knew about those records,' said Julie. 'If you'd told me about them before now, I could have told you exactly how you knew what would be there.'

'If you're going to tell us you're an angel light worker, Jules, can I be the first to say I never doubted you for a second and always thought angels would suffer from terrible wind after eating broccoli,' said Jeff. 'Still, at least you've got those wings for wafting the smell away!'

Everyone laughed.

'As much as I'd like to be a farty angel, no, I had met Pete Phillips from the auction rooms on my lunch break. He told me there hadn't been any other bids on the box of records, so Jeff had won them.'

'He knows his stuff, does Pete. I'm surprised he didn't snaffle them,' said Jeff.

'He'd been on holiday, just got back that morning, after the hammer had gone down, or he probably would have. Anyway, he told me what was there and where to find it...err...let's think, what was it again, ah yeah, Fairport Convention's *Liege and Lief* on the pink Island label, John Martyn's *London Conversation* first pressing, two Audience albums on pink Charisma at the front and the *Glastonbury Fayre* triple album at the back of the box. I told you this in bed but you'd dropped off to sleep. Your subconscious obviously heard it and then put the info into a dream. You're so mad about records that if there's one thing that your subconscious would be keen to remember, it'd be details about records.'

She put her hand to his cheek and laughed. Nick looked at her bright blue eyes and laughed too. 'Bloody hell. This is...I'm a total sap.'

'Aw, I wanted you to be psychic,' said Emily.

Nick sat back. 'Well, I didn't want to be special. It was really worrying me, actually. I like being ignorant of the future,' said Nick. 'I dreamt that I found you with knife in your back, Em and that really disturbed me.'

'Did you? Bloody hell,' said Emily, with a look of shock. 'You never said that before now. Why didn't you tell me?'

'I just didn't want to worry you. I dreamed I found you naked and dead.'

She paused and thought about it for a second. 'Well, that dream came true then, you did find me naked and dead and I was stabbed in the back, metaphorically, by Matty,' Emily said. 'You saved my life.'

Nick felt embarrassed. 'No, that was the paramedics that did that.'

Emily shook her head, 'No, recently, my doctor told me that I probably only pulled through because of the CPR you gave me. It gave me oxygen to my brain, enough to keep me from slipping away before they got my heart going. I can never thank you enough for that.' She made a flat smile, obviously upset by the thought.

Nick still found praise far harder to deal with than criticism, so he just shrugged. 'I just knew something bad had happened. I trusted my instincts.'

As he did so, Natalie's words returned to him when she'd said his dreams were all different. One was literal – the records – one was symbolic – the knife in Emily's back. That just left his dreams of his mother – the supernatural.

'Don't answer this if it's out of order, but given you were sort of dead, Em, do you remember what it was like?' said Mandy.

'Sorry, no. I passed out and I'm bloody glad I did. I remember nothing after that until I woke up in hospital. No go-to-the-light moment. Nothing.'

Mandy nodded. 'Good lass. You're a top woman. I massively admire how you've dealt with it all. Stay strong, sister. If I can ever be of help, let me know.'

'Thanks, Mandy. I appreciate that. I have to say, the sisterhood has been very supportive.'

'That's because every one of us understands what you've been through. Every one. The world is full of shitey blokes being shite. Every woman understands that. I'm a bit of a twat, but I'm here for you. Right?'

Mandy stood up and hi-fived Emily, her big fleshy hand twice the size of Em's.

Jeff pointed at Nick.

'So you saw Em in your dream, and you knew that the publishers would offer you two grand and a seven and half per cent royalty,' said Jeff. 'You dreamed that as well. So maybe you are a bit special.'

'Sort of. I told mam that's what they'd offer, but I'm still not sure if that's a dream or not...but anyway, it could easily have been an educated guess. I'd been researching typical sorts of deals and I know enough about the world of publishing to be able to guess what might be on offer. Not sure that's enough to think you're psychic or have precognition. I could've guessed this T-Bone would be about 25 quid and I'd have been right. That's not psychic, it's just experience.'

'Ah, right. So you're not psychic, you're not a visionary, you don't have precognition and you don't even make phones ring like you once did,' said Jeff, jokingly adding. 'Is there anything you're of any use for, Guymer?'

'Oh, he's got his uses,' said Julie, with a raised eyebrow. 'I can tell you that much.'

'Bloody hell, don't I know it? I've seen the video,' said Emily, to huge laughter.

***

'Hello, Nick.'

He opened his eyes. The clock said 4.27am. His mother was sitting in the wicker basket chair and was knitting what looked like a cream wool cardigan with cabling, the needles clicking together. It had been a constant soundtrack of his upbringing.

'Alright, mam. Why do you always come at 4.27am?'

'Do I? There's no time where I am. You've probably just made that up for some reason.'

'Funny you should say that, I've keep wondering if I've been making all of these meetings up or if they're real.'

She smiled and kept knitting. 'Well, what do you think?'

'I think I've probably...I don't know what the word is, probably conjured you up because I needed to work some stuff out about my relationship with you and because I miss you. Well, I miss you being healthy, anyway.'

'That's good, then. I've been telling you to trust your instincts, haven't I?'

'Yeah, you have absolutely drilled that into me and it served me well.'

'Well, then. Maybe you're just trying to help yourself. Don't worry about whether this is a dream or real.' She clicked away on the needles just as she always had done when he was a boy. 'It really doesn't matter. Dreams and reality are one and the same thing, our Nick. Like I said, you're a special lad, you always were and when you believe in yourself, you can achieve so much more.'

'Yeah, I can see that, now. I'll try and do that in future, mam.'

She smiled. 'There's a good lad.'

Her words made him shiver a little. When your mother calls a you a good lad, it somehow means more than anyone else saying it, or at least, it feels very different.

'Why are you knitting, mam? Do you need an Arran cardigan in the afterlife?'

She laughed a little. 'A good cardi never goes to waste wherever you are.'

Nick cast a look to his left as Julie moved, turned over and suddenly opened her eyes, took a moment to focus on his mother and said, 'Eee, hello, Mrs Guymer. How funny to see you here. Nick's been telling me about your visits.'

'Hello, luv. How are you feeling these days? It was a nasty business you and that little lassie went through last month.'

Julie propped herself up on an elbow. This was very weird. She had never taken part in one of his dreams before. 'I'm fine now, thanks. I've been having a bit of therapy to get over the attack, but I'll cope. I'm strong. Women have to be strong, we don't get a choice, do we?'

'Very true. You're a clever lass. My generation never talked about anything. We were told to swallow it all down, whatever it was and that wasn't healthy, Julie. So I'm glad you're getting help. You're certainly looking very well.' His mother smiled, and kept knitting.

'Thanks. You do, too.'

'And your bum still looks lovely.' She smiled almost cheekily at Julie. It wasn't a look he ever remembered his mother making before.

Julie laughed. 'It's just genetics. I should thank my mam, I suppose.'

His mother gathered up her knitting and put it into a canvas bag which had two wooden handles.

'Alright, well, I'll get off. I'm happy that you two are happy. Now get off to sleep.'

Nick watched as Julie lay back down and closed her eyes.

'Will you keep coming to see me, mam?'

'I don't know. That's up to you isn't it, luv?'

'Is it?'

'Of course it is. I suspect you'll see me from time to time. But I'm always with you, in all of the ways that matter. If you need me, I'll be here.'

'Thanks.' Tears glazed his eyes. That was just what he wanted to hear.

'Don't be daft. No need to thank me. I'm your mam. And don't forget your manners and just be a good lad.'

'Yes mam.'

She stood up, gave him a little wave and walked out of the room.

Nick smiled as she went. Julie was asleep again. He drank his glass of water, put it on the bedside table and lay back down, then turned to look at the clock.

4.36am.

What? Time had passed. Time never passed during her visits.

He woke up just as Julie was coming into the bedroom in an old loose white collarless shirt with two white china mugs of green tea. The curtains were drawn and the new morning sun shone in.

'Morning luv,' she said, climbing back into bed. 'Did you sleep OK?'

'Yeah. How about you?'

'Well, it was a bit weird.'

'Oh, yeah? Weird good or weird bad?'

'I don't know. I dreamed that I woke up and you were talking to your mother. She was sitting in the basket chair by the window knitting. She asked how I was and I was talking to her about having therapy. Then she said my bum still looked good. And that's all. It didn't last long, but it was very vivid. It felt...well...it felt real.' She turned to him. 'Why are you looking at me so funny?'

He took a deep breath and turned to look at the glass of water on the bedside table. His heart leapt. It was still empty, even though he'd only drunk from it in his dream.

'I dreamed that as well. I mean, exactly that. You woke up and talked to mam, then went back to sleep. We dreamed the same dream, together, and at the same time. And for the first time the clock changed from 4.27am to 4.36. I drank my water and the glass is still empty.'

They just stared at each other in silence. Finally, Julie spoke up.

'Well, you know what that has to mean, don't you?' said Julie.

'What?'

'It means it wasn't a dream at all. It means it was...'

'...real.'

THE END

Books in the Nick Guymer Series
Published by HEAD PUBLISHING

1. Teesside Steal (2013)
2. Queen Of The Tees (2013)
3. Teesside Missed (2013)
4. DJ Tees (2014)
5. Teesside Blues (2014)
6. Tyne Tees (2014)
7. High Tees (2015)
8. Teesside Meat (2015)
9. Teesside Shadows (2015)
10. King Tees (2016)
11. Teesside Dreams (2016)

Kindle/Paperback

http://www.johnnicholsonwriter.co.uk

About John Nicholson

John is a well-known football writer whose work is read by tens of thousands of people every week. He's a columnist for Football365.com and has worked for the Daily Record, The Mirror, Sky and many other publications over the last 14 years.

Books in the Archie Taylor Series
Published by HEAD PUBLISHING

1. The Girl Can't Help It (2014)
2. Sugar Mama (2016)

Kindle/Paperback

http://www.johnnicholsonwriter.co.uk

Other John Nicholson Books
published by Biteback Publishing

We Ate All The Pies -
How Football Swallowed Britain Whole (2010)

The Meat Fix -
How 26 Years of Healthy Eating Nearly Killed Me (2012)